Love Paul Finch's books? Get **#HookedonHeck**
and tell us what you think
@CrimeFix and @paulfinchauthor

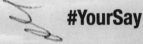 **#YourSay**

"Absolutely stunning."
★★★★★

"Easily one of my favourite books of the year."
★★★★★

"Clearly ranks alongside Rankin, Billingham and Kerley."
★★★★★

"Five stars are not enough."
★★★★★

"Loved the characters. Couldn't put it down.
I need the sequel ASAP."
★★★★★

"Bloodthirsty in the extreme, but driven along at pace…
proper thriller stuff."
★★★★★

"A

"Pure escapism   page turner."
★★★★★

"Sublimely written."
★★★★★

Paul Finch is a former cop and journalist, now turned full-time writer. He cut his literary teeth penning episodes of the British TV crime drama, *The Bill*, and has written extensively in the field of children's animation. However, he is probably best known for his work in thrillers, crime and horror. His first three novels in the DS Heckenburg series all attained official 'best seller' status.

Paul lives in Lancashire, UK, with his wife Cathy and his children, Eleanor and Harry. His website can be found at www.paulfinchauthor.com, his blog at www.paulfinch-writer.blogspot.co.uk, and he can be followed on Twitter @paulfinchauthor.

By the same author:

Stalkers
Sacrifice
The Killing Club
The Chase: an ebook short story

Dead Man Walking

PAUL FINCH

AVON

This novel is entirely a work of fiction.
The names, characters and incidents portrayed in it are
the work of the author's imagination. Any resemblance to
actual persons, living or dead, events or localities is
entirely coincidental.

AVON

A division of HarperCollins*Publishers*
77–85 Fulham Palace Road,
London W6 8JB

www.harpercollins.co.uk

A Paperback Original 2014
3

A catalogue record for this book is
available from the British Library

ISBN 978-0-00-755127-9

Set in Sabon LT Std by Palimpsest Book Production Limited,
Falkirk, Stirlingshire

Printed and bound in Great Britain by
Clays Ltd, St Ives plc

MIX
Paper from
responsible sources
FSC
www.fsc.org   **FSC™ C007454**

FSC™ is a non-profit international organisation established to promote
the responsible management of the world's forests. Products carrying the
FSC label are independently certified to assure consumers that they come
from forests that are managed to meet the social, economic and
ecological needs of present and future generations,
and other controlled sources.

Find out more about HarperCollins and the environment at
www.harpercollins.co.uk/green

For my children, Eleanor and Harry, with whom I shared many a chilling tale when they were tots, but whose enthusiasm is as strong now as it ever was

Prologue

The girl was quite content in her state of semi-undress. The man wasn't concerned by it either. If anything, he seemed to enjoy the interest she attracted as they drove from pub to pub that sultry August evening.

They commenced their Friday night drive-around in Buckfastleigh, then visited the lively villages of Holne and Poundsgate, before penetrating deeper into Dartmoor's vast, grassy wilderness, calling at ever more isolated hamlets: Babeny, Dunstone and finally Widecombe-in-the-Moor, where a posse of legendary beer-swilling reprobates had once ridden Uncle Tom Cobley's grey mare to an early grave.

The girl was first to enter each hostelry, sashaying in through the guffawing hordes, and wiggling comfortably onto the most conspicuous bar stool she could find, while the man took time to find a place in the car park for his sleek, black and silver Porsche. On each occasion, she made an impact. The riot of noise under the low, gnarly roof-beams never actually subsided, but it never needed to. Looking was free.

She wasn't behaving overtly flirtatiously, but she clearly revelled in the attention she drew. And why not? She had 'all the tools', as they say. A tall, willowy blonde, her shapely form showcased to perfection in a green micro mini-dress and strappy green shoes with killer heels. Her golden mane hung past her shoulders in a glossy wave. She had full lips, a pert nose and delicate, feline cheekbones. When she removed her mirrored shades, subtle grey shadow accentuated a pair of startling blue eyes. In each pub she made sure to sit prominently: back arched, boobs thrust forward, smooth tan legs sensually crossed. There was no denying she was playing it up, which was much appreciated by the taproom crowd. For the most part, these were beefy locals, countrymen to the last, but there were also visitors here: car-loads of lusty lads openly cruising for girls and beer; or bluff, gruff oldsters in denims and plaid shirts, down in Devon for the sailing, the fishing, or the moorland walking. They might only be away from their wives for a few days, but they too revealed an eye for the girls; in particular, an eye for this girl. It wasn't just that she smiled sweetly as they made space for her at the bar, or that she responded with humour to their cheeky quips, but up close it could be seen that she wasn't a girl after all – she was a woman, in her late twenties, and because of this even more of a taunting presence.

And still the bloke with her seemed oblivious to – or maybe was aroused by – the stir his girlfriend (or perhaps his wife, who knew?) was causing. He was well-dressed – beige Armani slacks, a short-sleeved Yves St Laurent shirt, suede Church's brogues – and of course, he drove an impressive motor. But he was plumpish, with pale, pudgy features – 'fucking snail', as one leery barfly commented to his mate – and a shock of carroty red hair. And he drank only shandies, which made him seem a little soft to have such a tigress on his arm – at least from the locals' point of view. And yet by the duo's body language, the man was the more dominant. He stood while she sat. He bought the drinks while she disported her charms, leaning backward against the bar, her exposed cleavage inviting the most brazen stares.

'Got a right couple, here!' Harold Hopkinson, portly landlord of The Grouse Beater, said from the side of his mouth. 'Talk about putting his missus on show.'

'She's loving every minute of it,' Doreen, his foursquare wife, replied.

'Bit old to be making an exhibition of themselves like that, aren't they?'

'Bit old? They're just the right age. Where do you think they'll be off to next?'

Harold looked surprised. 'You don't mean Halfpenny Reservoir?'

'Where else?'

'But surely they *know*? I mean . . .' Harold frowned. 'Nah, can't be that. Look, she's a bonnie girl, and he likes showing the world what he's got.'

Doreen pulled another pint of Dartmoor IPA. 'You really believe that?'

Briefly, Harold was lost for words. It all made an unpleasant kind of sense. Halfpenny Reservoir wasn't Devon's number one dogging location – it was a long way from anywhere of consequence – but it was well-known locally and it got busy from time to time; at least, it used to get busy before the panic had started. He eyed the fulsome couple again. The woman still perched on her bar stool, sipping a rum and lemonade. Now that he assessed her properly, he saw finger and toenails painted gold, a chain around her left ankle decorated with moons and stars. That was a come-on of sorts, wasn't it? At least, it was according to some of his favourite websites. Of course, it wouldn't have been unusual at one time, this. The swinger crowd would occasionally trawl the local boozers en

3

route to Halfpenny Reservoir – somewhat more covertly than this, admittedly, but nonetheless 'displaying their wares', as Doreen liked to call it, looking to pick up the passing rough that seemed to be their stock-in-trade.

Things were markedly different now, of course. Or they should be.

'They must be out-of-towners,' Harold said. 'They obviously don't know.'

'They'd have to be from another planet not to know,' Doreen replied tersely.

'Well . . . shouldn't we tell them?'

'Tell them what?'

'I don't know . . . just advise them it's a bad idea at the present time.'

She gave him her most withering glance. 'It should be a bad idea at *any* time.'

Harold's wife had a kind of skewed morality when it came to earthy pleasures. She made her living selling alcohol, and yet she had a problem with drunks, refusing to serve anyone she suspected of sampling one too many, and was very quick to issue barring orders if there was ever horseplay in the pub. Likewise, though she consciously employed pretty local girls to work behind her bar, she was strongly antagonistic to 'tarts and tramps', as she called them, and was especially hostile to any women she identified as belonging to the swinger crowd who gathered for their midnight revels up at the reservoir – so much so that when 'the Stranger' had first come on the scene, targeting lone couples parked up late at night, she'd almost regarded him with approval.

Until the details had emerged, of course.

Because even by the standards of Britain's most heinous murders, these were real shockers. Harold couldn't help shuddering as he recalled some of the details he'd read about in the papers. Though no attack had been reported any closer to The Grouse Beater than a picnic area near Sourton on the other side of the moor, twenty miles away as the crow flew, the whole of the county had been put on alert. Harold glanced around the taproom, wondering if the predator might be present at this moment. The pub was full, mainly with men, and not all of the 'shrinking violet' variety. Devon was a holiday idyll, especially in summer – it didn't just attract the New Age crowd and the hippy backpackers, it drew families, honeymooners and the like. But it was a working county too. Even up here on the high moor, the local male populace comprised far more than country squire and Colonel Blimp types in tweeds and gaiters; there were farm-labourers, cattlemen, farriers, hedgers, keepers; occupations which by their nature required hardy outdoor characters. And hadn't the police issued some kind of statement about their chief suspect being a local man probably engaged in manual labour, someone tough and physically strong enough to overpower healthy young couples? Also, he was someone who knew the back roads, so was able to creep up on his victims unawares, making his getaway afterwards.

There were an awful lot of blokes satisfying those criteria right here, right now.

The more Harold thought about it, the more vulnerable the young couple looked in the midst of this rumbustious crowd. Even if the Stranger wasn't present, the woman ought not to be displaying herself like that. The man should realise that several of these fellas had already had lots to drink, especially those who were openly ogling; he should know that temptation might get the better of them and that it would be so, so easy just to reach out and place a wandering hand on that smooth, sun-browned thigh. If that happened there might be trouble, swingers or not, and that was the last thing Harold wanted.

'We have to say something,' he muttered to Doreen, after they briefly stepped away together into the stock-room.

'What?' she sneered. 'Casually tell them all the local dogging sites are closed? How do you think that'll go down? They might just be show-offs. Might just have come out for a drink.'

'But you said . . .'

'Just leave it, Harold. We don't need you making a fool of yourself. Again.'

'But if they are swingers, and they go up there . . .?'

'They'll be taking a chance. Like they always take chances. Good God, who in their right mind would go looking for sex with strangers in the middle of nowhere?'

'But darling, if they don't know . . .'

'They're adults, aren't they! They should make it their business to know.'

Three minutes later – much to Harold's relief – 'the adults' left, the woman swaying prettily to the pub door, heads again turning to watch, the man digging a packet of cigarettes from his slacks as he idly followed. In some ways it was as if they weren't actually together; as if the man was just some casual acquaintance rather than a partner, which was a bit confusing. Still, it was someone else's problem now.

Harold edged to the diamond-paned window overlooking the pub car park.

The duo stood beside the Porsche, the man smoking, the woman leaning on the car with her arms folded, her bag dangling from her shoulder by its strap. They chatted together, in no apparent rush to go anywhere – perhaps they were just a dressy couple out for a few drinks after all? Harold felt a slow sense of relief. Probably a nice couple too, when you got to know them; it was hardly the woman's fault she was hot as hell.

It was approaching nine o'clock now and the sun was setting, fiery red stripes lying across the encircling moorland.

Maybe they were all set to go home? But then, when the man was only halfway through his cigarette, he stubbed it out on the tarmac and placed it in a nearby waste-container. And when they climbed into the Porsche together and drove away, it wasn't along the B3387 to Bovey Tracey, or even back through the village towards Dunstone and ultimately Buckfastleigh – it was along the unnamed road that ran due northwest from the pub. The next inhabited place it came to was Beardon, some fifteen miles away.

But long before then, it passed Halfpenny Reservoir.

It had been a vintage August day in the West Country, but the heat was finally seeping from the land, the balminess of the evening receding. An indigo dusk layered the hills and valleys of Dartmoor.

By the time they reached the reservoir it would be near enough pitch-black.

The woman checked their rear-view mirror as they drove. Fleetingly, she thought she'd glimpsed headlights behind, but now there was nothing; only the greyness of nightfall. Ahead, the road sped on hypnotically, the vastness of the encircling moor oppressive in its emptiness. Tens of minutes passed, and they didn't spot a single habitation – neither a cottage, nor another pub – though in truth they were too busy looking for the reservoir turn-off to indulge in any form of sightseeing. Even then, they almost passed it; a narrow, unmade lane, all dry rutted earth in their headlights, branching away between two granite gateposts and arcing off at a slanted angle amongst dense stands of yellow-flowered furze.

They slowed to a halt in the middle of the blacktop.

'This must be it . . .?' the man said. It was more a question than an observation.

The woman nodded.

They ventured left along the rugged route, bouncing and

7

jolting, spiky twigs whispering down the Porsche's flanks, following a shallow V-shaped valley for several hundred yards before starlit sky broke out ahead; the radiant orb of the moon was suspended there, its reflection shimmering on an expansive body of water lying to their right. Like most of the Dartmoor reservoirs, Halfpenny Lake was manmade, its purpose to supply drinking water to the surrounding lowlands. A row of wrought-iron railings flickered past in the glow of their right-side headlamp as they prowled the shoreline road, and the solid, horizontal silhouette of what looked like a dam blocking off the valley at its farthest end affirmed the mundane purpose of this place.

There were several sheltered parking bays along here, a dump site for used condoms, dog-eared porn mags and pairs of semen-stained knickers – though any such debris now would be old and rotted; there was no one present to add new mementoes.

Apart from the man and the woman.

They parked close to the entrance of the second lot, and there, as per the manual, turned the radio down – it was tuned to an 'easy listening' station, so was hardly intrusive in any case – opened all the windows, and climbed into the back seat together. Here, they sat apart – one at either end of the seat, exchanging odd murmurs of anticipation as they waited for their audience.

And so the minutes passed.

The stillness outside was near absolute; a gentle breeze sighing across the heathery moorland tops, groaning amid the tors. The couple's gaze roved back and forth along the unlit ridges. The only movement came from tufts of bracken rippling against the stars. It was almost eerie how peaceful it was, how tranquil. A classic English summer's night.

All the more reason why the fierce crackle of electricity jolted them so badly.

Especially the man, who stiffened and fell back against the nearside door.

It happened that fast. He simply froze, his eyes glazed, foam shooting from his rigidly puckered mouth. Then the featureless figure outside who had risen into view from a kneeling posture and reached through the open window with his Taser, now reached through again and opened the door.

All this happened too quickly for the woman to take it in. *Almost* too quickly.

As the lifeless shape of her beau dropped backward again, this time out onto the gritty tarmac, his head striking it with brutal force, she grappled with her handbag, unsnapping it and fumbling inside. It was a quick, fluid motion – she didn't waste time squawking in outrage – but their assailant was quicker still. He lunged in through the open nearside door. In the dull green light of the dashboard facia, she caught a fleeting glimpse of heavy-duty leather: a leather coat, leather face-mask, and a leather glove, as – *POW!* – his clenched fist caught her right in the mouth.

She too slumped backward, head swimming, handbag tipping into the footwell, spilling its contents every which way.

With thoughts fizzled to near-incomprehensibility, the woman probed at her two front teeth with her tongue. They appeared to wobble; at the same time her upper lip stung abominably, whilst her mouth rapidly filled with hot, coppery fluid. She coughed on it, choking.

And then awareness of her situation broke over her – like a dash of iced water.

She was lying on her back, but the intruder was now in the car with her, on the rear seat in fact, already positioned between her indecently spread legs. With one gloved hand, he kept a tight grip on her exposed upper left thigh; it was so high, his thumb was almost in her crotch. With his other hand, he was slowly, purposefully unfastening his coat.

From some distant place, the woman heard a new song on the radio. A rich American voice poured through the nicely central-heated car.

Wondering in the night what were the chances . . .

A beastly chuckle, hideous and pig-like, snorted from the leather-clad face. Still dazed, the woman strained to see through the greenish, pain-hazed gloom. Frank Sinatra, she recalled. One of her father's favourites. Old Blue Eyes, The Voice, the Sultan of Swoon . . .

'Looks like they're playing my tune,' the intruder said, as the final button snapped open and his coat flaps fell apart. If she'd had any doubts before, she had none now.

Strangers in the night . . .

He hadn't spoken before. Not a single word – not to her knowledge. But then who would know? The weird sex-murderer who'd begun his crimes by attacking anyone he encountered who was out after dark, but had then begun stalking lovers' lanes and dogging spots all over Devon and Somerset, had not left a single living witness. All those he'd targeted had been eliminated with precision, ruthlessness, and great, great enjoyment; the men with skulls crushed and/or throats cut, the women sexually mutilated in a ritual that went far beyond everyday sadism. Each one of them, man and woman alike, subjected to one final desecration, when their eyes were stabbed and gouged until they were nothing but jelly.

We were strangers in the night . . .

'Definitely my tune.' He chuckled again, using his left hand to fondle the array of gleaming implements in his customised inner coat lining: the tin-opener, the screwdriver, the mallet, the hacksaw, the razor-edged filleting knife.

The woman could barely move, yet her eyes were now riveted on *his* eyes: moist baubles framed in leather sockets; and on his mouth, the saliva-coated tongue and broken, stained teeth exposed by a drawn-back zipper. But that voice – it could only have been a whisper in truth, a gloating guttural whisper. But she would remember it as long as she lived.

It was Scottish.

The Stranger was a Scotsman.

The key thing now, of course, was to ensure that she *did* live.

Perhaps he was too busy drawing out that first instrument of torture – the tin-opener, an old-fashioned device with a ghastly hooked blade – to notice her right hand working frantically through the debris littering the footwell.

As he raised the tin-opener to his right shoulder – not to plunge it down as much as to tease her with the terror of it – her fingertips found something she recognised.

He kept her pinned in place with his other hand, a grip so hard in that soft, sensitive spot that it was now agony, as he crooned along to the tune.

They'd first dubbed him 'the Stranger' in the West Country press because of the sex-with-strangers scene he'd so viciously crashed. It now seemed even more appropriate. 'You're a taunting, godless bitch,' he added matter-of-factly, still in that notable accent. 'A whore, an exhibitionist slut, a prick-teasing slag . . .'

'And a police officer,' she said, pointing her snub-nosed Smith & Wesson .38 straight at his face. 'Move one muscle, you bastard . . . open that filthy yap of yours one more time, and I'll put a bullet straight through your fucking skull!'

The expression on his face was priceless. At least it

11

probably would have been, had she been able to see it. As it was, she had to be content with his sudden almost-comical paralysis, the whites of his eyes widening in cartoon fashion around his soulless black pupils, his gammy mouth sagging open between zippered lips.

'Yeah . . . that's right,' she said, thumbing back the pistol's hammer. 'The fun's over. Now drop that sodding blade.'

Of course, it couldn't be over in reality, and her heart pounded harder in her chest as this slowly dawned on her. He couldn't let it end like *this* – so abruptly, so unexpectedly; or in *this* fashion: trapped like a rabbit by one of the frail, sexual creatures he so brutally despised. Warily, she transferred the .38 from her right hand to her left, keeping it levelled at him as she lay there. With her empty right hand, she again reached into the footwell. Her radio was down there somewhere, but she was damned if she could find it. All the time, he sat motionless, nailing her with that semi-human gaze, strands of spittle hanging over his leather-covered jaw. And now she saw his mouth slowly closing, those discoloured teeth clamping together in a final, hate-filled grimace. He wasn't frozen with shock anymore, she realised; he was taut with tension – like a spring set to uncoil.

'Don't you do it!' she warned, but it was too late; he arched down with the tin-opener, intent on ripping her wide apart with its wicked, hooked point.

BANG!

The slug took him in the left side of his upper chest, just beneath the collar bone, flinging him backward out of the car and down onto the tarmac, where he lay silently twisting alongside the prone form of Detective Constable Maxwell.

She found the radio and slammed it to her lips as she threw herself forward through the cordite. 'All units, this is DC Piper! Converge on Halfpenny Reservoir! Repeat, converge on Halfpenny Reservoir . . .'

Her words tailed off as a stocky figure rose to its feet outside. For a half-second she tried to kid herself that this was Maxwell, though she knew it couldn't be. The DC's head had struck the tarmac with a hell of a whack.

Without a word, the figure swayed around and blundered across the car park.

'Repeat, this is DC Piper! Decoy unit Alpha. One shot fired. Suspect suffering a chest wound, but on foot and mobile.'

There was a scrabble of static-ridden responses, but even as Piper watched, the lumbering form of the Stranger scrambled over the car park's low perimeter wall, the dark blot of his outline swiftly ascending through the furze on the other side. He was hurt badly; that was clear – he lurched from side to side, but kept going in a more or less straight line, uphill and away from her.

'Suspect heading west . . . away from the reservoir, over open ground,' she added, clattering onto the tarmac in her tall, strappy shoes. 'We need an ambulance too.' She dropped to one knee to check the carotid at the side of Maxwell's neck. 'DC Maxwell is severely injured . . . he's received a massive shock from some kind of stun-gun and what looks like a head trauma. Currently in a collapsed state, but breathing, and his pulse feels regular. Get that ambulance here, pronto! In the meantime, I'm pursuing the suspect, over.'

She hurried across the car park, but once she was over the wall into the furze, her heels sank like knife-blades in the soft earth. She kicked the shoes off as she ran, flinching as twigs and sharp-edged stones spiked the soles of her feet, and thorns and thistles raked her naked legs. Very briefly, the Stranger appeared above her as a lopsided silhouette on the night sky. But then he was gone again, over the ridge.

'Get me that back-up now!' she shouted into her radio.

'*Gemma, you need to hold back,*' came a semi-coherent response. '*DSU Anderson's orders! Wait for support units, over!*'

'Negative, that!' she replied firmly. 'Not when we're this close.'

She too crested the ridge. The starlit moor unrolled itself: a sweeping georama of grass and boulders, obscured by patches of low-lying mist but rising distantly to soaring, tor-crowned summits. On lower ground now, but a hundred yards ahead of her at least, a dark blot was struggling onward.

The ground sloped steeply as she gave chase, ploughing downhill through soft, springy vegetation, shouting that he was under arrest; that he should give it up.

Perspectives were all askew, of course, so she wasn't quite sure where she lost sight of him. Though he wasn't a vast distance ahead, curtains of mist seemed suddenly to close around him. When she reached that point herself – now hobbling, both feet bruised and bleeding – she found she was on much softer ground, plodding through ankle-deep mud. He ought to have left a recognisable trail, but it was too dark to see and she had no light with which to get down and make a fingertip search.

Further terse orders came crackling over the airwaves.

Again, she ignored them. It occurred to her that maybe the suspect was wearing a vest and therefore not as badly injured as she'd thought. But if that was the case, why had he fled . . . why not use the advantage to go straight on the attack, ripping and mauling her in the car? No – she'd wounded him; she'd seen the pain in his posture. If nothing else, that meant there'd be blood.

Unless rain came before the forensics teams did.

'We need the lab-rats up here ASAP!' she shouted, cutting across the frantic exchanges of her colleagues. 'At least we'll have his DNA . . .'

There was a choked scream from somewhere ahead.

She slowed to a near-halt. Fleetingly, she couldn't see anything; liquid mist, the colour of purulent milk, drifted on all sides. But had that cry been for real? Was he finally succumbing to his wound? Or was he trying to lure her?

There was another scream, this one accompanied by a strangled gurgling.

She now halted completely.

This was Dartmoor. A National Park. A green and hazy paradise. Picturesque, famous for its pristine flora and fauna. And notorious for its bottomless mires. The third scream dwindled to a series of choked gasps, and now she heard a loud sploshing too, like a heavy body plunging through slime.

'Update,' she said into her radio, advancing warily. 'I'm perhaps three hundred yards west of the reservoir parking area, over the top of the ridge. Suspect appears to be in trouble. I can't see him, but it's possible he's blundered into a mire.'

There was further insistence that she stop and wait for back-up. Again she ignored this, but only advanced five or six yards before she found herself teetering on the brink of an opaque, black/green morass, its mirror-flat surface stretching in all directions as the mist seemed to furl away across it. She strained her eyes, but nothing stirred out there; not so much as a ripple, let alone the distinctive outline of a man fighting to keep his head above the surface.

There was no sound either, which was worrying. Dartmoor's mires could suck you down with frightful speed. Their bowels were stuffed with sheep and pony carcasses, not to mention the odd missing hiker or two. But all she could identify now were the twisted husks of sunken trees, their branches protruding here and there like rotted dinosaur bones.

Even Detective Constable Gemma Piper, of the Metropolitan Police – wilful, fearless and determined – now realised that

15

caution was the better part of valour. Especially as the mist continued to clear on the strengthening wind, revealing, despite the darkness of night, how truly extensive this mire was. It lay everywhere; not just ahead of her but on both sides as well – as though she'd strayed out onto a narrow headland. It was difficult to imagine that even a local man could have lumbered this way, mortally wounded, blinded by vapour, and had somehow avoided this pitfall. And if nothing else, she now knew their suspect was not a local man – but, by origin at least, from the other end of the country.

As voices sounded behind her, torches spearing across the undulating landscape, she sank slowly and tiredly to her haunches. The delayed shock of what had nearly happened back in the Porsche was seeping through her, leaving her numb. In some ways she felt elated; she'd almost nailed the bastard . . . but not quite. It was like a no-score draw after a football match. It was a result of sorts, but it was difficult to estimate how much of one.

Within an hour, the Devon and Cornwall Police, with assistance from Scotland Yard, had cordoned off this entire stretch of moor, were searching it with dogs, and had even brought heavy machinery in to start dredging the mire and its various connected waterways. At the reservoir car park, the conscious but weakened form of DC Maxwell was loaded into the rear of an ambulance. Gemma Piper meanwhile sat side-saddle in the front seat of a police patrol car, sipping coffee and occasionally wincing as a medic knelt and attended to her bloodied feet and swollen face. At the same time, she briefed Detective Superintendent George Anderson.

The hard-headed young female detective, already impressive to every senior manager who'd encountered her, had just assured herself a glowing future in this most challenging and male-dominated of industries. But of the so-called Stranger,

16

the perpetrator of thirteen loathsome torture-murders – as reported in the *Dartmoor Advertiser*: 'These crimes are abhorrent, utterly loathsome!' – there was no trace.

Nor would there be for some considerable time.

Chapter 1

There was no real witchcraft associated with this part of the Lake District. Nor had there ever been, to Heck's knowledge.

The name 'Witch Cradle Tarn' had been applied in times past purely to reflect the small mountain lake's ominous appearance: a long, narrow, very deep body of water high in the Langdale Pikes, thirteen hundred feet above sea-level to be precise, with sheer, scree-covered cliffs on its eastern shore and mighty, wind-riven fells like Pavey Ark, Harrison Stickle and Great Castle Howe lowering to its north, west and south. It wasn't an especially scary place in modern times. Located in a hanging valley in a relatively remote spot – official title Cragwood Vale, unofficial title 'the Cradle' – it was a fearsome prospect on paper, but when you actually got there, the atmosphere was more holiday than horror. Two cheery Lakeland hamlets, Cragwood Keld and Cragwood Ho, occupied its southern and northern points respectively. For much of the year the whole place teemed with climbers, hikers, fell-runners and anglers seeking the famous Witch Cradle trout, while kayakers and white-water rafters were catered for by the Cragwood Boat Club, based a mile south of Cragwood Keld, near the head of Cragwood Race; a furiously twisting river, which poured downhill through natural gullies and steep culverts before finally joining the more sedately flowing Langdale Beck.

The single pub at the heart of Cragwood Keld only added to this homely feel. A rather austere-looking building at first glance, all grey Westmorland slate on the outside, it was famous for its smoky beams and handsome oak settles, its range of cask ales, its crackling fires in winter and its pretty lakeside beer garden in summer. Its name – The Witch's Kettle – owed itself entirely to some enterprising landlord of decades past, who hadn't found The Drovers' Rest to his taste, and felt the witch business a tad sexier, especially given that most visitors to the Cradle were always awe-stricken by the deep pinewoods hemming its two villages to the lakeshore, and the rubble-clad slopes and immense granite crags soaring overhead. Its inn-sign was a landmark in itself, depicting a rusty old kettle with green herbs protruding from under its lid, sitting on a stone inscribed with pagan runes. It was just possible, visitors supposed, that current landlady, Hazel Carter, might herself be a witch – but if so, she was a far cry from the bent nose and warty lip variety.

At least, that was Heck's feeling.

He'd only been up here two and a half months, but was already certain that whatever magic Hazel wove, it was unlikely to be the sort he'd resist easily. Not that he was thinking along these lines that late November morning, as he entered The Witch's Kettle just before eleven, made a beeline for the bar and ordered himself a pint of Buttermere Gold. It was early in the day and there were few customers yet. Only Hazel was on duty. Like Heck, she was in her late thirties, but with rich auburn hair, which she habitually wore very long. She was doe-eyed, soft-lipped, and buxom in shape, a figure enhanced by her daytime 'uniform' of t-shirt, cardigan and jeans.

They made close eye-contact but only uttered those words necessary for the transaction. However, as she handed him his pint and his change, the landlady inclined her head slightly to the right. Heck pocketed the cash and sipped his beer, before glancing in that direction. Beyond a low arch lay the pub's vault, which contained a darts board and a pool table. One person was in there: a young lad, no more than sixteen, with tousled blond hair, wearing a grey sweatshirt, grey canvas trousers and white trainers. He looked once, fleetingly, in Heck's direction as he worked his way around the pool table, ignoring him thereafter. All the youth had seen, of course, was a man about six feet in height, of average build, with unruly black hair and faint scars on his face, wearing jeans, a sweater and a rumpled anorak. But he'd probably have paid more attention had he known that Heck was actually Detective Sergeant Mark Heckenburg of the Cumbria Constabulary, that he was based very near here, at Cragwood Keld police office, and that he was on duty right at this moment.

To maintain his façade of recreation, Heck found a seat at an empty table, pulled a rolled-up *Westmorland Gazette* from his back pocket and commenced reading. He checked his watch as he turned the pages, though this was more from habit than necessity. He felt he was following a good lead today, but there was no great pressure on him. Ever since being reassigned from Scotland Yard to Cumbria as part of the Association of Chief Police Officers' new Anti-Rural Crime Initiative, Heck had been well-placed to work hours of his own choosing and at his own pace. Ultimately of course, he was answerable to South Cumbria Crime

Command, and in the first instance to the CID office down at Windermere police station; he was only a sergeant, when all was said and done. But as the only CID officer in the Langdales – the only CID officer in twenty square miles in fact – he was out here on his own as far as many colleagues were concerned: 'Hey pal, you're the man on the spot,' as they'd say. There were advantages to this, without doubt. But it was never a nice feeling that reinforcements were always a good forty minutes away.

Heck's thoughts were distracted as two other people came down the stairs into the taproom. It was a man and a woman, the former in his mid-thirties, the latter in her mid-twenties, both carrying bulging backpacks. The woman had short, mouse-brown hair, and wore a red cagoule, blue cord trousers and walking boots. The man was tall and thin, with short fair hair. He too wore cord trousers and walking boots, but his blue cagoule was draped over his narrow, t-shirted shoulders. Neither of them looked threatening or in any way unwholesome; in fact they were smiling and chattering brightly. At the foot of the stair, they separated, the man heading to the bar, where he told Hazel he'd like to 'settle up'. The woman turned into the vault and spoke to the youth, who pocketed his last ball and grabbed up a backpack of his own.

The trio left the pub together, still talking animatedly – a family enjoying their holiday. As the door swung closed behind them, Heck glanced over the top of his newspaper at Hazel, who nodded. Leaping to his feet, he crossed the room to the car park window, and watched as the trio approached a metallic-green Hyundai Accent. He'd been informed by Hazel beforehand that this was the vehicle they'd arrived in two weeks ago, and had already run a check on the Police National Computer, to discover that its registration number – V513 HNV – actually belonged to a black Volvo estate supposedly sold to a scrap merchant in Grimsby nine months earlier. Without a backward glance, they piled into the Hyundai and pulled out of the car park, heading south out of the village.

Heck hurried outside – it was only noon, but it was a grey day and there was already a deep chill. Thanks to the season, the village was quieter than usual. Beyond the pines, the upward-sweeping moors were bare, brown and stubbled with autumn bracken.

Heck climbed into his white Citroën DS4, starting the engine and hitting the heater switch, but resisted the temptation to jump straight onto the suspects' tail. At this time of year, with traffic more scarce than usual, it would be easy to get spotted. Besides, there was only one way you could enter or leave the Cradle – via the aptly named Cragwood Road, a perilously narrow single-lane which wound downhill over steep, rock-strewn slopes for several hundred feet, sometimes tilting to a gradient of one in three – so it wasn't like the suspects could turn off anywhere, or even drive away at high speed. Of course, once the trio had descended into Great Langdale, the vast glacial valley at the epicentre of this district, it was another matter. So Heck couldn't afford to hang back too far.

As such, he gave them a thirty-second start.

It was about three miles from the village to the commencement of the descent, and Heck didn't see a single soul as he traversed it, nor another car, which was comforting – though it was useful to be able to hide among normal vehicles, an open road was reassuring in the event you might need to chase. As he began his descent, he initially couldn't see his target, but he refused to panic. The blacktop meandered wildly on its downward route, arcing around perilous bends and through clumps of shadowy pine. But when he finally did sight the Hyundai, it had got further ahead than he'd expected. It was diminutive; no more than a glinting green toy.

Heck accelerated, veering dangerously as the road dropped, taking curves with increasingly reckless abandon. He tried his radio, but received only dead-air responses. There was minimal reception in the Cradle, the encompassing cliffs interfering so drastically with signals that most communications from Cragwood Keld nick had to be made via landline. But it would improve as he descended into Langdale. In anticipation of this, he was already tuned to a talk-through channel.

'Heckenburg to 1416, over?' he repeated.

He'd descended to six hundred feet before he gleaned a response.

'*1416 receiving. Go ahead, sarge.*' The voice was shrill, with an Irish brogue.

'Suspects on the move, M-E . . . heading down Cragwood Road towards the B5343. Where are you, over?'

M-E, or PC 1416 Mary-Ellen O'Rourke, Cragwood Keld nick's only uniformed officer – she was actually resident there, bunking in the flat above the office – took a second or two to respond. '*Heading up Little Langdale from Skelwith Bridge, sarge. They still in that green Hyundai, over?*'

'Affirmative. Still showing the dodgy VRM. I'll give you a shout soon as I know which way they're headed, over?'

'*Roger that.*'

As Heck now descended towards the junction with the B5343, he had a clear vision both west and east along Great Langdale. This was a vastly more expansive valley than Cragwood Vale, its head encircled by some of Cumbria's most impressive fells; not just the craggy-topped Langdale Pikes, but Great Knott, Crinkle Crags, Bowfell and Long Top – their barren upper reaches ascending to dizzying heights.

By contrast, its floor was flat and fertile, and perhaps half a mile across, much of it divided by dry-stone walls and given to cattle grazing. Down its centre, in a west to east direction, flowed Langdale Beck, a broad, rocky river, normally shallow but running deep at present after a spectacularly soggy October and November. A hundred yards ahead meanwhile, at the end of Cragwood Road, the Hyundai passed onto the B5343 without stopping, following the larger route as it swung sharply south, crossing the river by a narrow bridge. Still hoping to avoid detection, Heck dallied at the junction, watching the Hyundai shrink as it ascended the higher ground on the far side.

'Heckenburg to 1416?'

'*Receiving, sarge . . . go ahead.*'

'Suspect vehicle heading south along the upper section of the B5343.' He glanced at his sat-nav. 'That means they're coming your way, M-E.'

'*Affirmative, sarge. I'm headed in that direction now. You want me to intercept?*'

'Negative . . . we haven't got enough on them yet.'

There was only one patrol vehicle attached permanently to Cragwood Keld police station: the powerful Land Rover Mary-Ellen was currently driving. Decked in vivid yellow-and-turquoise Battenburg, it was purposely designed to be noticeable on these bleak uplands; it even had a special insignia on its roof so air support could home in on it – but that was less useful on occasions like this, with stealth the order of the day.

'M-E . . . proceed to Little Langdale village, and park up,' Heck said. 'That way, if they reach your position and we still don't want to pull them, you can get out of sight.'

'*Wilco,*' she replied.

Heck hit the gas as he accelerated onto the B5343 and followed it across the valley bottom, taking the bridge over the beck. The Hyundai was still in sight, but high up now and far away; a green matchbox car. Shortly, it would dwindle from view altogether. Heck floored the pedal, the dry-stone walls enclosing the paddocks falling behind, to be replaced by swathes of tough, tussocky grass, which sloped steeply upward ahead of him. The fleecy white/grey blobs of Herdwick sheep were dotted all over the valley's eastern sides, several wandering across the road as he accelerated, scattering and bleating in response. Officially, the B5343 no longer bore that title at this point – it was now significantly less than a B-road, but it never rose as high as Cragwood Road, and in fact levelled out at around seven hundred feet. Once again, it banked and swung, though Heck kept his foot down, managing to close the distance between himself and the Hyundai to about four hundred yards.

The ground on the right had now dropped away into a deep, tree-filled ravine, through the middle of which a smaller beck tumbled noisily, draining excess water from Blea Tarn, the next lake on this route, located about five miles ahead. Before that, approaching on the right, there was another pub, The Three Ravens. In appearance, this was more like a Lakeland cottage, low and squat, built from whitewashed stone. Despite its dramatic perch on the very edge of the ravine, a small car park was attached to one side of it, though only one vehicle was visible there at present: a maroon BMW Coupe.

Heck glanced at his watch – it was lunchtime. This was the time of day the bastards usually pounced. His gaze flitted back to the Hyundai, the tail-lights of which glowed red, its indicator flashing as it veered right into The Three Ravens car park, pulling up almost flush against the pub wall.

Heck smiled to himself. They'd sussed this spot out

previously, and knew where the outdoor CCTV was unlikely to catch them.

'Heckenburg to 1416, over?'

The response was semi-audible owing to the higher ground, filtered through noisy static. *'Go ahead, sarge.'*

'We're on, M-E. Suspects have called at The Three Ravens pub, overlooking Blea Tarn ghyll. If I'm right, they're going to hit their next target somewhere between here and the tarn. It's perfect for them. Five miles of the remotest stretch of road in the Langdales. In fact, I think it's a must-hit. They won't want to chance it after that . . . too many cottages.'

'Received, sarge. How do you want to play it, over?'

'Bring your Land Rover up the B5343. Wait on Blea Tarn car park. But tuck yourself out of the way in case they carry on past, over.'

'Roger, received.'

Heck proceeded past The Three Ravens car park, catching sight of the lad from the Hyundai loitering about, now with his sweatshirt hood drawn up, while the two adults entered the pub, no doubt to size up any potential opposition. Mindful of indoor CCTV, the girl had affected a blonde, shoulder-length wig, while the man had donned a woolly hat with what looked like ginger hair extensions around its rim. Heck could have laughed out loud, except that unsophisticated precautions like these often hugely aided criminals. Though not on this occasion, if he could just get his timings right. Feeling that old tingle of excitement – something in distinct short supply these last two and a half months – he scanned the roadside verges for a lying-up point. A couple of hundred yards further on, he spied a break in the dry-stone wall on his left, a farm track leading through it and dropping out of sight into a hollow. Heck swung through and swerved down the stony lane, only halting among a thicket of alder, where he threw his Citroën into reverse, made a three-point turn and edged back uphill, halting some forty yards short of the gate. Jumping out, he climbed the rest of the track on foot, dropping to a crouch behind the right-hand gatepost and watching the road.

He wasn't sure how long this thing would take. If his suppositions were correct, the first thing this crew would do was establish whether or not their potential target was likely to be easy: an elderly couple or someone travelling alone would be preferable. Under normal circumstances they'd then ascertain which car in the car park belonged to said party. This was more simply done than the average member of the public might imagine, especially at a time of year when there were fewer cars to choose from. Maps and luggage, for example, would indicate visitors rather than locals; an absence of toys would suggest older travellers, which in its turn might be confirmed by evidence of medication or a choice of music or reading material – it was amazing what you could learn from the books and CDs that routinely littered footwells. In this case of course it would be even easier than usual – there was only one car. After that, it was a straightforward matter of disabling the car in question – previously this had been done by inflicting small punctures on the tyres with an air pistol – and following until it pulled up by the roadside.

A low rumble indicated the approach of a vehicle. Heck squatted lower. A soft-topped Volkswagen Sport roared past, leaves swirling in its wake. It was running smoothly, with no sign that it was suffering any kind of damage.

Heck relaxed again, ruminating for another fifteen minutes, reminding himself that patience and caution weren't just virtues in this kind of work, they were essential. So much of the success enjoyed by professional criminals was down to the fear they created with their efficiency – the way they came and went like ghosts, the way they knew exactly who

28

to victimise, exactly where to find such easy prey, exactly when to catch it at its most vulnerable. It bewildered and terrified the average man and woman; it was as though the felons possessed supernatural instincts. Yet in reality it owed to little more than thorough preparation and a bit of basic cunning, and in the case of distraction-thieves like this particular crew, a quick glance through the windows of a few parked cars. In some ways, that was impressive – you couldn't fail to admire someone who was so good at what they did, even something as callous as this – but it didn't make them the Cosa Nostra.

The radio crackled in his jacket pocket. *'1416 to DS Heckenburg?'*

'Go ahead, M-E,' he replied.

'In position now, sarge.'

'Stay sharp, over.'

'Roger that.'

Another vehicle was approaching, this time minus the low, steady hum of a healthy engine. Instead, Heck heard a repeating metallic rattle – as if something was broken. He tensed as he lowered himself. Two seconds later, the BMW Coupe from The Three Ravens car park chugged past, its driver as yet unaware he had two slow-punctures on his nearside. Unaware now maybe, though not for long.

Heck tensed again, waiting. The thieves wouldn't have dashed straight out of the pub in pursuit of the BMW's occupants – that might have attracted attention – but they wouldn't want to let them get too far ahead either. And right on cue, only half a minute later, the Hyundai itself came slowly in pursuit.

Heck dashed back to his Citroën, gunned it up the track to the main road and swung left. It was only a matter of distance now. With a single deflating tyre, it was possible an innocent motorist would keep driving, failing to notice, but with two, that was highly unlikely. Around the next bend, the road spooled out clearly for about two hundred yards, at the far end of which Heck saw the BMW wallowing to a halt beneath a twisted ash. The Hyundai prowling after it hadn't reached that point yet, but was already decelerating.

Heck hit the brakes too, swinging his Citroën hard up onto the nearside verge so that it was out of sight. He jumped out, vaulted over the wall, and scrambled forward along undulating pasture, staying parallel to the road but keeping as low as he could.

This was the ideal spot for an ambush, he realised. Brown Howe was a lowering presence on the left, Pike of Blisco performing the same function on the right. Utter silence lay across the deserted, bracken-clad valley lying between them. The dull grey sky tinged everything with an air of wildness and desolation. No tents were visible, no hikers; there wasn't even a shepherd or farm-worker in sight.

Heck advanced sixty yards or so, and moved back to the wall, where a belt of fir trees would screen him. The two cars were still visible, the Hyundai parked directly behind the BMW. Four people now stood by the vehicles' nearside. A dumpy balding man and a thin white-haired woman, both in matching sweaters, had clearly been the occupants of the BMW. But Heck also saw the girl in the blonde wig, and the lean young man in the woolly cap, who even now was stripping off his cagoule, no doubt offering to change one of the BMW's mangled tyres. Heck could imagine the advice he'd be giving them – mainly because the exact same spiel had been dealt to those others who'd suffered this fate in the Yorkshire Dales and the Peak District.

'A double blow-out's a bit of a problem,' the good samaritan would opine. 'But if you use the spare to replace the front one, you should be able to get down to the nearest town, where a garage can fix the rear one for you.'

Wise advice, delivered in casual, friendly fashion – and all the while, the third member of the trio, the youth, who the victims wouldn't even know was present, would be sliding unobtrusively out of the back of the Hyundai's rear and crawling around to the target vehicle's offside, from where he could open the passenger door and help himself to whatever jackets, coats, handbags and wallets had been dumped on the back seat. A classic distraction-theft, which even now – as Heck watched – had gone into play. The lad, still in his neutral grey clothing, snaked along the tarmac, passing the Hyundai on all fours.

Heck stayed in the field but ran forward at pace, climbing a low barbed-wire fence, and hissing into his radio. 'Thieves on, M-E! Thieves on! Move it . . . fast!'

Mary-Ellen responded in the affirmative, but it was Heck who reached the scene of the crime first, zipping up his anorak as he jumped the wall and emerged on the roadside, coming around the twisted ash before anyone had even noticed.

'Afternoon all,' he said, strolling to the rear of the BMW, where the youth, still on hands and knees, but now with a purse, a wallet and an iPad laid on the road surface alongside him, could only gaze up, white-faced. 'This is illegal, isn't it?'

The elderly couple regarded Heck in bemusement, an expression that only changed when he scooped down, caught the lad under his armpit and hoisted him into view. At once the younger couple reacted; the girl backing away, wide-eyed, but the bloke turning and sprinting along the road.

He didn't get far before Mary-Ellen's Land Rover, blues and twos flickering, spun into view over the next rise, sliding to a side-on halt, blocking the carriageway. The thief fancied his chances when he saw the figure who emerged from it: a Cumbrian police uniform complete with hi-viz doublet, utility belt loaded with the usual appointments, cuffs, baton, PAVA spray and so forth, but with only a young woman inside it – probably younger than he was in fact, no more than twenty-three, and considerably shorter, no more than five foot five. Of course he didn't know PC Mary-Ellen O'Rourke's reputation for being a fitness fanatic and pocket battleship. When she crossed the road to intercept him, he tried to barge his way past, only to be taken around the legs with a flying rugby tackle, which brought him down heavily, slamming his face on the tarmac. He lay there groaning, his fake head-piece hanging off, exposing the fair hair underneath. Mary-Ellen knelt cheerfully on his back and applied the handcuffs.

'Sorry folks,' Heck said to the astonished elderly couple, as he marched past, driving the other two prisoners by the scruffs of their necks. 'DS Heckenburg, Cumbrian Constabulary. We've been after this lot for a little while.'

'We've not done nothing,' the girl protested. 'We were trying to help.'

'Yeah, by lightening these good people's load while they were on their holidays,' Heck replied. 'Well don't worry, now you're going on *your* holidays. At Her Majesty's pleasure. You don't have to say anything, but it may harm your defence if you don't mention when questioned something you later rely on in court. Anything you do say may be given in evidence . . . in case you were wondering, you're getting locked up for being a set of thieving little scrotes.'

It was mid-evening when the arresting officers finally returned from Windermere police station, where they'd taken their prisoners for interview and charge. While Mary-Ellen headed to Cragwood Keld nick to sign off and close up for the day, Heck made his first port of call The Witch's Kettle, not least because on a cold, misty autumn night like this – the chill in the air had turned icy – the warm, ruddy light pouring from its windows was very alluring. Inside, a big fire crackled in the grate, throwing orange phantasms across the olde worlde fittings.

Lucy Cutterby, Hazel's only barmaid, was alone behind the bar, reading a paperback. 'Hi, Heck,' she said, as he approached.

Lucy was nineteen and worked here for bed and board only, because she was actually Hazel's niece, taking a year out to do some hiking, climbing and sailing and to get in some additional study time before she went to university, where she hoped to take a degree in Sports Science. At present, she looked trim and athletic in grey sweats and white plimsolls, her lush tawny hair worn high. With her blue eyes, pixie nose, and rosebud lips, Lucy had been a welcome addition to the pub's staff. Hazel assumed she'd attract men to the pub in droves, but on a night like this they'd be lucky to attract anyone. At present only a handful of customers was present: Ted Haveloc, a retired Forestry Commission worker, who now worked on everyone's gardens; and Burt and Mandy Fillingham, who ran the post office which also doubled as the village corner shop.

Lucy nipped upstairs to get her aunt, who trotted down a few minutes later. 'And?' Hazel asked, looking vaguely uneasy.

Heck shrugged off his anorak and pulled up a stool. 'Couldn't have done it without you.'

'You arrested them?' She looked surprised, but still perhaps a little shaky. Hazel was every inch a local lass – she was well-travelled but had never actually lived outside the Lake District, as her soft Cumbrian accent attested – and the thought of serious crime visiting this peaceful quarter was something she evidently wasn't getting her head around easily.

'All three of them,' Heck confirmed. 'Caught 'em in the act.'

She served him his usual pint of Buttermere Gold. 'So what was it all about? Or aren't you allowed to tell me?'

'Suppose you've a right to know, given the help you've provided. Several times in the last fortnight, tourists up here have been waylaid by distraction-thieves. It happened in Borrowdale, near Ullswater and down in Grizedale Forest. The usual form was the visitors stopped for lunch somewhere, but no sooner had they got back on the road than they had to pull over with a couple of flat tyres. A few minutes later, a young bloke and his girlfriend would conveniently stop to assist. Once these two had driven off again, the tourists found valuables missing from their vehicles.'

Hazel looked fascinated, and now maybe a little relieved that the crimes in question weren't anything more violent. 'I've heard about that on the Continent.'

'Well . . . it if works in France and Spain, there's no reason why it shouldn't work here. Especially in rural areas. All we knew was that the suspects were driving either a green or blue motor, which might have been a Hyundai. The victims were never totally sure, and we only got rough glimpses of it on car park security footage . . . on top of that we only ever had partial VRM numbers, and they never seemed to marry up. You won't be surprised to learn that after we arrested this lot, we found dozens of different plates in the boot, which they changed around regularly.'

'So this was like their full-time job?'

'Their career. The way they made their living. Anyway . . .' He sipped at his beer. 'As the crime spree only seemed to start around here two weeks ago, I made a few enquiries with other forces covering tourist spots – and I got several similar reports. A young male and female distraction team targeting motorists out in the sticks. It was always the same pattern. The boy offered to help with the tyre change, while the girl stood around chatting. In no case did the spree last more than two weeks.'

'They only booked in here for two weeks,' Hazel said.

'They never outstay their welcome. The upshot was I canvassed all the hotels and bed and breakfasts.'

'And that worked?' She looked sceptical. 'I mean, even in the off-season there are thousands of young couples who come up to the Lakes.'

'Yeah, but not so many who've got a gooseberry in tow.'

'I don't get you.'

'You may recall . . . I didn't ask you if there were any adult couples staying here. I asked if there were any adult *trios*.'

'Ohhh.' Now Hazel looked impressed. 'Who's a clever boy?'

'It struck me there'd have to be a third thief, someone concealed in the Hyundai. He would do the actual stealing while the others put on their show.'

'And one such trio was staying here,' she said. 'And they even drove a Hyundai.'

'And the rest is history.' He smiled. 'Mind you, I'm not saying we didn't get lucky that they happened to be rooming right here.'

Hazel continued mopping the bar. 'So long as they're gone. I mean I hope they haven't left anything behind . . . I wouldn't want them coming back.'

'I wouldn't worry about that. Quite a few forces want to talk to them. They'll be in custody a good while yet.'

Realising he hadn't paid for his pint, he pushed some money across the bar-top, but she pushed it back. 'On me. For a job well done. I'll tell you what . . . I'd never have had them pegged for criminals. Bit of a curious mix,

I suppose . . . mid-thirties, mid-twenties and a teen, but they didn't seem rough.'

'Successful crooks are rarely dumb. You want to infiltrate quiet communities, it doesn't make any sense to ride in like a bunch of cowboys. Not in this day and age.'

'Makes you realise how vulnerable we are up here, though.'

'Nahhh,' came a brash Irish voice. Mary-Ellen had materialised alongside them, now in a black tracksuit with 'Metropolitan Police' stencilled across the back in white. She leapt athletically onto the bar stool next to Heck. She was toothy but pretty, with fierce green eyes and short, spiky black hair. A champion swimmer, fell-walker and rock-climber, she radiated energy and enthusiasm – even now, at the end of a long, tough shift. 'You've got us two, haven't you?' she chirped. 'We're a match for anyone.'

'And here's the other girl of the moment,' Heck said. 'Wouldn't have been able to do it without her, either.'

'What'll you have, M-E?' Hazel asked.

Mary-Ellen gazed at Heck with mock astonishment. 'You buying, sarge?'

'*I'm* buying,' Hazel said. 'You two have taken some nasty people off the streets today. *Our* streets. And with the bad weather due, they could have been stuck around here for God knows how long. Who knows, we could have been murdered in our beds.'

'Don't think they were quite that nasty,' Mary-Ellen replied with her trademark rasping chuckle. 'But I'll have a lager, cheers. I'll tell you what . . . felt good getting our hands on some proper villains for a change, eh?'

'Too true,' Heck said, peeling away from the bar and heading to the Gents. 'Excuse me, ladies . . . too sodding true.'

Neither of the women chose to comment on that parting shot.

Mary-Ellen was a newcomer to the Lake District herself, having transferred up only a couple of months ago from the Met, just half a month after Heck in fact. But despite spending her last four years in Britain's largest urban police force, she had worked exclusively in Richmond-upon-Thames, a well-heeled area with relatively low crime rates, and lacked Heck's experience of inner-city policing and major investigations. But given that the most serious crimes they tended to have to deal with up here involved low-level drug dealing, thefts from gardens, and the occasional drunken incidents in pubs – she could understand how he might be feeling a little restless. He'd taken to this distraction-thefts enquiry giddily, like a kid in a toy shop, and had almost seemed disappointed they'd closed the suspects down so quickly. Of course, from Hazel's perspective, the whole thing had been fascinating but also a little unnerving – not just because it had revealed the presence of real criminals, but because it had allowed her a first glimpse of Heck's edgier, more adversarial character. In the real world, the handsome, homely landlady – newly divorced, thanks to her beer-bloated rat of a husband running off with one of his barmaids two years ago – should be the apple of every single bloke's eye. The problem was that there weren't that many single blokes in the Cradle. As such, it was perhaps no surprise Hazel and Heck had gravitated towards each other. But Mary-Ellen couldn't help wondering how long it could last.

Not that it was very clear to anyone, Heck included, what he and Hazel's actual relationship was.

Heck himself pondered this as he stood washing his hands in the bathroom. It had occurred by increments, if he was honest. With near-reluctance, as though both parties were trying to avoid being hurt, or perhaps trying to avoid hurting each other. But the mutual attraction had steadily grown: the furtive looks they'd exchanged, the occasional touching of hands, Heck finding himself perched comfortably at the end of the bar where the till and telephone sat, a position of familiarity that wouldn't normally be reserved for everyday customers. Despite all that, there were some confidences he wasn't yet prepared to share with Hazel – primarily a concern that he was wasting himself out here in the boondocks. Partly this was through fear. Hazel was so proud of this small, successful business she ran. She adored her tranquil life in Cragwood Keld, this 'haven in the mountains' as she called it. The idea of moving anywhere else was hardly likely to appeal to her. In that respect, Heck's increasing boredom with his current post was a subject he never gave voice to.

'Will I have to give evidence?' Hazel asked when he returned to the bar.

Heck pondered. 'Shouldn't think so. I mean, there's nothing they could cross-examine you on. I enquired if you knew anyone matching a certain description. You did and gave me a statement. After that, you had no further involvement. In any case, they've already coughed to the distraction-thefts up here in the Lakes, so the chances are that part of the case won't go to trial.'

'I may need that from you in writing if I'm not going to worry about it,' she said, moving away to serve Burt Fillingham.

'So what do we think?' Mary-Ellen asked Heck. 'Good day?'

'Very good day.'

'Hazel's right about the weather. Forecast's terrible. Freezing fog up here tonight and tomorrow. Maybe even longer. Visibility down to a few feet.'

'Great. Life'll be even quieter.'

'Hey . . .' She elbowed him. 'A few detectives I know'd be glad of that. Catch up on some paperwork.'

'To catch up on paperwork, M-E, you first have to generate it.'

She regarded him appraisingly. As a rule, Heck didn't get morose. But he was leaning towards glum at present. 'Heck, didn't you *volunteer* for this Lake District gig?'

'Yeah . . . sort of.' He waved it away. 'Sorry . . . quiet is good. Course it is. Means low levels of crime, people sleeping safe in their beds. How can I complain?'

She chugged on her lager. 'It won't be cakes and ale. There'll be accidents. People'll get lost, get hurt . . . there's always some bellend who'll come up here alone, whatever the weather man says.'

Heck pondered this. It was true – the fells were no place for inexperienced hikers, especially in bad weather. And yet all winter the amateurs would try their hands, necessitating regular and risky turn-outs for the emergency services. If this coming winter turned particularly nasty, the Cradle itself could face problems. With only Cragwood Road connecting it to the outside world, snow, sleet and even heavy rain had the potential to cut them off. The predicted fog would be even more of a nuisance as it might prevent the Mountain Rescue services deploying their helicopter.

'I think I can safely say,' Heck concluded, 'that even I would rather be tucked up warm in bed than dealing with that lot.'

'I'm sure that'll be an option,' Mary-Ellen said, as Hazel came back along the bar.

'Looks like there won't be much custom in here for the next few days,' Hazel commented.

'Just what we were saying,' Mary-Ellen said, drinking up. 'Anyway, I'm off. Thanks for the beer.'

'Bit early . . .?' Heck said.

'*True Detective*'s on satellite again tonight. Missed it the first time round.' She sauntered out of the pub. 'See you later.'

'*True Detective* . . .?' Hazel mused. 'Isn't that the one where they were after some kind of satanic killer?'

'Seem to recall it was,' Heck replied.

She mopped the bar-top. 'Not the kind of thing we get up at Witch Cradle . . . despite the name.'

'So I've noticed.'

'These sneaky buggers pinching people's handbags and wallets are about the toughest we're used to up here.'

'Let's hope it stays that way.'

She gave him a half-smile. 'Yeah . . . course you do.'

'Hey, I may surprise you.'

'Oh?'

'I'm adaptable. The quiet life has its attractions.'

'Such as?'

He shrugged. 'We're all adults. It's not like we can't find ways to fill these long, uneventful hours.'

Hazel smiled again, saucily, as she pulled Ted Haveloc a pint.

Outside meanwhile, a front of semi-frozen air forged its way across the mountains and valleys of northwest England, sliding under the milder upper air and gradually forming a dense blanket of leprous-grey fog which, in a region already famous for having very few streetlamps, reduced visibility to virtually nothing. The scattered towns and villages were shrouded. Cragwood Keld – a hamlet of only fifteen buildings – was swamped; one house couldn't see another. And of course it was cold, so terribly cold, with billions of frigid water crystals suspended in the gloom; every twig, every tuft of withered vegetation sprouting feathers of frost. By eleven o'clock, as the last few house-lights winked out and the full blackness of night took hold, the polar silence was ethereal, the stillness unearthly.

Nothing stirred out there.
These were foul conditions, they'd say.
It was a foul night all round.
The foulest really.
Abhorrent.
Loathsome.

Chapter 2

'We just have to get to lower ground,' Tara said tiredly. 'Then we can flag a car down or something.'

'I agree that's the obvious solution,' Jane replied, vexed, 'but don't keep saying it over and over, as if it'll be some kind of doddle and that it's somehow stupid of us to not have done it already. For the last three hours, the only way to get to lower ground has been over precipices or down vertical drops.'

Tara made no initial response, mainly through guilt.

It had been her idea to finish their week-long camping trip by taking a well-trodden hilltop path from Borrowdale, over High Raise and Great Castle Howe, and down into Great Langdale. On paper it had all looked so straightforward; in fact easier than that, and probably very rewarding. After a difficult week, it had felt as if she was plucking victory from the jaws of defeat. The campsite at Watendlath hadn't been all they'd hoped for, primarily because it was late November and the tourist season was long over. A few other hardy campers were present – hardier than Tara and Jane, it had to be said – but the site was largely empty, and its facilities operating at a reduced level; the toilets and showers were open, and that was about it. The weather conditions, while not exactly disastrous, were testing; the mornings damp and cold, the afternoons slightly drier but still cold, and the nights, freezing. On top of that, they were not experienced at this sort of thing. Their tent was old and somewhat mouldy; it was also single-skinned, which offered them zero protection against insects and condensation; they'd brought foam mats instead of truckle-beds, and their sleeping bags were old and filled with duck-down, which when it got damp stayed damp – and it had rained several times already that week; boy, had it rained.

None of this had made for a comfortable time. But worse still, they were bored. Neither Tara nor Jane classified themselves as party girls, but they were on their holidays and would have liked a drink now and then. Unfortunately, they'd used up all their spare backpack space on food supplies, and had assumed before arriving there'd be somewhere close by where they could stock up on booze once they'd got here – but there wasn't and neither had a car, so they couldn't just drive out. Jane had her iPad, so they could watch movies and listen to music – at least that had been the plan, but the device's battery had died within a day and Jane had neglected to bring her charger.

As such, Tara's sudden suggestion that they stop moping around the camp and actually get up into the wilderness – do some real walking, get some proper exercise and fresh air – had seemed like a godsend. It wouldn't even be that difficult, she'd said, as they pored over a map on the fourth morning. Watendlath to Elter Water was not a great distance. The guidebooks described it as a 'challenging route', but they weren't looking for a stroll in the park. If it took them all day, so much the better – they had nothing but time anyway. Once they reached Elter Water, they could catch a bus to Ambleside, stay overnight in a B&B, and head for home by train.

'I mean, how difficult can it be to just check the weather forecast?' Jane grumbled as they trudged doggedly on, their backpacks jolting their aching spines.

'With what, Jane?' Tara retorted. 'The club and bar were closed, so we had no access to a telly. Our phones aren't getting any signal up here. No one was selling newspapers on the site, and even if there'd been sufficient Wi-Fi for your iPad to be any use, the bloody thing ran out on us . . .'

'Alright, alright, for Christ's sake!' Jane's face reddened, and not just from the unaccustomed exertion.

On all sides, meanwhile, the midnight fog hung in impenetrable drapes. At this height and temperature it was like movie fog, a dense, grey mantle that rolled and twisted, obscuring everything. There hadn't been any sign of this when they'd set off that morning, in broad daylight – it had been clear as a bell. But even if it had still been daylight now, only a few yards of harsh, rocky ground covered with frost-white tussocks would be visible. And of course, it wasn't daylight; it was dark, which didn't so much obscure the surrounding landscape as obliterate it. Naturally, they'd neglected to bring a torch. The last few occasions they'd needed light – to try to make sense of a dog-eared map, which was now next to useless anyway, as some time back they'd unconsciously veered off the flinty footway that was their prescribed route – Tara had switched her phone on, using the dull glow of its facia. She was increasingly reluctant to do this now, as she didn't want to run its power down. It would be typical of their luck if they suddenly entered a better reception area and were able to make an emergency call, only for the battery to die.

The guidebook had predicted the journey would take six hours, meaning they'd finish well before nightfall, but they'd now been struggling along for at least twelve.

'Look . . .' Tara tried a more placating tone. 'If we can't find our way down to a road, we should maybe think about pitching the tent. Just camp for the night. Hopefully this fog will have lifted by morning.'

'Newsflash, Tara . . . it's perishing bloody cold!'

'So we wrap up.'

'Everything's wet, you dozy mare! We'll die from bloody hypothermia.'

Their voices echoed and re-echoed, creating the illusion they were in a chasm rather than on some open hillside. It was more than uncanny.

'Jane, it can't be a good idea to just keep ploughing on. We don't know where we're going, and this ground seems to be sloping upward.'

'We can hardly pitch the tent when we can't see our hands in front of our faces,' Jane said. 'Anyway, what if the fog hasn't gone by tomorrow? We're up on the fells, remember . . . not in some nice park a few yards from your mum and dad's nice little middle-class house.'

'*Alright!* You don't need to be such a bitch about it.'

'Anyway, what good is sitting tight going to do? No one'll come looking for us, Tara, because no one fucking knows we're here. Didn't it ever enter that air-filled brainbox of yours to tell someone what we were planning? And I don't mean that bloody campsite owner. I mean someone who might actually care about us, who might actually have been listening when you were talking to them. Like our fucking parents, perhaps! I mean, Jesus, how difficult can it fucking be . . .?'

45

'*Alright, I said!* Christ's sake, Jane . . . I'm in as much danger as you are!'

Jane muttered some incoherent, vaguely foul-mouthed response, and they trod along in silence for a few more minutes, hearing only their own grunted exertions and the hollow thuds of their feet. Fleetingly, oddly, Tara was uncomfortable with the otherwise complete silence. It was a stupid thought, of course. There was no one else up here, but why did she get the sudden feeling their latest outburst, which would likely have been heard for miles and miles on a night like this, might have drawn the attention of someone listening? Even if it had, that ought to be something they'd want – and yet there was a brief queasy sensation in her tummy.

'Sorry about the airhead thing,' Jane muttered self-consciously.

'It's alright,' Tara said. 'Sorry about the bitch.'

Tara Cook and Jane Dawson were able to converse like this, one minute at each other's throats, the next offering consolation, because they were close enough to be sisters, having grown up together in Wilmslow.

Jane was now a sales assistant at Catwalk, a clothing retailer whose branded products were strictly mid-range, while Tara had a bar job but was also studying for her PhD at Manchester Met. Money was tight for the both of them and, wanting to get away for a bit, it had been Tara's idea that they visit Cumbria.

'Let's just put everything on hold for a few days,' she'd said enthusiastically. 'Let's go camping in the Lakes. We both love it and it will do us a world of good.'

It was true, they did both love it. As children they'd holidayed in the Lake District many times with their respective families. But on those occasions, they'd stayed at hotels, rented cottages, or bed and breakfast accommodation. More to the point, they'd travelled up here in June, July or August – not November. Even so, Jane had thought the idea a good one.

'Let's do it,' she'd said.

It hadn't been difficult arranging it, given it was the off-season, and they'd been able to sort everything out that same evening. It was going to be great, Tara said.

It scarcely felt that way now: lost, frozen and well over a thousand feet up, and if that wasn't bad enough, the ground was indeed sloping upward again. It had been difficult enough coping with loose, ice-slippery stones, and clumps of spiky mountain grass – so much so that they hadn't initially noticed the shallow upward incline – but now it was steepening sharply. In addition, the fog seemed to be thickening, which was hardly helped by the clouds of soapy breath billowing from their lungs. Even walking shoulder-to-shoulder, they were only aware of each other as featureless phantoms.

'Look Tara,' Jane said, unconsciously lowering her voice. 'We need to get real about this. We're in pretty serious trouble here.'

'I know . . .'

And Tara did, though perhaps only now was it really dawning on her. When you were down in the Lake District's lower country on a bright summer's morning, taking tea and crumpets in whitewashed villages, it seemed such a benign environment. The stories you heard about people getting lost on the fells and dying from exposure surely applied to another time and another place.

And yet suddenly, bewilderingly, that time was now and that place was here.

The oft-quoted phrase, 'how did we get into this mess',

occurred to her with shocking force. It felt as if they'd led themselves blindfolded, for several hours, to this apparent point of no return.

'Well if we're not going to camp, we have to keep moving,' Tara said, doing her best to stay upbeat. 'That'll help us stay warm.'

'And will wear us down,' Jane argued, seemingly unaware she was contradicting her own position of a few minutes earlier. 'Reduce our ability to resist the cold. I can barely feel my hands and feet as it is.'

Tara knew what she meant. It was just before twelve o'clock now, but the temperature would continue to drop until well into the early hours.

'Can't feel our hands and feet, can't *see* our hands and feet more like,' she mused. 'We're disappearing by inches.'

'Not funny, Tara, Jesus!'

'Yeah, I know. I'm sorry.'

'At least the slope's levelling off.'

Thankfully, the gradient had flattened out again, and a second later they walked into a dry-stone wall. It came to roughly chest-height on Tara, higher still on Jane, and yet the fog was so impenetrable they blundered into it with enough force to induce pain and surprise. Tara switched her phone on. It created a minor capsule of dim aquamarine light around them, and shimmered over the smooth, neatly stacked stones. The wall led away to left and right, quickly vanishing.

Tara switched the light off again, plunging them back into darkness.

The wall wouldn't be difficult to scale, though both of them were aching and bone-weary, but at least it was a solid fixture, and it broke the surreal monotony of this place – not that it was something to actually be reassured by. Hundreds of miles of dry-stone walls snaked across the Lake District

National Park, through the lower valleys, up the teetering fell-sides, across the desolate tops of ridges and plateaux. Sure, it was a sign that civilisation wasn't too far away – as the crow flew, or if you were on horseback. Not so much if you were a tired, and increasingly cold and disoriented foot-slogger.

'So do we climb over it and keep going?' Tara wondered.

'Why?' Jane asked.

'What do you mean?'

'Why climb over it? Why not follow it?'

'It won't lead to a farmhouse, or anything like that.'

'At least we'll know we aren't walking in fucking circles.'

'Jane . . .' Tara tried to remain patient. It served no purpose to stand here sniping at each other in the murk. 'Look . . . people don't walk around in circles, okay? Not in real life. That only happens in the movies.'

'Oh, Jesus Christ . . . we're lost in the middle of nowhere, and you're giving me Halliwell's fucking Film Guide.'

'Jane, come on . . .'

'I've got a film for you, Tara. *The Shining*. Remember that . . . when he got lost, and in the morning he was dead, covered in ice?'

'That was up in the mountains.'

'*We're* in the fucking mountains!'

'Not in Colorado.'

'Look, Tara . . . below zero is below zero, whether it speaks with a Yank accent or Cumbrian.'

'Jane, panicking won't help.'

'I'll tell you what . . . let's get over this blessed wall. We have to do something soon, or I'm going to smack you one.'

Jane's voice had taken on a new, shrill intensity. Tara imagined that, were she to switch her phone on again, she'd see eyes like polished marbles straining from her friend's long, boyish face; the skin stretched like shiny parchment over those unattractive, hard-angled bones.

That was when they heard the whistling.

Or rather, Tara heard it.

'Wait, *shhh*!' she said, fumbling at Jane's arm.

'Don't shush me, Tara!'

'No, *listen*.'

Because she was in such a state that she'd grab at any straw, no matter how slender, Jane allowed her friend to speak. But of course, she heard nothing herself.

'Yeah, great . . . the silence that signifies impending doom.'

'No, I heard something.'

'What?'

'Listen!'

They fell quiet again, and now indeed there was something – a tune of some sort. At first it was very faint, as though being carried on the breeze. Except that there was no breeze. And the longer they listened, the clearer it became. Incredible though it seemed, someone relatively close by *was* whistling. Both of them recognised the tune, though neither could initially put a name to it, and now they were too excited to try.

'I don't believe it,' Jane said. 'Where's it coming from?'

'Over there, I think.' Tara indicated the other side of the wall.

'Hello!' Jane shouted at the top of her voice. 'Hello, is someone there?'

'Jane, don't,' Tara said.

'What's the matter?'

'I don't . . . nothing. It's just silly.' The misgivings Tara had briefly felt, about how vulnerable they were trekking through this endless gloom, had returned; suddenly, pinpointing their exact location seemed like a bad idea. But surely that was folly – a fear born of some ancient animal instinct, whereas logic advised that if there was someone out there, they should draw attention to themselves as soon as possible. 'I just thought . . .'

'*Shhh!*' Now it was Jane's turn to hit her friend's arm. Whoever the whistler was, he was persisting with it. He sounded closer, and yes, it *did* seem as if he was somewhere on the other side of the wall.

'Hello!' Jane shouted again, attempting to scramble up the bricks, which wasn't easy with feet numb inside frozen boots. Tara switched her phone back on, so they could identify hand and footholds. Jane reached the top of the wall first, and straddled it. 'Excuse me, we're lost! Can you help us?'

The whistling ceased.

'He's heard us,' she said.

'Hello!' Tara called.

The only reply was another dim echo of their own voices.

Nevertheless, they were sufficiently re-energised to clamber down the other side of the wall. 'Whoever it is, he probably can't believe there's someone else up here,' Tara said, laughing with relief. 'Excuse me . . . we're over here! I'd like to tell you which direction, but . . .' she laughed again, 'I don't know.'

The whistling recommenced. Now they were on the other side of the wall, it sounded as if it was coming from just ahead of them, but a way to the left.

'What the hell is he still whistling for?' Jane said. 'Didn't he hear us?'

'Oh God,' Tara replied. 'Suppose he's got earphones on, and he's whistling along to a song.'

'Oh shit. Okay . . . we'll just have to find him.' Jane started forward urgently, hoisting the straps at her shoulders with gloved thumbs.

'*Strangers in the Night*,' Tara panted.

'What?'

'That song he's whistling . . . it's *Strangers in the Night*. You know, the old Frank Sinatra number.'

Jane listened, and she too recognised the timeless ditty. 'Yeah . . . what a choice of song for a place like this. Quite apt for us though, eh?' She chuckled, though there wasn't much humour in it. 'Come on, Tara . . . we've got to find this guy.'

Tara also adjusted her pack, and hurried in pursuit. Again they were blundering through foggy blackness, their feet crunching on clumps of frozen grass. But the whistling was getting louder, clearer. Perhaps somewhere just ahead there'd be a campsite, maybe containing two or three climbers or fell-walkers. Their hi-tech canopies would be arranged around a small, neat fire. The guys themselves would be lean, rugged outdoor types, probably bearded, stoking the flames, eating peanuts, chocolate and other energy-enhancing foods, drinking hot coffee from a thermos flask; maybe it was laced with rum or whiskey to give it some bite.

But Jane and Tara found no such campsite.

They'd walked in what they were certain was the right direction for a good hundred yards, increasingly tired and irate again. And still the unlit reaches of fog extended on all sides of them. The whistling persisted somewhere ahead, but how far ahead they had no clue. And now, very abruptly, it ceased. Despite their own heavy breathing, the silence was ear-ringing.

'Hello!' Jane shouted again, with more than a touch of her normal petulance. 'Newsflash . . . there are people lost out here!'

They waited but there was no response.

'Come on, mate! You must have heard us by now!'

The whistling recommenced somewhere behind them. *Strangers in the Night* again. But now at a slower pace – deliberately slower, for effect.

'Is this guy taking the piss, or what?' Jane said, glancing backward.

'It must be the acoustics,' Tara replied. 'This landscape's really weird like that. I've heard stories about people hearing voices that have come from miles away.'

'Great, Tara. That's all I needed to know.'

'But listen . . .'

'Now what?'

'It's moving.'

The whistling continued – very clear, very precise, a slow and highly tuneful rendition of *Strangers in the Night*, but as Tara said, it was drifting from left to right, as though the whistler was strolling casually in that direction.

'Another atmospheric effect?' Jane wondered tartly. 'Or some dickweed playing stupid games?'

'Why would someone be playing games?' Tara asked, though it was a question she was posing to herself as much as Jane.

'Let's just find the bastard.'

They pressed on, heading right. As they did, the whistling steadily reduced in volume, as though the whistler was retreating from them.

'Hey, wait up!' Jane bawled hoarsely. 'You fucking idiot! We need help!'

'Jane, that's not the way you do it,' Tara hissed.

'Wait 'til I get hold of him, then you'll really hear something.'

The whistling stopped. They slid to a halt.

'Christ,' Tara said. 'It's like he just heard us.'

'Good, that's the idea.'

'Jane, I'm not sure about this . . .'

The whistling recommenced – closer than it had been, but now on their left.

'What the hell?' Jane said. 'Why is he walking around us?'

'Maybe he isn't . . . maybe it's like I said, the acoustics.' But from the tone of her voice – a breathless quaver – Tara knew she wasn't making a convincing case.

'Okay,' Jane said tersely but quietly, as if she too was suddenly unnerved by this curious behaviour. 'Let's go back to the wall.'

'The wall?'

'Put it between him and us . . . whoever *he* is.'

'I don't know the way back to the wall. I don't know the way anywhere. We've got turned around at least two or three times now.'

'*This* way.'

'Why?'

'It's as good as any.' Already walking, Jane scrunched the shoulder of her friend's orange cagoule in a talon-like grip. Tara fell into step beside her. Fleetingly, their fatigue was forgotten. It was all about covering distance now. 'Let's just accept that he's an arsehole,' Jane said under her breath; then louder, over her shoulder: '*You arsehole!*'

'Jane, no!' Tara's voice dropped to a whisper. 'Look . . . he's as blind as we are up here. Let's just walk away . . . right away. We keep it down and he won't even know we've gone.'

They strode quickly and quietly, the only sound their short, sharp breathing. They'd covered maybe a hundred yards unimpeded, their concern ebbing a little – when they head the whistling again.

No more than twenty yards to their right.

Almost on a level with them.

'Oh shit,' Tara whimpered.

They sped up until they were almost running, as a result

54

of which Jane tripped, falling full length. Tara stooped and groped around for her in the murk. 'You alright?'

'I'm alright, for Christ's sake! Just keep going . . . we have to keep moving.'

But the whistler was moving too, circling around behind them, still treating them to *Strangers in the Night*, though now at a raised tempo.

'Okay, okay,' Jane said. 'He goes left, we go right.'

She hooked onto Tara's cagoule again. They moved away, following a diagonal line. Both were now saturated with sweat, their lungs pumping. They again tried to move stealthily, only to find themselves on a loose, stony surface, which clattered and scraped under their soles.

'Oh, bloody hell!' Jane squealed.

It was scree; masses of broken rocks ramped sharply uphill in front of them.

'This way!' Tara said, pulling Jane in a different direction, but stones continued to crack and tumble beneath their boots, creating a racket that would carry across the night. 'He's stopped whistling at least. Probably lost track of us.'

'Don't be ridiculous. He can't *not* know where we are with all this hullaballoo.'

'Maybe he's just had enough then?'

Panting hard, the blood pounding in their ears, they forged on. They were on higher ground now, the chunks of debris larger. Soon they were having to pick their way between them rather than scrambling over them, though this at least was a quieter process. In fact, colossal boulders now lay in their path, which afforded a sense of protection. They slid between them in single file, their waterproofs hissing on the rugged stone.

'Don't worry, this is all good,' Tara whispered. 'Crooked passages. He can't come on us by surprise in one of these. We can lie low. Get down, wait a few minutes . . .'

'We should press on,' Jane said, in front, slapping her hands along the surfaces to either side.

'Let's at least stop, see if we can hear anything.'

They halted again, their breath furling in semi-frozen plumes. It took several seconds for the noise of this to subside, and then there were several seconds more of nothing – before they heard the whistling.

It was just above their heads.

They glanced upward.

He was only vaguely visible – an apelike silhouette crouched on top of the boulder on their left. His huge, misshapen head, almost certainly hooded, was inclined down at them. He stopped whistling half a second before he dropped. It was impossible to judge how big or heavy he was, but when he crash-landed on top of Jane, who, though stocky of build was only five feet four, she collapsed beneath him with a muffled shriek. Tara, standing rigid and helpless, didn't quite see what happened next, though she heard it: a succession of heavy blows. She thought a brawny arm was rising and falling, and maybe that was a jagged stone clutched in its gloved hand. With each impact, Jane gave a low, tortured moan.

'Stop . . . please,' Tara stammered.

The flurries of movement ceased. With a creak of waterproofs, the muffled shape turned its heavy, brooding head towards her. She heard a *thud* as the stone was released, saw an arm slide out of sight, heard a distinctive *click*. Tara knew very little about guns, but she'd seen enough of them on the television to recognise when a firearm was being cocked.

That was the tipper. The moment the adrenaline broke her paralysis.

She twirled around, fighting back along the crooked defile into open space, and there barked her shins against low, unseen edges. She barely felt the pain; the main problem was that she fell sideways, winding herself, another sharp stone digging into her hip. From here, she scrambled along on her hands and knees, sensing rather than seeing the humanoid form emerging from the defile behind her. She knew it would be pointing the gun in her general direction. Tears streamed down her face as she jumped to her feet and started running again, blindly but desperately, putting as much distance as possible between them: ten yards, twenty, thirty, forty. Surely she was out of sight now? He couldn't see her to shoot. Fifty yards, sixty . . .

Heck's eyes flirted open.

A first he wasn't sure what had disturbed him. Then he realised: a distant noise like a reverberating *boom*.

A gunshot . . . maybe.

He pushed the quilt aside, sat up and took his watch from the bedside table. Its neon numerals read: 00.18.

He hadn't been asleep long. He got up, wandered across the bedroom and shifted the thin curtain. It was impossible to see anything out there. The fog was like grey sediment swirling in liquid.

'What is it?' Hazel asked sleepily.

'Dunno. I thought . . . Did you hear something?'

'Outside?'

'I thought so.'

'Like what?'

'Not sure. Gunfire perhaps.'

She yawned. 'That wouldn't exactly be unusual around here.'

'No,' Heck conceded. He was still getting used to the idea that a much higher percentage of the population of this rural county held shotgun licences than they did back in the cities where he'd formerly worked. 'Bit late at night though, isn't it?'

'Car backfiring?'

'Perhaps.' He hung around at the window a few moments, until a gentle susurration from the pillow indicated Hazel had gone back to sleep. Eventually, wondering if he'd dreamed it, he drifted back to bed.

Tara covered another fifty yards before she realised she'd been shot.

Initially it had been like a blow on the back of her shoulder. A hard one, of course. It had driven the wind out of her, but sheer terror kept her on her feet, kept her motoring forward. Now however, very suddenly, her strength was draining, an intense pain spreading through the top right quarter of her body. The arm itself had turned numb – she had no sensation below the elbow. Under her clothing, that whole side of her body swam with hot fluid.

'Please,' she mumbled as she lost the coordination of her limbs. Her balance was all out, her legs wobbling. She realised the darkness filling her eyes was no longer just the darkness of night and fog. When she tottered over the precipice, she could hardly be blamed, because she hadn't even seen it.

Only vaguely aware she was falling, Tara spun downward for half a second, caroming outward from a jutting overhang made spongy by grass and rotted ferns, turning somersaults though icy emptiness, before hitting another shelf. This blow was phenomenal in its force, but again cushioned by sodden vegetation. Instinctively, she tried to grapple with it, but in mid-somersault all this did was wrench her left shoulder out of its socket and snap her humerus. In freefall again, she was engulfed by roaring, ice-cold water, and then hit by mud and rocks angled sharply downward, so that she slid on her back, until a heavy stone caught her feet and flipped her forward. Craggy edges tore at her ribs and rent her face, and then she was in mid-air again, descending through icy spume, the ear-pounding thunder of which overwhelmed all her senses.

Chapter 3

'It came over the wire during the early hours,' Mary-Ellen said to Heck as he checked into Cragwood Keld police station at eight the following morning.

It wasn't a real police station. It was located at the west end of the village, on a residential cul-de-sac called Hetherby Close, and was no more than a detached, whitewashed cottage which had been adapted for police use about ten years ago. It had stood empty for much of that time, only opening a few months back as part of ACPO's new rural crime initiative. A Cumbria Police noticeboard and an emergency phone stood on the front lawn, and wanted and mis-per posters decked its porch, but though it had a small front desk just inside the glazed front door – which was only open to customers temporarily, as Mary-Ellen had to patrol as well as answer call-outs – there was no facility to hold prisoners. The main office, where Heck and Mary-Ellen's desks faced each other over about three yards of carpet space, was in the rear of the building, where a large bay-window overlooked what had once been a garden, but was now a covered storage area for rescue and road-traffic equipment.

Heck yawned as he sipped his cup of tea.

Mary-Ellen read on through the email. 'Ambleside Mountain Rescue got a call from the owner of a campsite up at Watendlath. He's a bit concerned about two girls – a Jane Dawson and Tara Cook. Seems they checked out of his site a day early, said they were spending the last night of their holiday at Stagshaw View, which is a B&B in Ambleside. Then they set off on foot. He reckoned they must have been planning to yomp it through the northern Pikes. Trouble is, that was before the fog came down. He was already a bit worried, because he'd been observing them during the week and reckoned they were the most unprepared backpackers he'd ever seen. Around ten o'clock, when he saw what a pea-soup we were getting, he called Stagshaw View and was told the girls had never arrived. Called again at midnight, and at two – got the same response. He had emergency numbers for them – their own mobiles, which they weren't answering, and numbers for their parents back in Manchester. He got in touch with them too, but they hadn't heard anything from their daughters and didn't even know they were missing. Now of course, the mums and dads are panicking.'

'To be fair, *we* don't know they're missing yet,' Heck said. 'Not for sure.'

'They still haven't shown up.'

'If they got caught in the fog last night, they might just have camped.'

'The campsite owner said they wouldn't have stood a chance. Anyway, this fog's scheduled to last another day and night at least.'

Heck glanced through the connecting door to the front desk, and beyond that through the glazed front door to the outside, which was still concealed by an opaque grey curtain. It would be pretty nightmarish up on the fells, especially for someone with no experience and poor equipment.

'If they were headed to Ambleside from Borrowdale, that's some distance from here,' he said.

'Yeah, but Mountain Rescue reckon it wouldn't have been difficult for them to get turned around in the fog. They'd most likely have tried to come around Ullscarf and Greenup Edge, rather than go over the top. If they couldn't see their hands in front of their faces by then, it would have been easy to mistake High Raise for Calf Crag. If they did, that would bring them over Pavey Ark and down through Fiend's Fell to the east side of Witch Cradle Tarn. And in reduced visibility, well . . .'

She didn't need to elaborate. Heck was no mountaineer, but he'd been up there just to acclimatise himself to the region, and Fiend's Fell would be no laughing matter in fog. A notch in the White Stones crags, in appearance it was very dramatic – a vast, bowl-shaped grassland, windswept and strewn with boulders, and yet it ended abruptly, the land dropping precipitously away into the Cradle. There were various routes down from there – chimneys, ravines and even waterfalls – but these were strictly the domain of skilled and experienced climbers, not weekend adventurers.

'Think we should get the launch out?' Mary-Ellen asked.

'Yeah.' Heck finished his tea at a gulp. 'I do.'

In times long past, further back than anyone living in the Cradle could remember, Cragwood Ho, at the north end of Witch Cradle Tarn, had been little more than a remote farming community. Back in the day, when no one even maintained the roads leading up to this place, let alone provided gas, electricity and hot water, it must have been a spectacularly isolated spot.

It certainly felt that way today. 'The Ho', as it was known locally, was three miles due north of 'the Keld', and connected by a single-track lane, which proceeded in a more or less straight line along the tarn's edge, occasionally looping inward amid dense stands of pine and larch. Always to its left stood the steep, scree-cluttered slope ascending to Harrison Stickle. Though narrow, the road was usually bare of traffic during the off-season, and relatively safe. Though on this occasion, with visibility so appalling, progress was reduced to a torturous crawl. Veils of milk-white vapour reduced their vision to two or three yards, while even full headlight beams failed to penetrate more than a foot or so beyond that.

'Anyone lost on the fells in this is gonna be in real trouble,' Mary-Ellen said, zipping her black anorak. The Land Rover was warm inside, but it had a chilling effect just peering into the shifting blankness.

'Yep,' Heck muttered.

'Especially if they're new to the area.'

He nodded again. The Pikes were not hugely extensive, but they were dominant features even in the dramatic heart of the Lake District; colossal granite pyramids, with deep, wooded glens knifing through the middle of them, and fast becks tumbling and cascading down their rolling, rocky slopes. A playground for the fit and energetic, certainly; but a trackless region too, which required knowledge and athleticism to navigate on foot. And now, of course, something else had occurred to him.

'I don't want to overstate the importance of this, M-E, but just after midnight last night I heard what sounded like gunfire.'

She glanced sidelong at him as she drove. 'Where?'

'Up in the fells.'

'Any particular direction?'

'Impossible to say. It was only one shot too, so . . . I don't know, I might have been mistaken.'

Mary-Ellen pondered this.

'You didn't hear anything?' he asked.

'Nah. Hit the sack well before then. You know me. Sleep like a log.'

They cruised on at a steady six miles per hour, though even then it felt as if they were taking a chance. When a stag emerged from the fog in front of them, they had to jam on the brakes. The majestic beast had simply stepped from the vapour, little more than an outline in the misted glow of their lights, just about identifiable by its tall profile and the handsome spread of its antlers. It stood stock-still for a second, and then galloped off into the roadside foliage.

'Probably the last living thing we'll see out here,' Mary-Ellen commented, easing back onto the gas.

'Don't know whether to hope you're right or wrong,' Heck replied.

He'd often heard the saying 'no news is good news', and couldn't think of any dictum more worthless. At present, for example, they had almost nothing to go on. Before setting out, he'd checked with Windermere Comms, and had been given an update, which was mainly that there was no update, though they'd also been informed that, owing to the conditions, effective Mountain Rescue operations would be difficult – they might even be suspended – and it was certainly the case that no RAF helicopters could go up. Despite everything, it was deemed unlikely the two girls would have strayed from their intended route as far west as the Cradle, which was kind of encouraging, though the downside of this was that no extra bodies were being sent over here to assist. In the event there was a problem, Heck and Mary-Ellen were pretty much on their own.

Perched on the northernmost tip of Witch Cradle Tarn, Cragwood Ho was the archetypical Lakeland hamlet. Of its four houses, only two were occupied full-time. The empty units comprised a stone-built holiday let, once a working stable but still in the ownership of Gordon Clay, a farmer over Coniston way, and at this time of year almost always closed up, while the other, another former farm building, was now used as a second home by a family from south Lancashire. Aside from the Christmas season, this second house also stood unused during the winter months. Both of these premises were located on the west side of Cragwood Road. The hamlet's only two permanent residents lived on the east side of the road, next door to each other, right on the tarn's shoreline.

Cragwood Road itself ended in Cragwood Ho. As soon as it passed through the small clutch of houses, it ascended a few dozen yards into a gravelled parking area, where all further progress by normal vehicle was blocked by a dry-stone wall with a gate and a stile. Beyond that, a treacherous footway, the Cradle Track, snaked its way up into the Pikes; at its lower section this was just about wide enough for vehicle use, but most of the time the gate was kept barred. The car park was usually full during the spring and summer, walkers and climbers viewing this as the most immediate access to the Central Lakes massif, while the early autumn saw no shortage of visitors either. But at present, as Heck and Mary-Ellen coasted up into it, the Land Rover's tyres crunching to a halt against its rear wall, they appeared to be alone.

Visibility was still negligible. They couldn't even see the entirety of the car park. Further wafts of milky vapour flowed past as they climbed out, pulling on their gloves and woolly hats. As usual, Mary Ellen was in uniform, while Heck, as a CID officer, wore his regulation sweater, canvas trousers and walking boots, though on a day like today both also pulled on hi-viz waterproof overcoats with POLICE stencilled across the back in luminous letters.

'Quiet as the bloody grave,' Mary-Ellen said, her voice echoing eerily.

Heck took the loudhailer from the boot. 'At least if these lasses are stuck somewhere nearby, it shouldn't be difficult getting them to hear us.'

They set off down the side path which dropped steeply from the car park, and led along the front of the two houses on the water's edge.

The house on the right was called Lake-End Cottage, and its inhabitant was a certain Bill Ramsdale, a onetime married man and academic who now, in his mid-fifties, had become a reclusive loner and apparently, a writer, though Heck had never seen his name in a bookshop, either online or in the real world. His house was a small, scruffy cottage, the downstairs of which was almost entirely taken up by his study, but it was also surrounded by acres of untrimmed lawn, which rolled impressively down to the waterside and terminated at a private jetty. Given the usual prices in the Lake District, such a plot ought to have cost him a pretty penny. Whether he was rich or poor, Ramsdale was notoriously ill-tempered about his privacy. Twice he'd been spoken to by Mary-Ellen for showing a belligerent and even threatening attitude to hikers who'd strolled down across his land to the tarn's edge, unaware they were trespassing thanks to most of his perimeter wall having collapsed and his grass being overgrown.

The second resident, Bessie Longhorn, was an altogether more likeable sort. Just turned twenty, she was a little rough around the edges – only poorly educated, and thanks to a lifetime of semi-isolation in the Cradle, minus a fashion sense or any real knowledge about youth culture in general – but she was a friendly kid and always eager to please, especially when it came to Heck. Bessie's cottage, formerly a farmhouse and so considerably larger than Ramsdale's, with numerous run-down outbuildings attached, belonged to her mother, Ada, who was only sixty-five but in poor health and residing in sheltered accommodation in Bowness. For obvious reasons, Ada considered it important that Bessie get used to being independent, even though this meant the younger woman didn't get to visit her old mum as often as they'd both like. For all that, Bessie was a happy-go-lucky character, who filled her time doing odd jobs for the residents of Cragwood Keld at the other end of the tarn. She'd once offered to help Ramsdale by mowing his unruly lawn, but the surly neighbour had responded by telling her to 'keep the fuck away', so now Bessie, who was reduced to tears quite easily, did exactly that.

Perhaps the task she prized most highly was minding the keys to the police launch. This was convenient for all concerned because the boathouse in which the launch was kept was part of Bessie's property. Approximately the same size and shape as a suburban garage, the boathouse was propped up on stilts and in a generally dilapidated condition, its timbers tinged green by mildew – but it was better than nothing. The cement path leading down to it crossed the middle of Bessie's neatly-trimmed back garden, so it was always necessary to call on her first.

They halted before walking up Bessie's front path, and looked towards Ramsdale's house, his presence indicated by a very dull glow from one of its windows and the pale smoke issuing from its chimney.

'Wouldn't have liked to be one of the two girls if they came looking for help and knocked on that miserable sod's door,' Mary-Ellen said.

'Neither would I, now you mention it,' Heck replied thoughtfully. 'But it's a good point.' He veered back along the road and down the path towards Ramsdale's house. 'Go and check with Bessie, would you?'

'Who the fuck is it?' came a muffled response to Heck's full-knuckled knock.

'Detective Sergeant Heckenburg, Mr Ramsdale,' Heck replied. 'Cragwood Keld police station. Can you open up please?'

What Heck always thought of as a guilty silence followed. Whenever you arrived at someone's house and announced yourself as a copper, it was the same – whether it was some flash manse in the suburbs, or a scumhole bedsit in the urban badlands. Everyone, it seemed, no matter what their station in life, had some itsy-bitsy secret that occasionally kept them awake at night.

A chair finally scraped on a stone floor and heavy feet thudded to the door. It opened, but only by a few inches, and Ramsdale's big frame filled the gap. He wasn't just burly, he was tall – at least six-three – and permanently dishevelled, with a head of shaggy, iron-grey hair and an unkempt grey beard, all of which when combined with his tarnished earring, had a distinct air of the scuzzy. Today's attire did little to offset this: a shapeless white t-shirt stained by tea or coffee, baggy stonewashed jeans torn at the knees, and a pair of floppy, moth-eaten slippers. He also smelled strongly of tobacco. And it wasn't just the householder who was a less than wholesome sight. Heck caught a glimpse of the room behind. There was a desktop computer on a table and a wall of lopsided shelving crammed with buff folders, while the floor was buried under a mass of disordered paperwork.

'How can I help, detective?' Ramsdale asked, regarding Heck over the tops of his reading glasses. His anger had abated a little, but his tone implied hostility.

'Just a quick one really, Mr Ramsdale. We've got two people missing in the Pikes.'

'You don't say.'

'You've heard about it already?'

'No, but it's the silly season, isn't it? Same thing every year. First bit of really bad weather and all the idiots come out to play.'

'Yeah, well . . . we're pretty worried about these two. Their names are Jane Dawson and Tara Cook. Young girls, both aged twenty-four. They were last seen yesterday, rambling south from Borrowdale. As far as we know, they weren't planning to come down into Langdale, but they could easily have got lost up on the tops. Just wondered if you'd seen or heard anyone coming down the Cradle Track late last night?'

Ramsdale remained blank-faced. 'I'm hardly likely to, am I?'

That was a fairer comment than it sounded. The walls in these old farm cottages were several feet thick, and at this time of year all doors and windows would be closed, while both Ramsdale's house, and Bessie's house next door, were a good fifty or so yards from the parking area at the foot of the Track.

However, Ramsdale's scathing tone provoked Heck into prolonging the interview. 'They'd have had to be well off-course, I suppose . . .'

'That could never happen, could it?' Ramsdale scoffed. 'Bunch of kids left to their own devices. Fucking up.'

'These weren't kids, sir.'

'Oh, excuse me. Twenty-four years old. I bet they've seen everything.'

'It just struck me that if they did get lost and come down this way, it would be the middle of the night . . . so they might have knocked on the door, asked for shelter.'

'Nobody did. I just told you.'

'Maybe a drop of tea . . . to warm them up?'

'Sorry.'

'Or just to ask directions. I'm sure even *you* wouldn't have had a problem providing those, Mr Ramsdale.'

Ramsdale smiled thinly. Despite his blustery exterior, he was no bully; he didn't reserve his anger for those who couldn't fight back. But he was intelligent enough to know not to get on the wrong side of the Cumbrian Constabulary. 'Like I say, no one came here. But if you want to do a thorough job, Detective Heckenburg, it might be worth having a word with Longhorn next door.'

'That's already in hand, Mr Ramsdale. Just out of interest . . . you're not going away anywhere are you?'

Ramsdale looked puzzled. 'No.'

'Good.'

'Why?'

Heck shrugged as he backed away along the path. 'We've got to stay on high alert until these girls are found. That means maintaining contact with all persons of interest.'

'Persons of interest?' Ramsdale's cheeks reddened. 'Are you trying to be funny?'

'Do I look like I'm laughing, Mr Ramsdale?'

The tall figure in the cottage doorway diminished into the fog as Heck walked back to the road. There was a thumping *CLAP!* as the door was slammed closed.

Heck turned in along the next path, and found Mary-Ellen and Bessie Longhorn standing by the side of the house, the exterior of which – mainly whitewashed pebble-dash – had been more recently maintained than Ramsdale's.

'This is a right how'd-you-do, isn't it, Sergeant Heckenburg?' Bessie said with her characteristic froglike grin. She was about five foot seven and of stocky build, though much of this was running to plump, with a mottled pink complexion and an unruly thatch of thinning gingery hair. As usual when outdoors, she wore an old duffle-coat and a shapeless chequered hat, which Heck suspected might have enjoyed a former existence as a tea-cosy. An electric torch was clutched in Bessie's mittened hand.

'Sure is, Bessie,' Heck replied. 'You got that right.'

Her cheeks turned a ruddy hue at the sound of her own name on Heck's lips. It was Mary-Ellen who'd first concluded that their local handywoman liked the 'tall, dark-haired detective sergeant', and though it was something he hadn't noticed before then, the impression was now impossible to shake.

'I've got the keys for you,' Bessie said, jangling said articles as she turned and led them primly down the cement path, the angled outline of the boathouse materialising ahead of them.

'Bessie didn't see or hear anything,' Mary-Ellen said.

'Dead quiet round here last night,' Bessie said over her shoulder.

'Mr Ramsdale didn't hear anything either,' Heck responded.

'It's a bad business, isn't it, Sergeant Heckenburg?' Bessie chattered as he unlocked the corrugated metal door. 'If these lasses haven't come down from the fells by now, something bad *must* have happened to them.'

Heck didn't initially reply. There was something vaguely disturbing about that simple and yet undeniable logic.

'Lots of places up there where they could just have got lost, Bessie,' Mary-Ellen said. 'It's not necessarily bad news.'

The door creaked open on the boathouse's fetid interior. Bessie lurched in first, switching on her torch. The Witch Cradle Tarn police launch was actually a small outboard now adapted for official purposes. Despite it almost never needing to be used, it was old and in degraded condition, its hull scraped, its metalwork tarnished. Only its recently applied turquoise and yellow Battenberg flashes looked new.

For all this, it was more than adequate to take them across the tarn to the east shore, which the two missing girls, if they'd followed the route Heck and Mary-Ellen suspected, might well have descended to, or in the worst-case scenario, could have fallen down to. The boat currently sat between two concrete piers, normally in about four feet of mucky brown water, though at present, owing to the heavy autumn rain, the tarn's level was significantly higher.

Bessie handed the keys to Mary-Ellen, and walked to the end of the starboard pier, where she used a crank-handle to raise the roll-up door at the entry-port for the boat. Mary-Ellen climbed aboard, taking the wheel. Heck untied the mooring ropes, then jumped aboard as well, and the craft rumbled to life.

'Just give us a knock when you get back, so I can lock up,' Bessie called as they chugged out into the chill, foggy air.

'No probs, Bessie!' Heck called back, to which she no doubt blushed again.

With the tarn already having risen to its winter levels, the normal straight channel they'd follow for about a hundred yards through dense bulrushes before reaching open water was almost hidden. Only the tips of browning vegetation were visible, which made it considerably more difficult to steer along, especially in this monotone gloom. The last thing they needed was to get ropes of rotted herbage meshed around their propeller. But as with so many outdoor pursuits, Mary-Ellen was more than a dab hand. She stood at the helm, keeping them on a dead-straight course as they processed forward. If visibility had been bad on land, it was even worse over frigid water. Within seconds of solid ground disappearing behind them, they found they could see no distance in any direction. The outboard's headlights were already activated, but Heck turned on the prow spotlight as well. This normally drove a broad wedge of luminescence for several hundred yards, though on this occasion it revealed nothing and in fact was reflected back on them with interest. He turned the spot on its pivot, but wherever it pointed there was a glaring backwash from the semi-liquid whiteness, every tendril of fog, every twist and spiral glowing as if phosphorescent.

'East shore?' Mary-Ellen asked, raising her voice over the engine.

'Yeah, steady as you go though.'

'Steady as I go.' She cackled. 'Aye aye, skip . . .'

'You know what I bloody mean.'

Despite the potential seriousness of the situation, Mary-Ellen bawled with raucous laughter. 'Only funning. Hey you're my line-manager, Heck . . . I would never take the piss out of you for real!'

Mary-Ellen might only have been in the job four years, but she was a copper through and through. With a dark sense of humour and generally relaxed persona, she enjoyed her work and didn't get fazed by its more onerous prospects. She had that all-important burning desire to 'get up and at 'em!', as she was fond of saying, and that was something Heck heartily approved of. You couldn't play at being a copper; to be effective in the job, you had to fully absorb yourself in it. So many learned that on the first day. Those with sense got out quickly; those who hung on, looking constantly for inside work, only made life difficult for all the rest. Not so Mary-Ellen. Her previous beat, Richmond-upon-Thames, was pretty sedate by normal London standards, though it also encompassed both banks of the Thames and boasted over twenty miles of river frontage, so she was no stranger to pulling bodies out of the drink – which gave an additional explanation for her irreverent attitude now. That said, she was still unlikely to have scoured any body of water quite like this one.

Witch Cradle Tarn was the child of a geophysical fault long predating the glaciers that had broadened out the valley above; it was a cleft in the mountains formed by ancient tectonic forces, and for its size it was astonishingly deep – nearly seven hundred feet – and abysmally cold. Its sides shelved steeply away beneath the surface, but its eastern shore, which was almost flush against the cliff-face, was heaped with glacial scree, which intruded some distance into the water itself, creating semi-invisible shallows comprising multiple blades of rock, none of which were marked by buoys and any one of which could pass through the keel of a boat like a knife through the belly of a fish.

For several minutes they ploughed through turgid mist, Heck only sighting the surface of the tarn if he glanced over the gunwales, where it flowed past as smooth as darkened glass. The fog shifted in bizarre patterns and yet remained impenetrable. The quiet was unearthly. Even the drone of the engine was muffled, and yet whenever they spoke a word, it echoed and echoed.

'You really thought you heard a shot last night?' Mary-Ellen asked.

'I dunno.' Heck shrugged again. 'Strange sounds in these mountains. I've only been here two and a half months, but I've already realised how deceptive things can be.'

'Sure you weren't dreaming?'

'I can't definitively rule that out, either.'

'I can make some calls later, if you want,' she said. 'We've got a list of all licence-holders.'

'Yeah, do that. Ask some searching questions – like what the hell they thought they were doing discharging firearms in the wee small hours. Go at them hard, M-E. Make it sound like we *know* they were up to something. Even if they

74

were shooting rats in a barn or something, they're unlikely to cough unless we press them, and we can't dismiss them from any enquiry otherwise . . . unless we find something nasty out here of course, in which case it's a whole new ball game.'

Heck didn't hold out much hope for that, but they were now approaching the tarn's eastern banks, so Mary-Ellen cut the engine and lifted the propeller, letting them drift inshore. There were no proper landing places on this side of the tarn, no quays, no jetties – in fact there were no paths or roads either, though it wasn't impossible to explore this shore on foot. Further back from the water's edge, pines grew through the scree, creating a narrow belt of woodland. This was just about visible as Mary-Ellen kept a steady course from north to south, the vague outlines of trees standing spectral in the mist.

'Jane Dawson! Tara Cook!' Heck said, putting the loud-hailer to his lips. 'This is the police . . . can you hear us?'

He waited thirty seconds for a response, but there was nothing. Without the engine, the silence was immense, broken only by the lapping of wavelets against the rocks.

'Jane Dawson, Tara Cook!' he hailed again. 'This is the police. Can you respond please? Even if you're injured and unable to speak . . . throw a stone, bang a piece of wood on another piece of wood. Anything.'

The lack of response was ear-pummelling.

'Can you get us a tad closer inshore?' Heck said.

'I'll try. Just be prepared for the worrying sound of grinding, cracking timbers.'

'Don't even joke about that.'

'Who's joking?'

They veered a few yards to port. Heck could clearly see the submerged juts and edges, like serrated teeth, no more than a couple of feet below the surface. Meanwhile, the rocks exposed along the waterline were piled on top of each other haphazardly and yet resembled those huge, manmade defences that guarded the entrances to Elizabethan-age harbours.

'Okay, that's far enough,' he said, grabbing the boat-pole.

Mary-Ellen corrected their course. They continued to glide forward, veils of murk opening in front of them. The shore and its rows of regimented pine trunks was a little more visible, but not greatly so.

'Perhaps start up the engine, eh?' Heck said over his shoulder. 'The noise might let them know we're here.'

Mary-Ellen complied, while he hailed the girls another five times, always leaving thirty-second breaks in between. All they heard in response was the dull chug of the engine, until a few minutes had passed and this was subsumed by the rumble of churning water. Just ahead, the fog cleared around a protruding headland of vertical rock with a greenery-matted overhang about thirty feet above. Thanks to the heavy autumn rain, one of many temporary rivulets descending from the surrounding fells was pouring down over this in a minor cataract. The space beneath the overhang was filled with shadow. Heck directed his spotlight into it, just able to pick out a few clumps of shingle against the innermost wall. Normally, if memory served, there would be a small beach there, but the tarn's high level had inundated it. Either way, no one was taking shelter.

They pressed on, the cataract falling behind them, its roar dwindling into the all-absorbing vapour. They'd now traversed a quarter of the tarn's length.

'Starting to think this is a long shot,' Mary-Ellen said. 'Couldn't we be more use back at the nick, manning the phones?'

'Let's go down as far as the Race,' Heck replied. 'After that, we'll come back . . . hang on, what's *that*?'

Mary-Ellen stared where he was pointing, catching a glint

of colour in the grey; a flash of orange. It could have been anything, a tangle of bobbing rubbish, a plastic shopping bag scrunched between two semi-submerged rocks – except that you didn't as a rule find shopping bags or any other kind of rubbish in Witch Cradle Tarn, which normally was far beyond the reach of unconscientious slobs. Of course it could also have been a cagoule, and now they looked closely, they could distinguish a humanoid shape; two lengths of orange just below the surface (legs?), the main bulk of the orange (the torso?) above the water-level, thanks to the two boulders it was wedged between. When they drew even closer they saw that it wasn't solely orange either, but spattered black and green by moss and dirt, and streaked with crimson – as was the third length of orange (an arm?) folded over the back of it.

'Christ in a cartoon . . .' Heck breathed. '*They're here!* Or one of them is!'

Quickly, Mary-Ellen cut the engine again. 'The anchor!' she shouted.

He scrambled to the back of the craft, took the small anchor from the stern locker and threw it over the side, its chain rapidly unravelling. Other items of kit were also kept in the stern locker, including a zip-lock first-aid bag and two sets of rubberised overalls and boots, which the crew were supposed to don if they ever needed to wade out into deep water. There was no time now for a change of costume, but Heck grabbed the first-aid kit and moved to the gunwale, peering down. Heaped scree could still be discerned below. It wasn't just jagged and sharp, it would be loose, slimy – ultra dangerous. But again, this was no time to start thinking about health and safety. Heck pulled on a pair of latex gloves, before zipping his phone inside the first-aid kit and then climbing over the gunwale and lowering himself down.

The tarn's gelid grip was beyond cold, but now the adrenaline was pumping. Heck's boots found a purchase about three feet under. Holding the kit above his head, he pushed himself carefully away from the craft, pivoted around and lurched towards shore. Behind him, he heard Mary-Ellen shouting into the radio, asking for supervision and medical support. It was a futile gesture – there was usually no radio up here, but it had to be worth trying. A second later there was a splash as she followed him over the side. They struggled forward for several yards, closing the distance between themselves and the body – but actually making contact with it wasn't easy, as it was lodged at the far end of a narrow passage between rocks, the floor of which constantly shifted, threatening to collapse at either side, creating suction currents strong enough to pull a person under. To counter this, they clambered on the rocks along the edges, slick and greasy though these proved to be.

It was indeed a body, by the looks of it female, but in a woeful state: much more heavily bloodied than they'd seen from the boat, at first glance lying motionless and face-down in the water, its string-like fair hair swirling around its head. At the very least, its left arm, the one folded backward, was badly broken, while the other was concealed from view because the bedraggled form was wedged on its right side.

Heck leaned down, placing two fingers to the neck. It was ice-cold and clammy; there was no discernible pulse.

'Shit,' he muttered. He felt around under the face to check the nose and mouth were elevated from the water. Now that it was slopping and splashing, it covered them intermittently, but it hadn't done this sufficiently to wash away a crust of congealed blood caking the nostrils and lips. Heck scraped what he could of that away, to free the air-passages. 'I know it's non-textbook,' he said, 'but we've got to move her from here right now. If we don't, she'll drown. You got a filter valve?'

'In the first-aid kit,' Mary-Ellen said. 'Hang on, you're saying she's still alive?'

'Dunno, but she was still bleeding when she washed up here. Here!' He tossed his phone over to her.

'Heck, there's no signal . . .'

'Never mind that, get a couple of quick shots – the body and the location where we found it. Every angle. Hurry.' Mary-Ellen did as he asked. 'Okay,' he said. 'We can't drag her, so we're going to have to lift. Take her legs.'

Mary-Ellen plunged into waist-deep water, and manoeuvring herself into place, wrapped her arms around the body's thighs.

'Try and keep her horizontal, okay?' Heck said, sliding his own hands under the armpits, supporting the casualty's head against his thigh. 'Minimum twisting and turning. Her left arm's bent the wrong way over her back – looks horrible, but it's best to leave it that way.'

'Yeah, yeah.'

'Okay . . . three, two, one . . .'

The girl's body lifted easily. She wasn't particularly heavy. But on raising her above the water, Heck saw something that shook him. The cagoule fabric covering her front right shoulder had burst outward, along with tatters of the woollen and cotton layers worn underneath, and what looked like strands of muscle tissue. Below that was a crimson cavity, from out of which red-tinted lake-water gurgled.

'Christ!' he said. 'I think . . . I think she's been shot!'

'What?'

He craned his neck to survey the back of the victim's right shoulder, and spotted a coin-sized hole in a corresponding position.

'She's been shot from behind.'

Mary-Ellen had turned chalk-white. 'You serious?'

'Quick, get her to shore.'

They splashed through the shallows until they mounted a low, shingle embankment a few yards in front of the pines, and laid the lifeless form carefully down. Heck applied the sterile valve and they attempted resuscitation – to no effect. They persisted for several minutes longer, still to no effect. No matter how good a copper you were, unless you also held a medical degree, you weren't qualified to pronounce death – but this girl was just about as dead as anyone Heck had ever seen. Aside from the gunshot wound, she'd been severely brutalised, suffering repeated contusions to face and skull. That didn't necessarily mean she'd taken a beating; it might be in accordance with the girl having fallen. The only way down to the tarn from the east fells was via steep gullies and perilous slopes.

Either way, this was now a crime scene.

'I shouldn't really do this,' Heck said, feeling carefully into the girl's pockets, 'but on this occasion, establishing ID is pretty vital.' He extricated a small leather purse containing credit cards. The name on all of these was Tara Cook.

'So where's the other one?' Mary-Ellen wondered, giving voice to Heck's own thoughts. He glanced at the foggy woods. Thick veils of vapour hung between the trunks. Nothing moved, and there was no sound.

'Jane Dawson!' he shouted. His voice carried, but still there was no response.

'We need to get up on the tops and have a look,' Mary-Ellen said.

Heck disagreed. 'Two of us? Covering all those miles of empty fells? In fog like this? Be the biggest waste of police time in history. Besides, this is now a murder scene. We need to preserve it, and start the investigation. We also need to alert the local population – we don't know if this danger has passed yet.'

'I hear all that, Heck, but the other girl's still missing. We can't just ignore her.'

Heck chewed his lip with indecision. That Tara Cook was dead, a clear victim of homicidal violence, did not bode well for the vanished Jane Dawson. But climbing the fells to look for her – just the two of them – would be a hopeless, point-less task even if there hadn't been dense fog. To have any hope of getting a result in these conditions would require extensive search teams experienced in mountain rescue, not to mention dogs, aircraft, the lot. But Mary-Ellen was right about one thing – they couldn't just do nothing about the missing girl.

'Perhaps check along the shore,' he said. 'If Jane Dawson made it down to the tarn as well, she might still be alive.'

Mary-Ellen nodded and disappeared into the trees, while Heck tried his radio again as he stood alongside the corpse, but gained no response, not even a crackle of static. He spent ten minutes on this before finally turning to the trees and calling for Mary-Ellen.

Now she didn't respond either. He called again.

The maximum depth of the east shore wood could only be fifty yards or so, before the gradient sharpened upward and the mountainous scree became too harsh for any vegeta-tion to have taken root there. Of course, that didn't mean she couldn't have wandered for a significant distance to the north or south.

'Mary-Ellen!' he called again, advancing into the woodland gloom, not liking the way his voice bounced back from the cliff-face towering overhead.

Behind him, the glare of the outboard spotlight penetrated through the trees in a misty zebra-stripe pattern. He moved a few dozen yards north, trying to avoid clattering the loose debris with his feet. That Mary-Ellen hadn't so much as called back to him was not reassuring. How far could she have ventured in ten minutes? As he sidled away from the boat, the murk thickened. Soon the stanchions of the pines were no more than upright shadows. He halted again to listen – and to wonder for the first time how it was that a female hiker had been shot while rambling in this wilderness, and who by.

'Mary-Ellen!' he called, pressing on a little further. At his rear, the glow of the boat's spotlight had diminished to a ruddy smudge.

He listened again. An incredible silence. Even if the police-woman had been doing no more than mooching about, he'd surely hear her.

But could someone else have heard her too?

Had that person already heard her and taken appropriate action?

As Heck backtracked towards the boat, he tried to calculate how much time had elapsed between now and the gunshot he'd heard the night before. A glance at his watch showed that it was just before nine-fifteen. He'd been disturbed in bed at quarter past midnight or thereabouts. So, nine hours in total. More than enough time for the killer to have long left the area. Assuming he actually wanted to leave.

Heck bypassed the point where the boat was moored. The corpse of Tara Cook lay where they had left it.

It would be impossible to second-guess the killer's next move, because they had no clue about motive. But just suppose the fatal shot had been fired somewhere much higher up – on Fiend's Fell for example – and the body had fallen down the cliff-side. With the tarn down here to break the fall, how could the killer be sure the victim was dead? Wasn't it at least conceivable he would try to get down here, to check out the scene for himself? Heck headed south along the shore, more cold, dark fog embracing him. Even if the killer had clambered down here, nine hours was more than enough to locate the corpse, establish death and high-tail it away again.

Again though, that question – what if he didn't want to high-tail it?

And what about the other girl? Heck knew one thing for certain – he'd only heard a single shot. Then of course there was Mary-Ellen – where the hell was she?

He stopped again. In this direction, what looked like straight avenues lay between the ranks of waterside trees, though a little further ahead progress was impeded by several trunks that had fallen over. This wouldn't have been completely unusual in a wood at the foot of a scree-cliff – heavy chunks of rock would occasionally fall, smashing and flattening the timber; but they made difficult obstacles. He climbed over the first diagonal trunk, and crawled underneath the second, increasingly suspecting that Mary-Ellen would *not* have gone to so much trouble to make a quick, cursory inspection of the shoreline. Beyond the fallen pines, the woods seemed to close in, the rising ground on the left steepening, and on the right falling away towards the tarn's edge. Heck veered in the latter direction until he was virtually on the waterline. As before, the smooth surface rolled away from him, flat as a mirror, black as smoke. At this time of year there wasn't a *plop* or *plink*; neither frog, newt nor fish to disturb the peace.

Further progress was impossible in these conditions, he concluded.

He turned back, but it was as he stooped to clamber underneath the first fallen tree that he heard the whisper.

If it *was* a whisper.

It could have been the wind sighing through meshed evergreen boughs. That was entirely possible too. But it *had* sounded like a whisper.

Heck whirled around, unable to see very much of anything, *until* . . .

Had that been a faint, dark shape that had just stepped out of sight about twenty yards away on his left? Heck's heartbeat accelerated; his scalp prickled.

Suddenly it seemed like a very bad idea to be here on his own, especially as this character was armed. He set off forward, moving parallel with the tarn, heading back in the direction of the boat, eyes fixed on the spot where he thought he'd spied movement. And now he heard a sound behind him – a snap, as though a fallen branch had been stepped on. He twirled around again, straining his eyes to penetrate the vapour, unable to distinguish anything. When he turned back to the front, someone in dark clothes was standing nearby, leaning against a tree-trunk.

At first Heck went cold – but just as quickly he relaxed again.

Recognising Mary-Ellen, he walked forward. For some reason she'd removed her luminous coat. To lay over a second body maybe? Except that these days you weren't supposed to do that. And now, having advanced a few yards, he saw that he wasn't approaching Mary-Ellen after all. A bundle of interwoven twigs and bark hung down alongside the trunk. The outline they formed was vaguely human, but was mainly an optical illusion, enhanced by a shaft of light diffusing through the wood from the boat and exposing the place where the bark had fallen, which had created the impression of a face.

Heck heard another whisper.

This time there was no doubt about it.

He glanced right. It had come from somewhere in the direction of the upward slope. Ten seconds later, it seemed to be answered by a second whisper, this time from behind, though this second one had been less like a whisper and more like a snicker – a hoarse, guttural snicker. Heck gazed into the vapour as he pivoted around, wondering in bewilderment if all this could be his imagination.

For a few seconds, there was no further sound. He took several wary steps towards the upward slope, the rank autumnal foliage opening to admit him – and then closing again. Needle-footed ants scurried across his skin as the fog seemed to thicken, wrapping itself around him, melding tightly to his form. For a heart-stopping second he had the overwhelming sensation that someone else was really very close indeed, perhaps no more than a foot away, watching him silently and yet rendered completely invisible. Heck turned circles as he blundered, fists clenched to his chest, boxer fashion. He wanted to call out, but his throat was too dry to make sounds.

More alert than he'd ever been in his life, Heck backtracked in the direction of the waterline; this at least was possible owing to the slant of the ground. When he got there, he pivoted slowly around – to find someone directly alongside him.

'Coast appears to be clear, sarge,' Mary-Ellen said.

Heck did his best to conceal his shock – though he still almost jumped out of his skin. 'What the . . . *Jesus wept!*'

'What's the matter with you?'

'Creep up on me, why don't you!'

'Sorry . . . heard you clumping around. I presumed you heard me.'

'Well, I bloody didn't!'

'Getting jumpy in your old age, or what?'

'Don't give me that bollocks. Why didn't you reply when I shouted?'

'Sorry.' Mary-Ellen shrugged. 'Never heard you.'

'Hmmm. Suppose these acoustics are all over the place,' he grunted. They trudged back to the boat. 'You didn't hear anything else, though? No one farting around?'

'Farting around?'

'Whispering . . . chuckling.'

She looked fascinated. 'For real?'

'Shit, I don't know.' He glanced back into the opaque gloom. 'More atmospheric weirdness, maybe. Or the local wildlife. The main thing is there's no second corpse?'

'Didn't find one.'

'Well we can't get any help up here to do a proper pattern-search until this weather clears.'

They'd emerged onto the bank, back into the glare of the outboard's spotlight. Tara Cook lay as before. Heck angled back towards her, and knelt. He didn't want to disturb the scene more than he already had and would avoid making further contact if possible, but it had belatedly occurred to him to check for any lividity marks, maybe even signs of rigor mortis, as either of those could give a clearer indication how long the girl had been dead. He reached down towards her and suddenly the body twitched. Heck froze. For several helpless seconds he knelt rigid, as, without warning, the 'corpse' reached a violently shuddering hand towards his face, and drew five carmine finger-trails down his cheek. Still, neither he nor Mary-Ellen were able to respond.

Tara Cook's head now lolled onto her shoulder. Her puffy eyes were still swollen closed, but slowly, almost imperceptibly, she opened her mouth. A low moan surged out, along with globs of fresh blood, which spattered down the front of her filthy cagoule.

'Good Christ!' Mary-Ellen breathed.

'Good Christ indeed!' Heck said urgently. *She's only bloody alive!*

As they worked frantically on the girl, her moan rose in volume and intensity until it was a prolonged, keening screech, which rebounded from the cliffs overhead and all across the misted, semi-frozen lake.

Chapter 4

'Gemma Piper,' came the voice on the line. It was clipped, efficient. Time hadn't softened that aspect of his ex-boss's personality. Not that much ever did.

Time, though. It had actually only been two and a half months since he and Gemma had had the mother of all fall-outs, yet in some ways, it seemed like a lifetime.

'Ma'am,' he said.

'Heck?' He couldn't tell whether she was pleased to hear from him or not. The probability was she was more surprised. 'Where are you calling from?'

'Cragwood Keld nick, South Cumbria.'

'Oh . . . right.' Perhaps she'd fleetingly wondered if he was back down in London for some reason.

'Currently buried in the muckiest November fog I've ever seen,' Heck added. 'The whole of the Lakes is in lockdown at present, ma'am. Nothing's moving.'

She'd sounded curious about his call, but her patience, as always, was wearing thin, especially now he'd got onto the weather. 'What can I do for you, Heck?'

'We've just had an attempted double homicide.'

'I see. Local to your subdivision?'

'Right on it.'

'Good job they've got you there.'

'Thing is, ma'am, I think this one may be of interest to you.'

'You said two *attempted* homicides. Have you actually had any fatalities?'

'Not sure.'

'Doesn't sound like an SCU job, Heck. Give it to South Cumbria Crime Command in the first instance. That's what they're there for . . .'

'No . . . I think it may be of interest to *you*, as in you personally, rather than SCU.'

'Okay . . .?' Now she sounded cautious, not to say sceptical, but she knew Heck well enough to at least give him a hearing. 'Go on . . .'

'It was a blitz attack, seemingly without motive. Two girls hiking in the Langdale Pikes got themselves lost in the fog. The next thing they know, they're being followed by someone who attacks them. The first one he beats down with a stone. The second one he shoots.'

There was a lengthy pause. 'This is news to me. When did it happen?'

'Last night, around midnight.'

'Nasty stuff, but I still don't see . . .'

'Two female hitchhikers alone on a dark night? Getting jumped by a single assailant, who takes one of them out ASAP with a lump of rock?'

'That would be a common sense strategy for any random attacker attempting to overpower two people at the same time.'

'I'm not sure this is a random attacker, ma'am. While he was stalking them through the fog, the assailant was whistling something.'

'Whistling?'

'It was a song you're quite familiar with . . . *Strangers in the Night.*'

Now there was a much longer pause, and the sound of paperwork being shuffled. Heck could picture Gemma filching a pen from her drawer, shoving documentation aside as she opened a fresh daybook on her desk. Gemma was in the habit of starting a new log for every crime that was referred to her personal office. 'Give me the details, Heck.'

He told her what they knew, which in truth wasn't very much. Namely, that Tara Cook and Jane Dawson had gone astray while following a challenging route through the Langdale Pikes, at which point they'd been assailed first by that eerie whistling, and then by a strong, stocky figure, whose physical features had not just been concealed by fog, but by a full head mask and heavy outdoor clothing. He'd beaten Jane Dawson savagely – though whether it was to death was as yet unknown, as the sole witness, Tara Cook, had fled, only to be shot from behind. She'd survived the wound, but in a subsequent delirious state, had fallen down a waterfall, finishing up in Witch Cradle Tarn, where Heck had found her only an hour and a half ago.

Gemma listened long and hard, clearly undecided about the import of what he was telling her. While she tried to make her mind up, Heck glanced back from the Cragwood Keld front desk into the rear office, the little bit of floor space in there now taken up by a camping bed, on which the casualty, her more serious wounds dressed and bound, was reclining. Mary-Ellen was crammed in there alongside her, scribbling anything Tara could recollect into her pocket-book. The ambulance scheduled to take the casualty down to the Westmorland General Hospital, in Kendal – the nearest medical facility capable of dealing with a gunshot wound – had still not arrived. Nor had any supervision units from Windermere. In the meantime, they'd done the best they could, bringing Tara Cook directly back to Cragwood Keld in the police launch, which was now tied up down at the public jetty near to The Witch's Kettle, and applying as much first aid as possible. Their cause was assisted by Tara Cook's apparent determination to survive. She'd suffered a nasty-looking wound, but in reality the attacker had only winged her, which was understandable in such poor visibility. This started Heck thinking again.

'Ma'am,' he said, 'the Stranger was never accounted for, was he?'

'Heck . . . that was ten years ago. And I shot him through the left side of his chest. That wound had to be fatal.'

'But you didn't see him die. The Stranger taskforce never found his body, and they dragged that mire for days afterwards.'

'Why would he suddenly reappear now?'

'I don't know, but I'd be interested in finding out.'

'Did he try to rape or rob these girls?'

'We don't know what he did with the girl he clobbered. We haven't been able to get up there yet, and there's no sign of a body down at this level.'

'You say he shot the second girl? Well that wasn't the Stranger's MO, Heck. He never carried a firearm.'

'Which he's probably always considered a big mistake. I mean, it all went swimmingly for him until the night he met a nice-looking chick packing a .38.'

There was another long pause. Gemma was the arch-professional. Not just a top-notch administrator, but a highly organised investigator. She rarely let emotion get in the way of cool-headed logic, but he knew she'd been haunted all her career by the very close call she'd had at the hands of the Stranger back in 2004.

Despite that, she was clearly making an effort to be realistic. 'Heck, as far as British law enforcement is concerned, the Stranger is dead. Not just because he suffered a deadly wound, but because no further victims were reported.'

'Suppose he modified his MO. Suppose he didn't just start carrying a gun when he went on the job, suppose he cleared off to another part of the country to do it. I mean, we know he's a Scot. Up here in the Lakes, he's only an hour from the border.'

'Ten years ago, Heck . . .'

'Yeah, but like you say, you shot him. Suppose he survived but was badly damaged. It might have taken a decade for him to recover his health.'

She sighed, though it didn't sound like a sigh of frustration; more a sigh of puzzlement. 'Heck . . . what do you want me to do about this?'

'Well, now you mention it . . . nothing.'

'Come again?'

'I'm drawing this to your attention, ma'am, because I still respect you. And because I'd like to think we're still friends to some degree. Plus I thought you might be interested. And you are, I can tell. If you remember, the Stranger taskforce never publicised that intelligence about the Frank Sinatra song.'

This was another key factor in Heck's thinking. The original investigation team had avoided any public mention of *Strangers in the Night*. Firstly on the grounds the song was actually irrelevant to the case at the time, but secondly because cranks had a habit of putting themselves forward as serial killer candidates, so it was always useful to withhold one small detail.

'What's the current status of the enquiry?' Gemma asked.

'It's not even started. I'll be accompanying the casualty down to Westmorland General just as soon as the ambulance gets here. And then liaising with DI Mabelthorpe from Windermere nick.'

'And this assault happened around midnight?' She sounded unimpressed. 'That's almost eleven hours ago. Life moves at a slower pace up there, eh?'

'Ma'am, we only found Tara Cook an hour and a half ago. And this fog is literally so bad we can't get a chopper up to examine the main crime scene. In fact, we don't even know where the crime scene is. Tara Cook reckons they'd been wandering for hours, lost, when they were attacked.'

'Heck . . . this couldn't just be some wandering maniac?'

'The chances of that are a hundred to one, ma'am. First of all that any such person would exist up here without us already knowing it, especially as he's armed. Secondly that he could have run into these girls in the fog purely by accident.'

'You think he'd stalked them from earlier?'

'Somehow or other he must've known where they'd be. I mean, stalking would be the Stranger's style, wouldn't it? From what I remember. He used to pick his targets in the pubs around the West Country, followed them for a couple of hours before they'd parked up somewhere and got down to it . . .'

Gemma went silent again, and this time he heard her fingers hitting a keyboard. The Serial Crimes Unit, which she headed, was one of the busiest offices in Scotland Yard's elite National Crime Group. It existed solely to investigate or assist in the investigations of series or clusters of connected violent crimes, wherever in England and Wales they might occur. It was a near-certainty she'd have other important tasks to be getting on with as well as this.

'Anyway, that's it, ma'am,' he said. 'Just thought I'd give you a heads-up . . .'

'And this suspect was definitely whistling *Strangers in the Night*? The witness is quite sure?'

'Yeah.'

'You didn't prompt that from her in any way?'

'Definitely not.' Tara Cook had begun mumbling the moment Heck had carried her out to the boat and laid her on the deck, but they'd been halfway across the tarn, en route straight to the Keld, before he'd realised what she was actually saying. With her reeling senses and battered mouth, it had been difficult getting anything intelligible from her. She'd clutched at him and Mary-Ellen with hands like talons, burbling, weeping, showing remarkable animation for someone so badly hurt. 'Din' see his face. No face . . . but that song. *Stran' in the Ni'*. Kept on whistling it while he was creeping after us. *Strangers in the Night . . .*'

'That was the main thing she remembered about him,' Heck said. 'The song. Absolutely petrified her. Sounds like he was playing cat and mouse with them for quite a while before he struck.'

As he relayed all this, Heck wondered again about his own experience on the tarn's east shore, specifically the chuckle he thought he'd heard. Hadn't Gemma once described her assailant on Dartmoor as having a snorting, pig-like chuckle? Of course, there was no guarantee he'd actually heard anything. He'd been so isolated at the time by the mist and the trees and the icy, ear-numbing silence that his senses had been scrambled.

'I'm not sure I'll be part of this investigation once it kicks into action, ma'am,' he added. 'But if you're interested, I'll try and update you regularly.'

'Do that by all means . . . if you wish.'

'Excuse me?' he said. 'If *I* wish?'

'The song's most likely a coincidence, Heck.' By her tone, she was quite decided on that. 'For all we know, your perp could be some kind of crooner obsessive. And the fact he ran into two girls is exactly how it sounds – he *ran* into them. He got lucky.'

94

'Just like the Stranger did ten years ago, you mean? Having carefully trawled for his victims first.'

'Heck, it's more likely some opportunist headcase than a middle-aged madman who survived a bullet wound in the chest and a dunking in a Devonshire swamp, and then suddenly, over a decade later, decided to recreate the best night of his life four hundred miles away on a frozen mountaintop.' She paused. 'Don't you think?'

Heck was unwilling to admit that what she said made pretty good sense. Because still, some deep gut instinct advised him there was much more to this.

'Like I say, ma'am, I'll keep you informed.'

'And like *I* say, Heck . . . if that's what you want.'

'I thought you liked to get ahead of the game, Gemma?'

'I've always been a believer in the Golden Hour principle.'

'And what about the JDLR principle? Remember that, from when you were a street cop? Just Doesn't Look Right.'

She sighed. 'I'm onside with that too. How could I have tolerated *you* for so long if I wasn't? But the thing is, Heck . . . I'm not your supervisor anymore. You need to address these concerns to this DI Mabelthorpe. If there is something in this for us, I'm sure we'll get the message through the usual channels.'

'Okay,' he said, disgruntled. 'See you around, ma'am.'

'Yeah. See you, Heck.' And she hung up.

When Heck ambled back into the rear office, Mary-Ellen was gazing expectantly up at him. Though she'd only been a kid at the time, she knew all about the infamous Stranger enquiry. There was barely anyone in Britain who didn't. She hadn't leapt excitedly a few minutes ago when he'd first mentioned there were possible similarities between that case and this, but she was clearly fascinated to know more.

'What does Superintendent Piper think?' she asked.

Heck shrugged. 'She doesn't want to know.'

'But what does she actually *think*?'

He chuckled without humour. 'That's always tougher to ascertain.'

Chapter 5

It might have been a signature of the Stranger that he always destroyed his victims' eyes by stabbing or gouging, but he wasn't alone in that, Gemma reminded herself. Okay, it wasn't a common feature of serial sex murders, but occasionally the eyes had it – so to speak. And yet considering this was such a momentous thing to do, quite often those responsible would offer only garbled explanations as to why.

One had professed an ancient, long-discredited belief that an image of the last thing the victim saw before death would be imprinted on the internal optical structures, allowing identification of the murderer on the pathologist's slab – though no one had taken it that seriously, given this was the educated twenty-first century. Another had described it as a convoluted act of remorse, saying he'd sought to remove all sense that his victims were human beings. 'As the eyes go, so goes the soul,' he'd whined in a voice that almost pleaded for his interrogators' sympathy. 'It's easier to tear and mutilate a doll than a living person.' A third had adopted the polar opposite viewpoint, coldly claiming his victims' eyes as trophies, and keeping them in jars on the shelves in the 'workshop' located in his cellar. The idea they were somehow sentient had excited him. In his eventual confession, he'd admitted: 'I was aroused by the thought they were being protractedly tortured, trapped indefinitely in sealed glass containers, unable to vocalise their suffering, unable even to blink away the sight of me, their captor, in my endless triumph.'

Gemma hadn't memorised any of these details, but then she didn't need to. Even before Heck had hung up, she'd accessed Serial Crimes Unit Advisory, or SCUA for short – the unit's own intelligence databank, and now called up one case file after another on the screen in her office. Purely on principle, she would never have let Heck know she was doing this. He'd always been a chancer; he took risks and gambles, but so often they paid off because his instincts were very well-honed. She'd benefited from them hugely, but that didn't mean she could openly approve of this approach, even indirectly, by attaching undue credibility to it. But it was unfortunate, or maybe fortunate depending on your view, that Heck hadn't mentioned anything about the assailant up in the Lake District going for his victims' eyes – if he had, that would have been a smoking gun no one could ignore. In the original Stranger investigation, the aspect of the eyes being attacked had been of crucial importance.

Gemma opened the files in question, for the first time in quite a few years. Immediately, all kinds of memories flooded back. The crime scene photographs ensured that, along with the hundreds of statements taken, the intelligence and analysis reports and the many, many names involved – not just the other officers on the case, but the victims and their families, and the numerous suspects who'd slowly, steadily and very frustratingly been ticked off the list as their alibis checked out. She imagined she could smell again the rankness of the reservoir that stifling hot night, could hear the wind whispering through the thick, dry grass on the Dartmoor ridges, could feel the heat rising from the sun-beaten landscape. But more than anything else, she could clearly visualise that bestial, leather-clad face with its frothing, gammy-toothed mouth. Despite the many awful things she'd seen since then, the small hairs at the nape of Gemma's neck stiffened at the mere memory.

It didn't affect her quite the way it used to. She didn't dream about the Stranger anymore – at the end of the day he had given her a soaring career, so she could hardly complain. But like so many other cases for which no real and satisfactory solution had been provided, the subject came up in conversation with discomforting regularity. There'd never been anything to suggest the killer was still alive, but perhaps deep down it wouldn't have surprised her if something did. Very little about that enquiry had actually been straightforward. The guy had murdered indiscriminately, yet at times had behaved more like a professional assassin than a sex case, never leaving a trace of physical evidence, covering his tracks with amazing skill. And yet all the way through he'd behaved as if he was on a kind of learning curve, constantly modifying and adjusting his methods – so much so that in the initial stages of the investigation, before Gemma was actually attached, West Country police forces hadn't immediately been sure they were dealing with a serial killer. Had it not been for the brutal stabbing of all the victims' eyes after death, which rapidly became the Stranger's trademark, they might have set up separate enquiries.

With her usual painstaking thoroughness, she now ran back through the primary crime reports.

The first known Stranger attack had involved the death of a lone householder, an elderly man living in a remote cottage on the edge of Exmoor in north Devon. He had died in the armchair in front of his fireplace on a cold February night in 2003, as the result of a flurry of blows to head and body, probably delivered with a stone taken from the wall outside, and several vicious stab-wounds to his neck and chest, one made with a spike-like object that was removed from the scene by the killer, the others caused by the victim's own household implements – a carving knife and a wood chisel, both of which were left standing in his gaping wounds.

Though there was no sexual interference with this victim and nothing of value had been stolen from the scene, the initial assumption was that a burglar was responsible – that he'd simply not been able to find anything he wanted, and that the post-mortem stabbing out of the old man's eyes had been a ghoulish act of vindictive anger.

The second attack had occurred on a quiet country lane in Somerset, the following July. It was late at night, and two teenage girls had been hitchhiking home from the Glastonbury Festival. Someone had stopped a car alongside them, but with no intention of offering a lift. This hadn't been an out-and-out sex attack either, but it was closer to that than the first. One of the two victims, the heavier built of the two, who also, coincidentally, had worn her hair cut very short – which conceivably, in the dark, had led the attacker to mistake her for a male – had been felled with a single skull-crushing blow from behind, delivered with a heavy stone. The other victim had then been dragged into a roadside ditch and forcibly divested of her jeans, though not her underwear, before being subjected to a severe beating, at the end of which she was ripped and slashed with several edged imple-ments. Once again, both girls' eyes were gouged post-mortem with some kind of steel spike, which forensics examiners concluded was a sharpened screwdriver. If there was any lingering uncertainty they were dealing with the same killer as before, that disappeared when the old man's DNA was discovered in both female victims' eye-sockets, implying the same screwdriver had been used in both attacks.

These initial three slayings constituted what investigators would later come to refer to as 'the first string of murders', primarily because they hadn't yet fully adopted the Stranger's trademark MO.

The 'second string' would commence within a few months. These would be more organised and less opportunistic in nature, and as they'd focus primarily on courting couples and doggers, would comprise the crimes for which the Stranger would best be remembered. He was clearly learning fast by this stage, because in these cases all the new victims were stalked beforehand, covertly and professionally. But he was also enjoying himself more – possibly because the females in these cases were 'dressed for sex', and because the very isolated locations in which he found them allowed him to take his time. Whatever the reason, the methods used to eliminate these latter victims were increasingly more gruesome, a wider variety of implements used, the females in particular suffering ever greater and more prolonged savagery.

Gemma perused the raw detail with her usual unemotional eye, though even for someone who had been physically present at several of the crime scenes, the final few photographs made harrowing viewing, while the accompanying medical reports were sufficient to put the most experienced homicide investigator off her lunch. Of course, in all this mass of information there were only three obvious connectors to the case Heck had just reported from the Lakes. As he'd said, the unsuccessful assault on the two walkers was vaguely similar to the successful assault on the two hitchhikers near Glastonbury. But that could be coincidental. Likewise the second possible connector, which was the blitz assault with the heavy stone; again, the use of such a crude weapon would not be atypical of the average opportunist offender. But the third connector was more difficult to dismiss.

Strangers in the Night.

The press had only come to dub the killer 'the Stranger' when the second string of murders was well underway and he'd settled on his targets of choice: sexual adventurers looking to hook up with strangers. But as far as Gemma was aware, that was the only reason they'd given him such a moniker. By pure chance, the song *Strangers in the Night* had happened to be on the radio during his final attack – the one in which she had been the intended victim – but the investigation team had never publicised this fact. The only other non-police person who could have known about it was the Stranger himself.

On its own, this fact perhaps wasn't quite enough to chill the blood, but then Gemma would have been lying to herself if she didn't admit she hadn't spent at least some part of the last ten years wondering where the Stranger's body lay.

Or if indeed it lay anywhere at all.

She ruminated on this for several minutes, before standing up, straightening her skirt and leaving her office. The main detectives' office, or DO, as it was known, was located at the far end of the department's main corridor and filled with chattering keyboards and idle discussion. As usual, about half the team were on base, and one of these was big, bearded Detective Sergeant Eric Fisher. SCU was not a cold-case unit, but Gemma always believed in keeping half an eye on the past, and it fell within DS Fisher's remit, along with his many other analytical roles, to regularly review all their open and unsolved cases, particularly in response to new and possibly relevant info flowing in from more current enquiries.

'Eric, what are you doing?' Gemma asked.

He glanced up from the nest of paperwork over which he'd been slumped.

'Homework, ma'am.'

'Excuse me?'

'I'm at Winchester Crown tomorrow. Regina v Smallwood.'

'If you're giving evidence tomorrow, I'd have hoped you'd be on top of it by now.'

'So would I.'

'Yeah, well drop it for the time being.'

Fisher sat back, his swivel chair creaking beneath his vast girth. 'Ma'am, I . . .'

'This won't take a minute.' Gemma leaned with folded arms against the filing cabinets alongside him. '*Strangers in the Night* . . .?'

'Okay . . . nice song.'

'That's all it means to you?'

'Well . . .' He adjusted his glasses as he pondered this. 'Believe it was originally part of a movie score. Frank Sinatra released it sometime in the mid-60s . . .'

'No comedians today, Eric, please.'

'Sorry, ma'am.' He pawed the spillage of paperwork on his desk. 'Always get nervous when I'm going to Crown. Just trying to lighten the load. Erm . . .' He squinted as if it would help him recollect. 'The Stranger referred to it as his tune, or something like that . . . on the night you shot him.'

Gemma pursed her lips. 'Who else knew about that, Eric?'

'Aside from a select few in the Stranger taskforce, and SCU, no one.'

'That's what I thought.'

'That intel's accessible via SCUA and HOLMES 2, but only if you know what you're looking for beforehand. If I remember rightly, a strategic decision was taken back in 2004 to withhold that specific detail from the public.'

'That's correct,' she said. 'And no one has reversed that decision at any time since?'

'Not to my knowledge.'

'Okay, Eric . . . thanks for that.' She moved to a big grimy window overlooking Victoria. It was shortly before noon, but the dull, damp greyness of late November pervaded the city. Many shop-fronts were lit, vehicles shunting along Broadway in a river of headlights.

'Something wrong, ma'am?' Fisher asked.

'No, it's okay.'

She didn't elaborate, so he shrugged, spun around at his desk and recommenced his homework.

'But I'm going to be away for a couple of days,' she added as an afterthought.

He spun back again. 'Anywhere nice?'

'Normally, yeah. But at this time of year I'm not so sure. Cumbria.'

He arched a bushy, red-grey eyebrow. 'You're not by any chance seeing . . .?'

'Don't ask me that, Eric . . . okay? *Just don't!*'

Immediately, she regretted her curtness. Two and a half months ago, Eric Fisher had only been one of several SCU detectives to express dismay that Heck, in his opinion the most proficient investigator in their team, was transferring north. In fact, despite Gemma having so adversarial a rep inside the National Crime Group that she was quietly referred to as 'the Lioness', the normally affable DS Fisher had been so forthright in his view that she'd 'catastrophically mishandled' her latest disagreement with Heck that she'd almost suspended him. She'd only resisted that ultimate sanction because she'd known where such impertinence stemmed from – a genuine conviction they were making a big error letting Heck leave.

'Maybe,' she admitted. 'Possibly. Yes alright, probably.'

Fisher nodded, quietly pleased. 'Cool.'

'There's nothing cool about it, trust me,' she said. 'I'd much rather stay here.'

'You going up there alone?'

'For the moment.'

He seemed puzzled. 'So . . . what's the case?'

'There isn't a case just yet. Not for us.' Understandably, he looked none the wiser. 'It's a ghost if you must know, Eric.' Sensing several others earwigging from different corners of the DO, she lowered her voice. 'Can you believe that? I'm chasing a bloody ghost.'

Chapter 6

Though it was only a journey of twenty-five miles, it took the ambulance two hours to arrive at Cragwood Keld from Kendal. The last few miles saw it crawling along Great Langdale and uphill into Cragwood Vale at less than a snail's pace. It was the worst fog any of the ambulance crew had seen, but you didn't play Lewis Hamilton on these roads even in blazing sunshine. It would be similarly slow progress heading back to Kendal; despite having a seriously injured person on board, there would be no police escort to clear the way – Mary-Ellen's Land Rover was still at Cragwood Ho, and though Heck intended to travel down to the hospital in his own car at the first opportunity, there were a couple of things he needed to do up here first. But at least Tara Cook would now have health professionals alongside her and could be drip-fed painkillers.

Heck stood in the doorway of the nick and watched as the ambulance pulled slowly away, its tail-lights dwindling like fish-eyes sinking into ocean gloom. Only now, outside in the cold again, did it occur to him that he was still wearing damp, musty clothes. He turned to Mary-Ellen. She'd already got changed. Organised to a tee, there always seemed to be a second uniform pressed and ready in M-E's wardrobe for occasions such as this.

'I'm nipping to the Section House to get some dry togs,' he said. 'Can you knock on a few doors . . . get everyone over to the pub?'

'Sure, but I thought you were going down to Kendal with the ambulance.'

'I'll follow the ambulance. I want to speak to everyone else first.'

'No probs,' she said, eagerly, still enjoying the unaccustomed action. 'I'll get up and at 'em.' She strode off across the road.

It had often struck Heck as odd that an all-action character like Mary-Ellen had consciously sought reassignment to Cragwood Keld. He didn't buy into her glib explanation that the moment she heard Heck was being posted here, she wanted to hook up with him because she'd read about his antics in the police press. It was a complex deal, swapping forces; the paperwork alone was off-putting. Heck knew, having done it several times. Plus, he couldn't imagine what kind of action she'd thought she was going to get up here. Then again perhaps, as she'd also once said, she just loved the great outdoors.

'I should have been a park-ranger, me, sarge,' Heck remembered her once sniggering. 'Gimme a horse, some buckskins and a whole range of empty mountains, and you can shag me any time you want.'

Promises, promises, he thought as he headed down a ginnel opposite the station which connected with the village green. So long as she got the villagers together, that would do for the time being. On the right, at the end of the ginnel, was 'the Section House', as they called it – a one-up/one-down built of whitewashed stone, which, as it had had no permanent occupant for years, had been refurbished and taken on a long-term rental by Cumbria Constabulary. As police digs went, the Section House was actually pretty good. Okay, it was a bit compact – split-level, with the lounge, diner and kitchen all crammed into a single space downstairs, while the 'bedroom' was actually a timber balcony, accessible only by a loft-type ladder. But it was double-glazed and centrally heated, and it had all the mod cons Heck could need.

He scrambled 'topside', as he thought of it, stripped off, towelled down, and then pulled on jeans, trainers and a hooded blue sweatshirt. As a rule, Heck tended not to view himself in mirrors anymore than he needed to. He was only in his late thirties, so he was hardly old, but his face had taken more than its fair share of kicks and punches over the years, and these days looked . . . well, 'lived-in' would be a polite way to describe it. At least he still had a full head of black hair, even if it was its usual unruly mop. He dragged a comb through it, before grabbing his phone, his radio and his cuffs, locked up and crossed the leaf-strewn green to The Witch's Kettle, in which several of the villagers were already waiting.

Hazel and Lucy stood behind the bar, regarding him curiously. As Hazel was the only person offering bed and breakfast accommodation in the vicinity, Heck had rung her shortly after getting back to the nick with Tara, to check no visitors had arrived unexpectedly. The reply had come in the negative, but he hadn't had time to elaborate further.

'We got everyone?' he asked, approaching the bar.

'What do you mean?' she said.

'Where's Mary-Ellen?'

'Here,' the PC said, coming in after him with another woman. This was Bella McCarthy, a former investment banker from the Home Counties who lived in the Lakes in early retirement with her husband, James. He was already present in the pub. She sat down alongside James at the foremost table, the pair of them in matching green wellies and waxed overcoats.

'That's everyone, sarge.' Mary-Ellen sidled to the bar.

'Good.' Heck turned to face the crowd, who were also seated but watching him expectantly.

There weren't too many of them actually. As well as the McCarthys, Ted Haveloc had arrived, along with Burt and Mandy Fillingham and a pair of spinster sisters, Dulcie and Sally O'Grady.

'Hello, everyone,' Heck said. 'Thanks for dropping what you were doing and getting over here so promptly. By the way, does anyone here not know who I am?'

There was no reply. He was pretty sure he'd spoken to all of these people, for various reasons, over the past two and a half months. 'Okay . . . I'll get right to the point. I'm afraid there's been an incident. A pretty vicious attack in fact, not too far from here. Two young girls were walking in the Pikes when they were assaulted. Just the other side of the tarn, in fact.'

The crowd listened in stony silence. But already, worried frowns were appearing.

'I'm not saying there's a specific threat to this community,' Heck added. 'But I wouldn't be doing my job if I didn't at least warn you. We've no idea who the perpetrator is, but this was fairly serious violence. On top of that, we've got reason to believe he may be armed.'

'You mean with a gun?' Burt Fillingham said, looking uncharacteristically bewildered. He was a short, squat man in late middle-age, with thinning, straw-blond hair and a curious line in tank-tops, ties and tinted spectacles; he was normally a rather superior, disapproving character, who viewed himself as an authority figure. He certainly knew everybody else's business, which sort of went with the postmaster territory, Heck supposed, at least in a rural enclave like this.

'Yes,' Heck said. 'We don't know what kind yet, or how much ammunition he's got . . . or even how willing he is to use it. The thing is, this attack occurred sometime last night. On which subject, I don't suppose anyone heard anything out of the ordinary?'

'I heard what sounded like a gunshot?' Sally O'Grady said in a querulous tone. Around fifty, she was the younger of the two sisters by about ten years, and by far the most nervous, but both were physically similar to each other; tall and thin, with short grey hair. 'It was a long way off though, I thought.'

'What time would that have been?' Heck asked. 'Early hours maybe? Four o'clock? Five?'

'Oh no, much earlier than that. I'd say around midnight.'

'Okay.' Heck threw a discreet nod at Mary-Ellen, who nodded back, acknowledging that he wanted her to take a statement from Sally later.

'You folks don't need me to tell you how vast and empty the Lakes can be at this time of year,' Heck said. 'I mean, this guy . . . he could have legged it in any direction. He could be miles and miles away by now. He might even have left the county. We've no clue about his transport capability.'

'If this attack was up in the Pikes in the middle of the night, he must be a robust sort.' This came from Ted Haveloc, a rugged, sun-wizened character, whose tattoos, broken teeth and chaos of wiry grey hair indicated a life spent largely outdoors and made him look much older than his sixty-two years.

'We can't make assumptions about anything,' Heck replied. 'We don't know the first thing about him. We haven't even had a chance to get up there and look yet.'

'The attack happened at around midnight, and you haven't been up there looking?' Burt Fillingham said.

110

'The fog's impeding our best efforts, but the latest forecast is that it's due to clear by around midday tomorrow.'

'That's twenty-four hours off,' Bella McCarthy said. 'What do we do in the meantime?' She was a tall, trim blonde of around fifty-five, always decked in the latest rural fashions and a famous local sportswoman, playing a prominent role at the Cragwood Boat Club. But at present she sounded so dismayed that her small-statured husband, who despite his dyed brown, crimped hair, was ten years her senior, took her jewellery-coated hand in his. James McCarthy was another boat enthusiast and one-time big noise in the City, and yet was inclined to extreme mousiness in his wife's presence, which might explain why she seemed less than impressed by his attempts to comfort her.

'That's what I've gathered you all for,' Heck said. 'As I say, I've no reason to assume this man will come down to Cragwood Keld. Most likely he'll be far away by now. But it's not impossible. I mean, the Cradle Track is the most direct route up into the Pikes. It's also the most direct route down.'

'But would he really come this way?' Mandy Fillingham – Burt's plain, dumpy wife – asked, evidently seeking reassurance. 'I mean, knowing there are villages here and people . . . and that he's wanted by the police?'

'I don't know,' Heck said. 'The best advice I can give you at present is to go home and lock your doors and windows. Report anyone wandering the village who you don't know, and certainly don't admit anyone to your house. In fact, don't even open the front door until you've looked through your peephole or living-room window and established who it is.'

'So we're prisoners in our own homes?' Bella McCarthy said.

'Kind of,' Mary-Ellen agreed.

111

'Oh my God!' Sally O'Grady looked appalled to hear it in such bare terms.

'*Sally!*' her sister said warningly.

'But only until tomorrow,' Mary-Ellen added.

'Assuming the fog clears tomorrow,' Bella retorted. 'I mean this is the Lake District, you know. And it *is* November.'

'Bella, there's zero chance of this guy coming here,' Mary-Ellen said.

'How can you say that if you don't know anything about him?'

'The thing is, Mrs McCarthy,' Heck said, 'you've got a police office right in the middle of Cragwood Keld. I can't stress how unusual that is in this day and age. It exponentially reduces the chance of an offender setting up shop here. You've got officers right on the spot.' He indicated Mary-Ellen. 'PC O'Rourke and I will remain permanently on duty until this guy is arrested or until we can be absolutely sure he's left the area.'

Some looked relieved by that. There were several murmurs of gratitude. The inhabitants of Cragwood Keld had got quite used to Mary-Ellen in the relatively short time she'd been here; they admired her spirit and enjoyed her sense of humour, but they also liked that she was a toughie who could look after herself and, if need be, them.

However, one person who didn't seem relieved was Burt Fillingham.

'But this man's got a gun,' he said. 'If that's the case, he could force his way into any building. He could force his way into the police station. There'd be nothing you or PC O'Rourke could do then.'

This thought had crossed Heck's mind too, but the last thing he wanted now was an unofficial evacuation of the village. Despite the limited numbers, it could still turn into a stampede, and in these conditions that would be fraught with difficulty and danger, and it was probably unnecessary in any case.

'The firearms issue's being taken care of.'

'How?'

'Well . . . I'm hoping to get a couple of firearms officers posted here for the next day or so. I haven't had time to organise that yet, but I'm going to sort it at the first opportunity.'

'We didn't mention that before because we didn't want to alarm you,' Mary-Ellen explained.

'What about Cragwood Ho?' Sally O'Grady asked in a shrill tone. 'That's much closer to the Cradle Track than we are. And those poor people don't even know . . .'

'We've already made contact with Bessie Longhorn and Bill Ramsdale and have given them exactly the same advice we're giving you,' Heck answered.

In actual fact, that was a little white lie. They hadn't yet been able to personally warn the folk who lived at the north end of the tarn. Mary-Ellen had tried to call, but as Bessie Longhorn didn't even have a landline, she'd been forced to concentrate on Bill Ramsdale – from whom there'd been no reply, despite her trying three times. This wasn't a cause for knee-jerk concern; Ramsdale was known as a guy who wouldn't bother answering his phone if he was busy or in a mood. On the third occasion, she'd left a detailed voicemail, with a request that he pass the info on to his neighbour as well.

'PC O'Rourke will be setting off to Cragwood Ho very soon,' Heck added. 'Just to check everyone there is okay.'

This wasn't quite as much of a lie. First and foremost, Mary-Ellen had to take the police launch back across the tarn, to mark out the one crime scene they so far knew about with tape and a tent, and to preserve any potential exhibits she might find. She then had to return the launch to its shed and retrieve the Land Rover which was still sitting in the car park up at the Ho, so she'd be visiting that end of the tarn in due course anyway. Of course, this would take a little longer than they'd prefer, but there was nothing else they could do.

'Any questions, guys?' Heck said.

'Yeah,' Hazel said from behind the bar. He turned, looking at her closely for the first time since he'd made the announcement. She had noticeably paled in the cheek. 'You haven't told us much about this attack up in the fells. What's the reason for it?'

'We don't know,' Heck said.

'You said the victims were two girls. I mean, was . . . was it sexual?'

'Yet again . . .'

'He doesn't know,' Burt Fillingham replied on Heck's behalf.

'Whether it is or isn't, the same rules apply,' Heck said. 'Keep your doors and windows locked and everything will be fine.' He turned to the rest of the pub. 'If any of you are really worried, there's nothing to stop you doubling up for the night. You know, sleeping in others' houses – set up a camp bed downstairs, or whatever. Strength in numbers, as they say.'

They absorbed this quietly, which wasn't always a good sign. But sometimes there was no alternative but to give people the facts. If there was the slightest danger, the public needed to be put on their guard.

'We've also got these.' Heck laid a bunch of contact cards on the bar-top. 'Everyone take one, please. They've got direct lines to Cragwood police office and the radio suite down at Windermere. It's also got mine and Mary-Ellen's mobile numbers.'

'Lot of good mobile phones are up here,' Burt Fillingham grunted, as if the rest of them didn't already know that.

'It's only until tomorrow,' Mary-Ellen said again. 'Seriously folks, there's no need to be upset.'

There was a brief contemplative silence, during which the fire in the hearth crackled and spat. The thick grey mist hung so close to the window it was like a layer of dirty cotton wool pinned on the outside of the glass.

'Okay,' Heck said. 'That's it.'

With subdued murmurs, the less-than-happy band broke up, some talking together quietly, others shuffling to the door.

'What now?' Hazel asked Heck. 'We can double up for the night, lie low and all that, but what are *you* going to do?'

'I've got to go down to Kendal,' he replied. 'Get a report from the hospital.'

'Okay.' She nodded glumly.

'Hey . . . M-E's nearby. I mean, she's got a few jobs to do first, but she'll not be too far away. And believe me, she's as good in a fight as any bloke I've ever met. On top of that, I'll be back by tea-time, I'm sure.'

'It's just that I think there may be another problem.'

'Go on.'

'You haven't mentioned Annie Beckwith.'

'Beckwith?' The name didn't ring any bell of familiarity with Heck.

'Oh shit, yeah,' Mary-Ellen said quietly. 'That's the old lady who lives at the top of the Cradle Track.'

'Someone lives at the top of the Track?' Heck was astonished. He had some vague idea there was an old farm building up there, but he didn't know someone lived in it.

Mary-Ellen nodded. 'Bit of a local character. At least, she would be if she wasn't so reclusive. She's very self-sufficient. Grows her own food, makes her own clothes, keeps a chicken or two. She lives in Fellstead Grange, which was built sometime in the 1700s and hasn't been renovated since. There's

115

no power, no phone, no computer, nothing. The Track leads to it, but no actual road. And she's completely alone.'

Heck wasn't quite sure how he was supposed to respond to this.

Hazel looked even more worried. 'That puts her in the danger zone, doesn't it?'

'How far up the Track does she live?' Heck asked.

'About fifteen minutes' walk. And it's all uphill.'

'You say she's an old lady. How old exactly?'

'Must be nearly eighty,' Hazel said.

'Seriously, and she lives up there alone?'

'It's her farm – she came into full ownership when her parents died.'

'Which was about five decades ago, if I heard rightly,' Mary-Ellen added.

'Yeah, and now she won't leave the place,' Hazel said. 'She's been offered the market value loads of times, but she won't sell. And why should she, Mark?'

'Why should she? Well . . . how about no heating, total isolation, working the land at that age, next to no money . . .'

'It's her life,' Mary-Ellen shrugged.

'Well . . .' He rubbed his chin. 'She may not be in as much danger as we think. First of all, like I say, this guy might have left the area. Secondly, he may not even know she's there. Thirdly, if he does, she may not be his type . . .'

'His type?' Hazel said. 'So he *is* going for more victims?'

'It's way too early to make that assumption,' Heck replied.

'Even though you clearly have?'

'Hazel, it's my job to prepare for the worst. Annie Beckwith's in a vulnerable position, and we'll get up there at some point to check, but I'm not sure there's anything we can do for her right at this moment.'

'Why don't I go up there?' Hazel suggested.

'What?'

'You two have got things you need to do. I know Annie better than you two, anyway. I can drive to the Ho, and walk up the Track.'

'I'm really not sure that's a good idea,' Heck said. He didn't elaborate, but his head was suddenly full of images from the Stranger enquiry back in the West Country all those years ago: 'Police Eyes Only' photos of female victims lying in the back seats of cars, stabbed multiple times, genitals torn, eyes gouged.

Mary-Ellen may have been thinking the same. 'I don't reckon it's a good idea either, Hazel.'

Hazel glanced from one to the other. 'Well . . . you can't actually *stop* me.'

Hazel was a sweet woman, very patient, very quiet in her manner, but only now was Heck starting to detect the iron at the core of her independent spirit. Hazel ran her own business and led her own life. She'd been manipulated in the past by a worthless philanderer of a husband, but she couldn't be pushed around any longer, it seemed. And yet Heck was surprised at how disquieted, not to say alarmed, this suddenly made him feel. He and Hazel had no formal arrangement together. From the outset, they'd agreed to see each other purely on a casual basis – whenever they felt like company, whenever they needed sex, with no emotional entanglement. It had suited them both, he'd thought.

Irritated, he tried to put this from his mind. 'I can't stop you,' he agreed. 'But I can *ask* you not to go up there . . . for the sake of your own safety. And because as the police officers on the scene, we'd be even more worried and distracted if you did this . . . which would not be a help.'

Briefly it seemed as if Hazel's quiet but innate wilfulness would defy even this earnest request. But eventually she nodded.

'You promise?' Heck said.

She nodded again, though a little half-heartedly, he thought.

'You can be more useful to us running the pub,' Mary-Ellen said, adding a welcome dose of practical common sense. 'People are going to feel lonely and scared this next twenty-four hours. Might be a good idea if they all pile in here, have a drink, sit round the fire together . . .'

'I won't close,' Hazel said. 'But I don't think it's going to be much of a party.'

'Yeah, but just think of the one you're going to have when this is over.' Heck winked, then took her hand and squeezed it.

She greeted this with a brave smile.

'There's something else I want you to do,' he said. 'Keep your ears open.'

'Of course . . .'

'No, I mean if someone you don't know comes into the pub. Treat them as normal, serve them ale, whatever. But if they show a propensity to whistle, take note of it.'

'Whistle . . .?'

'Don't spread that around by the way,' Heck added, going on to describe the harmonious whistling heard by the two hikers just before they were attacked.

'*Strangers in the Night*?' Hazel looked perplexed.

'It may be nothing,' Mary-Ellen said. 'A complete red herring . . . but we can't take any chances.'

'But seriously . . . *Strangers in the Night*? That's a love song, isn't it?'

'Takes all sorts, I'm afraid,' Heck replied.

He glanced out of the window. The fog was dense and silent. Already, as instructed, everyone else had retreated to the safety and security of their homes.

'What do you *really* think about Annie Beckwith?' Mary-Ellen asked after she and Heck had stepped outside together.

118

He blew out a long breath. 'Depends on our boy's motivation, doesn't it?'

'You mean if he's after a bit of crumpet, some scrawny old octogenarian's not going to do it for him?'

'The Stranger tended to go for the younger end of the market. Mainly went after doggers and courting couples, when the girls were dressed like porn queens. You wouldn't have thought he'd get much of that up on the tops, especially from old ladies in run-down cottages . . . then again, his first known victim was an old fella living alone.'

'A fella? The Stranger was bi?'

'No, that wasn't a sex attack; it was like a trial run or something. Profilers at the time theorised the offender was a wannabe killer and was testing himself, seeing if he could actually take a human life . . . so the old man was a target of convenience. You know: vulnerable, isolated, easy. Personally, I'm not so sure. When I've read the case notes, I've always wondered if Devon and Cornwall might already have had a seasoned killer on their hands, who happened to be between MOs.'

'That happens?' Mary-Ellen sounded fascinated. That was something else about her: she was always willing to learn. Heck didn't think she'd ever asked him the same question twice.

'Yeah, but it's rare,' he said. 'Usually it's because the law is getting close, so the offender needs to change his pattern to throw them off. Likewise, he might force himself into a prolonged fallow period, to try and make everyone think he's gone away. You'll have heard the phrase "he's either left the area, died or gone to prison"?' He chuckled grimly. 'If only it was that simple. Course, he'd have needed a lot of self-control to pull that off, and it may have been that he was trying his best, but then came across an easy target, perhaps by accident, and couldn't resist taking another life.

That could have been the trigger that started the whole thing off again. Who knows?'

'Where would his murders before the West Country have occurred?' she asked.

Heck shrugged. 'Like I say, I don't know . . . I wasn't even involved in the Stranger enquiry. The other thing is we can't just *assume* it's the same guy. The Stranger got shot, ten years have passed, yadda yadda. The chances are much higher it's just some wandering fruitcake.'

'Either way, it puts Annie Beckwith in danger.'

'Not saying it doesn't.' Heck dug his car keys out. 'But I've still got to get down to the hospital. I need to interview Tara Cook again . . . properly, when she's more comfortable and coherent. Plus, I've got to run this lot by DI Mabelthorpe. All of which is going to take time.'

'Well look, don't worry about Annie,' Mary-Ellen said. 'I'll go and check on her as soon as I've secured the crime scene and taken the boat back to the Ho. Won't take me long to get up the Track.'

Briefly, Heck doubted that, wondering if for once her enthusiasm might have outstripped her actual abilities. It would be a tall order getting through that list of jobs before the late-autumn darkness descended. Securing the crime scene alone would be a complex task for an officer flying solo – first checking for any clues they'd missed, such as bullet fragments that might have bled out from the wound, not to mention the basics: deploying the incident tape, erecting the forensics tent, establishing a common entry point – which in its turn would necessitate finding an anchorage on the lake shore a sufficient distance away from the scene to prevent contamination, and so on. And that was assuming Mary-Ellen was able to find the right place, which wouldn't be easy in this murk, and then get ashore with all the correct gear. The mind boggled. But at the end of the day, someone had to get up there, so it might as well be the young power-pack he was so fortunate to have at his beck and call. Of course, despite Mary-Ellen's fearless approach and physical super-efficiency, Heck still wasn't completely comfortable sending her over there alone. It was difficult to imagine the assailant would still be hanging around on the east shore after all this time, if he'd even come down from the fells in the first place. But even a small percentage chance was something to worry about. And yet what else could they do? It was needs must; the crime scene had to be secured, and at present they could only spare one officer to take this duty on.

'Okay . . .' He started walking. 'Don't mess around though. Once all that's done, we need you back at the nick.'

'We wanted big crime, didn't we, Heck?' she called after him. 'The real deal?'

'I always do,' he replied, glancing back. 'And then, when it happens, it always scares the crap out of me.'

Chapter 7

Don't be a dick.

It was a simple, straightforward concept; nothing vague or ambiguous about it. It was also the tenet by which professional people, authors especially, were supposed to lead their lives. As a professional author you could never rely on your talent alone. The fact you had talent was only the start point. Beyond that, you required the skills of a good agent, a good editor, a good publisher, and a good bookseller. And it was these individuals, in whose equal interest it was that you be successful, whose instincts you had to take consideration of and not live in a constant state of hostility towards, or behave as if you were only tolerating their involvement under extreme sufferance. It also helped if you were nice to your readers. Okay, it might be disappointing that there weren't millions of them, but even a few thousand could trumpet your cause effectively these days thanks to social networking, so it rarely paid to be disdainful of them, or rude and dismissive whenever they managed to make contact.

Of course, on reflection, most of this could be filed under Common Sense.

Hence that oft-quoted phrase: 'Don't be a dick.'

The problem was that Bill Ramsdale rarely adhered to this rule, as he rarely adhered to any rule, for the simple reason he considered himself above the mundane conventions of normal life. He knew that such rebellious notions would do him no good long-term, and it infuriated him. But then lots of things infuriated Bill Ramsdale. As Professor of English Language and Literature, formerly of Birkbeck College, he knew he ought to have a deeper insight into the human condition than he actually did. But that had never been the case, even when he was teaching. If students hadn't been annoying him, it was his wife, Joan, or his mistress, Tamsyn, a third-year student who'd become increasingly demanding of his time and attention – and all the while, he'd been trying to write *that* novel, which he eventually had done, though no thanks to those around him.

The real irony though, was that it was his second novel – composed in the peace and isolation of Cragwood Vale, his day job, his wife and his mistress no longer fixtures in his life – which was proving such a headache now.

Primarily because no one would buy it. Not an insignificant problem when your cash reserves were running as low as Bill Ramsdale's were.

He strolled his cluttered lounge/kitchen/study, dragging on a cig and swilling coffee, his normal state of grumpy frustration even more aggravated than usual because he was awaiting an email from his agent in which she apparently was about to propose a solution, and yet twenty minutes earlier, for no obvious reason, he'd been kicked offline. These internet crashes were only usually a temporary thing, of course, but they were never less than fucking enraging.

Ramsdale stared again at his blank computer screen. It was as grey and featureless as the fog outside. For the third time, he rebooted the system, only to get the same result.

He smoked another cig to try and calm himself, glancing

at the window and the motionless gloom beyond. That reminded him about the visit he'd had earlier from that shit-arse cop Heckenburg – another proletarian bully-boy. Not that Ramsdale gave a fuck about the cops, with all the other things he had to worry about. Or those two so-called missing girls. No, they damn well didn't call here at Lake-End Cottage the previous night. He'd have given them short shrift if they had; stupid idiot bitches, fell-walking in these conditions. He couldn't help but picture them as a pair of Tamsyn lookalikes: freckle-faced and blue-eyed, with snazzy blonde ringlets – and nothing whatsoever between the ears.

'Sod it!'

There was no point delaying. He might as well pick up the phone and speak to his agent in person. This wasn't something he enjoyed doing, as she was an old pro and rarely took his tirades and accusations on the chin. As such, many of their discussions descended into blazing rows; on the last occasion he'd threatened to fire her. But the wolf was increasingly close to the door, and sometimes even Bill Ramsdale knew he had to swallow his pride. Shaking his head, he picked up the phone.

But there was no dialling tone.

It sounded completely dead.

Ramsdale banged the receiver back on the cradle – one, two, three times, and put it to his ear again. Still there was no tone.

'What the fuck!'

No dialling tone? What the Goddamn hell did that mean? Were the lines down because of a bit of bloody fog? That would be typical, that would! Incompetent bloody Britain at its best! The only country on earth where autumn leaves prevented trains from running, where kids were sent home from school if it snowed, and now where fog brought the fucking telephone lines down!

He tried two or three times more, but there wasn't a spark of life in the device. Only as an afterthought did he look towards the skirting board, wondering if he might inadvertently have pulled the flex out himself, perhaps if it had got wrapped around the caster of his office chair. But it hadn't.

Ramsdale stood with hands on hips, seething, unable to think straight, let alone figure out how he might resolve this. If nothing else, he supposed, it explained why he'd lost the internet connection. But who did he speak to about this, and how did he contact them? Mobile phones were no good in the Cradle. Of course, the joke was on him in that respect, as this had been one of the things that had first appealed to him about Cragwood Ho – that he could cut himself off, put himself out of reach of those buffoons and time-wasters who'd so hindered his writing career when it first started.

And then another thought occurred to him – completely out of the blue.

The phone line connected to Lake-End Cottage via a junction box located under the eaves on its southeast corner. Could it have frozen solid? The temperature outside was hovering about two degrees above zero, but it had fallen well below last night. Ramsdale was no electrician, but if the thing was encased in icicles, who knew what impact that could have.

He pulled his scruffy quilted jacket on and left the cottage by its front door.

The fog still swamped everything – it was dense, almost tangible, like a breathable fluid, and it was damp of course and perishing cold, which made it harsh on the throat. It didn't just restrict his vision down to a couple of feet; it muffled the sound of his footsteps as he made his way along the paved path around the exterior of the house. He passed various windows en route, each emitting only dull, weak light. But the weakest light of all came from the open

125

door next to the northeast corner, the door to the storeroom, which was built into the side of his cottage like a small washhouse.

Ramsdale slowed down as he approached.

The storeroom door stood ajar. Even though the electric light in there wasn't the strongest – usually emitting little more than a dim, brownish glow – he could see a tall, vertical slice of it in the vapour.

Ramsdale halted, rigid.

His shaggy hair didn't exactly prickle, though he knew immediately that he wasn't responsible for the light being on; he hadn't been into his storeroom any time in the last couple of weeks.

'Longhorn,' he said under his breath. *'Longhorn!'*

He dashed forward, blocking the storeroom doorway with his body so there could be no escape. There was no particular reason to assume his dull-witted neighbour would be in the storeroom at this actual moment, nor did he have the first clue why she might have done this in the first place – except that she was the only person who lived nearby. But fleetingly Ramsdale was so incandescent with rage that all logical thought had flown. Only slowly did it occur to him that innocent, law-abiding Bessie was the last person to go pilfering his garden tools, such as they were, or that it was highly unlikely she'd even come near his property after the last time he'd shouted at her.

The storeroom was empty anyway, aside from its usual heap of dingy equipment: bits of rotted garden furniture stacked against the wall, coils of old hose, shovels, rakes, hoes, a long-defunct lawnmower and some rusty, tarry old barbecue kit that Ramsdale had inherited on moving here and was never likely to use. It smelled as it usually did, of dust and grass-cuttings. But there was nobody in there, nor any sign anyone had been – until he noticed something was missing.

His twelve-rung stepladder.

He scanned the junk-laden cubby hole, but the ladder was definitely absent.

Ramsdale backed outside as his mind started to join the dots, lurching on around the house, and heading quickly to its southeast corner. The ladder loomed out of the fog directly in front of him, propped up against that corner of the building, directly underneath the junction box. Ramsdale reached it and gazed up. And now his hair finally did prickle, because he didn't need to be an expert to recognise the damage that had been done, the various leads and cables hanging severed from a box that had been all but disembowelled.

It seemed too ludicrous to be true, but some bastard had deliberately . . .

But why? What was to be gained by . . .?

His thoughts trailed off as he realised the upright object just faintly visible in the fog some ten yards away on his left should not be there. Whatever it was, *whoever* it was, it was simply standing there, indistinguishable in the murk, watching him. Then it realised he'd seen it, and it turned and scrambled away, vanishing into nothingness.

'Hey!' Ramsdale called, his voice morphing into an aggressive bark. *'Hey, you bastard!'*

He ran after it with heavy clomping feet, stumbling out into the middle of his lawn where milky suds of mist swirled around him, absorbing the house almost immediately, bringing him to a tottering halt. He'd only run for a few yards, but the breath was already rasping in his lungs. Ramsdale was a big guy and wasn't in great health. He did little fitness work, fed himself poorly and of course he smoked and drank way more coffee than was good for him.

'What the bloody hell do you think you're playing at?' he bellowed. 'You moron!'

But nothing was visible in front of him now, or on either side. He could hear water lapping sluggishly at the tarn's edge. That was another thirty or so yards away on his left, but suddenly that distance seemed terrible. Were he to venture all the way down there, the refuge of the house wouldn't feel close. Ramsdale's rage ebbed. Sure, he was angry – he was bloody furious – but none of this made sense, and that was always enough to create at least a pang of unease. How could someone do this? How could they know where to find the junction box, or to find the ladder with which to get up to it? *Why* would they do it?

He'd offended a few people during his time here, primarily down at Cragwood Keld. But they were adults and for the most part typical Middle England types; there were no kids or chavs among them who might be responsible for this. He thought again about Bessie Longhorn, the only other person in this vicinity. From this position he could normally see her cottage, but it was currently wrapped in impenetrable grey. She perhaps had more reason than most to damage his property. But at the same time, Bessie was timid. She'd sobbed her heart out when he'd sworn at her.

Then he heard the whistling.

At first he thought he was hearing things, but there was no mistake.

Someone close by was whistling a tune – a clearly recognisable tune. To his disbelief, Ramsdale realised he was listening to a melodious rendition of that famous ditty from the 1960s, *Strangers in the Night*. He turned in a slow circle, unable to nail the actual direction. 'Who is it?' he shouted.

The whistling continued without a blip.

'Hey, this is not a fucking joke! I need my telephone for work, alright? So what you've done is costing me money!

That means you hang around here, and you're gonna be in a lot of trouble! I advise you to piss off right now!'

The refrain rolled on.

Ramsdale felt worse than helpless. He had no option but to backtrack towards the house, all the time shouting, swearing, making gruff, blustery threats. If nothing else, he'd make sure the bastard knew he wasn't dealing with some effete tosser who lived in fear of his own shadow. Not that Ramsdale was showing himself to be much of an outdoorsman. Thanks to the all-enveloping vapour, though he'd thought he was making a diagonal beeline to the northeast corner of his house, he found himself stumbling through the overgrown rockery at the far north end of his property. 'Fuck!' he hissed, turning an ankle, and having to limp due west, before finding the house again and then feeling his way between that and the old Honda Civic parked on his drive. *'Fucking shit!'*

As though in direct response, the whistling which, rather creepily, had sounded as if it was encroaching on him, ceased. Ramsdale spun around again, peevish eyes narrowed. But still he saw no one and nothing behind him.

'You think you've got some kind of upper hand over me? You think because I'm in the middle of nowhere and haven't got my telephone, I'm going to shit my pants? Why don't you show your face . . . we'll see who shits their pants then! You'll be shitting blood into yours after I've kicked your belly for half an hour!'

He continued to glance backward as he made these promises – but something about the whistling stopping so abruptly had unnerved him. He groped his way along the side of his car, still glancing over his shoulder, half-expecting that featureless shape to re-emerge from the blankness – for which reason his hands detected that his car's bonnet had been forced open before his eyes did.

Ramsdale gazed down at the severed pipes and bashed-in cisterns of his mangled engine, numbness spreading slowly through his body.

At least he was now at the house's northwest corner, and could see the dim oblong glow of its open front door. He hobbled hell for leather towards it, coughing brackish phlegm into the icy air, and blundered inside, red-faced, the sweat spraying off him. He stumbled across the room towards the bin alongside his work-station. Somewhere amid all the screwed-up papers that had overflowed down there, he kept a cricket bat, its willow surface notched crimson by a hundred drives to the boundary. But this wasn't just a fond relic of his days at Harrow. After he'd first split up with Joan, he'd lived briefly in a crummy bedsit in Tottenham, surrounded – or so he'd assumed – by thieves and smack-heads. It had been a handy bedside accoutrement in those days, and maintaining it for that role had become a habit ever since, even up here in the leafy Lakes. He rummaged madly through the heaps of crumpled documents before locating the thing, but as his hand closed around its tape-wrapped handle, he heard the thump-click of the front door closing behind him.

Ramsdale spun around, bat in hand, but even after every-thing that had happened, he didn't quite expect to see the figure advancing coyly across the interior towards him, hands behind its back, as if it was somehow shy. In truth, he was panicking so much that he only caught a fleeting glimpse of it: it was shorter than he was, but then almost everyone was shorter than he was, but it was broad of build, its stocky frame entirely covered in thick, plasticky waterproofs, its face concealed by what looked like a leather 'rapist' mask, a mocking pink tongue poking out through its zippered mouth.

A bellow of combined fear and rage tore itself from Ramsdale's chest as he lumbered forward and took a wild, two-handed swing.

The two-handed grip was his first mistake of course, because if he missed, it would put him off balance. His second was that he aimed at the head, because that made it much easier for his opponent to duck, which he duly did.

Ramsdale never saw the low, hard counterpunch that caught him in the groin, squashing his genitals, driving the wind from his lungs on a tide of nausea. Nor the second blow, which wasn't delivered with a gloved fist, but with something made of hard, flat steel, and which smashed upward across his nostrils, breaking his nose and snapping his head backward, filling his eyes with hot, peppery tears.

The one-time professor fell heavily into his swivel chair, thoughts spinning, every inch of anger and belligerence knocked out of him. Pain and sickness cramped his whole body, and yet, through the desperation of necessity, he managed to focus on his assailant, who it was now apparent had stolen something else from the storeroom as well as the gardening ladder.

Unlike most of Ramsdale's outdoors equipment, his hedge-shears were in good condition, their blades clean and rust-free, their hinges so well-greased they slid open easily to their fullest extent.

'Wait,' Ramsdale stammered, as the masked form advanced up to him in a predatory crouch. 'Please . . .'

Its only response was a guttural, pig-like chuckle.

Ramsdale coughed, snorting blood. 'I haven't got . . . haven't got much, but . . .' He raised a hand to ward the figure off. 'Anything you can find, you can have . . .'

The blades slammed together with an axe-like *CHOP!*

Four digits fell to earth.

Ramsdale shrieked like a child.

The figure chuckled on, as it drove the blades together again.

And again, and again, and again . . .

Chapter 8

Cragwood Road was dangerous and difficult enough under a blanket of fog, but that was only the start of the journey from the Cradle down to Kendal. Heck knew the route well enough, but even to his experienced eye, it was astonishing how different everything now looked. To start with, he almost missed the turn at the bottom of Cragwood Road, and found himself shooting across the B5343, which could have been fatal if anyone else had been unwise enough to be out and driving at this remote end of Great Langdale.

The B5343, winding down through the dale, was itself a narrow route, in some parts single lane, so Heck could only edge forward at ten miles per hour or less. Even then, the occasional vehicle coming towards him would materialise through the gloom with only yards to spare, headlights reduced to dim angler-fish orbs. Needless to say, quite a few of these characters were driving too fast. There was much screeching of brakes and squealing of rubber. On one occasion, the other driver – a solid, mannish woman in a jumper, a green quilted doublet and a silk scarf – jumped out of her Toyota Land Cruiser and began to harangue Heck in an accent more Buckinghamshire than Cumbria. His reaction was swift, simple and to the point. He jumped out as well, displayed his warrant card, pointed at the verge and said: 'Can you move your Chelsea tractor, ma'am. I'm responding to an emergency and you're holding me up.'

'Excuse me,' she responded, looking only vaguely fazed by this. 'But I'm perfectly within my rights to . . .'

'And I'm within my rights to arrest you for obstructing an enquiry if you don't do precisely what I say, right now!'

Inevitably there were further delays. When Heck finally got down to Skelwith Bridge and joined the A593, the fog was no less smothering but there was heavier traffic. At Clappersgate village, there'd been an accident. A clutch of vehicles now blocked the carriageway, a Vauxhall Astra having struck a Fiat 500 coming from the opposite direction, a Chevrolet flat-bed having tail-ended the Astra, and a Mini Cooper having shunted the Chevrolet. There was much shouting and arguing in progress, while splintered metal and other bits of debris were scattered across the blacktop. It was clear this wasn't going to be resolved quickly. With no choice, Heck reported the accident – his radio was receiving signals again, albeit intermittently – then turned his Citroën around and headed south, this time taking the B5285 to Hawkshead and following the shore of Esthwaite Water, beyond which the road began looping like crazy and grew steadily narrower, leading ultimately through Far Sawrey to the Windermere car ferry.

Heck didn't expect the ferry to be operational on a day like today, and had half a mind to continue south via the back roads until he reached Newby Bridge, though that would be very much the long way around. However, rather to his surprise, the ferry was in service. More to the point, in such foul weather the usual traffic jam awaiting it was absent. In fact, Heck's Citroën was the only vehicle on board as the barge rumbled slowly across the flat grey sheet that was Windermere's narrow neck.

Climbing from his car, Heck stood by the barrier and gazed out at nothing. His mobile began buzzing in his pocket – a rare event these days, given that he spent most of his time higher up in the fells where there was no reception. He fished the device out, and was surprised to see the name of the caller.

'So I'm finally able to get through to you,' Gemma said.

Heck was caught on the hop. 'Erm . . . the signal's unreliable up here, ma'am. At best.'

'Good job I'm coming up in person then.'

'I'm sorry?'

'I'm coming up today. I'm on the two-thirty from Euston to Oxenholme.'

'Oh . . . okay.'

'I considered driving, but if the fog up there's as bad as you say, it'll be probably be traffic jams to infinity.'

He could hardly deny that. The Lake District boasted relatively few main roads, and they were bad at the best of times.

'Can you pick me up at Oxenholme?' she asked. 'I'm due to get in just over two hours from now . . . around five-fifteen.'

'Ma'am, are you really sure you want to . . .'

'Heck, you've pricked my interest. Is that not what you wanted to hear?'

In truth, Heck wasn't actually sure what it was he'd wanted. Or why he'd even called her. He and Gemma had once been lovers, long ago now, when they were junior detectives together in East London. At the time, their partnership had been firm, their relationship intense. But over the years things had got in the way, not least the Stranger enquiry. They'd remained reasonably close after the break-up – as work

135

colleagues if nothing else – but on the whole tried to avoid each other, each coming to the Serial Crimes Unit at Scotland Yard by different routes, though by then Gemma was of much higher rank. Mutual respect had made a working relationship between them possible, but the near-decade they'd then spent in SCU together hadn't all been hunkydory. By necessity, the higher Gemma rose in the job, the ever straighter bat she'd become, whereas Heck, whilst never consciously bucking the system, had always preferred a trickier approach. The last case they'd worked on together had seen them hunting a gang of professional rapists and kidnappers called the Nice Guys Club, whose sadistic rampage through the heart of Britain had been assisted by corruption and conspiracy at high levels. That incident was now two and a half months in the past, yet it was still raw to Heck. One of the most painful episodes in his police career – if not *the* most painful, mainly because at the end of it he and Gemma had rowed spectacularly. Things had been said that could never be unsaid. Afterwards they'd both decided it would never be possible for them to work together again. Hence, Heck's new career in the low-crime paradise of the Lake District.

'Heck? . . . Heck, I'm talking to you.'

'Oh . . . sorry, ma'am.'

'Can you pick me up at Oxenholme, or not?'

'Ma'am . . . where are you going to stay when you get up here? It's not going to be a one-night stopover.'

'It's a holiday area, isn't it? I'm sure there'll be rooms.'

'I wasn't exactly planning for this. I'll have to okay it with the SIO . . . when someone's appointed.'

'Leave that to me.' Gemma spoke with her usual airy confidence. 'This isn't just personal, Heck . . . from what you've told me, it actually does fall within SCU's remit. Five-fifteen at Oxenholme. I've not had a "yes" or "no" out of you yet.'

Even then, it wasn't as straightforward a question as it sounded. Heck had voluntarily left SCU so that he could be as far from Gemma as possible. His sense of betrayal after the Nice Guys enquiry hadn't just hurt him, it had put him into a state of shock. Of course, these things always seemed a hundred times worse coming from someone you'd trusted and respected.

There was a keen silence on the line as she awaited his decision.

Heck couldn't deny that he was going crazy up here. Mostly, it was less-than-divisional CID work he was engaged in. ACPO could chunner all they wanted about needing to install experienced detectives in isolated rural areas, but there were more sheep in the Langdales than humans. The last couple of days had been unusually busy, but they had been the exception, not the rule.

'Yeah, I'll be there,' he said sourly.

She hung up.

From Bowness, which was busy – everything moving at a crawl – he ploughed straight on into the hills again via the B5284. This was yet another perilous road in thick fog, but at least it was free of other cars, not that the occasional sheep straying directly into his path made life any easier.

As a result, Heck reached Kendal just short of two hours after he'd set off.

When he entered the Westmorland General Hospital, he learned the ambulance had only arrived twenty minutes earlier, but this had been sufficient time for Tara Cook to be taken straight through to theatre. There was no chance Heck could interview her again until at least this time tomorrow. All he could do now was ensure the girl's clothing and belongings were all bagged for forensic examination, and then wander frustratedly through to the empty ICU waiting area, where he got himself a watery coffee from the vending machine. As he did, two other figures ambled in; DI Don Mabelthorpe and DS Kealan Walker from Windermere CID. The former was a squat, tubby guy in his late forties, rather porcine in appearance; balding on top, which was why he normally wore a tweed hat, and yet blessed with thick red sideburns. The latter was much younger, somewhere in his late twenties, but studious-looking, with short black hair and steel-rimmed glasses.

'Looks like we can't speak to her 'til tomorrow,' Heck said, handing over the evidence bags.

'Yeah, I heard,' Mabelthorpe replied, distracted as he examined them.

'Tomorrow at the *earliest*,' Walker corrected them both. 'Which is probably a good thing. Both the girls' parents are on the way up, but they're driving, so they probably won't arrive until much later this evening, if not the early hours tomorrow . . . the last thing they'll want is to get here and find a bunch of hairy-arsed bobbies crawling all over their semi-comatose daughter.'

Heck nodded, unable to deny this logic.

'Still no chance of getting the chopper up there, I'm afraid,' Mabelthorpe said. 'We'll have a whole search party standing by late tomorrow morning. I'm putting a small taskforce together as well, to investigate the assault. You want in, Heck?'

'Absolutely,' he said.

'I'm having some space cleared at Windermere to set up the Incident Room.'

'You get the initial assessment report I emailed you, sir?'

'Yeah.' Mabelthorpe scratched behind his ear. 'To be frank, I don't know what to make of it. Especially those notations you added about the Stranger.'

'It's a long shot, I admit,' Heck replied, 'but if I hadn't mentioned that, I wouldn't be doing my job properly.'

'Well, we've pulled the files on the Stranger.' Mabelthorpe

shrugged. 'But it's the same rule as ever . . . they'll flip out on the top floor if we start talking serial killers.'

'To be honest, there isn't much evidence to suggest it's him,' Heck acknowledged. 'But I think it's something we ought to bear in mind.'

'*Much* evidence?' Walker said. 'There's no evidence at all. We don't even know for sure there's been a murder, so it's a real feat of mental acrobatics to link this to an unresolved series from Devon ten years ago.'

'DSU Gemma Piper didn't think that,' Heck responded. 'I told her exactly what I told you, and she's on her way up here as we speak.'

The two divisional detectives glanced at each other.

'SCU are on their way already?' Mabelthorpe visibly reddened in the cheek. 'Before we've found the other AP? Before we've even ascertained there's been a homicide?'

'Not SCU, sir . . . Detective Superintendent Piper. She knows the Stranger case better than anyone.'

'Heck,' Walker said. 'This is pretty damn spurious . . .'

'I know, I know,' Heck made a helpless gesture. 'The links are tenuous. But the MO matches one of the Stranger's earlier attacks, the victimology's right, plus I keep thinking, *Strangers in the Night.*'

'Yeah, well . . .' Mabelthorpe pondered. 'That *does* bear further consideration. When's Piper due to arrive?'

Heck glanced at his watch. 'Soon. I'm picking her up at Oxenholme.'

'She's not bringing a team with her?'

'Don't think so.'

'She's coming on the train . . . on her own?' Walker sounded surprised. 'So is this in an official capacity, or not?'

'That's up to her,' Heck replied.

'Well it's not going to hurt,' Mabelthorpe said, 'having an experienced homicider on the plot.'

'One thing I'm a bit concerned about, sir,' Heck said, 'is the villagers in the Cradle. Both Cragwood Keld and Cragwood Ho are dangerously close to the crime scene, and at present, apart from a single unarmed policewoman, there's no one there to protect them if this nutter comes back.'

'We've thought about that,' Mabelthorpe said. 'Lads . . . in here if you please.' A couple of uniformed officers, both wearing fluorescent anoraks, who'd been loitering out in the corridor, now sauntered in. 'DS Heckenburg, you know PCs Mick McGurk and Dan Heggarty.'

Heck knew them vaguely. McGurk was a doughty, hard-bitten Scot from the Borders. A former Royal Marine, he was now in his mid-forties and prematurely grey, but still in good shape, with a strong build and stony, pockmarked features. When stripped to his shirt-sleeves, both his brawny arms displayed tattoos commemorating his role in Desert Storm. Even now he wore a rubber *Help For Heroes* band on his thick, powerful wrist. He'd formerly been a DS up in Carlisle, but some unspecified incident – which might or might not have had something to do with the brutalisation of prisoners – had seen him kicked down a rank and back into uniform. Heggarty was younger than McGurk, mid-twenties, and taller – about six foot three, with a lean, rangy physique, short black hair and a trim black moustache. Heck didn't know Heggarty personally, but was aware he had a reputation for sticking religiously to procedure, which didn't make him the most popular guy to have around.

At present, both men sported black body-armour under their hi-viz anoraks.

'We can't get anyone up onto the fells at present,' Mabelthorpe said. 'Even if we had a load of spare bodies available – which we don't at this short notice – the conditions won't allow it. Way too dangerous. Mountain Rescue were prepared to chance it on foot, but I've pulled them back too – with guns on the plot, we can't authorise civvie involvement until we know exactly what we're dealing with. However, I know you could use some help at Cragwood Keld, Heck, so for the time being you've got these two. They're on an extended shift until midday tomorrow. Use 'em any way you see fit.'

'Okay, good,' Heck replied. 'You lads got your own wheels, only I can't take you back up to the Cradle straight away?'

'No worries, sergeant,' Heggarty replied. 'We'll take the patrol car.'

'An officer from Kendal nick will be babysitting the casualty while she's in Recovery,' Mabelthorpe added. 'Whoever it is, they'll be briefed to keep their ear open for a dying declaration, though from what I hear, that's not going to happen. And I've passed your request for firearms support up the chain of command too. You should have a unit with you by the end of today. They'll want to check out the crime scene on the lakeside too, just to make sure there's no unexploded ordnance lying around.'

'All the better,' Heck said. It had been worth the difficult journey down from the Cradle just to hear that. Suddenly it felt as if the odds had tipped a little way back in their favour.

Chapter 9

Though Oxenholme railway station was only a few minutes' drive from Westmorland General, it was rush-hour, so the fog-clogged streets were additionally gridlocked with grumbling, slow-moving cars.

It took Heck fifteen minutes longer to get to the station than he'd anticipated, and when he arrived, Gemma was already waiting on the forecourt. It looked as if she'd headed straight to Euston from the Yard, as she was wearing her normal office attire of skirt, blouse, heels and beige overcoat, while the only piece of luggage she had with her was a blue zip-up holdall. Like most good SIOs, she kept a grab-bag permanently at hand, containing a change of clothes, toiletries, waterproofs, forensics gear, clean notebooks and so forth, so she could be ready to respond in an instant. Like now.

'See what you mean about the fog,' she said, throwing her bag into the back and sliding into the front passenger seat, not wasting time on a 'hello' or 'how are you?'

'Wait 'til you get into the hills,' Heck said, pulling away from the kerb. 'On top of that, they reckon it's going to freeze again tonight . . .'

He drove them back across the west side of the town, having to negotiate yet more log-jammed traffic, though the only vehicles actually visible were those in the Citroën's immediate vicinity. The lights of shops were little more than smudges in the murk; pedestrians were filmy shadows flitting past. Overhead, the streetlamps infused the grey canopy with a sodium-yellow tinge, but themselves were invisible.

It took another half-hour to break free of the Kendal conurbation. Even on the B5284 heading towards Windermere, no noticeable acceleration was possible. The road rose and dipped as it ascended the Crosthwaite fells, and every so often the traffic would slow and the glaring red eyes of tail-lights abruptly emerge in front. Heck stole a covert glance at his passenger. Gemma didn't look much different from the last time they'd met, and why should she? He had to keep reminding himself it had only been two and a half months. That said, there were some slight alterations. Her fair hair was longer now, cut to shoulder length and styled in a neat bob, which he was forced to admit was rather fetching.

If she was aware he was appraising her, she didn't respond, merely gazed into the turgid gloom.

'How's life at the Yard?' he asked, before the silence became awkward.

'We've got a couple of interesting cases,' she said. 'But nothing that requires my attention hands-on.'

'Well, this one doesn't either, if I'm honest . . . ma'am.'

She was a little slow to respond. 'Not the impression you gave on the phone.'

'I could have been a bit previous with that call.'

'Now you tell me.'

'Don't get me wrong. Nothing new has come up. We still haven't found the missing girl. The one we did find is in critical care, incommunicado 'til tomorrow at the earliest. But the local factory are a bit surprised you're here.'

'Wasn't it ever thus. Who's SIO?'

'At present, Don Mabelthorpe, DI at Windermere nick. He's alright, to be honest. I tried to explain the situation, but . . . like I say, he was a bit surprised.'

Gemma produced her mobile. 'Give me his number and I'll put him in the picture.'

'You'll be lucky to get a signal up here.' But Heck gave her the number anyway, and drove on while she fiddled with her phone for several seconds before silently acknowledging he was right by putting it away again.

'Well, whether there was any point to it or not, I'm here now,' Gemma said. 'So you might as well tell me what you know. And don't leave anything out.'

Point by point, Heck reiterated everything that had happened, embellishing it here and there with his own thoughts and theories.

'The gunshot Tara Cook suffered,' Gemma interrupted. 'Have you retrieved the slug?'

'No, it passed clean through.'

'No bullet fragments left in the clothing or wound?'

'No results on that yet.'

'So thus far we've no clue about the make or model of the firearm?'

'None whatsoever. If it was the same gunshot I thought I heard, I'm guessing a high calibre.'

'Loud?'

'Very loud, but there's no guarantee even about that. The sound effects up here, especially in the mountains, can get seriously distorted.'

'What about publicity?'

'Thus far the case has only been publicised in the immediate environment.'

'Nothing to the press?'

'South Cumbria Crime Command are taking charge of

that. They'll be getting some search parties out tomorrow too. Mountain Rescue can deal with the peaks, but there's a lot of lower ground to cover as well.'

'Any reason why there's no one up there now?' Gemma wondered.

'Apart from the conditions, which would make even a ground-level search next to impossible, and would also mean we'd have no air-cover, there is the potential presence of firearms. It'll be a risk sending out civvie search parties in daylight, even though it's one we'll have to take . . . but deploying them in darkness and fog is too horrific a prospect, I suppose.'

She considered this. 'At the risk of asking a painfully obvious question . . . this *is* the countryside. This girl couldn't have been shot by accident?'

'I'm hoping Mary-Ellen's been making some calls about that.'

'Mary-Ellen?'

'Mary-Ellen O'Rourke. My PC up at Cragwood Keld. But the girl herself was quite adamant she and her mate were attacked.'

'And is that statement reliable? I mean, was she semi-conscious, delirious maybe?'

'What she told me wouldn't stand up on its own. That's why I want to speak to her tomorrow, get a proper statement before local plod gets too involved.'

'*You're* local plod now, Heck.' Gemma said this flatly, without emotion, without so much as glancing at him.

'Yeah,' he grunted. 'Thanks for reminding me.'

They descended into Bowness, where, alongside Windermere's frigid waters, the fog was even thicker and the evening traffic snarling itself up again, the flow of which was further hampered by various shunts and collisions. The hold-ups this caused were endless, so Heck opted to head towards Ambleside

145

and the road around the north end of the lake, rather than chance the ferry again.

'*I've* got a question, ma'am, if you don't mind,' he said.

'Sure.'

'Why are you here?'

Despite her previous comment, which had felt like a deliberate barb designed to irritate him, Heck was more curious about her interest in this case than hostile. He supposed he *ought* to feel hostile. At the end of the day, he was the one who held the moral high ground. At least, in his own mind he did.

'Surely the real question is, why did you contact me?' she replied.

'As a courtesy.'

She peered through the windscreen. Fog eddied past. 'Since when have you shown me any courtesy, Heck?'

'Just seemed the right thing to do, to let you know what was going on. And . . . well . . . I was maybe thinking about picking your brains.'

'You don't expect me to believe that, do you?' Gemma pursed her lips in that stern, humourless way of hers when approaching a problem she'd already figured out. 'That tone you used on the phone. I've heard it before. About a thousand times. It was your tally-ho tone.'

'My what?'

'Your eager-beaver tone, your raring-to-go tone, your "we're onto something here, ma'am" tone.'

'Well if it was . . . I've had more time to think about it since.'

'So now you *don't* think we're dealing with the Stranger?'

'That was my first idea, but I'm still undecided. You must admit, it seems unlikely.'

'Well, just in case it's worrying you, I still won't consider this a wasted trip. This is what we do in Serial Crimes, Heck

. . . I didn't think you'd have forgotten so soon. One of the criteria for the murder cases we consult on is *odd*. You know . . . unusual, weird. And now we're looking at what . . . a dead man walking? They don't come much weirder than that.'

'This isn't officially a murder case.'

'Do *you* believe it isn't?'

'No ma'am, I certainly don't believe *that*.'

Tara Cook's description of the attack on her friend, Jane Dawson, had been pretty graphic, even if her view of it had been obscured by fog. She'd talked about repeated blows with a heavy stone. She'd also placed special emphasis on that eerie whistling, which she'd said had persisted for ages as they were trailed across the fell. It was difficult to imagine that had all been part of some workaday mugging.

'Doesn't matter anyway,' Gemma said. 'I've already spoken to Detective Chief Superintendent Wilcox. I called him while I was on the train.'

Heck realised he ought to have expected that. Alan Wilcox was senior supervisor at Cumbria Crime Command. It was typical of Gemma to go straight to the top.

'He doesn't see that me being on the plot can hurt the investigation,' she added.

'So long as SCU are writing your cheques, eh?'

'See . . . you do have a grasp of the job's political dimensions, after all.'

'It still begs the question, ma'am, why *you're* here? As in you personally. I mean, if this was just another SCU dig-out, you'd have sent some of your minions. Gary or Shawna, or whichever DS you've got in to replace me.'

'I got no one in to replace you, Heck. As of now, that post is still open.'

For some reason that pleased him, though he didn't quite know why. Several weeks ago he'd finally – after a few days of introspective self-brutalisation – admitted to himself that he was missing the Serial Crimes Unit. Not just the action, but the whole thing: the chaos, the noise, the frenetic atmosphere of life at the sharpest tip of British law enforcement. But he was damned if he was going back to the bastards, cap in hand. *He was bloody damned if he was!* As far as Heck was concerned, his absence from Scotland Yard was punishing Gemma. It wasn't the other way around.

'The question stands,' he said.

'Does it really?' She glanced sidelong at him. 'You were more aware than most, Heck, that I was one of the investigators on the Stranger taskforce? That I got closer to him than anyone else – intimately, in fact. Bearing that in mind, would it make sense to send someone else instead? Someone who wasn't even there?'

Regardless of this eminently reasonable explanation, Heck persisted. 'I was wondering if it was more to do with this being the one that's always bugged you . . . you know, if this was the one that got away?'

'Rather like you and the Nice Guys, you mean?'

'Not to put too fine a point on it, yes.'

The whole crux of Heck's bitter argument with Gemma two and a half months ago had concerned the hunt for the Nice Guys. A team of ex-military personnel with severely blotted copybooks, the Nice Guys had set themselves up as a professional rape club. Heck had hunted them down on two different occasions, obsessively refusing to give up the chase until he'd put an end to their operations in the UK, several times flouting the very laws he'd first joined the police to uphold. But now he was fascinated to know if Gemma had a few obsessions of her own.

'The Stranger can't be regarded as anything other than the one who got away,' she grudgingly said. 'As you're perfectly well aware, I shot him in the chest. From point-blank range. It's a mystery he made it any distance at all, let alone completely vanished.'

'A mystery it's long been your personal ambition to crack, eh?'

'It's a bit more than just personal ambition, Heck. This was one of the worst murder cases in British history, and though it's now officially closed, not many of us who worked on it actually feel that way.'

'You suspected he was still alive then?'

'No . . . I just didn't know where he was, or what had happened to him. None of us did. It was a very dissatisfying way for the enquiry to end.'

'All that work, eh? All that worry and risk . . . for no tangible result?'

'Uh-huh.'

'If only you'd been given a bit more time and space to look it over, eh? To see if there was something you'd missed? Some way to bring closure?'

She shrugged, and they drove on in silence. Having reached the north end of Windermere, they were back on the A593, heading west towards Clappersgate and Skelwith Bridge. The scene of the major accident earlier had been cleared, but a sprinkling of glass and other detritus sparkled in their head-lights as they rumbled past.

'You know, Gemma,' Heck said slowly, 'you hauled me over the sodding coals because I felt exactly the same way about the Nice Guys Club . . .'

'It's not the same thing, Heck! Now stop right there!' She aimed a warning finger at him. 'You went AWOL on two occasions to catch the Nice Guys. That's two occasions more than any other police officer in this country would get away with. And I covered your back both times.'

'You couldn't very well do anything else. The first time

you signed off on it, the second time I could have gone to the newspapers and told them everything I knew.'

'The point is you broke some of our most sacred rules, and in so doing endangered not just yourself but other police officers and members of the public.'

'The only ones who died, ma'am, died because the Nice Guys murdered them.'

'You were like a man possessed. You were at war.'

Gemma paused as the road ahead rose steeply. They hadn't passed another vehicle for several minutes now – sure proof they were returning to the high country. As the streetlamps fell behind, the fog thickened until it was more like smog flowing from a hundred funeral pyres. Heck turned his full beams on, though the extra intensity made little headway through the sluggish vapour.

'That's not what's happening here,' she added. 'I've travelled up to Cumbria to assess the evidence, such as it is, and then give you any assistance I can . . . on the basis I've spent many years as a homicide investigator, and that I have a unique personal experience of the so-called Stranger. Now, is that alright with you?'

'You've got a bee in your bonnet.'

'I have not got a bee in my bonnet!' Her temper finally flared. 'You say that one more time, DS Heckenburg, and I'll have you kicked out of Cumbria too!'

'You think they could get anyone else to work CID in this wilderness?' Heck laughed without humour. 'Due west from here it's seventeen miles to the coast. The entire population that whole distance is probably no more than a hundred.'

'You don't seriously expect me to feel sorry for you?'

'No, I suppose not. But I don't feel sorry for you either.'

'Loath though I am to ask . . . what do you mean by *that*?'

'Well ma'am, you may think you'll enjoy bringing the

benefit of your experience to us carrot-crunchers, but look at this lot . . .' By necessity, they'd now slowed to less than ten miles an hour. Only a few feet of road were visible in front. To either side, they caught hints of grassy, stony verges. The rest was obsidian blackness. 'Whether you're here to consult or actually investigate, you can trust me on one thing . . . this isn't going to be fun.'

Chapter 10

Bessie was glad she didn't have animals anymore. When her mother had lived up here with her, they'd kept a goat and some chickens. It had only been one of Bessie's many duties to feed and look after those gentle creatures, but it had been the one she'd enjoyed the most. Now however, in terrible weather like this, it would have been quite difficult. It wasn't that Bessie was too frightened to go outside. Fog was just fog – it was cold mist, and they got lots of it up here in the Cradle – but when you couldn't see anything, even your own back garden felt different and strange. Despite having a torch to hand, she doubted she'd easily be able to find the coop where the chickens had once roosted, or the shed where she'd used to milk the goat.

At present, she was settled down in her cosy little living room in front of the television, with a nice fire in the grate and a pile of darning next to her on the couch. It wasn't her favourite task – despite her mother putting in long hours trying to teach her, Bessie simply wasn't very good with a needle and thread – but it needed to be done, and she was happy to get on with it, because keeping busy was very important. That said, it was still difficult to ignore the black-grey nothingness outside. She kept trooping to the little window next to her front door and peeking out, hoping for signs the fog was dissipating. She certainly hoped it would have gone by tomorrow, because she was due to make a trip to Cragwood Keld to see if there were any odd jobs she could do, while there were also some bits of shopping she needed to pick up. All that, and the weekly village bus service wasn't due for another three days. The last thing she wanted was to *walk* down that lonely tarn-side road in a pea-souper like this. It was bad enough when it was so cold that the road was slippery with ice, but this was the worst – when you couldn't see anything or anyone, and could only hear your own breathing and your own footsteps. She shivered just to think of it.

It pleased her that she'd be able to ask Constable O'Rourke when the fog was expected to clear. The police officers would be bringing their launch back at some point soon this evening, and they'd definitely know about the weather. It was quite unusual for the police to be out on the tarn for this long – by Bessie's reckoning they'd had the boat almost the whole of the day. She glanced at the big wooden clock on the mantel, and was surprised to see that it was after six. Yes, that was a long time for the police to have their boat out, but Bessie knew it was an important job they had to do. Those poor missing lasses. Presumably the officers would have to keep looking for them, whatever had happened. It might be ages yet. And there was no reason to get worried either, because being the police, they weren't likely to run into trouble. They would certainly know how to look after themselves, especially Sergeant Heckenburg.

Bessie blushed cherry-red just thinking of him. That warm feeling flooded through her again. She knew what it meant, and that it was probably a hopeless thing, but it was all new to her and very, very nice. It had happened the first time she'd seen him, two and a half months ago, and on all the occasions since. As such, Bessie took every opportunity she could to talk to him. And he always chatted back. He was never cold or stuffy with her, the way other people tended to be, even those she was looking to do chores for. Okay, maybe he was sometimes a little distant, like he had stuff on his mind, but that was understandable. He had lots to do. Especially today, with those two missing girls. That thought made her wonder again why they were so late getting back. It occurred to her that maybe Heck and Mary-Ellen had already got back and she hadn't noticed, though normally she'd have heard the boat as it came chugging into the boathouse, and nearly always in the past Constable O'Rourke had knocked on the door to let her know and to give her the key.

Bessie crossed her cluttered living room to the window. On the other side, the fog was solid – as if a blank wall had been erected only a couple of feet away. She went through to her tiny kitchen to peer out of the small window over the sink. This one looked down towards the boathouse, but there was less chance of seeing anything down there. Even if the boat was docking at this moment, she was unlikely to notice, as its lights wouldn't be able to penetrate the fog. She hung around for a minute or so before going back to the living room. She'd already made herself some peanut butter and jam sandwiches, but she wasn't hungry yet, so she settled back in front of the telly to continue darning and watch the game shows.

These were the programmes she liked the best. She liked films too and most television shows, though some of those could get a bit scary, and that wasn't ideal at this time of year, with the long dark nights and no holiday-makers in any of the other cottages. Winter could be a difficult time when she only had Mr Ramsdale to share it with.

There was a loud rapping on the door.

Though she'd been half expecting this, Bessie jumped off her sofa and hurried across the room. She lifted the latch and opened the front door, expecting the police officers to be on the step, but seeing only swirling fog.

Puzzled, Bessie stuck her head out, looking left and right. Nobody was there. It didn't bother her too much. One of them had probably just nipped around the front to knock on the door and let her know they were here and had now returned to the boathouse. Bessie would meet them down there. She grabbed her duffle-coat, her mittens and her hat, and dashed through the kitchen, drawing the bolt on the back door and stepping out.

There was less light on this side of the house, so the fog was almost black. She took the torch from her coat pocket and switched it on. But the beam illuminated nothing.

'Hello, I'm here!' Bessie shouted as she blundered forward, feeling her way down the gentle slope of the garden with cautious steps.

In these conditions, she didn't expect that she'd be able to see the lights from the boat, even though it was only about thirty yards away. But it surprised her that she didn't hear anything. If the boat was already in the shed with its engine turned off, she'd have thought she'd at least be able to hear their voices.

But she heard nothing.

Puzzled, she pressed on, finally reaching the boathouse – walking right into it in fact, only her outstretched hands preventing her banging her nose on its rickety timber wall – and still she couldn't hear anyone. She shone her torch the length of the building. The entrance door stood open. It wasn't locked while the boat was out, but she was sure she'd closed it earlier. In fact, she knew she had. She moved forward curiously. This surely meant they were here. Yet, again, why could she not hear them? Why could she not see any lights from the open door?

'Sergeant Heckenburg?' she said, sticking her head through.

Bessie's voice echoed from the hollow chamber. Her torchlight struck rippling liquid shadows from the muddy water in the docking bay – but then caught something else. To Bessie's astonishment, the boat *was* in there, moored, and yet riding so low that it was partially submerged. In fact, it was largely submerged. Only the tops of its gunwales were visible above the surface. She couldn't even think how this might have happened; she had a vague idea the craft must have sunk while it was in here, or else how would they have brought it back? Another thing caught her attention.

On the opposite side of the boatshed interior was something completely new. At first she had to blink because she thought she was seeing things in the gloom – but it looked like big handwriting on the wall opposite; graffiti of some sort. She shone her torch over it.

REMEMBER ME?

Bessie was utterly bemused. The two words meant nothing to her. Remember who? And from when? And how had the graffiti artist even got in here?

But she didn't stay bemused for long, before another emotion slowly took over.

The large spiky letters, which were at least half a foot tall each, were bright red. Crimson, even. And they'd dribbled a little.

Paint might dribble, or ink – but she knew without needing to be told that this message was composed of neither of those innocent substances.

All Bessie could think about as she stumbled wordlessly out through the boathouse door was those two missing lasses on the fells. Good God, what had happened to them? Oh good Lord . . . good, good Lord! Was the same terrible thing about to happen here?

The breath groaned out of her as she staggered blindly up the garden, stabbing the torch wildly in every direction. She ran into her back door the way she'd almost run into the boathouse, though this time she didn't stop in time. Her nose smashed on the hard oak planking, spattering it with gore. She barked her knees as well, and yet none of this meant anything to her. Nor did the fact the door was now mysteriously closed and locked.

Bessie wheezed frantically as she toppled around the side of the house. It didn't matter about the back door. The front door would still be open. She could get inside that way, and then she could lock it behind her, and she'd be safe.

But the front door wasn't open either.

When she finally reached it, it too had been closed, its latch falling into place on the other side. She beat on it madly, squawking – making that terrible sound she'd tried to restrain for so long. That sound she'd only got on top of as a young teenager, when her mother had said it made her sound like Jemima Puddle-Duck.

Bessie gasped, sucking in the ice-edged air with such force that it briefly froze her throat and sinuses. None of this made sense. How could she be locked out? How could someone have been writing with blood in the boathouse? Why would they do it? What was wrong with them?

It had to be something to do with the missing girls. The ones Sergeant Heckenburg was looking for.

Then she heard the whistling.

She looked slowly around, her broad face bathed in sweat.

157

At first it was almost friendly, as if someone was whistling a nice song.

'Sergeant Heckenburg,' she said under her breath. 'Sergeant Heckenburg!' she tried to shout, but it came out as a cracked whimper.

Almost instinctively, Bessie realised that whoever this was, it was no friend.

She flicked her torch off. The only light now came from the window beside the front door, and was nothing more than a pale, grimy smear. Even so, she stepped aside so that she wasn't framed in front of it. Now he, whoever he was, was standing in deep darkness – just like her. In fact, maybe the fog could help her. This wasn't like they were standing in a room with the lights out; it was like they were standing in a room with the lights out and blankets thrown over them. He wouldn't know where he was anymore than she did. In fact, things might be worse for him than they were for her – she knew her own garden very well.

Almost on cue, as though the whistler had been reading her thoughts, he stopped.

A piercing silence followed.

Did that mean he was approaching? Sliding towards her through the fog?

But he couldn't be, because he didn't know where she was. And yet – he might have seen her light, and she was still standing near the same spot.

Bessie lurched away to her left, only to stumble over a plant pot, managing by a miracle to keep on her feet but sending it clattering along the side path. Frantic, she tried to hush it, at the same time struggling to recollect what lay between here and the path leading up to the road. That would be the best thing, the path that led to the road. It was all flat paving-stones. She could walk up that in complete safety. And along the road it was only three miles to Cragwood Keld. She'd walked that distance lots of times. So she could easily run it now.

But maybe *he* could run it too. Maybe he was up there now, waiting on the road, because he knew that was the way she'd come. Instead, why not go to Mr Ramsdale's house, which was the next one along? He hated her; he would doubtless shout at her again, but at least in his house she'd be safer than out here. That said, Mr Ramsdale's house was a good sixty yards away. Would she be able to make it that far?

The whistling started again, now from somewhere on her right, whereas previously she'd thought it was to her fore. It also sounded a lot closer.

Bessie continued lurching left, almost running, kicking over another couple of plant pots. Away from the front window, it was so dark she could easily have bypassed the path leading up to the road, but by now she didn't care. The outbuildings were on the south side of the house: two ramshackle old structures that she hardly used anymore. But there were lots of hiding places around there. He'd never find her, and once he'd moved on, she'd hurry on over to Mr Ramsdale's. He had a telephone too, so they could call for help.

She reminded herself that however frightened she was, she shouldn't make a sound from this point on. As such, she tried to make progress with stealth. But now she was in the uncut grass, amid bits of rubbish that had spilled from her dustbins – so her feet kept striking tin cans or crunching plastic cartons. It didn't help that she whimpered each time and kept shushing herself.

And then she collided with the first outbuilding. Thankfully, her hands were in front of her again, so though it was noisy, at least she wasn't hurt. It was the rotting old timber shed, the one she'd always thought of as 'the stable', though it had never been a real stable in her lifetime. The reverberations of the blow resounded through the night. Tears flooded Bessie's cheeks as she groped her way to the eastern end of it. Beyond this point there was a gap, and then the building she always thought of as 'the garage', though again it had never been used as a garage, because neither she nor her mother had ever owned a car. This one was in an equally poor condition to the first, but built of bricks and covered with pebbledash, with a sagging tarpaper roof. She'd been planning to hide inside this, but now it occurred to her that there was only one way in – a single entrance around the back, which was also the only way out. It suddenly seemed a much cleverer plan to insinuate herself into the passage between the two; that way she'd have an exit at either end. The passage was about two feet wide, so she could work her way along it easily enough. It was filled with old thorns and weeds, which in summer reached to waist-height, but now they'd turned to desiccated bracken. At least it was damp though, so there was no loud crackling as she thrust her way along it. Bessie hunkered down somewhere around the middle of the passage, and waited, listening.

The sweat beading her face slowly turned cold. It was amazing, she thought – the fog even penetrated into this narrow space. She couldn't see the entrance ahead of her. Or, when she craned her neck around, the one at her rear. And this was good because he wouldn't be able to see in here either.

He wasn't whistling anymore, she realised. In fact suddenly she couldn't hear anything. Did that mean he'd gone? Had he given up?

Bessie knew better than to take such a chance at this early stage. So she waited, clutching the torch tightly, the moisture on her palms seeping through her woollen mittens, making its handle slippery. The heart was banging in her chest so loudly it was more like a drum. But aside from that, there was no sound at all. She couldn't even hear the gentle lapping of the tarn, which was kind of a pity. She'd always loved that sound; it had never failed to remind her she was home. But what sort of home was this now, where people she didn't know could come in whenever it suited them and write strange, horrible messages? And then, five seconds later, she *did* hear something – a dull, hollow thud.

Bessie stiffened where she crouched.

Now she heard another thud, followed by a low scraping sound.

Slowly it dawned on her that these sounds were issuing from the stable, which was just on her right. Still she didn't move.

He couldn't know she was here. He was probably just bumping around in the fog, like a silly idiot, or some daft, spoiled lad kicking at doors and stuff, angry that he couldn't find her. But the next thud sounded as if it came from the stable roof. As did the one after that, which was much louder and heavier, and the one after that, which was heavier still – and much closer.

Bessie stood up, but before she could get out of there, she sensed movement directly above her. She gazed up, her face drenched with sweat, and saw a bulky form – it looked like a man's head and shoulders in heavy clothing and a hood – leaning out over the edge of the stable, peering intently and silently down at her. With duck-like squawks, Bessie turned and fled along the narrow passage. On exit, she fought her way through briars and thickets. There was only one thing for it now. She had to make a run for it. With luck, she could still make it to Mr Ramsdale's. As

Bessie scrambled forward through the sodden undergrowth separating their two properties, she realised there was an old fence somewhere around here. She wouldn't see it until she ran into it. But it was flimsy and decayed, and indeed, when she struck it thighs-first, the whole thing collapsed. Of course there was a strand of barbed wire in there too, which half-tripped her and tore at her duffle-coat as she climbed over it. But she didn't care about any of that. She just ran, kicking through more tussocky grass, and then slipping and tottering over what had once been an ornamental rockery. The angular shape of Mr Ramsdale's house loomed in front of her, blurry light shimmering from its windows. From the first one she ran to, she could see straight into the downstairs living area. And she could see him as well.

He was sitting at his table, with his back turned, working on his computer.

'Mr Ramsdale!' she shouted, banging on the mullioned glass.

He didn't look around, too engrossed in his work.

A rotten twig snapped somewhere behind her.

With more squawks, Bessie buffaloed along the side of the house and around the corner to the front door. Mr Ramsdale would hear that for sure. He had a knocker, and she would bang it loudly – so loudly he would get angry. But she didn't care, so long as it brought him out to see her.

And yet, when she got there – wonder of wonders – the door was open. Only a little bit, slivers of light shining around its edges, but so what? Without waiting for an invitation, Bessie pushed the door open.

'Mr Ramsdale!' she panted. 'Mr Ramsdale?'

He was still at the desk with his back turned. She stomped

across the room in heavy, uncoordinated fashion. She was exhausted now, her throat raw, breath ripping in and out of her lungs. But she was here, she'd made it – she didn't care if he shouted and bellowed. She was safe, and the relief flooded through her.

'Mr Ramsdale!' Midway across, the stone floor turned slippery; she skidded a couple of feet but somehow kept her balance. She grabbed at his right shoulder, shaking it hard. *'Mr Ramsdale!'*

Bessie stood bewildered as, with the creaking of the chair's oily pivot, he turned slowly around, jerking to a halt when he faced her. The expected foul-mouthed tirade didn't come. It would never come. Mr Ramsdale's head was slumped stiffly to one side, his white face twisted into a rigid rictus of horror. And only now did it strike her that the mysteriously slippery floor was red, that her neighbour's desk and computer were red, that the entire front of his clothing was red, that the streaks running down from his empty eye-sockets were red, and that the sickle-shaped, double-edged cleft where his throat and larynx had been crudely butchered was monstrously red.

She spun around, screaming hoarsely, slipping and sliding back across the greasy, gore-clotted floor – to be confronted by a rectangle of fog where the open doorway stood, and that whistling again, from somewhere on the other side of it.

This brought her to a slithering halt. Frantic, Bessie tried to hobble backward, this time losing her feet properly and landing hard on her front, her chin smacking the floor with such force that sparks shot before her eyes. For seconds Bessie lay dazed – until approaching footfalls drew her attention to a pair of heavy boots tramping in from the fog. Her dimmed vision roved upward, catching a momentary glimpse of a stocky body dressed all in black, and of a black leather-gloved hand clasping and unclasping around the hilt of a large, hook-bladed tin-opener. Too groggy and feeble even to moan, she lay helpless as those feet came thumping towards her.

Chapter 11

Rather to Hazel's surprise, the pub drew custom that evening. She'd intended to keep the front door locked, but had told all the locals she'd still be open for business – they needed only to knock.

The first knock came shortly after six; Burt and Mandy Fillingham. This was perhaps expected. Fillingham, as a gossip merchant, would hear a lot less sitting behind locked doors at home than he would in The Witch's Kettle. Half an hour later, Ted Haveloc showed up. In this case, it was more of a surprise. For a grizzled sixty-two-year-old, Haveloc was the most robust occupant of the Keld, a long-term outdoorsman with the gnarled hands and cracked black fingernails to prove it. But he lived alone of course, so perhaps even he felt more vulnerable than usual on a night like this. The O'Grady sisters, Dulcie and Sally, lived together, social-ised together, did almost everything together, and yet they turned up a short time later too, having made the quick trip across the green at a scurry and knocking frantically and continually on the pub's heavy oaken door until Lucy opened it. Half an hour after that, Bella McCarthy and her husband did exactly the same thing. In their ones and twos, the customers settled around the fire, drank alcohol and conversed in quiet, subdued tones.

'Strength in numbers, I suppose,' Lucy said, as she and her aunt stood behind the bar.

'Yep,' Hazel replied. 'Do me a favour, Luce. Go upstairs, check all the windows are locked . . . yeah?'

Lucy nodded and trotted away. Hazel glanced at her watch. It was just after six-thirty.

'Is there anything to eat, Hazel?' Ted Haveloc called across the taproom. 'I haven't had a meal all day, and I'm famished.'

'Erm, yeah . . . sure,' she said, unable to think of any reason why the normal menu wouldn't be operating. They had plenty of food in the larder, and neither she nor Lucy would have much else to do for the rest of the evening. 'Give us a minute, okay?'

She breezed through into the kitchen, turned the ovens on and, as an afterthought, opened the top panel in the window over the sink. It was a relatively small kitchen and would quickly get hot and stuffy when they started cooking.

Then Hazel heard the ululation – the distant, eerie ululation.

Astonished, she turned to the window.

Several seconds passed as she wondered if she'd imagined it. Because it had sounded like no human cry she'd ever heard, and yet some disconcerting inner sense told her that was exactly what it was.

Beyond the window lay the yard where her maroon Renault Laguna was parked, and various crates and barrels awaited collection by the drayman. Even with the gates barred, as they were now, someone could get in there easily enough – the walls were only seven feet high. But briefly, that didn't matter.

166

Hazel knew what she'd heard.

She opened the back door and stood on the step, listening. The air was bitter, the fog thick, grimy and fluffy as cotton wool. Was it possible there was some kind of error here? Had someone been fiddling around with the jukebox in the taproom? But now she heard the cry again – this time prolonged for several seconds longer than before. Weird, ululating, so filled with angst and torment that it barely sounded human. Abruptly, it snapped off.

Hazel stood rooted to the spot, deep shivers passing down her spine.

When she finally went back inside, she ensured to lock the door behind her. Almost certainly the rare atmospheric conditions were partly responsible for her hearing that sound. She had no doubt it had travelled a long distance. The normal acoustics in the Cradle would also have assisted. Whenever the drag-hunt was around, she'd hear the yipping of the hounds and the drone of the hunting horn when the pack was way up at the north end of the valley.

Two words formed in her mind – for about the twentieth time that day.

Annie Beckwith.

Hazel seriously doubted that even on a night like this, noises at Fellstead Grange would be audible in Cragwood Keld. But that poor old dear was such a long way from help should she need it, and of course she had no idea she was in danger. Lucy reappeared in the kitchen doorway, so abruptly that Hazel jumped.

'Ted Haveloc's still asking if there's any food on tonight?'

'Erm, yeah, yeah . . . sure. Give them the menus. Listen, Lucy . . .?'

Lucy glanced back in.

'You'll have to cook it yourself. That okay?'

Lucy looked briefly puzzled, but then shrugged. 'No problem.'

While Lucy went back out into the taproom, Hazel crossed the kitchen and retrieved one of the police contact cards. The first number she tried was Heck's mobile. Predictably, there was no response. Following that, she tried Mary-Ellen. That gained no reply either. She went out into the bar and tried the police station from the landline, but it was the same outcome.

'Anyone up at Cragwood Keld police office, Ted?' she asked Ted Haveloc. As he lived closest to the police station, he was the most likely to know.

'The lights were on when I came out, Hazel, but I didn't see anyone moving around,' he replied. 'The Land Rover's not there, nor Sergeant Heckenburg's Citroën. At a guess, the place is still locked up and they're out and about.'

'Thanks.'

Cumbria prided itself on the sense of community preserved in its small, close-knit towns and villages. Hazel supposed this had developed naturally in an environment where all occupants were lumped together. Encircled by bleak moors, fathomless forests, and high, wind-riven mountains, there was a sense of embattlement, and of course they had terrible winters here – the worst rain, the worst snow, and now it seemed, the worst fog. Lake District residents needed to get on well together and look out for each other, just to endure.

As such, Hazel wondered when it was that she'd last seen Annie.

A couple of years ago, easily. The old dear had reluctantly come down to the pub to celebrate Ted Haveloc's sixtieth, and even then she'd been all skin and bone, wearing ragged clothes. Ted, who knew Annie better than anyone because he occasionally went up to help with chores on her run-down farm, might have seen her more recently, but not, as far as Hazel was aware, in the last few months. The water company truck went up there reasonably regularly too, to empty the septic tank, but would its crew have any interaction with the old girl? Would they even know she was there while they were working?

None of this was good enough, Hazel decided. Mark had said they'd get up there at some point, but he hadn't held out much hope it would be anytime soon, and it probably wouldn't be because he and Mary-Ellen would have a lot to do. But in the meantime someone had to look out for that nice old lady.

Hazel slipped out around the bar to the foot of the stairs. Nobody noticed; they were all too busy giving Lucy their food orders. Upstairs in the flat, she put on her walking boots and her fleece-lined jacket. She decided that she'd try to persuade Annie to come back down here, offer to put her up for a few nights free of charge. If nothing else, the old lady could have a hot bath, get a proper night's sleep, and sit out the crisis in relative safety. Failing that – because Hazel knew Annie, and she could be stubborn as an ox – she'd take her some supplies up; some eggs, milk, bread, some packets of tea and dried soup, some chocolate and biscuits. She didn't know what Annie lived on half the time. She'd once kept cows and pigs. She'd even had a pony for her trap, though said trap was now most likely decaying in some forgotten outbuilding. Ultimately, Annie had become too infirm to tend her stock, though she'd often tell anyone who'd listen that they were her only real friends. Apparently, she still grew her own fruit and vegetables, but in all honesty how easy could it be to eke out your existence like that, especially when you were an OAP?

Feeling guilty at not having done this before, Hazel quickly went back downstairs and straight into the kitchen before anyone could query her. She got everything together, placed it in a wicker basket and covered it with a fresh tablecloth. She also grabbed herself an electric torch.

Then she had another thought.

Perhaps it was a bit silly – maybe an overreaction, maybe a *massive* overreaction, but Mark had seemed genuinely concerned earlier on. She knew a little bit about his background. He'd been in a few scrapes, to say the least. Surely it would take a lot to discomfort him as much as he'd looked discomforted today? In which case, assuming this menace wasn't imaginary, she left the basket on one of the kitchen work-tops and trotted back upstairs. As she did, she felt a different kind of guilt – about breaking her word. Before he'd set off on his travels, Mark had strongly advised her to stay in the pub and provide a safe haven for the occupants of Cragwood Keld. Definitely not to go to the far end of the Cradle and up the Track to Annie's farm. But Mark had only been here two and a half months. He was a good man, but a child of the urban sprawl. He likely had no idea how much they all cared for each other in these rural outlands. Hazel made a mental commitment to teach him that – if he opted to stay with her and give it a go.

And she wasn't ignoring his concerns either. That was why she was now back up here in the flat, why she was rummaging through the closet among her ex's old sports gear and fishing tackle. The item she was looking for was right at the back, in a zipped canvas case. She lifted it out. It was old now, not quite an antique, but it had belonged to her father and to her grandfather before him. Slowly and cautiously, she drew the zipper down and extricated the object inside.

It was a double-barrel Purdey shotgun, a twelve-gauge.

With its walnut stock, open scroll coin engravings on its sidelock, and blued carbon steel barrels, it was an exquisite piece of craftsmanship, and had been her father's pride and joy when he'd used to go duck hunting. Even now it was in excellent working condition. Over the years, she'd disassembled and reassembled it several times, oiling it regularly. Both Mark and Mary-Ellen knew she had it in her possession, but while the two cops didn't exactly approve, they weren't about to turn her in. Mark would probably do his nut if he knew she kept it in an old cupboard in her lounge, but the truth was she didn't really have anywhere else.

The one big problem of course, was the absence of ammunition. There was a cartridge box in the closet, on a high shelf. Mark had told her she was supposed to keep the ammunition away from the firearm – but as the box only contained two cartridges it hardly seemed worth the trouble. There'd only been two as long as Hazel could remember. She broke the breech open just to check, then snapped it closed again, slid the gun back into its case, and shoved the cartridge box into her fleece pocket.

Before descending the stairs, Hazel took off her fleece and draped it over her shoulder, to conceal the weapon. No one in the taproom noticed, but in the kitchen Lucy was now hard at work. She'd already spotted the basket of supplies, and when she saw the shotgun as well her eyebrows arched dramatically.

'Don't tell anyone,' Hazel said. 'But I'm going up to Fellstead Grange.'

'Annie Beckwith's place? Why?'

Hazel didn't mention the cry she'd heard earlier. She was starting to think that had been nothing significant; an animal or some rare bird. There were plenty to choose from in the heart of the National Park. But the others wouldn't rationalise it that way. They'd try to stop her going.

'I don't like the idea of her being alone up there.'

'Heck said it wasn't a good idea,' Lucy argued.

It's easy for him to say that,' Hazel replied. 'He doesn't know Annie. To him, she's just a name.'

'He knows what he's talking about. Anyway, M-E said she'd go and look.'

'Will Mary-Ellen take Annie some spare food? Will she suggest she come down here and stay for a few nights in the pub?'

Lucy had no answer for that.

'It's not a problem,' Hazel added. 'I'm driving to the Ho, and walking up the Track to Annie's farm. I'll be forty minutes, tops. And if anyone tries to mess with me . . .' she hefted the shotgun, 'I've got this.'

Lucy looked more than a little sceptical. 'Have you ever fired that thing?'

'You point it and pull the trigger. How hard can it be?'

'In this fog you won't know who it is until they're right on top of you.'

'No one's going to be on top of me,' Hazel said with an airy confidence she didn't feel. She pulled a bob-cap on, zipped her fleece and took her gear to the back door. 'Close the gate after I've gone, and make sure you put the bolt on. Then lock the back door and look after our customers. They're your responsibility while I'm gone. Like I say, I'll be forty minutes, max.'

Lucy gave her further arguments, but knew from experience that when her Aunt Hazel's mind was made up, there was no changing it. Hazel had a disarmingly gentle manner, but for several years she'd survived comfortably in an isolated environment which in winter was as challenging as they came. Many was the time Lucy had seen her carrying piles of firewood through the snow, chipping ice from frozen water pipes, fixing broken roof-tiles and gutters, tasks which didn't remotely faze her. For all her soft exterior, Hazel was gutsy and independent, and she cared about her neighbours; that latter aspect of her character, in particular, was non-negotiable. So in the end Lucy did as she was asked, closing the back gate straight away after Hazel had reversed out through it in her Laguna, and ramming the bolt home; then going back indoors to cook everyone their tea.

Slowly and cautiously, Hazel's heavy car rumbled its way around the exterior of the pub, joining Truscott Drive, the single lane that ran upward across the green and through the centre of the village. Very little was visible, even with full headlights, the beams draining ineffectively into impenetrable murk. In some ways it was encouraging, she thought, as she finally reached the top of the Drive and swung left onto Cragwood Road. Because whoever she couldn't see out there, they presumably couldn't see her either. Though merely thinking in those terms – that there *might* be someone out there – was surprisingly unnerving.

'There's no one here,' she assured herself as she coasted north through sheets of opaque mist. Whatever had happened to those girls, it had been way up in the fells. Anyway, the police had already admitted they didn't know for sure what the incident involved. It could have been an accident.

Hazel had told Lucy she'd be there and back in around forty minutes, but in fact so slow was her progress that it took her over twenty to drive the three miles to Cragwood Ho. She pulled up in the car park at the foot of the Cradle Track, and turned off her engine. She was uncertain how she felt about seeing the police Land Rover sitting there. On one hand, it might mean Mary-Ellen had now gone up the Track herself to check on old Annie, which would be great news. But it could also be that she was still on the other side of the tarn, having not yet returned in the police launch, in which case Hazel was still here alone.

She checked her phone. It was just past seven-twenty; evening was now turning into night. Even so, she sat behind her steering wheel for several minutes longer, listening. The silence was absolute, the vapour shifting past her windows in solid palls. Briefly, she could sense the towering, rock-strewn slopes as they rose inexorably to her left and right, eventually reaching the heights of Pavey Ark and Blea Rigg, though all Hazel could see in the glow of her headlights was the dry-stone wall in front of her. When she switched the lights off, even that vanished.

Several more seconds passed, while she worked up the courage to climb out.

She hadn't expected to be frightened, but suddenly all that stuff about the fog hiding her as effectively as it might hide someone else seemed like over-optimistic nonsense. Feeling as if she was crossing some kind of Rubicon, Hazel reached into the back seat, slid the shotgun from its case and inserted the two cartridges. Snapping the weapon closed again, she climbed from the car, circled around, took the basket of supplies out from the other side, and shut the door.

The thud of the central locking system echoed in the dimness. She loitered by the vehicle as she listened to it. A few seconds later, she tried both Mark and Mary-Ellen on their mobile phones once more, but again there was no contact. She glanced down across the car park to the other houses. They were only fifty or so yards away, but the blanketing mist concealed all lights. Now that she thought about it, Hazel wondered if she ought to be concerned about the others who lived at this isolated end of the valley as well.

Okay, they'd already been given a heads-up by the police, though that was no guarantee Bessie Longhorn would be safe. Hazel made a decision to call at Bessie's cottage on the way back, and check she was okay. Maybe take her down to the pub for couple of days as well. She might even, if she felt particularly charitable, offer the same option to Bill Ramsdale, though she expected she'd get short shrift on that – which would probably be a good thing. Bessie and Annie would be hard work enough – but wasn't that what communities were all about?

Hazel switched her torch on and ventured along the wall to the point where the gate and the stile were located. On the other side, the Track snaked uphill into the gloom. It was composed mainly of broken slate, which had deluged from the slopes above, and slithered and cracked underfoot when anyone stepped on it. It closely followed the edge of a barren, rock-filled ravine, and though at this lower level it was broad enough for a narrow-gauge vehicle to pass along it, Hazel didn't personally know anyone who'd be crazy enough to try that in this weather.

She slid through the stile and started upward, only now realising how challenging a hike this would be. Fifteen minutes minimum, she reckoned, and all the while the gradient increasing. It wasn't a straight track, either. It bent and looped. The ravine, though it was cloaked from view, lay close on her left and grew progressively deeper, its sides ever more sheer, as she ascended, while the miasma turned steadily thicker. She'd often assumed that, as fog was heavy, the higher up into it you climbed, the thinner it would become. Earlier that day, she'd tried to imagine what this fog would look like from the point of view of a chopper lofting high above the Pikes: bare rocky islands slowly emerging from an oozing grey ocean.

Here and there on her right, clutches of young pine grew

175

amid the jagged piles of slate. She occasionally glimpsed them through the torch-lit vapour, but there was nothing cute or Christmassy about them. Many were fantastically warped and twisted by the wind and cold. Equally unnerving, and for some reason Hazel could never fathom, climbers and fell-walkers traversing this route in the past had chosen particularly hefty shards of slate, some of them three or four feet in length, and had then used smaller pieces to prop them upright on both sides of the path – usually every hundred yards or so. What they were supposed to be – distance-markers, or even some variety of crude outdoor art – she never knew, but the illusion they created was of gravestones. Or, if one of the largest ones – some were maybe as tall as five or six feet – suddenly loomed from the fog, of malformed figures standing close by.

She ignored them as she trudged on, the crunching impacts of her boots resounding loudly. By now she was breathing hard, her knees and ankles aching as she leaned forward with each step, occasionally slipping or skidding. A couple of times she thought she heard movement – a scrape or rattle of pebbles. She would always stop on these occasions, only to be greeted by unearthly stillness. Each time it was entirely possible she'd heard an echo, though it set her nerves on edge. She filched her phone from her fleece pocket to see how long she'd been here, and was dismayed to find it was only a couple of minutes.

Sweat chilling on her body, Hazel dragged herself up the Track, which grew ever more uneven and rugged. Only after what seemed much longer than fifteen minutes, closer to half an hour maybe, did it at last level out again, and diverged into two distinct routes. The left-hand route continued ahead, still rising slowly into the Pikes, but from this point only as the narrowest of footpaths. The right-hand route remained broad enough for vehicle passage, just about, and led beneath the darkly woven branches of several firs, before crossing a low bridge into the rocky corrie where Fellstead Grange was located.

In good weather, this was a stunningly beautiful spot. Fellstead Corrie was a natural amphitheatre in the hillside, its gentle slopes thick with bracken, gorse and springy heather, and ascending on all sides to high, ice-carved ridges. The farmhouse itself stood close to a bubbling pool at the foot of a cataract, which poured from the dizzying heights of High White Stones like a helter-skelter. At its rear there was a network of allotments, greenhouses (mostly dingy with mould and filled with brambles), decrepit barns and sheds which all belonged to Annie, and swathes of overgrown pasture for which there were now no animals to graze upon. The building, which was early eighteenth-century in origin, was large and sprawling, comprising various wings and gables, and built from solid Lakeland stone with a roof of Westmorland slate. Spruced up, it would be magnificent, and in a location like this it would make a superb country house or holiday inn. But in its current state of semi-dereliction, it was an eyesore. Both the walls and roof were crabbed with lichen, the rotted iron gutters stuffed with mosses and bird's nests. But of course, none of this dilapidation was visible at present.

With the basket over her left wrist and the shotgun cradled under her right arm, Hazel felt her way across the rickety bridge. Fellstead Beck gurgled past underneath, having circled around the farm from the waterfall plunge-pool. A few dozen yards to her right somewhere, it dropped down a narrow gully into the lower valley, eventually at some point – Hazel wasn't sure exactly where – flowing into the tarn.

On the other side of the bridge, beyond a pair of moss-clad gateposts, she entered the farmyard proper, her feet clipping on aged paving stones as she approached the darkened structure just vaguely visible in the fog. When she halted again, the only sound was the distant rushing of water. Meanwhile, not a single light shone from the eerie edifice. In the icy murk, it resembled an abandoned Viking long-hall; the remnant of some Nordic nightmare rather than a family home. Disconcertingly, the darkness beyond its windows seemed even darker than the darkness outside. Annie Beckwith had no electricity, no gas . . . but surely she would keep a fire in her living room? Didn't she even have candles?

Hazel checked her phone again. It was now after seven-forty. Too early even for Annie Beckwith to go to bed. She approached the front door. If the old lady was sleeping, Hazel didn't like the idea of disturbing her. But she'd not come all this way to turn back without at least trying to make contact. She knocked several times on the warped, scabby wood. There was no thunderous echo inside; the door was too thick and heavy. Likewise, there was no reply.

Hazel tried again – the same.

She fumbled for the handle, a corroded iron ring, which, when she twisted it, turned easily. There was a clunk as the latch was disengaged on the other side, and the door creaked open an inch. To open it the rest of the way, she had to put her shoulder against it, grating it inward over the stone floor.

This was also a tad discomforting. It wasn't common practice for folk in this part of the world to keep their doors permanently locked, but surely a lone OAP like Annie would do so at night, especially living all the way out here?

'Hello!' Hazel called into the blackness.

Again, there was no response.

She sidled through, unbidden, and was hit with an

eye-watering stench, the combined aromas of grime, mildew and decay.

Hazel shone her torch around the room, which was so cluttered with broken and dingy furniture that it was more like a lock-up crammed with rubbish than an actual living space. Dust furred everything, so that colours – the fabrics in the upholstery and lampshades and the many drapes and curtains – were indiscernible, each item a uniform grey-brown. And yet, evidence of the fine old farmhouse this had once been was still there. The fireplace was a broad stone hearth, elaborately carved around its edges with vines and animals, though currently filled with cinders, burnt fragments of feathers and what looked like chicken bones. The mantel above was a huge affair, again constructed from Lakeland stone and heavily corniced, and yet dangling with tendrils of wax from the multiple melted candles on top of it. A mirror was placed above the mantel, so old and tarnished that only cloudy vagueness was reflected there. Ancient sepia photographs hung in cracked, lopsided frames, the faces they depicted lost beneath films of dirt. These added to the house's melancholy air, but also created the eerie sensation that eyes were upon her. Hazel turned sharply a couple of times, imagining there was someone hidden in a corner whom she hadn't previously noticed, perhaps peering out through one of those veils of dust-web, eyes bloodshot, yellow peg teeth fixed in a limpid, deranged grin.

'For God's sake, woman, what's the matter with you?' she said to herself in a tight voice. Her and her bloody imagination. 'Annie?' she called out. 'Annie, it's Hazel Carter! You know, from The Witch's Kettle!'

There was no answer, but her voice echoed in various parts of the house. Immediately on her left, an arched doorway led into a passage that Hazel thought connected with the kitchen and dining room, but the blackness down there was so thick it was almost tangible. She ignored it, moving into the centre of the lounge, only to freeze at a skittering, rustling sound. She turned, just as a whip-like tail vanished beneath the web-shrouded hulk of an age-old Welsh dresser.

Hazel had to fight down a pang of revulsion. The place was clearly unfit for human habitation as it was, but if it was crawling with rats as well . . .

A furry, grey body scuttled along the mantel, casting a huge, amorphous shadow as she followed it with her torch. Stubs of candles went flying to the floor, their ceramic holders shattering. The rat leapt after them and moved in a blur of speed down the passage towards the kitchen.

There was no question, Hazel decided – they had to get the social services onto this. Annie would hate them for it, but what choice did they have?

But this was assuming Annie was still alive.

At least there was no sign of forced entry, or that there'd been any kind of struggle in here. Not, if Hazel was totally honest, that it would be easy to tell.

Hazel glanced at the brown-stained ceiling, realising with a sense of deep oppression that she had yet to check the upstairs. So unwilling that it was difficult to set her legs in motion, she advanced across the room to a square entry in the facing wall, which led to other rooms, as well as the foot of the main stair. She approached it and gazed up. Even without fog, the darkness at the top was impermeable. It seemed to absorb the glow of her torch rather than retreat from it. Hazel hesitated before placing the basket of food on a side-table and, with shotgun levelled in one hand and torch extended in the other, slowly ascended. The hair was stiff on her scalp. It was actually a terrible thing she was doing here; she'd entered someone's home uninvited, and was now processing from one area to the next with a loaded firearm.

But she couldn't leave. She'd called out and no one had responded, and with the house unlocked, implying someone was at home, she knew there was some kind of problem here. The temptation to call again was strong, but now some basic instinct advised her that stealth was a better option.

Hazel reached the top of the staircase. The landing was all cobwebs, bare floorboards and plaster walls, the plaster so damp and dirty that it was falling away in chunks, revealing bone-like lathes underneath. Various doorways opened off it. The doorway to the room that Hazel thought Annie might use as a bedroom was at the end of a short passage on the left. When she directed her torch in that direction, the door was partly open, more blackness lurking on the other side. Someone could easily be waiting in there, watching her, and she wouldn't see them from here.

Despite this, Hazel trod slowly forward, only halting when she was right in front of it. Even close up, the room was hidden from view. There was insufficient space between the door and its jamb for her torch to illuminate anything beyond. But now there was something else too – a faint but rather fetid smell, like open drains.

Hazel knew she was going to have to say something. It wasn't the done thing to barge unannounced into someone's private room, especially with a gun, not even if you were concerned for their wellbeing. Steeling herself in the face of an urge to hurry back downstairs and leave the building, she spoke loudly and clearly.

'Annie? Are you alright in there? It's Hazel Carter . . . you know, from The Witch's Kettle down in Cragwood Keld.'

Again there was no response, but the silence was beyond creepy. It was intense, weird; a listening silence. Despite every molecule in her body telling her to flee this odious place, Hazel propelled herself forward, pushing against the door, and as it swung open, entered with torch in one hand and shotgun balanced over the top of it.

What she saw in there had her blinking with shock.

And then screeching with horror.

Chapter 12

Heck made no attempt to conceal his annoyance. 'She's gone up to Fellstead Grange? On her bloody own?'

'You know how stubborn Hazel can be,' Lucy protested, almost tearfully. She'd never seen Heck shout before, so only now was it dawning on her how serious this might be. 'She's all sweetness and light usually, but when you try to stop her doing something, she just won't listen.'

'And you tried?'

'Course I tried!'

'Great! Just bloody great!'

He'd have said more – he felt like bellowing the pub down – but what purpose would that serve? In addition, he sensed they had an audience. They were standing at the bar in The Witch's Kettle. Having driven past the police station, where they spotted McGurk and Heggarty's Astra patrol car parked outside, and at least one of the two uniforms moving about inside, Heck and Gemma had driven on to the pub so that she could book in, take a quick shower and get changed. The villagers were still gathered around the fire, but all conversation between them had ceased as they listened in fascination.

'Let's go somewhere private,' Heck said.

Lucy, looking more than a little worried, lifted the hatch on the bar and moved to the kitchen door.

'Do you have an update for us, sergeant?' Burt Fillingham asked loudly.

'No, I'm sorry everyone,' Heck replied. 'Except to say that no news is good news, eh?' That didn't sound convincing even to his own ears, and Heck was an expert at lying to himself. 'If it's any consolation, folks, this is Detective Superintendent Piper . . . from Scotland Yard. She's one of the top homicide investigators in Britain, and we've got her for the duration of this enquiry.'

Gemma, cool and unruffled as always, nodded politely.

'And does that make us any safer?' Bella McCarthy asked, her voice made brasher than usual by the number of G&Ts she'd plied herself with over the last hour.

'You'll be perfectly safe as long as you do what I tell you,' Heck replied. 'Which is to stay together behind locked doors.'

'Stay together in here, you mean?' Ted Haveloc asked. He too was beside the bar, having ordered his sixth pint of Buttermere Gold. 'Seems like a plan.'

'It *is* a plan, actually,' Heck said, glancing at Lucy, implying they were all likely to be a lot safer together in here, rather than dispersed through their own cottages. 'How late were you planning on staying open for?'

She shrugged. 'Hazel's the boss, and she's not here.'

'Well, everyone stay in the pub for the time being,' Heck said. He circled the bar with Gemma, and followed Lucy into the kitchen. 'What happened?' he asked, once they were out of earshot of the others.

Lucy still looked scared. 'I don't know why she suddenly decided she was going up there. I think she's been worried about Annie for some time.'

'Funny how it all came to a head tonight.'

184

Lucy's cheeks coloured. 'Well, there *is* a killer on the loose . . .'

'We don't know that,' Gemma interjected calmly. 'So far we've got one case of GBH, and it wasn't fatal. Why don't we all just relax a little, eh?'

'On the subject of which,' Heck said quietly, consciously making an effort to calm himself down, 'it might be a good idea to close the bar.'

Lucy looked surprised. 'But you just said . . .'

'Let them stay in the pub, by all means. But it's not going to do us any good if they all get smashed out of their communal tree.'

'There isn't much to do in The Witch's Kettle if you can't drink,' Lucy said. 'Hazel's never had a telly in here.'

'Obviously your granddad never took you around the pubs when you were a nipper.' Heck headed back to the door. 'Give them some dominoes and a few bags of crisps . . . they'll be fine.'

'Where are you going now?' Lucy asked, dismayed they were leaving so soon.

'Back to the nick to see what's been happening,' Heck replied. 'And then up to Fellstead Grange to bring your bloody auntie back, hopefully with Annie Beckwith in tow.'

'Just be careful . . . Hazel's got that shotgun. You know . . . the one she's not supposed to have.'

The two cops halted and glanced at each other. Lucy's cheeks turned even pinker as she wondered if she'd spoken out of turn.

'That's something, I suppose,' Heck finally said.

'Yeah, but there are only two shells for it,' Lucy said.

'Let's hope she doesn't fire them off willy-nilly.'

'Let's hope she doesn't fire them at all,' Gemma stated, 'if she's not supposed to have this weapon.' She eyed Heck closely. 'Did *you* know about it?'

'Hazel's a special case,' he said. 'She's not a criminal. But I'll give her a damn good telling off when I see her. Should be fun.' He glanced at Lucy. 'I don't suppose Mary-Ellen's been in during our absence?'

'I haven't seen her since she left here with you around lunchtime.'

'Didn't look like she was at the nick, either,' Heck said, as he and Gemma left the pub together, the door slamming closed behind them. 'She had a lot to do, I suppose. Cordoning off that crime scene on the east shore. After that, she was going up to Fellstead Grange. Even so, I'd have expected her back by this time.'

'Why not give her a call?' Gemma threw her bag back into the rear of his Citroën.

'There's no mobile phone network at all in the Cradle.'

'No . . . silly me. Why would I have expected otherwise?' She glanced around. Aside from the pub's entrance and front windows, everything else was obliterated by murk. 'I understand there are people who like to get away from it all, Heck . . . but this place is like something from a Vincent Price movie.'

'It has its charms.'

'They've just been put away for the off-season, I suppose.'

'Well, yeah, that's exactly the case.' As he climbed in behind the wheel, Heck supposed Gemma was hardly seeing his new home at the ideal time. The apparent harshness of Cragwood Vale was more than a little deceptive. Things were so much different here on a fine summer's day. When the rising sun bathed the encircling summits rose-pink and the last threads of night mist dissipated over the mirror-still waters of the tarn, a deep tranquillity lay on this high, pristine valley. As the day ascended, the thickly treed shores would turn a lush, vibrant green and the higher, heather-clad slopes shimmer with purple. Picturesque didn't always mean perfect, of course. Wildness and isolation did not suit everyone, but the wildness of Cragwood Vale was not the wildness of Siberia, or Colorado, or even the Cairngorms. It was a homely, folksy kind of wildness. A safe wildness. Usually.

Gemma climbed into the back seat and closed the door, while Heck fastened his seatbelt and started the car. Only then did he notice that she'd kicked her shoes off and was in the process of unbuttoning her blouse.

'What're you doing, ma'am?'

'What does it look like? I'm getting changed.'

'In here?'

'Well there's clearly no time for me to get settled into my room. Eyes front, if you don't mind.'

'We're only two minutes from the nick.' He turned the ignition and put the car in gear.

'Drive slowly then.'

Not that there was much option about that. Thanks to the fog, they cruised laboriously up Truscott Drive, the rapid rustling of clothes from the back seat suggesting Gemma was working at a faster pace.

'If you adjust that rear-view mirror one more time, sergeant, I'll have you on a disciplinary,' she snapped.

'Sorry, ma'am. But I need to know what's going on behind me.'

'Yeah, I bet you do. Does this nice lady, Hazel, whose own crimes you're mysteriously cuffing, know what she's getting into, I wonder?'

'Probably not.'

By the time they'd rolled up at the police station, Gemma had changed into jeans, walking boots, a hooded black sweat-top, and a black waterproof jacket. The nick was unlocked, Heggarty behind the front desk, stripped to his shirt-sleeves. He buzzed them through into the back office. Heck introduced

Gemma, but the PC regarded her blank-faced – clearly the name 'Gemma Piper' meant nothing to him, though he acknowledged her rank with a curt, if surprised, nod. Half a second later, introductions were made again as Mick McGurk arrived.

'Taken a turn around the village,' he said, removing his hat and unzipping his hi-viz coat. He used a thick, hairy forearm to mop a sheen of sweat from his brow. 'Nae'n around anywhere.'

'No sign of Mary-Ellen either?' Heck asked. 'I see no Land Rover.'

McGurk gave a laconic shrug. 'Didn't see her, sarge.'

'I don't know where she is either,' Heggarty said, though his tone implied this was a more complex question than Heck realised. 'Is she still on shift, for instance?'

'Shift?' Heck replied.

'Me and PC McGurk are officially on overtime now. I presume PC O'Rourke is too, but I see no overtime charts on the walls here. And as you're her skipper . . .'

'And is that your priority at present, PC Heggarty? How much you're getting paid?'

'People need to go home sometime, you know, sarge.'

'*This* is Mary-Ellen's home. She rooms in the flat upstairs.'

'She's nae there either,' McGurk said. 'We checked up there soon as we got here.'

Heck eyed Heggarty warily. On closer inspection, the rangy young constable didn't just look the sort who'd be a stickler for procedure, but probably for workplace fairness as well; which would be reasonable enough in normal circumstances – there were far too many middle-aged, middle-management skivers in the police – but it was hardly a consideration at present.

Heck pushed past him and hit the playback button on the messaging machine. There were several missives waiting from

Windermere Comms, none of which told him anything he didn't know, apart from the last one.

'DS Heckenburg . . . we've had a Met Office update. The fog's definitely set to clear by mid-morning tomorrow. Maybe earlier. Mountain Rescue are going up into the Pikes at first light. The chopper will be in the air as soon as it's safe. Probably around the same time . . .'

'Jane Dawson will have been missing about thirty hours by then,' Heck muttered, unable to contain his frustration.

'We can't control the weather, sarge,' Heggarty replied. 'There are also several search parties headed your way first thing tomorrow, though some are going up via Dungeon Ghyll as well. They include PSUs, off-duty officers, members of the public who've volunteered and even some Territorial Army lads who've been camping in the Kirkstone Pass, so we won't be short on numbers. The low-level search will be under the control of Chief Inspector Dewhurst from Kendal. DI Mabelthorpe will be on his way up to Cragwood Vale first thing as well, with dog units, photographic and SOCO. The MIR's down here at Windermere, but he wants to open a subsidiary Incident Room at the Cragwood Keld office . . . can you call us back and let us know if you don't think that's practicable?'

Heck glanced around the narrow confines of his small workplace. 'Practicable, no . . . possible, probably.'

Heggarty was duly shocked. 'They'll be like sardines crammed in here, sarge.'

'It'll only be temporary . . .' Heck glanced to Gemma for support, but she was now poking casually around the office, oblivious to the conversation.

'Temporary or not,' Heggarty said, 'HR'll go mad if the conditions aren't conducive to . . .'

'We've got a cellar too,' Heck interrupted him. 'Plenty of room down there if we chuck all the junk out.'

'A cellar!'

'Look, we'll find somewhere. There're cottages-to-let up at the Ho. We'll commandeer one of those. Plenty light and ventilation there.'

'But . . .'

'I'm not doing CID admin's job for them,' Heck retorted. 'If they can't be arsed calling the Force Buildings Officer and checking the blueprints, that's not my fucking problem. I'm much more concerned about the situation at Fellstead Grange.'

'Perhaps it would help if you enlightened the two constables,' Gemma suggested. Apparently she'd not been quite as distracted from the conversation as Heck had thought, though she'd now taken a dog-eared scrapbook down from the shelf above his desk; it was the scruffy old tome in which he kept mug-shots of all those murder victims he'd gained convictions for during his career. She leafed through it. 'Put them in the picture, like . . .'

'Erm, yeah, of course.' In the whirlwind of recent events, Heck hadn't stopped to consider there were some folk here who knew even less than he did. He filled the PCs in as quickly as he could, emphasising how vulnerable Annie Beckwith was, and how vulnerable Hazel probably was too, even though she'd gone up there gun in hand.

'In that case, we should wait for armed support,' Heggarty stated flatly. 'I mean, if there are guns on the plot . . .'

'There are guns on the plot anyway,' Heck reminded him. 'Our suspect has already shot someone . . . which is why SFOs are en route. Just don't ask me when they'll get here. They've got to travel all the way down from Penrith.'

'But if this bloody madwoman's carrying a loaded shotgun . . .'

'Hazel is not a madwoman.'

'It's foggy, sarge . . . there could easily be a misidentification.'

'So we proceed with caution. At the end of the day, she's only got two slugs. If it's really bothering you, Heggarty, make sure you're the third man in.'

'So you aren't going to make any kind of formal risk assessment?'

'I already have,' Heck lied. 'And it's acceptable.'

'Acceptable?'

'We're the police, Heggarty. Sometimes it's beholden on us to take risks.'

'It won't look good if one of us gets injured . . .'

'It'll look even worse if two women die because we're too busy watching our own arses.' There was a long silence at this, Heggarty's face tingeing bright red.

Gemma shoved the scrapbook back onto the shelf. 'Anymore questions?' she asked.

'Yeah.' This time it was McGurk. 'We *all* going?'

'Not this time,' Heck said. It was tempting – strength in numbers again, but the landline at the nick was the only working phone they had, so it needed manning. The question was, who did he take? He assessed the two uniforms. Heggarty was the prig, and clearly the most likely to query instructions. In addition, he was young, inexperienced and a physical beanpole. Leaving him here, where he was out of the way, would be ideal. By contrast, dour combat-veteran McGurk would be much more use up on the fells, though he'd also be useful protecting the villagers here at Cragwood Keld. If something kicked off here and civilian lives were put in danger, did they really want Heggarty in charge?

'PC McGurk,' Heck said, 'you okay holding the fort?'

McGurk shrugged. Which seemed to be his answer to almost everything.

'Obviously report developments down to Windermere by the landline,' Heck said. 'Keep your eye on the pub too. It's just the other side of the green, but that's where the locals are gathered at present. And make your presence visible. Go round there once in a while. It'll reassure them.'

McGurk nodded.

'Keep the Astra too,' Heck said as an afterthought. 'PC Heggarty, you can ride with me and DSU Piper in the Citroën. Okay, everyone . . . let's get cracking.'

Heck and Gemma filed back out of the station, Heggarty tagging at the rear, looking vaguely disconsolate as he re-donned his hat and hi-viz coat.

'Thanks for the magnificent amount of help by the way,' Heck said quietly.

Gemma didn't look at him. 'What are you talking about?'

'When Citizen Smith back there was having a pop.'

'Easy, sergeant. He'll probably end up being Chief Constable.'

'So will you, ma'am . . . most likely. But you weren't exactly chucking your weight about when I needed it.'

'And would it really have helped if I was? You know these guys. I don't.'

'I *don't* know these guys.' Heck unlocked the Citroën. 'Not really.'

'Anyway . . .' Gemma slid into the front passenger seat. 'You seem to have everything well in hand. Including the local landlady.'

He realised she'd spotted the calendar hanging next to his desk. It was a locally produced piece of promotional work on behalf of The Witch's Kettle, depicting both Hazel and Lucy, looking uncharacteristically glamorous in bright make-up, short, tight dresses, high heels and fancy hair-dos, posed outside the hostelry on a glorious summer day; the tarn lay like a flat mirror behind them, vividly reflecting the azure sky and purple/green mountainsides.

'Don't tell me that's bugging you?' he smirked. 'I mean . . . for real?'

'No, but it's interesting. In your former life there was never much time for love.'

'Yeah, well in *this* life there's plenty of time for everything. Until these last few days of course.'

Heggarty now clambered into the back seat, and they pulled away from the kerb, prowling west to Cragwood Road, and then heading north towards the Ho. As before, they could only advance at a frustrating crawl.

'What's that for?' Heck asked, noticing through the rear-view mirror that Heggarty was inscribing something on a clipboard.

'I don't like to work directly into my pocketbook,' Heggarty replied. 'His eyes flirted towards Gemma, and he flushed. 'Sorry about that, ma'am . . . it's just to make sure I get everything right before it goes down on official paper.'

'It's okay, PC Heggarty,' she replied. 'They may not teach you that when you're being puppy-walked, but I think it's a good idea.'

'I'm dead keen on good paperwork,' Heggarty added. 'Only like to hand mine over for inspection at the end of each shift when it's bang-on. Every i dotted, every t crossed, spelling and grammar all present and correct.'

'Like there's not enough writing in this bloody job,' Heck grunted.

'You'd rather we ran around being totally unaccountable?' Heggarty asked.

'It's not that,' Gemma said. 'It's just that in his eighteen years in the job, DS Heckenburg's form-filling skills have never been better than execrable. I know . . . I've had to sign most of them off.'

'Paperwork's a pain in the arse, I'd agree,' Heggarty said. 'But it's a necessary evil and we've got to be professional.'

'And what are you being professional about now?' Heck asked him.

Heggarty tapped his clipboard. 'We've already got a number of offences to look into. Obviously the assault on Tara Cook is the main subject of the enquiry. But there may be care and neglect issues around this old lady, Annie Beckwith. And then we've got the unlicensed shotgun, not to mention the fact it's being carried around in public and may be loaded.'

'The important thing, though, is to remember why we're here,' Gemma said.

'Of course, ma'am.'

'And not let ourselves get side-tracked.'

'No . . . I understand that . . .'

'It's also important we get there in one piece.' She glanced at Heck. 'So why don't we slow down a bit?'

Heck eased his foot off the gas, having not noticed they'd slowly accelerated to thirty miles per hour. 'Listen,' he said, 'if we meet Hazel coming the other way, or Mary-Ellen, I'll be a happy bunny. Even if we hit them head-on.'

'Well, writing cars off has always been a habit with you. At least this time it won't be coming out of *my* budget.'

Gemma said this without humour, her eyes roving the turgid blackness enshrouding the car, occasionally narrowing as she caught fibrous hints of foliage along the roadside. In all the years they'd been work colleagues, and especially when they'd lived together as boyfriend and girlfriend, Heck had seen every kind of emotion from Gemma. This aloof ice-maiden was the image she reserved for television interviews or appearances before public inquiries, while the human spitfire was the one he and his fellow officers were more familiar with – Gemma did not suffer fools lightly. But he'd never seen her look afraid or even unnerved, and she'd faced down dozens of hardcore criminals in the past. Now however, perhaps for the very first time, she looked a little uneasy. It was possible that as an officer who'd seen most of her service in the big city, she was feeling like a fish out of water in this country wilderness, but perhaps she was also bewildered to have discovered that such conditions as these could actually exist in the real world.

'We're high up, here,' Heck said by way of explanation. 'If it's not fog, we get low cloud. And then there's the tarn. It's ultra-deep and always freezing cold. We've had mist lying in this valley for hours after it's cleared everywhere else.'

'By the sounds of it, it hasn't cleared anywhere just yet,' she replied.

'Fifteen hours to go, the Met Office reckons, ma'am,' Heggarty piped up.

'Hmmm,' she agreed. 'Sounds quick when you say it like that, doesn't it?'

Chapter 13

The first thing they noticed on arrival at the Cragwood Ho car park were the two empty vehicles sitting side-by-side: Hazel's Renault Laguna and Mary-Ellen's police Land Rover. Heck jumped out, checking all around both cars, but there was no sign of damage. They had simply been parked and locked. That was probably reassuring, though once again the strength of his concern for Hazel discomforted him slightly. It wasn't like she was his wife, or even his girlfriend. They had an informal arrangement; that was all. Or so he kept telling himself.

'So the question is, are they together or separate from each other?' Heggarty asked.

'I'm hoping Hazel ran into Mary-Ellen when she arrived here, and that they've gone up the Track together,' Heck said. 'Course, we won't know unless we go up there ourselves.'

'Perhaps there are other residents down here she wants to check on,' Gemma said.

'Only two,' he replied. 'One of whom has some keys to the boatshed. We'll have a look down there afterwards if she's not up at Fellstead Grange. Annie and Hazel have got to be our priority at present.'

They zipped up and pulled on gloves, as the temperature had dropped significantly. Furls of smoky breath hung from their lips, adding to the general miasma, which was now so thick it was like something from the early days of TV sci-fi. The dull, echoing silence only added to this. Heck could sense the immense, towering rock forms that rose on all sides at this end of the Cradle. It wasn't just eerie, it was other-worldly. He had to struggle to remind himself how normal this place was in ordinary times. How, with fine conditions prevailing, there'd be climbers on the overlooking cliffs, hot sunshine pinpointing them like tiny blue and orange beetles as they made their cautious way across the ancient, weathered faces. Bands of student backpackers would joke and shout to each other as they yomped ahead, ascending the flinty Track with preposterous energy, while families would stick to the lower levels, laughing and calling out while they explored the lakeside nature trails, throwing sticks into the water for their yapping pooches. And at the end of it all, with the azure sky turning indigo and the sun melting in embers on Harrison Stickle, spilling its dazzling glimmer across Witch Cradle Tarn, they'd all reconvene in The Witch's Kettle beer garden to eat trout and chips, and join in a rousing, ribald chorus that would be heard as far south as Cragwood Race. Heck didn't like admitting it, but he wished he was there now, doing exactly that.

Gemma brought him back to reality, her boots crunching as she moved to the gate. 'How come neither car was taken up to Fellstead Grange?'

'Even in the police Land Rover, the Cradle Track isn't for the faint-hearted,' Heck said. 'You'd be taking a horrendous risk. No one will chance it in this fog. M-E doesn't spook easily, but trust me, ma'am, you see this route and you'll understand what I'm talking about.'

They clambered through the stile, and with all three torches spearing ahead of them, set off up the Track side-by-side. It steepened steadily, and soon they were huffing and grunting with the exertion, their torchlight flickering over the various ghostly totems erected alongside it.

'Looks like someone had nothing better to do,' Gemma commented.

'Artists,' Heck said. 'Of one kind or another.'

They proceeded for several more minutes, then, at Heck's insistence, they stopped. When Heggarty queried this, Heck signalled for silence.

They listened, but heard nothing.

'What?' Gemma finally asked.

'Thought I heard a voice. Only briefly, but it sounded like . . . laughter. Some way off though, I must admit.'

'These gullies and canyons can amplify sound,' Heggarty said. 'Whoever it was, they could be miles away. Climbers maybe, campers.'

They listened a little longer. Still nothing.

'You couldn't have been mistaken?' Gemma wondered.

'Maybe,' Heck said thoughtfully. 'When I found the injured girl on the shores of Witch Cradle Tarn, I thought I heard something then. Whispers . . . laughter. But there was no one there.'

'Weird kind of offender,' Heggarty said. 'Hanging around at the scene of the crime, laughing.'

'Be under no illusion, PC Heggarty,' Gemma advised him. 'There are some *very* weird offenders.'

They pressed on, and about ten minutes later they reached the right-hand turn leading into Fellstead Corrie. Despite the cold, all three were now damp with sweat and breathing hard. Again they halted and listened. Heck gazed up the remainder of the Track, which, though they couldn't see much of it, from this point was no more than a scant footpath. He turned, looking back down the section behind them.

'More laughing?' Heggarty asked.

'No . . . nothing.'

'Okay. Good.'

But to Heck's mind it wasn't good. Like so many detectives who'd spent years and years investigating serious crime, he'd developed an internal alarm system for when something didn't feel right. It was that old hunch thing so popular in the era before the Police and Criminal Evidence Act, when time-served coppers worked largely on instinct. And it was real. There was nothing magical or mystical about it. Years of experience taught you, particularly in a job like this where observational skills were vital, to subliminally checklist everything your five senses were absorbing, and to stick up a red flag if there was anything that didn't seem kosher.

He thought he'd heard laughter up here; he thought he'd heard laughter down near the tarn. So did that mean he'd been mistaken *twice*? It seemed unlikely. As Heggarty said, there could be a normal explanation. Climbers or campers, but in this weather that seemed unlikely too.

'Well?' Gemma asked him.

Heck shrugged. 'Nothing. Let's check the farm out . . . but let's turn these lights off first. And no talking either, unless it's absolutely necessary. This guy's armed, remember . . . he doesn't need to see us to be able to shoot at us.'

They crossed the bridge, their feet unavoidably thudding on the hollow timbers. For several seconds after that they had no reference points at all, and advanced through a world of pure anonymity. It was difficult even to imagine they were progressing forward. Then they passed a gatepost on their left, connected to a tumbledown stone wall covered in desiccated brambles; after that, the rugged ground gave way to old, uneven paving. A few seconds later, the angular shape of a house heaved itself out of the murk.

They halted, stunned.

'Remember that block of hellhole flats in Salford where I found Ron O'Hoorigan's body, ma'am?' Heck eventually asked. 'After he'd been disembowelled alive?'

'Yeah,' she said.

'I wish we were there now.'

Fellstead Grange was easily the gauntest, most desolate structure they had ever seen. From its silent, featureless bulk, it might have been a derelict ship emerging from an ocean-fret, or an ancient, rusted sub on the floor of a sediment-filled sea.

In light of this, Heck was truly astonished Hazel had come up here on her own. He would never have called her timid, but he knew she was uncomfortable with stories about violence and crime. And yet she must have remarkable depths of strength and character. Either that, or she'd come here in company with Mary-Ellen. Either would be good, though he'd prefer the latter.

They regarded the house for several seconds, finally advancing to its gable wall, which had been built from rough stone and was covered in moss. They tracked along it, moving around the exterior, passing a couple of windows with curtains closed on the inside but fitted with glass so grubby they were impenetrable anyway. When they found what looked like the front door, it was standing ajar. Deep blackness skulked beyond. They slid through it one by one, their torchlight springing to life again, the beams criss-crossing as they flashed around the decayed room, illuminating the dirt and debris. Though they were indoors, there was no discernible change in the icy temperatures and yet despite this a stale fetor hit them; not quite the 'urine' stink of a long abandoned building, but a grotty, dank odour.

'This old girl was living *here*?' Heggarty said.

'I'm hoping she still is,' Heck replied.

'The fact there are no lights on anywhere suggests she's absent at present.'

'Keep it down, eh? Everyone listen up.'

This time they heard something. Three heads turned to the arched black entrance on their left. What sounded like a piece of crockery had clattered somewhere down the passage beyond. Immediately, Heck and Gemma fell one to either side of the arch, left and right respectively. When they passed through, they proceeded down the passage by sliding along its walls.

Heggarty copied them, bringing up the rear behind Heck.

The passage was laid with an old carpet, dingy and gummy, curled along its edges. As they advanced, the stench worsened. Rotted food, Heck realised – they must be approaching the kitchen. But in one way that was good; it meant an occupant had prepared meals here relatively recently. He glanced across the corridor at Gemma, who nodded at the doorway approaching on the left.

Heck stopped alongside it. Only darkness lurked inside, but that was where the spoiled food aroma emanated from. There was another door on Gemma's side of the passage, a yard past the kitchen door. Gemma indicated to Heggarty to keep an eye on that one. He nodded back, but didn't look as though he fully comprehended. Of course, this whole process was flawed: they were dealing with an armed suspect, though none of them were armed themselves. But there was no real option. Police officers in Britain were routinely unarmed, and yet faced villains toting guns every day; it was part of their job description – all they could do when it happened was take action to minimise the terrible threat. As such, Heggarty nervously extricated the baton from his belt, easing it open rather than 'snapping' it in the time-honoured style.

Heck glanced at Gemma. She nodded again.

He whirled across the left-hand entrance to its opposite side, his torch directed into the far left corner of the room beyond. Gemma darted over too, taking the other side of the door, driving her own beam to its far right corner.

'Clear!' Heck said.

It was indeed a kitchen, with a paved floor, a cinder-filled hearth, ancient oak fittings, and an age-blackened kettle-cum-teapot on the hob. Again, dust sheathed everything, and a canopy of webbing hung overhead, multi-limbed monstrosities scampering away from the light, seeking refuge in cracks or crevices. Directly facing them was a stone sink heaped with crockery caked in a detritus of dried food. Two rats, having presumably been digging around amid said crockery, leapt out and bolted in different directions. One scuttled through a broken lower panel in the window over the sink; the other hit the floor and streaked past them across the corridor and through the other doorway. Heck followed it with his beam – and shouted a warning at the sight of a human shape standing there in the recess.

The other two reacted as one, spinning to face this new threat – but just as quickly relaxed. It was a mannequin, the sort you'd find in a department store window or on a display pedestal. Probably sometime in the 1940s.

Heck approached it, bewildered.

It was made from the usual flesh-toned plastic. It had no hair, but its painted features had faded through age; the blue of the eyes and the pink of the lips were barely recognisable. How it had arrived in Annie Beckwith's possession was anyone's guess, though she'd clearly been making use of it. Heck now remembered that she'd designed and made her own clothes. By its short hair and V-shaped physique, it was supposed to be male, but it wore female garb – an old woollen cardigan with hooks instead of buttons, and what looked like a patched-up tweed skirt.

Heck pushed the figure aside, shining his torch into the room behind. This might once have been a dining room; it was large enough, with a properly beamed ceiling and ancient wainscoting. But now it was hung with ragged clothing, both men's and women's – he also remembered hearing that Annie had once lived here with her parents. Jackets, pairs of trousers, skirts and frocks adorned every wall, suspended along what had once been the curtain rail and from the lintel over a doorway connecting with yet another darkened room. The scent was exclusively rancid. Annie might well use and re-use her old family garments, which in some ways was laudable, but she didn't have hot running water, so how could she wash these things effectively? Meanwhile, what might once have been a handsome dining table took up the central space. It was dented and scuffed and covered with melted wax from candles that had burned down into puddles. The long dark of the Northern English winter was difficult at the best of times, but the thought of facing it without gas or electricity was horrific.

An Edwardian-era sewing-machine, powered by foot pedal, occupied the far end of the table. The sight of this aged mechanism – which stirred so many memories of Heck's indomitable grandmother – put a barb of sadness through him, reminding him more than words ever could that they were dealing with a real person here; an elderly lady who'd struggled against the elements all her life, putting in backbreaking hours just to survive. He moved around the table to the next door, but this led only to a walk-in wardrobe hung with yet more tattered relics. Gemma now entered the dining room, Heggarty standing behind her in the doorway. Before anyone could speak, there was a dull thud somewhere overhead. They swapped glances. Another thud followed; it sounded like a foot impacting on timber.

They followed the corridor back to the living room. The front door stood open as they'd left it, but now they noticed another door, beyond which their torchlight picked up the bottom of a staircase. Heck halted briefly at the foot of it, staring at what looked like a recently-placed basket of consumables, complete with a fresh tablecloth over the top, sitting on a side-table. This was all the proof he needed that Hazel at least had been here. But why had he not seen her yet? Why couldn't he hear her voice as she conversed with old Annie? Why did the place still feel silent and dead? Swiftly, Heck led the way upstairs. They stopped at the top – and heard what sounded like a suppressed whimper. It came from a passage on the left. Heck went down there first.

'Heck!' Gemma hissed.

He barely heard her, homing in on a door at the end, coincidentally the only door on the landing that was closed. At the last second his old instincts kicked in again, and he slid to a halt.

There was a soft metallic *click*.

Heggarty had come up behind, but Heck spun from the door, slamming an arm across the tall bobby's chest, knocking him back against the wall. Gemma, about five yards behind, dived to the left. With a shuddering *BOOM*, and a gale of smoke and splinters, the entire lower half of the door was blasted outward.

'*Shotgun!*' Heck shouted. 'Gemma, you're still in the line of fire! Get downstairs!'

'Fu . . . uck me!' Heggarty stammered, ashen-faced. He

tried to struggle upright, but Heck slammed him backwards again, so they were both flush against the wall.

'Downstairs!' Heck shouted again. 'Right now!'

But then he heard another voice – wavering, almost childlike.

'Mark? Mark . . . is that you?'

'Hazel? What the . . .?'

'I tho— thought . . .' The voice stuttered unintelligibly. 'I thought you were . . .'

'Yeah, it's me!' he called. 'And I've got two other police officers with me. Put the gun down, okay? You're safe now.'

There was a clunk of metal on wood.

'It's down.' She sounded tearful.

'You sure?'

'It's down, I said!'

Heck pushed what remained of the door aside and shone his torch through. Gemma appeared alongside him, adding her light to his. Their combined glare was dazzling – so much so that Hazel, who was crouched in a corner of the bedroom, had to cover her eyes. Though the figure lying on the heavy, iron-framed bed did no such thing.

Even from outside on the landing, Heck and Gemma could see why.

First of all, it lay twisted and still, the shapeless shift it wore so wadded with congealed blood that it was plastered over the skeletal proportions beneath. They couldn't see the face from where they were standing, but the feet and exposed shanks were rail-thin and mottled purple, the hands at the ends of the sleeves little more than emaciated claws. The reek pouring off the shrivelled form suggested it had been dead for at least a couple of days.

Heck ventured forward, only for Hazel to cross the room

205

in a blur, throwing herself into his arms. He staggered, almost dropping his torch.

'Thank God!' she wept. 'I thought . . . I thought . . .' Her hair was in disarray, the mascara stained down her cheeks indicating she'd been crying. 'Thank God . . .'

'What's going on?' he asked, as Gemma slid past, already replacing her woollen gloves with a pair of latex disposables. The room was a cluttered hovel. Aside from the discarded bed-sheets, musty clothing was heaped everywhere, also stained with blood. The walls were green with damp, the ceiling smothered in layers of dust-web.

'I came up here . . .' Hazel jabbered, breaking off to kiss Heck on the mouth again and again, though they were kisses of relief rather than desire.

Gemma, having made a cursory but unsuccessful check for vital signs, circled around the bed and picked the shotgun up by its stock, gently disengaging its second hammer and breaking it open to unload the remaining barrel. On her signal, Heggarty also checked the prone figure, just about managing to avoid gagging as he probed. Not that there was any obvious need for this. Even from over the back of Hazel's shoulder, Heck could tell that the old woman, whose face was more like a decayed rubber mask, was dead. What looked like a deep stab wound yawned in the middle of her throat. There was another between her withered breasts, and more tellingly than either of these, her two eyes had been gouged to pulp.

Heck and Gemma swapped glances, neither initially commenting.

'I came up here . . .' Hazel stammered. 'I wanted to help Annie . . . and I found her like this . . . I mean, good God!'

'Okay,' Heck said. 'Okay. But why'd you shoot at us?'

'I don't . . . I don't know what I was thinking.' Fresh tears brimmed onto Hazel's cheeks. 'I was so . . . so frightened . . .'

'You need to calm down, Ms Carter,' Gemma said with what Heck thought was unnecessary firmness. 'You've just opened fire on the police with an unlicensed shotgun. Now alright, it may have been unintentional. But we need to know why.'

Hazel nodded, trying to get hold of herself. 'I'm so, so sorry about that . . .'

Heck cupped her face. 'Just tell us what happened.'

'I came in here and found Annie like . . . this. I mean she's obviously been murdered. Her eyes, oh God, her eyes . . . look, I'm so glad you're here. I'm just . . .'

'Tell us exactly what happened, Ms Carter,' Gemma prompted her.

Hazel shook her head, visibly quaking. 'Well . . . I didn't know what to do. I mean, there's no phone here. Mobiles can't get a signal in the Cradle . . .' She fought to regain control. 'Then I heard this whistling.'

The officers listened intently.

'Whistling?' Heck said.

Hazel's eyes glinted with fresh tears. 'Oh my God, it was *Strangers in the Night.*'

'You're sure about that?' he asked.

'Absolutely.'

'You didn't think *Strangers in the Night* because that's the song I happened to mention to you in reference to those two hikers?'

'I know what I heard, Mark!'

'Where did this whistling come from, Ms Carter?' Gemma asked.

'At first it was outside, and then it was downstairs in the house. I could hear someone moving around. And it was loud too, and tuneful. Like they weren't trying to hide.'

'So whoever it was, he didn't know you were here?'

Hazel shuddered. 'He might have, he might not.'

'When was this?' Heck asked.

'Twenty minutes ago . . . half an hour.'

Gemma turned to Heggarty. 'Look around . . . let's make sure he's not still here.' Nodding, the PC left the room. They heard his heavy feet clumping downstairs.

'I was so frightened,' Hazel stammered, more tears dabbling her lashes. 'Especially when the whistling just stopped. It was weird, like a switch had been thrown – for a moment then I was certain he'd heard me. Though he'd probably seen that basket of supplies I left downstairs.'

'I'm surprised he didn't,' Heck said.

'I know. Anyway, all I could do was sit in that corner with the gun . . . you know the rest.'

Gemma glanced at Heck, her expression blank, which in his experience of working with her meant she was seriously concerned. Almost unconsciously, she retrieved the shotgun from the wall where she'd propped it.

'Can you honestly blame me for shooting?' Hazel asked them.

Heck mused. 'It's not a good idea in times of crisis to make a blazing shotgun your default option, but I think on this occasion it may just be forgivable.' He looked at Gemma, who was peeking around the curtain and, rather surreptitiously, had broken open the shotgun and was sliding the remaining shell back into its breech.

'What about Annie?' Hazel asked in an increasingly shrill tone. 'Why's he killed her . . . a harmless old lady? For God's sake, why did he take her eyes . . .?'

'Ms Carter, why don't you go onto the landing,' Gemma said. 'The air's fresher out there.'

Hazel looked confused by the request. She glanced at Heck.

'Better if you go and wait at the top of the stairs,' he said, steering her out of the fetid room and along the landing. 'The bedroom's a crime scene now.'

She leaned against him as they went, their bodies briefly melding into one another. He couldn't deny it anymore; he was developing a protective urge. Perhaps it was inevitable after all they'd been through together, but that didn't make it any easier. He just hoped Hazel didn't detect it. All through their short-lived acquaintanceship, though she'd never admit it, he'd suspected Hazel was looking, or maybe hoping, for a little more commitment from him.

Heggarty now re-ascended from below. 'No one else here, sarge.'

Heck nodded, allowed the PC past and sat Hazel at the top of the stairs. 'Listen, you've done incredibly well,' he said, kneeling next to her.

'Not well enough,' she sniffled.

'You think you could have saved her? How? By the looks of her, this happened a couple of days ago.'

'By coming up here months back and checking she was alright.'

'That still wouldn't have saved her.'

'It's just the thought of her . . . alone, in this horrible place . . .'

'Hazel, Annie chose to live this way.'

'And does that mean the rest of us had no responsibility?' New tears coursed down her cheeks. 'I only came up here tonight because I heard . . .' Her words tailed off. She looked too horrified to say more.

'Heard what?' he asked gently.

'I don't know. I was down at the pub, and I heard this ungodly wailing. Oh Lord, Mark . . . what pain must she have suffered to make a noise like that?'

Heck considered this. 'Hazel, you must've heard something

else. Something completely unconnected. Annie was already dead by this evening.'

'Hell of a coincidence, Mark!'

'Coincidences happen. Look . . . you heard a noise travelling half the length of the Cradle? Not just that. All the way down the Cradle Track as well? Annie was old and probably sick. Imagine the pair of astonishingly powerful lungs it would have taken to project any noise over such a distance . . .'

'So you're telling me this didn't happen? That we've imagined this terrible thing?'

'Of course not . . .'

'If only I'd checked on her sooner.'

'If anyone's to blame, it's me,' Heck said. 'I'm the closest thing around here to a chief of police, and I didn't even know Annie Beckwith existed.'

'I should have ensured you did.'

He put his arm around her again. 'People die . . . okay? It's a bag of crap, but it happens. And yet always I meet grief-stricken friends and relatives who blame themselves, which is total bloody bollocks. The fault for Annie's death lies with the person who killed her. Nobody else. You get that, Hazel? Other folk can make innocent mistakes. Can be unintentionally neglectful. But murders happen because murderers commit them.'

She wiped her eyes. 'That doesn't make me feel a lot better.'

'Very little will in these situations. But don't beat yourself up. You came all the way up here on your own to try and help Annie. How brave is that?'

Hazel looked vaguely surprised. 'You're not cross about that?'

'Yeah, sure . . . but I'm proud of you as well.' He squeezed her shoulders, pecked her cheek. 'I need to ask you this though, Hazel . . . did you have any physical contact with the body? Any at all?'

She shook her head numbly. 'As soon as I got close . . . saw what he'd done to her, I just . . . I just couldn't.'

'Okay, good. Now you just sit tight a couple of minutes. I've got to get back in there and help Gemma.'

Again, Hazel nodded.

When Heck re-entered the bedroom, Heggarty was standing unobtrusively to one side while Gemma had produced her phone and was stepping carefully around the bed, making as detailed a photographic record as she could. She broke off to nod at a discarded item lying in a corner. It was one half of a pair of rusty old sewing scissors. Heck squatted down, using the light of his own phone to examine it more closely. It was coated with dried blood.

'Rigor's been and gone,' Gemma said. 'At a rough guess, time of death happened a couple of days ago. Course we'll need confirmation.'

'That's what I thought too,' he said. 'At least twenty-four hours before the attack on the two girls. Murder weapon improvised from yet another household item, I see.'

'In the original case there was a theory he'd improvised his entire murder kit from household implements that he'd pillaged from the house where he launched his first attack,' Gemma said. 'Possibly added to it with other items later on.'

'So we think he's got himself a new kit together, eh?' Heck indicated the half-scissors. 'And maybe left this behind because it was broken?'

'I was talking about the original case,' Gemma replied. 'Not necessarily this one.'

Heck turned to Heggarty. 'I take it there's no sign of forced entry?'

'The front door was open, sarge . . . like you saw. But it hadn't been forced.' Heggarty turned to Gemma. 'Isn't it time we got divisional supervision up here, ma'am? And a doctor to certify death?'

'By all means try and get someone if you can,' she replied.

Heggarty put his lapel transmitter to his lips. '7438 to Charlie Two, receiving?' There was no response; not even a crackle. 'I'll see if I can get a better signal outside.' Gemma nodded as he strolled along the landing, asking 'Ms Carter' to 'mind out' and clumping downstairs again. '7438 to Charlie Two, urgent message . . . 7438 to Charlie Two, receiving, over?'

'So, what do we think?' Heck asked.

'You mean do I think is this the Stranger?' Gemma replied.

'It's familiar stuff, you must admit.'

'You're long enough in the tooth, Heck, to know that other offenders have gone for the eyes.'

'I'm aware of that, but the eyes are only part of the pattern . . .'

'Where are the extensive mutilations?'

'If I recall rightly, the Stranger worked his way up to that last time. In the first instance, it was a home invasion in a remote spot. Then, like now, there was no sexual interest . . . so the occupant, a lone householder, was killed relatively quickly. It was almost like a trial run. An easy hit on a vulnerable target. And then the real thing afterwards – the attack on the two hitchhikers.'

'There was a much longer cooling-off period last time,' Gemma said.

'He's not a newbie anymore. He's taken a few years off, but for whatever reason, he's suddenly got a taste for it again and he's raring to go.'

She glanced at him curiously. 'You're a hundred per cent sold on this, aren't you?'

'No, but what does the evidence tell us?'

'Evidence can be fabricated.'

'I know, I know. This whole thing bears much deeper investigation. But . . . now is not the time.' He shook his head. 'If you want my honest opinion, ma'am . . . we should get the hell out of here. I don't know about you, but I can sense when the odds are against me. Right now we're far out of our comfort zone. This guy might not be.'

'You're suggesting we abandon a crime scene?'

'Preservation of life and limb always takes priority over the needs of an investigation, you know that. Look, Gemma . . . whoever we're dealing with here, he could hold all the aces, while we're blind as moles. Not only that, we have a civilian on the plot.'

Gemma glanced with interest at the open door to the landing. It wasn't just any old civilian out there of course – it was Hazel. 'Heck, we walk away from this now and he'll have all the time he needs to clean this place from top to bottom.'

'This fog will be gone tomorrow . . . we can come back then, in force.'

'There might not be a scrap of physical evidence left.'

'Whatever physical evidence there is, he can't afford to let us sit on it 'til the circus arrives.' Heck lowered his voice to ensure Hazel didn't hear. 'He's going to counterattack . . . and he's got a gun he isn't frightened of using, while the best we can muster is the Salford Caution. Look, Gemma . . . we don't need to leg it all the way back to the Keld. If we can make it down to Cragwood Ho, one of the houses there has a landline installed, so we can call Windermere Comms. We can even draw straws to see who gets to stay here and stand guard over the insecure premises, if you like . . . but there's only three of us, and splitting us up further doesn't sound like a plan to me.'

She pondered this; it went against all her CID instincts, but there was no doubt about the danger they faced. Outside meanwhile, they heard Heggarty's muffled tones. '7438 to Charlie Two, receiving, over?'

Heck tugged the curtain aside to glance down.

The tall shape of the rangy bobby was about ten yards from the house. He still held the transmitter to his mouth. In fact, so intent was he on this that he never even heard, much less saw, the hooded form materialise out of the fog directly behind him.

Heck was fleetingly frozen. Then, as the indistinct figure lifted its left hand to the back of Heggarty's skull, he jerked to life, shouting a warning, pounding on the glass.

But it was too late. The gunflash blew off Heggarty's hat. And the top of his head.

Chapter 14

'Kill the lights!' Heck shouted, as he charged along the landing, snapping his own torch off in the process. He met Hazel at the top of the stairs. She'd heard the shot and tried to grab hold of him, but he thrust her in the direction of the bedroom. 'In there with Gemma, lie low . . .'

Before she could reply, he was galloping down the stairs and across the darkened lounge towards the open front door.

For half a second, he expected a black-clad figure to emerge through it, pistol levelled. But Heck reached it first, banging it closed with his shoulder, then scrabbling around for a lock. Rather to his surprise, his fingers alighted on a central bolt, which he rammed home with no difficulty. When he felt around the top of the door, there was one there too, which also moved freely and easily.

Heck threw himself to one side, flattened against the jamb.

Even through the thick farmhouse walls, he could hear the whistling. Though he'd been half expecting it, and though he'd heard it so many times before, *Strangers in the Night* had never sounded so menacing. Yet the song was fading – as if the whistler was already departing the scene. Half a minute later, sweat trickling down his face, Heck risked glancing from the window. Nothing moved out there, though the crumpled form of Dan Heggarty lay where he'd fallen, a dark pool spreading sluggishly around him.

Heck switched his torch back on, but kept its beam lowered as he crossed the lounge to the stairway passage, passing the staircase itself, and darting from one ground-floor room to the next. Most were dank and uninhabitable, draped in webs and crammed with all manner of aged junk. But currently he was more concerned about their doors and windows, and in the main these were securely locked, including the back door.

Overall, the house looked secure, though there was no guarantee of that.

He trotted up the stairs and back along to the bedroom. 'It's me,' he said as he entered. The two women were well away from the window, crouched in separate corners. They waited expectantly while he squatted down. 'I'm pretty sure Heggarty's dead.'

Gemma nodded. 'His body's still out there . . . it hasn't moved.'

There was a brief contemplative silence.

'So . . .?' Hazel had again been struggling to choke back sobs, but now sounded shocked. 'You're just going to leave him?'

'Do *you* want to go out?' Heck asked her. 'The bastard's probably working on the basis at least one of us will try.' He mopped a sweaty hank of hair back from his brow. 'He's obviously been watching this place closely. Cragwood Vale, Fellstead Grange . . . he must have done that in order to identify Annie as a possible target.'

'And?' Hazel wondered again, sensing something else was coming.

'Think about it,' Heck said. 'There are two bolts on the front door. They work properly. There's no sign that door was broken open any time recently. Nor with the back

216

door. I've checked all the windows too. They aren't in brilliant condition, but no one has smashed any of them to get in here.'

Hazel shook her head. 'What are you saying?'

'I'm saying whoever this guy is, when he first got in here a couple of days ago, he didn't have to break and enter.'

'Annie may have left the door unlocked.'

'She may have done,' Gemma said, picking up on Heck's thought process. 'But how likely is that, living all the way out here on her own? Especially given that she was in bed when this attack took place.'

Hazel looked horrified. 'You mean there's another way in?'

'Shit, this is not good.' Heck's voice was taut. 'He's up here in the hills. Watches Annie pottering around the farm. Sees her coming and going, identifies an entry point. Uses it when Annie's in bed. Murders her, most likely while she's asleep.'

'Oh my God . . .'

'It's worse, I'm afraid. Somehow or other he knew we'd end up coming up here. Don't ask me how . . .'

'And that's why he left the front door unlocked,' Gemma interrupted. 'To get us all into the house.'

'Yeah.' Heck felt fresh sweat on his brow. 'To make us fish in a barrel.'

'If you're right,' Hazel whimpered, 'that means he could be here . . .'

Heck nodded. 'I know . . . *now*!'

The door burst open, slamming the wall as a dim figure forced its way through.

'Everyone down!' Gemma shouted, throwing the shotgun to her shoulder. Heck dived to the floor, dragging Hazel with him. *BOOM* – the payload spread as it crossed the room, shredding the woodwork to either side of the entrance, and hitting the figure full-on, hurling it backward onto the landing.

Heck scrabbled after it on all fours, wafting at dust. He levered himself to his feet and flattened his body against the fragmented jamb, angling his head to peek around.

And seeing something incredible.

There wasn't one body lying out there. There were two, one on top of the other.

The one on top was dead, though it would be more accurate to say it had never lived. It was the mannequin from downstairs. The shotgun blast had broken it in half. One of its arms had become detached. However, the body underneath it was fully intact, and far more animated. Even as Heck watched, it kicked aside what remained of the dummy and lurched quickly to its feet. Heck ducked back into the room, but caught a fleeting glimpse of heavy boots, dark waterproofs, a full-head leather mask, and in its gloved right hand, a six-shooter.

The bedroom door was only partially intact, and when Heck banged it closed, it came loose around the hinges, which had been mangled by shot.

'The bed! Get me the sodding bed!'

The women jumped to their feet, though Hazel was too frozen with shock and horror to do much more. She goggled at the sight of Gemma unceremoniously throwing Annie Beckwith's corpse to the floor, and inserting herself behind the heavy cast-iron bedframe as she tried to shove it across the room.

'Give me a hand!' Gemma gasped.

Belatedly, Hazel joined her. The bed screeched forward, its un-wheeled feet chewing through floorboards. Heck added his strength too, and they slid it into place, ramming it against the door – and not before time. Half a second later, there were three detonations, and a trio of holes was punched through the planking. Three corresponding impacts struck the far wall, knocking out fist-sized chunks.

'Heck . . . I may have killed us here,' Gemma panted. 'I wasted our last cartridge.'

'We're not bloody beaten yet!' He pivoted around, grabbed at the curtains and yanked them down in a mass of dust and rotted fabric.

The window beyond was deeply recessed, set into a stone wall that was at least three feet thick. But its four panes of glass, though heavy and grimy, relied on a central cruciform frame that was badly decayed.

'Both of you get down,' he said, tearing off his jacket and wrapping it around his fist. Behind him meanwhile, the door was assailed. Kicks and blows rained down with anger and exertion, then three more gunshots followed, ripping through the jamb.

'He must have ammo to spare!' Gemma shouted.

'This whole thing's been well planned.' Heck drove his padded fist hard at the window, which exploded out in a cascade of jangling shards. A few teeth of glass remained in the aged frame, but he knocked these out too. 'Okay . . . quickly!'

Hazel hung back like a frightened rabbit. 'What . . . what's on the other side?'

He didn't answer, just grabbed her around the waist, lifted her up and placed her on all fours in the window embrasure, pushing her bottom until she vanished and he heard the double-thud of her feet alighting on a hollow surface.

'You next, Gemma.'

'No . . . *you* next,' she said. 'I'm the senior rank, and I screwed up. So it's my arse.'

'It's your arse I'm thinking about. Be a hell of a shame to lose it.'

'I could say the same about yours . . . now get out!'

219

He leapfrogged into the recess, and scrambled forward on hands and knees, poking his head out and seeing a lower section of slanted roof about five feet below, covered in broken, lichen-covered slates. Hazel was already halfway down it on her backside. She'd shortly reach the eaves, from where it would be no more than a seven-foot drop. Heck scrabbled out in pursuit, landing hands-first on the sloped surface, shattering a dozen more tiles, hearing the woodwork crack underneath, but now rolling sideways, coming up hard against Hazel's back, causing her to yelp.

He glanced backward and up. 'Gemma?'

'I'm okay,' she said, appearing in the window. 'Just go!'

Heck and Hazel leapt from the roof side-by-side, Gemma following half a second later. Without stopping to talk, they ran forward and away from the house. Heck looked back once, seeing a black aperture where the hatch to an old coal-cellar had been pried open – which clearly explained how the killer had first gained access to the property. Not that there was time to ponder this. They ploughed through icy fog, which seemed even denser than earlier, keeping their torches switched off; the gunman would hear them easily enough without them leaving him a beacon. And yet almost immediately they came unstuck. Within a few dozen yards, they were staggering across strips of ground cordoned by knee-high net-wire fencing, some planted with rows of vegetables, others filled with rubbish and old straw. Beyond these, they stumbled between chicken-sheds and other dilapidated structures which they had to veer around or scrabble over. As such, they lost all sense of direction, only keeping together because they clung on to each other.

From behind them, there was an echoing thump.

'Front door,' Heck breathed. 'He's coming after us. Keep moving.'

But now they hesitated. Low sheds lay on all sides. Alleys led in various directions.

'Which way?' Gemma said. 'We can't just run blind. If we come to that beck, or to a scree slope or something, and he's right behind us . . .'

'Keep heading away from the house in a straight line,' Hazel advised, panting.

'How do we know it's a straight line?'

'As long as all these paddocks and farm structures are here, we know we're crossing Annie's farmyard. Most of them are directly behind her house.'

'And then what, Ms Carter?' Gemma asked.

'There's a path up into the hills.'

'You mean the Track?' Heck said.

'No, a smaller one. Annie once told me she didn't like it when walkers used it, as it brought them down into the corrie behind her house.'

'How steep is this smaller path?' Gemma wondered.

'It's just as steep for him as it is for us,' Hazel replied tartly.

With no option, they hurried on, coming to a broad thoroughfare of beaten earth running straight through the middle of the allotments.

'This is the main passage across the yard,' Hazel almost shouted. 'It leads straight to the hills.' She took off quickly, the other two hurrying in pursuit.

'And what do we do when we get up into these hills?' Gemma asked Heck quietly. 'How is that going to help us exactly?'

'Hazel's a local,' he answered. 'She knows her way around.'

'She's a pub landlady, for Christ's sake!'

'Yeah, but she's been up here thirty-eight years, whereas I've been here two and a half months, and you've been here . . . what, four hours? And what's all this "Ms Carter" stuff? I think she'd prefer Hazel.'

'And I'd prefer it if you weren't so bloody close to her. We're doing a job here, not playing out some romantic melodrama.'

'Hey . . . she's just found a friend dead and now she's being chased by a madman. So cut her some bloody slack, eh!'

'Watch your tone, sergeant . . .'

'I don't need to watch anything. I'll defer to your rank . . . ma'am. But as I'm the one with operational command, you're not my bloody gaffer. Or anything else.'

But five minutes later, when they slid through another stile and found themselves on a path that ascended sharply, mainly by forming switchbacks through heaps of fallen slate, he began to wonder.

'Hazel . . . where are you taking us?'

'I told you . . . the hills.'

'Where in the hills?'

'Anywhere away from Fellstead Grange, don't you think?'

'This is great,' Gemma said. 'If we'd stopped and thought, we could probably have worked our way back to the Track, and then it would all have been downhill.'

'You think we'd have made it, Superintendent Piper?' Hazel wondered as they tottered upward. 'We'd have had to go right past the house. What if he'd intercepted us there?'

'He probably wouldn't even have seen us,' Gemma retorted.

'That'd be a gamble,' Heck said. 'He hasn't had a problem seeing us so far.'

Gemma glanced sideways at him. 'What are you talking about?'

'I'll be honest, I'm thinking thermal imaging . . .'

'Dear God!' Gemma said. 'If he's got something like that, he can spot us up here on the fell-side as easily as he could down in the farmyard.'

222

'Agreed. So we've got to get a move on . . .'

Renewed fear fuelled their uphill flight. Lungs working like bellows, muscle-blood pumping hard, they continued up a path which in some sections was more like a stepladder, ascending tier after tier of broken ground, tripping on ruts and loose stones. To make life worse, the path branched several times. On each occasion Hazel dithered, uncertain of the route, but Heck always urged her on. Once they were past the aprons of scree, the fell-side steepened to the point where it became impassable, the path meandering sideways, a ledge hanging above a mist-filled abyss. They scrambled along it in single file, all the while thinking how badly exposed they were, how their foe might be scoping the fog with some hi-tech device. Abruptly, they slid to another halt. Hazel, who was at the front, slammed her torch on.

'Ms Carter, that's not a good idea!' Gemma said.

'I need to,' Hazel replied. 'We've already passed so many of these, I don't know where we are anymore.'

The path had branched again, the right-hand route tilting back downhill, the left-hand route ascending sharply.

'Which way?' Heck said.

'I'm thinking . . .'

'Which bloody way?'

'Stop rushing me, Mark . . . we could have gone wrong half a dozen times already.'

He glanced over his shoulder. The torchlight limned the vapour with a near-phosphorescent glow. Nothing stirred. He strained his ears, but all he initially heard was the wheezing of his own breath, the thunder of blood in his ears.

'Left,' Hazel decided.

'Uphill again?' Gemma said wearily.

'We go back down into the corrie, he could be waiting there for us.'

'Not if he's chased us up the path.' Gemma glanced around at Heck. 'Any sign we're being followed?'

Heck motioned for quiet. Still they heard nothing, which gave them no clue either way. It might be the madman was down there somewhere, watching, waiting for them to re-descend. On the other hand, he could have prowled up after them, and even now was stealthily encroaching.

'If we keep going uphill, we make it harder for him,' Hazel said, snapping off her torch. 'Besides, you ever tried running down a scree-track in the dark?'

'No disrespect, Ms Carter,' Gemma said. 'But we need a better plan than this. We know he's been up in these fells before. He may know them like the back of his hand, he may be perfectly kitted out for them. But *we* aren't.'

Hazel considered this. For several seconds, all Heck could hear was the declining rate of her breath. It was undeniable that plunging endlessly on into this blind, frozen wilderness would gain them no obvious advantage when they had no clue who their pursuer actually was, or even whether he was anywhere near – though that latter issue was resolved half a second later when they heard a scraping of slate on the path behind, and then a casual, tuneful whistling.

As always, it was *Strangers in the Night.*

They stood rigid. Thanks to the crazy mountain acoustics, he could still be over a hundred yards away. Alternatively, he might be much closer.

Heck pushed the women forward. 'Go, go . . .'

'Which way?' Hazel moaned.

'It doesn't matter, just go . . .'

She took the left-hand path, heading to higher ground again. They were no longer concerned about noise. It was impossible to move quietly anyway. Loose slate clattered under their feet as they grunted and groaned their way up a zigzagging path that was so steep it might have been

224

designed for goats. Only after ten minutes did it level out again, though now the ground ramped up both to the left and right of it, forming a gully. They ran on regardless. Soon walls of sheer rock hemmed them in from either side. After a few minutes, Heck, who was at the rear, stopped to listen – perhaps in some vain hope that merely keeping going would have been enough to put their pursuer off. It was amazing how quickly the clamour of Gemma and Hazel running on ahead faded. But it was equally amazing how the sound of someone advancing up the path behind them – heavy breathing and stumping footfalls – grew.

Heck sped on, thirty yards later running into the back of Gemma, who had halted for some reason, bowling her over.

'What the hell . . .?' he stuttered.

'We've got trouble!' she said, jumping back to her feet.

Hazel snapped her torch on. Its beam played over the rough surface of a plank barricade, which blocked all further progress along the path.

'Oh God,' Hazel said weakly. 'I forgot all about this.'

The barricade had been painted with crude crimson letters:

DANGER! DO NOT USE
VIA FERRATA UNSAFE!

'What does this mean?' Heck demanded.

'It's a Via Ferrata . . . don't you know?' Hazel was ash-pale in the torchlight; her hair hung in sweat-sodden strands. 'Via Ferrata . . . it's Italian, it means "iron road".'

'Oh . . . bloody hell,' he said.

Gemma still looked perplexed.

'They have these in mountains everywhere,' Hazel added. 'It's like a fun thing. You know, for climbers and hikers. Plus it helps them get from one ridge to the next.'

'You'd know it as a cable-walk or monkey run,' Heck explained.

'You mean like a rope bridge?'

'Bit more solid than that.'

'Except that this one's closed,' Hazel said. 'It's been closed for about five months. The pins will have rusted or the cables frayed, or something.'

'So . . . is that it?' Gemma asked, incredulous. 'This is as far as we go?'

Heck turned his torch on and shone it up the canyon walls on either side, but they were sheer, offering no visible escape.

A shot was fired.

It was difficult to say how far back along the passage it was fired from. And thankfully it wasn't a clear shot, caroming from the left-hand wall and ricocheting from the right, before smashing a hole through the planking on the left of them. Both Gemma and Hazel dropped to crouches, the latter just managing to suppress a scream. Heck spun to face the barricade.

'Either he can't see us, or he's a crap shot, or both!' he said, tearing with his fingers at the splintery-edged bullet hole, then stepping back and kicking with his right foot. 'Either way, we've no choice now!'

'You're going across the bridge?' Hazel said, eyes bugging.

'Not just me,' he responded.

Gemma joined him, ripping and rending, pulling the planks apart until there was space for a body.

'Go!' Heck ushered her through, then leaned down and grabbed Hazel by the arm.

'I'm not going through there,' she said hoarsely.

'Hazel . . . if this guy's who I think he is, he used to open women up like tins of dog-meat.'

'But it's not safe . . .'

'We've got to try.' He yanked her to her feet and hauled her through the shattered barricade after him.

On the other side, they crossed an open flat area like a small plateau, before hitting a rusty iron safety-barrier, which was the only thing stopping them pitching over an edge into a terrible gulf.

'Here!' Gemma said, emerging from the fog on their left.

They felt their way along the barrier, the plateau narrowing until soon they were on another ledge. This narrowed too until it was replaced by a timber catwalk. The safety-barrier now gave way to a row of upright steel pegs, each about three feet tall, equidistant from each other and connected by chains, though both the pegs and the chains were corroded, and in some cases missing. The footing comprised loose, uneven planking, which creaked and shifted. Just thinking about the bottomless mist underneath it stiffened Heck's hair. Again, they could only progress in single file and now did so by hugging the left-hand rock-face, which though it sloped as it ascended away from them, was rubbed smooth by the numberless hands and bodies that had sidled along it, offering no purchase if the structure suddenly collapsed – which it threatened to constantly, shaking, shuddering, pins swivelling in their holes.

Some fifty yards later, they reached a chunk of timber decking jutting from the cliff-face. This at least felt secure, though it was small, no more than four feet by four. From here, the only progress possible lay out across the chasm courtesy of the Via Ferrata. In appearance, it was a V-shaped bridge constructed entirely from steel cables so old and rotted they were crabbed with rust. Two cables in particular served as hand-rails, one on either side at roughly waist-height, connected by occasional lengths of wire to the single cable serving as the footway. This was thicker than the other two, but any person walking along it would have to tread with care, each foot planted crosswise as though he were traversing a tightrope. By the foggy light of their torches, the structure protruded no more than ten yards before this too was hidden in fog.

They stood there, paralysed.

'If this thing's unsafe,' Hazel said in an eerie monotone voice, 'we surely can't risk it all at the same time. I mean, the combined weight . . .'

Immediately, the wires and cabling along the ledge behind began to vibrate. Heck stared at Hazel, then at Gemma – even *she* wore an expression glazed by fear. The metallic vibrations resolved themselves into repeated heavy clanking: the sound of footfalls approaching. Still none of them moved.

'How far to the other side?' Heck asked dry-mouthed.

Hazel swallowed, as though about to vomit. 'Two hundred yards . . . maybe.'

He gazed down into the mist. 'And how far to the bottom?'

'Rough guess . . . a thousand feet.'

Chapter 15

'Mark, you cannot be serious!' Despite the clattering approach of those heavy feet, Hazel hung back. 'We haven't got harnesses or safety-lines.'

'Hazel, we've no choice,' Heck said. 'Look, let Gemma go first. I'll bring up the rear.' He caught Gemma's disbelieving eye. 'Gemma . . . you know this guy's going to kill us all. He wanted to do that before – that's why he lured us up to Fellstead. We're the protectors of this place, so he needed to eliminate us first. But now he *really* has to do that. Listen to me, he *can't afford* to let us live!'

Gemma clearly couldn't believe what he was asking of her. But by the same token, she knew he was right. Abruptly, she took a breath and, turning back to face the bridge, tucked her torch into a side-pocket and zipped it tight, so that it shone ahead. Planting a firm grip on its two hand-rails, she slowly, extremely tentatively, set her first foot on the cable-walk. A second step followed, and a third, and now she was out over the abyss. The bridge shuddered and sang and appeared to sag. There were deep groans from the network of lesser cables connecting it to the cliff-side. But conversely, the approaching footfalls fell silent.

Gemma glanced back. Heck did the same, expecting a gun-toting figure to emerge from the wall of blankness behind them.

It made no sense that one didn't.

What was the bastard waiting for? Did he want them to try and cross the bridge? That didn't bode well. Was he thinking he could make this whole thing look like an accident? Either way, they couldn't hang around.

'Go, Gemma,' Heck said. *'Just go!'*

She went, foot over foot, hand over hand, moving further and further from the platform. The flimsy metal structure shuddered and thrummed.

'Now you, Hazel.' Heck placed his hand in the small of her back. Hazel was rigid, like a post. She resisted the pressure, so he increased it, pushing her gently but firmly forward. 'Come on, now . . . there's no other way.'

Seeming to get hold of herself, she ventured onto the bridge. As it didn't immediately fall apart in a welter of lashing, snapping cables, she was able to steel herself further, going forward in pursuit of Gemma, who had now almost vanished into the vapour. They were both of them stiff as pegs, hands clamped around the safety-rails like talons. Swallowing a lump of bile-flavoured saliva, Heck stuck his own torch into his belt, and started after them, trying to ignore the perilous drop beneath his feet, but already fighting to keep his balance. It went against all the rules of logic of course. Every bone in his body told him this was a bad idea.

Danger! Unsafe!

A wooden barricade had been erected to prevent people doing exactly *this*.

But the alternative could be worse, particularly for the two women.

He glanced back, sweat beading his face. With his

torchlight angled upward, the platform behind was already shrouded in darkness. A figure could have appeared there by now, it could be gazing silently after them, and they wouldn't know. That said, if whoever it was had a thermal imager, he could still pick them off with ease, which thought goaded Heck to greater efforts, sending him blundering on along the slender cable, gloves sopping with sweat as he slid them over rusted, twisted steel. The bridge juddered in response, dipping and bouncing the further over the gulf he proceeded.

A thousand feet down.

Heck did his damnedest not to think about that – and in some ways it was easier than expected, because this was close to the most unreal experience of his life. On all sides, above and below as well, hung only swirling mist – it was like a studio set, partly negating that gnawing sense of vertigo. Ahead, he could no longer see the two women, could merely hear the clunking of metalwork, the vibrations passing backward with a force he felt through the rubber soles of his trainers. He tightened his own grip as he swayed from side to side. A small whimper floated back to him.

'Stick with it, Hazel!' he shouted. 'Couple of minutes and this'll be over.'

He didn't know if that was true. What rate of progress were they actually making? Could they really cover two hundred yards in two minutes?

He tried to increase his speed, but a couple of times his feet slipped, shooting downward either left or right, leaving him dangling, lopsided. Though he never let go of the handrails, these were moments of the purest terror – yet thanks to the unseen presence behind, he always levered himself to his feet and pushed on with reckless speed.

Were they out in the middle of it yet? It seemed unlikely, but it was impossible to judge. When a yelp of horror came echoing back, Heck initially froze, but then stumbled forward as fast as he dared, the bridge swaying and tilting horribly. Two seconds later, he came up behind Hazel. Gemma was just in front of her, but she too had lost her footing, and was in the process of slowly, carefully raising herself up.

'We can't fart around,' he said. 'We've got to keep moving.'

Gemma threw him a baleful glance. It looked as if she was about to voice some very choice words, but then came a shuddering impact from their rear, a mighty *THUNG* resounding through the entire structure.

'What was that?' Hazel said, in a tone so querulous Heck barely recognised it.

'Don't bloody know,' he muttered.

Another impact followed, and another. A horrendous realisation dawned on the two cops at the same time.

'He's trying to de-anchor us,' Heck said. 'Trying to tip us into the valley. Quickly, forward . . . *forward!*'

The women needed no second telling. Gemma lurched her way along at the front, the bridge swinging wildly.

'He can't cut through those cables, surely?' Hazel said, breathless.

'Let's not wait to find out,' Heck replied.

She turned to push herself on, only to shriek deafeningly as both feet slid off the cable-walk together. She dropped hard on her crotch and tilted to the right, legs pumping against nothing. For several seconds Heck thought she was going to pitch clean through and plummet into the chasm. He jerked his right arm down and grabbed her hood, though this meant he only had one hand in place himself. For several spine-freezing seconds they were locked together in the middle of nothing, wrestling to maintain their mutual balance, Heck's left arm straining hideously under the combined weight.

232

Slowly, barely breathing, he managed to haul her upright again.

All the time, shocks were passing through the bridge, repeatedly, getting increasingly heavy.

'He can't . . . can't cut those cables,' Hazel stuttered again, teeth chattering.

'I don't know whether he can or can't,' Heck replied. 'But a lot of those pins were loose. How many does he have to knock out before gravity does the rest?'

'Oh my God!'

'Don't think about it, just keep going!'

A deeper impact sounded behind them, followed by a *squeeeaaal* of splintering metal and then a reverberating whip-lash as the bridge lurched downward several feet. Hazel shrieked again. Twenty yards ahead, Gemma dropped to a crouch, arms rigid as she clutched the rails. She glanced back, white-faced.

'Keep moving!' Heck shouted. 'It can't be too far.'

'We're miles away,' Hazel moaned, lunging desperately on.

Further thudding impacts shuddered past them.

Heck held his position, a crazy thought spinning. Slowly, he shuffled around and began to retrace his steps backward. It was several seconds before Hazel noticed.

'*Mark!*' she screeched. 'What the hell are you doing?'

'If he's busy trying to de-anchor this thing, he might not be watching,' Heck called back. 'I might be able to get on top of him!'

'Mark, for God's sake!'

'Just get moving . . . get to the other side!' Heck pressed on back. The reality was they couldn't have progressed more than a hundred yards. It seemed highly unlikely they'd make it to the other side if someone didn't do something to distract the bastard.

'Gemma, stop him!' Hazel cried.

'Heck!' Gemma called.

'Gemma, get Hazel to safety!'

'Sergeant Heckenburg, get back here this fucking instant!'

'Go!' he shouted again, almost overbalancing as another thunderous blow struck the bridge. The flimsy structure lurched to the left, and he had to clamp the cable on the right with both hands. A fog-filled chasm yawned directly beneath him.

What in the name of God was he doing?

It only struck Heck now that if the bridge collapsed while he was near the broken end of it, he'd have far less chance of surviving. Even clinging on, he'd have a much longer distance to travel.

'Okay . . . *okay!*' he said, forcibly getting hold of himself, suddenly baffled that he could ever have thought this was anything more than the stupidest idea in history.

He *might* die going the other way, but he'd certainly die going this way.

Fingers locked painfully into rusted steel, he pivoted back around, and began struggling forward again. All around him metalwork shuddered, one massive vibration following another as the suspension cables were assailed.

'How you guys doing?' he shouted, no longer able to see the two women.

This time there was no reply, but there was so much noise from the bridge that any responses were likely lost. He advanced with rash speed, leaning precariously to the right but not letting that worry him as he took longer and longer strides. It was still impossible to judge how much distance he was covering; there were no points of reference. With a reverberating *CLUNG*, the bridge sagged again, tilting even further to the right. Muffled shrieks tore through the fog. Yet the women had to be almost at the other side by now. It might have been Heck's imagination, but the footway

234

appeared to be sloping upward, as though he'd passed the dip at its centre.

'Heck, where are you?' someone called back. It was Gemma. Relief was palpable in her voice. 'We've made . . .'

'I'm almost there,' he shouted, gravity tugging on him as he sidled along, corroded metal burning through his gloves, digging into the muscle and bones of his fingers. The bridge was definitely angling upward now. 'Couple of min—'

It fell away beneath him.

Heck didn't even hear the fatal blow.

All he knew was that another sharp vibration rocked the structure and that it flipped all the way to the right, before collapsing in a chaos of whining, whipping wires and cables. Heck's body plummeted through mid-air, but by sheer instinct his left hand remained wrapped around the cable – and half a second later he wasn't dropping like a stone so much as swinging like a pendulum.

The Via Ferrata had held its mooring on the far side.

One breathless second later, a granite wall hung with tufts of vegetation came hurtling towards him out of the fog. Heck gazed at it, goggle-eyed, knowing that any such impact would break him to pieces. But all the time he was losing altitude, and now he dropped below the level of the rock-face, heading instead for a steep, bracken-clad embankment. The next thing, he was crashing through layers of dead vegetation with pile-driving force. As well as knocking every ounce of wind out of him, the collision yanked him loose from the mass of twisting, screaming cable, and then he was falling backward downhill, turning head over heels, somersaulting through rotted, semi-frozen foliage, bouncing, spinning, hammering every part of his body on the shifting, ragged-edged rocks underneath, yet still protected by the bracken, which meshed itself thickly around him. Finally, after what seemed like minutes but was probably only seconds, he came to a dizzying, bone-numbing halt.

After that, there was only darkness.

And pain.

Chapter 16

Heck had no clue how long he lay there for.

Firstly, because he was only semi-conscious. Secondly, because it was one of those slow disbelief moments, the sort people experience after emerging from terrible car crashes; when it seems somehow unjust that they've survived, when they probe gingerly and nervously around their limbs and body, increasingly baffled by the absence of extensive damage. Heck did exactly this, and though he discovered cuts and bruising, nothing appeared to be out of place. His vision was still obscured, but this time by broken stalks and tatters of brown leafage.

Heck rent all this aside as he sat slowly upright. He was still bathed in sweat, in fact his clothes were sodden, and it was noticeably chilling – aside from the warm stickiness caking the left side of his face. When he fingered this, he discovered that his left brow had split open. However, blood was only leaking out, suggesting even this wound was super-ficial. Still groggy, he gradually became aware of the jagged jumbles of rock underneath him, digging into his pummelled body, and of a distant ghostly voice calling his name from somewhere far overhead.

Despite the loose hillside shifting under his trainers, he rose painfully to his feet.

'*Mark!*' a frantic voice called again. '*Mark!*'

It actually sounded like two voices. Hazel and Gemma.

'I'm okay!' he tried to holler back, but he struggled to get enough air into his lungs. He took a second to compose himself – his back was hurting, his neck was hurting, his chest was hurting. Every damn part of him was hurting.

'It's okay,' he bellowed, though the mere act felt as if someone had clobbered him in the ribs with a sledgehammer.

There was an abrupt, lingering silence, as they perhaps wondered if they were hearing things. 'Mark . . .?'

'I said I'm . . . I'm okay.' Heck shook himself; just craning his head back to gaze upward was enough to send him dizzy, but at least the acoustics of the chasm enabled him to shout and be heard reasonably clearly. 'Look, I don't know how far down I am.'

'You're actually okay?' That was Gemma. She sounded incredulous.

'Think so . . .'

'Anything broken?'

'Not sure. Nothing that isn't bruised, that's for certain.'

'Are you stuck?'

'Seem to be at the top of a slope. I can probably work my way down from here, but I doubt there's any way I can get up to you.' There was another brief silence. He imagined them discussing the situation. 'Does Hazel know where she is?' he called up. 'Can she work her way back into the Cradle?'

'Yeah, I think so,' Hazel replied. 'You *sure* you're okay?' She didn't sound as if she believed it either. 'I thought you'd been killed for sure . . .'

'No chance,' he replied. 'But you two may be. If he's got a rifle, you'll still be in range, so you need to back away from the edge. Make your way into the Cradle on foot. If nothing else, at least he'll be off your back for the time being.'

'But what're you going to do?'

'Same . . .'

'Do you even know where you are?'

'No, but heading downhill's got to be a start.'

Chapter 17

Hazel and Gemma walked through the fog for at least fifteen minutes after leaving the Via Ferrata, before encountering a rutted, unmade road, which, though Hazel felt she recognised it and said they should follow, seemed to weave a pointless course across the high, desolate fell-tops. Hazel said she thought she knew where it led to, though she wasn't completely sure. Gemma was prepared to give her the benefit of the doubt, and followed her without speaking.

For a few moments back then Gemma had seriously thought Heck was dead. Not for the first time since they'd been working together, though on this occasion it had happened in front of her eyes – or at least it would have done, had the fog not screened him from her. It still surprised her how the breath had caught in her throat, how the heart had almost stopped throbbing in her breast. The near light-headed sensation when his voice had come echoing up to them had been startling. The brief tears Gemma had found herself blinking away had been tears of shock more than anything else – but it still peeved her.

Typical bloody Heck. The only bloke, apart from her father, who'd ever been able to make her cry. And he still managed to drive her up the wall even now, though they were based nearly three hundred miles apart. Of course, all this was explainable. They'd been together so long, emotionally as well as professionally. They were *so* familiar with each other. You couldn't just switch off those kinds of feelings. But that was all it was now. Heck was a police colleague and a sometime friend. No wonder she'd been horrified to see him drop into that chasm.

This was what Gemma told herself.

Meanwhile, the road they were following didn't actually seem to lead anywhere except to occasional sets of iron gates built into dry-stone walls, which were always chained and padlocked. On no occasion was there a stile to climb through, which indicated they were well off the hiker/tourist route. On all sides there lay only emptiness, unseen stretches of desolate moorland, swamped in monotonous grey. Inevitably, it took her back to the last time she'd encountered the Stranger. She'd had to get used to wild, dreary moorland on that occasion too. Of course, back then the boot had been on the other foot. That time it was the Stranger facing an imminent demise.

He *should* have been, after taking her bullet in his chest.

But it had been a momentous incident for all kinds of reasons, not least because it had seen Gemma commence her meteoric rise through the police ranks. Up until then she'd been a no-nonsense, hard-working detective constable; one among hundreds, no more likely a high-flier than so many others. But that night, she'd really made her name.

Of course, there'd been other after-effects too; a less savoury kind of fallout.

The case seemed such a long time ago now, ten years. But there was no point in pretending it hadn't happened. And in this place, it seemed she had nothing but time with which to mull over it, no matter how reluctant she might be . . .

* * *

241

The Stranger taskforce occupied an entire floor at Newton Abbot police station. The MIR was its central hub, though there were numerous smaller side-offices connected to this. One of these was allocated exclusively to the decoy units, who completed each shift by typing up and logging all their observations from the night before, even the most seemingly insignificant of which they would then send to the Document Reader, who would assess them in detail before attaching them to a Policy File that now had more entries than the unabridged Gideon's Bible.

Given the events of the previous shift, there were no decoy units on duty today. In fact the only person present in the small side-office was Gemma, scrubbed of her 'war-paint' – as DSU Anderson had referred to it – and dressed sensibly in a sweater and jeans. Oddly, she felt more shaken now than she had done when she'd first come off Dartmoor; she was tired and slightly nauseous, but she had a report to complete nonetheless, and it was already a couple of hours late.

The door stood open, admitting the usual chaos of raised voices and trilling phones in the MIR, though this morning, perhaps understandably, there was a more jovial atmosphere than previously. In fact, part of the delay on Gemma's paperwork was down to a succession of well-wishers from the rest of the squad breezing in to see her, first to check she was okay, then to congratulate her, and then to mug her for all the juicy details. So it was a bit unexpected when someone bothered to knock.

She glanced up and was surprised to see Heck standing there. It wasn't yet ten in the morning, but by the looks of it, he'd come straight off nights and then driven all the way from London. His jacket was crumpled, his tie hanging loose.

'Any chance I can come in?' he asked.

She smiled and sat back. 'Sure.'

He crossed the room for the customary affectionate peck. Her mouth was bruised and swollen, so she offered him her cheek. Reluctantly, he indulged her on that, then dragged one of the other office chairs to her desk and slumped down into it.

'So . . . what are you doing here?' she asked.

'I happened to be passing?'

'Yeah, right.'

'Seriously . . . what do you think I'm doing here?'

'I'm fine,' she said. 'As you can clearly tell.'

'You seen a dentist?'

'Yep. At the hospital last night. Front two teeth got knocked loose, but they'll soon firm up. They may be a teensy bit crooked, but I'm reliably informed some guys find that sexy.'

'Okay. And aside from that?'

'I told you I'm fine. In fact, I'm bouncing.' Sensing that he didn't think she looked to be *bouncing*, she added: 'I got him . . . didn't I?'

'You're sure of that?'

'Damn sure.'

'No body,' he reminded her.

'No body *yet*.'

'No blood.'

'It was pouring rain by this morning.'

'What if he was wearing body-armour?'

'I have a gut feeling he wasn't.'

'No disrespect, Gem, but it's *his* gut feeling that counts. If there's a bullet in it, the job's a good 'un. If there isn't, because it's stuck in a Kevlar vest, this whole thing could kick off again.'

She shrugged. 'If that's the case, we'll find out soon enough.'

'You should have gone for a head-shot.'

'Hey, I'm really sorry! But it was dark and it all happened in the blink of an eye!'

243

'Whoa, whoa . . .' He raised his hands. 'Just winding you up.'

She sniffed as she resumed typing. A second passed while Heck stood up and strode to a noticeboard on the left. It had been pasted with crime scene glossies, the three first-string murders along the top; the ten second-string murders along the bottom.

'Do you really need these in here?' he asked.

'They're a reminder, apparently.'

'You girls needed reminding?'

'Of what could happen to us if we got this thing wrong.'

'Or of what very nearly happened to *you* anyway.'

She eyed him warily. 'You know, Mark . . . many other-halves would have driven all the way down here to the West Country to offer their congratulations.'

'That's one of the reasons I came here . . . the main reason, in fact. But it doesn't mean I wasn't scared and shaken when I heard what nearly occurred.'

'Not as scared as me.' She went back to her keyboard.

'You realise I was only informed about it this morning?' he said. 'When it was all over?'

'Of course. You aren't part of the enquiry.'

'Gemma, we've spoken on the phone nearly every day since you came down here. Would it have hurt to tell me you've spent the last couple of weeks on decoy duty?'

'You'd only have worried. What would be the point?'

Heck turned away, hands jammed into his pockets. Frustrated, he reassessed the display. Devon and Cornwall photographic had captured the victims from just about every angle, in unstinting detail and deluxe colour. The first string was somewhat less graphic. A variety of household items had been used: pliers, scissors, tin-openers, hammers. But in most cases death had resulted quickly, without prolonged sexual torture. However, in the second string – the slayings of the young couples – it was a different story. Okay, the men had all been despatched with speed, usually by having their skulls battered, but the women, who were beaten half-senseless first (or if they were lucky, until they were completely unconscious), had been stripped of their clothes and under-wear and laid out as though on a dissection slab. The usual wholesale slashing and stabbing had followed, no part of their bodies left unravaged, though extra attention had always been paid to the abdomen and genital area. Even then, towards the end of the series, progressively more recognisable bloodlust was visible, the maniac attacking each new victim with ever greater savagery, to the point, in the final couple of cases, where full evisceration had resulted. Even with the eye of an experienced and detached investigator, it was diffi-cult not to flinch back from these glossy, brightly coloured images of young women spread-eagled and sliced open.

Whatever part of the process had actually killed them, the madman had always completed each task with his usual *coup de grâce*: a brutal blow to either eye, delivered with a specially sharpened screwdriver, and with such force that it penetrated through to the brain. In fact, the two cavernous holes in the slashed, bloody face of Sarah Bunting, the last female victim before the Stranger had attacked Gemma, revealed that he'd plunged his steel four or five times through either socket.

'God knows what he'd have done to *you* if you hadn't got that shot off,' Heck muttered, his stomach churning.

'Well I did, didn't I?' Gemma replied primly, still typing. 'So there's nothing to be upset about.'

'How's Maxwell?'

'Single fracture to the skull . . .'

'Small change for letting himself get zapped the moment the bastard showed up.'

'But there are no complications . . .'

'He'd have another one by now if your pic was being added to this gallery.'

She glanced up hard. 'So he's going to be alright . . . I'm sure that's the answer you were actually looking for.' She sat back and folded her arms. 'Let's cut to the chase, Mark . . . what're you *really* doing here? You don't think I should have volunteered to be a decoy, do you?'

'It's not just that . . .'

'Oh, it's not *just* that?'

'Look . . . I don't like the way, every time one of these sex maniacs cuts loose, we respond by finding every female detective we've got, sticking her in a short skirt and sussies, and sending her out on the streets to see if she can pull him.'

'I wasn't wearing sussies. You'd be so lucky.'

'This isn't a joke, Gemma!'

'What . . . you're telling *me* that?'

'There must have been a dozen other ways you and the rest of the girls could have been more useful in this enquiry.'

'And do you really believe that, Mark? Or is it actually the case that you mean there were a dozen other ways *I* could have been more useful?'

He shrugged, awkward. 'Obviously you mean more to me than the others . . .'

'Thirteen victims, Mark. And no main lines of enquiry. And on top of that, a decreasing cooling-off period between each attack. It was needs must.'

In truth, Heck couldn't dispute that.

'You didn't want me to take this Devon and Cornwall attachment in the first place, did you?' she said. 'Even before there was any talk of us using decoys.'

'Because the moment I heard D&C were checking with other forces for female officers who were authorised and experienced with firearms, I knew the long-term plan was to put them out there as bait . . .'

'No, you didn't. You *thought* it might. But even that was enough to give you the willies.'

'Am I not supposed to be concerned about you?' he said. 'I mean, throw your mind back nine months – when I cornered that nutter who'd been chucking acid in people's faces. I chased him across the railway bridge at Mile End, remember, even though he'd threatened me with a butcher's knife as well as the usual jar of concentrated sulphuric. I managed to nab him. And what happened when I got back to the nick? You slapped me across the bloody face!'

'You saw him and recognised him. We could have picked him up afterwards, team-handed. In perfect safety. He'd have been bang to rights.'

'He could have gone to ground, he could have stayed on the streets for days. Besides, I was confronted by him in the course of an investigation. A split-second decision, and I had to chase . . .'

'Everything okay in here?' the squat, bull-like shape of DS Harry Jenks wondered from the open doorway.

'Everything's fine,' Heck snapped.

Jenks glared at him, unconvinced.

'Seriously, Harry,' Gemma said. 'Everything's okay.'

'Hmmm.' Unconvinced and clearly unwilling, Jenks withdrew.

'The point is, Gemma,' Heck said, 'you didn't get this decoy gig thrust on you, you weren't railroaded into it. You volunteered *after* careful consideration. You consciously put yourself in extreme danger.'

Gemma heard this out in a growing fury, but by the same token she could tell that Heck was upset; he was pale-cheeked, almost breathless. She'd come close to getting hurt many times in the job; it happened regularly to all of them, but he'd never responded this way before – and now she had an inkling why.

'Of course I volunteered,' she said slowly. 'Would you have expected the married women on the team to step forward? The women with families?'

'Isn't that what *we* were planning?' he said.

Stoically, she resumed typing.

'Gemma, seriously . . . is it so wrong of me not to want my wife-to-be volunteering for this kind of duty again?'

She shook her head. 'You can't lay those kinds of stipulations on me, Mark.'

'I'm not saying I don't want to be married to a hotshot lady detective. Of course, I do. You're a force of nature, Gemma. That's what I love about you. But I don't want the mother of my kids sitting in anymore cars at midnight, or standing on street corners, providing a honey-trap for homicidal maniacs . . .'

'That is so unfair!' she said, hot-faced. 'We face risks on a daily basis, but you more than most . . .'

'Look, *I'm* . . .'

'Please don't say it, Mark . . . that you're the man and I'm the woman. Or, let's put it into the correct parlance, you're the bloke and I'm the bird. I suppose it sounds slightly better that way.'

'*I'm* . . . not saying you can't make arrests,' Heck said patiently. 'Or that you can't run down violent offenders. I just don't like what happened last night.'

'It happens once in a blue moon, and you know it. But you want me inside, don't you – in a nice warm office, checking process cards all day. Maybe working Area somewhere, showing kids across the road, holding hands with little old ladies.'

'That isn't true, Gemma . . . but we can't both be buried in this job to the point where our lives and health are on the line. That's hardly a basis for starting a family.'

'Good job we've got no *immediate* plans, then, isn't it?'

When Gemma hit the keyboard this time, it had an air of finality. She didn't shift her eyes from the screen.

A second passed, then Heck walked to the door. 'Well done on last night's takedown,' he said. 'An extremely fearless piece of work. You've got guts of steel, love.'

'Careful, Mark . . . you almost sounded as if you meant that well.'

He turned in the doorway. 'Look, Gem . . . there's a refs room down the corridor. Let's go and have a coffee.'

'No.'

'Just so we can have a quick . . .'

'No. I've too much work to do. And I'm sure you have too . . . soon as you get back to Bethnal Green and get on with it.'

That hadn't been the end of them, Gemma reflected, as she and Hazel trudged on. But it had been the beginning of the end. She'd pondered it long and hard ever since, wondering if she could have handled it differently. Sure, Heck had done his usual thing, come crashing in feet first, leaving wreckage all around, but, though he could have been a lot more considerate given what she'd just been through, his concerns had only been those any genuinely caring partner would have felt. It had continued to enrage her until long after she'd been promoted and thus was raised beyond the reach of such sordid escapades as decoy work, but maybe she ought to have been more touched by his attitude at the time than she actually was.

He'd certainly been right about one thing. If both of them were to run a daily gauntlet of risk, that was hardly the ideal start-point from which to raise a family. But she knew Heck intimately well – better than anyone else in the job – and she was all too aware he'd *never* be the one to step back from the more menacing demands of his work. His was a positive, pathological need to remain on the front line. He'd turned down an offer of promotion once because he wanted to stay on the streets rather than 'spend his days administrating'. It was unhealthy, with Heck. It went beyond courage or a sense of duty, into self-destructive obsession. The acid-attacker had been a good case in point. Only someone with no concern for his own safety would have tackled the suspect in that situation – on a narrow footbridge over a railway line, the only angle of approach from directly in front, the madman armed to the teeth with his 'instruments of vengeance', as he'd told the press in his rambling, spidery letters. Yet Heck had gone at him full-on, at a hundred miles an hour. And by some miracle had emerged unscathed, with collar in hand.

Too right she'd slapped his face afterwards. She'd slap it again for the same reason, if she thought it would do any good.

But ultimately, what was she supposed to do? This wasn't just her job, it was her life. Gemma's father had been a copper too; he'd died in the line of duty. Maybe, as such, she was a tad on the obsessional side herself – her mother had always said she and Heck were perfectly designed for each other – but Gemma was in this for the long haul. She always had been, with no turning back. How could she progress if she only opted for the safe work, the indoors work, the boring work?

Even now, Gemma still wondered if she could have been nicer to him that day. A bit more understanding that he too had been badly shaken. It had passed without either of them really noticing at the time, but he'd said something revealing – 'that's what I love about you'. Up to that point, though they'd loosely been planning a future together, he'd never used words like 'love' and 'you' in the same sentence. Neither had she, for that matter. It wasn't that they weren't very close; they'd been exceedingly close. It wasn't that they weren't happy together; they'd been happy, too. That said, Gemma had often wondered if that happiness might ever become strained if she, as she hoped and expected, had begun to rise through the ranks, while Heck – thanks to his always playing fast and loose with the rulebook – had progressed more slowly. Even so, after a few months of seeing each other, she was more than willing to move in with him, and not just for the sex. She'd shared all her confidences with him, her thoughts, her desires. Oh yeah, she'd been smitten, and was more than content to play those games that only real lovers play, sometimes even falling out with him to test him, teasing him in the process, tormenting him, but always ultimately rewarding him. She'd cheerfully indulged in all those highs and lows and in-betweens of feeling – and soon she'd known she was ready to build a life with him.

Maybe it was just that words like 'love' had still seemed incongruous in that rather tough environment. Incongruous, maybe even melodramatic. And perhaps a little risky – because, like it or not, people had a habit of dying in their line of work.

Of course knowing that, the fact the word had slipped out of Mark in the honest heat of the moment had made it all the more credible. Little wonder that forever after Gemma had wondered how she'd have responded if she'd picked up on it at the time; whether she would have moderated her exasperation enough to save the situation. But it was too late now, as she kept on reminding herself. It was way too late now.

Struggling to suppress a sigh, Gemma clambered over their fourth farm-gate of the night. 'You certain you know where you're going, Hazel? We seem to have been following this road for ages.'

'I think so,' Hazel replied, waiting on the other side.

'We've not by some chance stumbled upon the one place on earth where roads actually lead nowhere?'

'If it's the road I'm thinking of, it leads to the other end of the Cradle. There's a path from there, which dips down to the south end of the tarn. We should be able to get back to the Keld that way. It's a long walk, mind.'

'And do you *think* that too?' Gemma wondered. 'Or in this case do you actually *know*?'

Hazel shot her a look. 'I'm doing the best I can, Superintendent Piper. I haven't been up on these fells for quite a few years.'

'I thought you were supposed to be a local?' Try as she may, Gemma couldn't keep the weary irritation from her voice.

'You're a Cockney . . . do you know every backstreet in London?'

'No . . . but the difference is I wouldn't go wandering them in the dark when there's a madman loose with a pistol.'

They plodded wearily on.

'You don't like me very much, do you?' Hazel eventually said.

'I think you probably mean well.'

'Oh . . . "probably"?'

'Well, let's not beat around the bush. Let's say what we think. Going up to Annie Beckwith's farm on your own was extremely reckless, and as a result one police officer is dead and the rest of us are in a raft of trouble.'

'Was I supposed to ignore Annie's plight?'

'From what I saw, you people had done a pretty good job of ignoring her up 'til now.'

'I . . .' Hazel hesitated. 'I can't deny it, but I don't think that's the reason you dislike me. You were Mark's girlfriend once, weren't you?'

'So he's been talking, has he?'

'No fury like a woman scorned, eh?'

Gemma glanced around. She opened her mouth, but a second passed, and thinking better of speaking, she strode on.

Hazel made sure there was a yard or so between them as she followed. 'I see you're not trying to deny it.'

'You supposedly know where you're going. Why don't you concentrate on that, Ms Carter? And in the meantime do us both a favour, and zip it!'

'Zip it?' Despite her growing fatigue, Hazel was startled. 'How bloody dare you! It may be such a new predicament for you that you can't grapple with it, but I'm not under your command . . . okay? I'm not some junior bloody officer you can boss around all day just because it's your time of the month.'

Gemma threw her another sharp glance, this one so threatening that Hazel edged away from her, though she continued her tirade.

'Who do you think you are anyway . . . a queen? Because I've got news for you, *Ms Piper* . . . out here, you're nothing. A spring lamb would have more chance surviving in this wilderness than you. So you can kick the bully-boy act. It might have worked with Mark . . . in fact it *did* work with him. He's a lovely guy, but he's miserable as sin up here. Which by the looks of it, is exactly what you wanted . . .'

'Have you quite finished?' Gemma asked, rounding on her.

Hazel held her ground defiantly.

'Have you?' Gemma asked again. 'Because you're making an awful lot of noise and not actually saying anything. Let me tell you what *I* know about *Mark*, shall I! Up here – in this bloody wilderness – is exactly where he needs to be. You understand that, I hope. He is in *totally* the right place. You see, once upon a time Heck was consistently the most productive officer in my department. But he was extremely difficult to manage, even for me. He doesn't do subtle, he doesn't do discreet, he doesn't do politics . . . not even the office variety. He's a wild-card and a supervisor's nightmare. And where he is now, king of a castle no one else cares about, is the inevitable result of that.' Gemma jabbed a finger. 'And you can pretend to be outraged all you want, but the fact remains we almost died tonight, thanks to you. If you *were* under my command, Hazel, you can be damn sure I wouldn't have left things at "zip it"!' She turned and stalked on.

Hazel followed, disconsolate rather than angry. 'And are you going to take him back with you? Because that's what he wants.'

Gemma snorted with contempt.

You're not my bloody gaffer. Or anything else.

'You could've fooled me,' she said.

Chapter 18

The vegetation Heck was now trying to climb down through, though it was mostly dead, was still luxuriant, not to mention littered with fragments of cable from the collapsed bridge. In addition, the scree surface underneath it made treacherous footing. It could have been worse of course. Had the entire structure simply dropped, rather than swung over to this side of the canyon, he would have plummeted a thousand feet. He didn't even like to contemplate the odds stacked against him when the aged metal had first given way. To say he'd been fortunate would be the understatement of all time.

That said, though it was a broad slope, so there was no danger of falling over a precipice, the descent was trickier than he'd anticipated. Heck had no light with which to guide himself, his torch having flown from his belt during the fall, and so ended up on his backside at least six times before the gradient at last began to flatten out. Long before he reached level ground, he heard the trickling of a beck, but only actually located it after descending a couple of hundred metres. It was clear and shallow and about twenty yards in breadth as it meandered along the valley bottom, weaving between embankments crammed with mature pines.

Heck was cold and aching all over, but he also had a raging thirst. He picked his way across loose, heavy cobble-stones cluttering the water's edge, and scooped it up in cupped hands. The icy refreshment cut sharply down his phlegmy throat. He threw a couple of handfuls over his head as well, washing the wound on his temple, and mopping back his hair. It probably wasn't the most sensible move; the temperature was only just above freezing, after all. But the only real solution to any of this was to get back down into the Cradle as quickly as possible. Heck still didn't have the first idea where he was, but following the course of the beck seemed like a plan. At present it only progressed in loops and whorls, but it was bound to spill into the tarn eventually. He tried his phone as he limped along, though that was an act of hope rather than realism, and as usual hope proved ill-founded.

Then he heard the whistling.

It was that same song, the one Heck now knew he'd never forget for the rest of his life. He darted to the nearest pine trunk, slamming his body upright against it. The whistling came from somewhere to his left; it sounded distant and higher up than he was. Could the lunatic still be perched on the platform, whistling his deranged tune to no one in partic-ular? Or had he seen that Heck was alive down here and was he seeking to torment him again? Heck held his position for several minutes, fresh sweat forming in globules on his brow, stinging his wounded temple. Slowly, the whistling dwindled, as though the whistler was moving off into the distance. That didn't prove anything of course – it certainly hadn't done the last time.

It still seemed likely the guy had some kind of thermal-imaging device. It was too much of a risk to assume anything else. Holding his breath, Heck dashed away from the tree, determinedly following the course of the beck. His body was briefly re-flushed with adrenaline, which helped him over-come his bumps and sprains, but the stony ground along the water's edge proved difficult. He slipped and tripped, turning his ankles repeatedly. The beck snaked constantly from side to side, at some points narrowing, at others broadening until he couldn't see the far bank. The fog was burdensome beyond description, hanging in dingy drapes. Again, it dulled Heck's senses, reducing his ability to read position or distance. He'd been lumbering along the waterside for what seemed like minutes now, but with no idea how far he might have trav-elled, or how far he might still have to go. Again thirsty, he moved back to the water's edge and knelt down to drink, at which point what he first thought was a twisted rock form on the far side appeared to resolve itself into a human outline.

Heck went rigid, his hair prickling.

Then he relaxed a little. He'd been caught out like this before, of course. Such conditions as these were ideal for optical illusions. He swigged another handful of water, then blinked twice, focusing on the shape again, trying to discern exactly what it was. And slowly turned numb as he realised he'd been right the first time.

Someone was standing on the other side of the beck. A strong, stocky figure, clad head to foot in black. Even as he gazed at the figure, it raised its right hand as though to point at him – but it wasn't pointing a finger.

The muzzle-flash was blinding; the sound of the shot thundered between the valley walls, the impact on the tree beside Heck cacophonous as a slug kicked out a wad of splinters. He ducked away, running blindly, zigzagging through the trees. A second shot followed, equally loud. The missile whipped past, ricocheting from a boulder.

There was a loud splashing as someone waded across the beck.

Heck glanced over his shoulder. Briefly the fog screened

them from each other. He changed direction, haring back towards the water, plunging in to his knees and wading in the opposite direction, barely breaking speed as he stumbled up onto dry ground again. On this side, the hillside was near enough sheer, so he had no option but to keep following the beck. At least the going here was softer, pillows of pine needles silencing his footfalls. A third shot roared behind him, but Heck couldn't tell where this bullet went. The bastard might have thermal vision, but he clearly wasn't the best marksman.

Not that it would matter if he managed to get close.

There was a renewed splashing. The guy was also coming back across, by the sounds of it at speed.

Heck lengthened his own stride. Now the strip of land he was following broadened out, the upward slope on his left furling away. The cover of the trees fell behind, and suddenly he was heading downhill onto open moorland. But even here there was no easy escape. The ground undulated, and was covered in tussocky grass that was slick with icy dew. He slid to a halt, desperately trying to get his bearings. His heart thudded in his chest, drowning out all other noise. He spun first to the left, then to the right, scanning the grey emptiness and seeing nothing. But this killer was adept at stealing up on people. It was impossible to imagine he wasn't somewhere close by.

Heck dropped to a crouch.

And heard the whistling again.

That haunting, old-time melody drifted through the dead air, emanating from somewhere to his rear, perhaps thirty or forty yards away. Instead of running on in a straight line, Heck went left, keeping low. Some sixty yards further on, he stopped and sank down again.

The whistling had ceased, which somehow was even more eerie.

Heck scampered on, and half a second later the squat,

258

angular outline of a single-storeyed building loomed into his path. He skidded to a halt.

It was actually less than single storey, and built in the familiar dry-stone style, indicating it was a farm outbuilding of some sort. He groped his way around its exterior. On the far side there was a small enclosure, a corral about twenty yards by thirty, fenced with old planking. A sheep fold, Heck realised. From this side, the building, which was nothing more than a shelter, stood wide open. He vaulted the fence and entered, digging out his phone to try and make use of its fascia light, wondering if he might be able to put his hand on a weapon: a pitchfork or scythe, though neither seemed likely, given that up here it was mainly sheep-farming.

What he did find, however, was even better.

In the dim green glow, there were two large, bulky objects shrouded by musty canvas. He lugged the first sheet away, exposing the tarnished metal frame of an ATV, or quad-bike. It was battered and dinted all over, caked with mud and grass-pulp, suggesting it was used for working rather than posing. But even at first glance he could identify a powerful model, most likely with a four-stroke engine. When he tore the second sheet away, there was a similar machine.

Even more useful, keys hung from both their ignition ports.

Chapter 19

The road trailed interminably on as Hazel and Gemma slogged heavy-footed along it. They'd barely exchanged a word since the argument about Heck, but were now so drained that even feeling hostile towards each other felt like too much of an effort.

'You hungry, by any chance?' Hazel delved into one of her jacket pockets.

Gemma shrugged. 'Nothing a chicken dinner with all the trimmings wouldn't fix.'

'All I've got is *this*.' Hazel handed over a thick white slab wrapped in blue and silver foil.

Gemma took it from her. 'Kendal Mint Cake . . . haven't had this since I was a kid.'

'It's icky-sweet, but it's good energy food.'

Gemma nibbled at it. It was ultra-sugary and strongly flavoured with peppermint, but it went down well. Remarkably quickly, she felt stronger, even sturdier on her feet. She took another two large bites. 'You always carry this around?'

'It's not a bad idea, living up here,' Hazel said.

Gemma wrapped what remained of the confection in its foil, and handed it back.

There was an awkward silence, and then she said: 'Despite everything that's happened tonight, you seem like a nice lady, Hazel. If things work out between you and Heck, I'll be very happy for you.'

Hazel didn't initially reply. She wasn't going to pretend she didn't ultimately hope for that. Like Mark, she'd entered this arrangement in adult, open-minded fashion. They'd been attracted to each other, they'd enjoyed the mutual company, the no-strings sex. They'd neither been looking for much more than that. But the better you got to know someone, the more your emotional relationship to them changed.

'You honestly don't have feelings for him yourself?' Hazel asked.

'Heck makes that difficult,' Gemma replied.

'That isn't answering the question.'

'Look . . .' Gemma shrugged. 'I know it sounds terrible, but . . . Heck would like to come home each night after a long, tough day at work, to find his beautiful wife wearing heels and a miniskirt while she cooks him an excellent supper. Not because he's sexist or a chauvinist. He isn't. But because that's the only thing that's going to take his mind off the job. And . . .' she shook her head, 'that just isn't me.'

'It isn't me either,' Hazel said defensively. 'I have a career just like you . . . maybe more like you than you think.' Conscious of Gemma's sceptical glance, she added: 'I run The Witch's Kettle because I love it, not because it pays a load of money . . . which it doesn't anyway. What I mean is . . . oh hell, whatever I say, you're just going to see me as another silly, inconsequential woman, aren't you?'

'I never made *that* comment,' Gemma replied.

She might not have done, but Hazel certainly felt silly and inconsequential with her smudged make-up and tousled hair, especially in the presence of this handsome, athletic

261

policewoman, who even now was only wearing a light sweat, whose lustrous blonde locks, though messed up after all the running around they'd done, appeared to be reverting to a fetchingly curly state, whose aloof, supercool attitude would have been reassuring had it not been so intimidating.

'You know, Mark's spoken about you a lot since he's been up here,' Hazel said. 'He holds you in the highest regard as a fellow officer. He just feels you betrayed him, that's all.'

'Maybe I did, when all's said and done.' Gemma sensed Hazel glancing around at her. 'There, I've admitted it . . . you happy? I hope so, because I haven't been . . . not since it happened.'

'Well, they say confession's good for the soul. Personally, I'm not so sure.' They plodded on side-by-side. 'Anyway, I wonder where he is now?'

Gemma laughed without humour. 'Wherever it is, it'll mean a shed-load of paperwork for someone.'

The two quad-bikes frequently rode neck and neck as they chased each other across the open moor.

Heck had no idea which direction he was travelling in, or even how fast. Both riders had hit their headlight switches, but this revealed nothing in front except vapour. His speedo was coated in grass and dried mud, and he hardly dared spare a hand to scrape it clean; but surely they'd reached forty miles per hour by now at least. It had never been his plan for the killer to mount the other ATV in the sheep fold and come racing after him. Heck had even taken its key and jammed it into his pocket. But somehow or other, his opponent, who was nothing if not versatile, had managed to get it started and had come ploughing in pursuit.

Torn turf sprayed behind the duo as they roared back and forth, twisting and turning across the glistening, dew-slick fell-side. Every manoeuvre Heck made, his opponent copied it. A couple of times, when they were close together, he glanced around, and on each occasion saw the masked figure pointing a pistol at him. Heck lowered his head, though this wasn't easy – he was already lying forward until he was almost flat, like a MotoGP racer, and yet weirdly, no shots were fired. Only now did it start to occur to him that this guy – this maniac, this madman – was actually enjoying himself. This whole thing was great sport for him; possibly it had turned out better than he could ever have hoped for.

On the third occasion the gun was turned his way Heck spun his machine left, the twosome spreading apart, engines grinding. Heck throttled down a sharp descent, at the bottom of which he hurtled along a deep furrow. The ground down there was soft and boggy, liquid mud spurting every which way as he slewed across it. This slowed him somewhat, so he hit the gas harder – just as his opponent came veering down the right-hand slope, attempting to head him off.

Heck took such swift evasive action that he found himself running on two wheels, the vehicle about to tip. He fought the handlebars desperately until he was able to bring it back onto all fours. As he swung up the left-hand slope, his opponent aped the manoeuvre. They blazed along neck and neck again, their flanks almost touching, clods and divots spinning from their wheels as the surface dipped and rose. Heck glanced across, saw the black rapist mask, the strange fierce eyes in its leather sockets fixed on him with eerie intensity. Seconds seemed to pass as they sped along in this mesmeric embrace, neither of them watching where they were going. The pistol, a chunky Colt Python revolver with a four-inch barrel, was still in the killer's right hand, but now clamped against the handlebars as he kept a tight grip on them. Of course, just because he wasn't able to shoot at present, that didn't mean he wouldn't take a chance very soon – especially not if Heck gained some kind of advantage. There was no option but to try and outpace the son of a bitch, but that was proving difficult. They ran on and on, still not watching the ground ahead. Not that this made a great deal of difference, as they couldn't see more than a few yards anyway in the fog – until the terrain to the left tilted sharply up onto another ridge. Heck swayed in the saddle as he rocketed up, the killer again copying his action. The ground on top was dry, but rutted and uneven, and now the duo found themselves jolting and bouncing across rocks. And boulders too, large ones.

As they swerved to avoid these, they were funnelled together into a natural passage, which very quickly became a ravine, maybe a hundred yards long and with no visible exit at the end. Heck throttled up, though he knew this was a terrible risk. They were touching sixty now, easily, and still he couldn't see more than a few yards ahead. When he struck a heavy stone with his front nearside tyre, it was a massive blow, which lifted his ATV sideways off the ground – for a second or two he was sailing through mid-air. He landed with brutal force, but managed to stay upright, and yet there was worse to come. They were on open ground again, still blistering forward – at which point Heck's opponent seemed to brake, to swing his machine violently sideways, as though he'd suddenly had enough of the whole thing.

Heck wondered what the guy had seen, or knew about in advance. And then he saw it himself.

But only at the last second, as it came rushing out of the fog.

Another dry-stone wall, built completely transverse to his angle of approach – aside from a small gap where the old stones had tumbled down in heavy weather. The gap was four feet across at the most; Heck wasn't sure if that was even wide enough, but he aimed for it all the same, veering crazily so that he could meet it head-on, at the same time realising he'd at last gained the edge.

Only to abruptly realise something else.

In what might be his last moment of coherent thought, he understood why the maniac had pulled away. Because they weren't just on any old moorland here, he realised – they were on Fiend's Fell. Heck thought about braking, but knew it was too late. Now all he could do was slam his head down and throttle his machine to the absolute max. He shot through the gap in the farm wall, roaring up the naturally ramped ground beyond it, and sailed far out into the abyss over Witch Cradle Tarn.

Chapter 20

'What time is it now?' Hazel asked, glancing over her shoulder.

Having left the moorland road, they were moving single file along a snaking hillside path. Gemma, who brought up the rear, dug her phone from her pocket. 'Half past midnight.'

'Christ,' Hazel groaned. 'I thought it'd almost be morning. Seems to have been dark for hours and hours.'

'The good old wintertime, eh. At least we're heading downhill.'

'Yeah.' Hazel didn't even sound enthused by that, mainly because the blisters she'd developed over the last mile of rough ground had reduced her progress to an agonised limp.

'You *do* know where you're going, don't you?' Gemma asked.

'Like I said, we're now on our way down to the south end of the tarn.' Hazel stopped and swept with her hand at the general area behind them and to their right. 'If it wasn't for this fog, you'd have one of the best views in the Lake District from here.'

'That's Witch Cradle Tarn down there?' Gemma asked.

'I'm certain of it.'

'You don't sound certain.'

'I'm as close to being certain as I can be.'

They listened, not quite sure what they expected to hear. Calling out to see if their voices echoed would be the dumbest of dumb ideas, given that they were possibly still being hunted. Besides, any sounds that came back to them could just as easily be the result of atmospheric conditions as from some vast gulf.

None the wiser, they pressed doggedly on. Gemma was used to leading, not following, and it grated on her having to rely on someone else to make all the decisions, but one thing her reluctant guide had said earlier was definitely true. She'd be in a real mess if she was up here on her own. Okay, this was only the Lake District, not the Wild West, but it was astonishing how disorienting a lack of light could be, either artificial or natural, not to mention a lack of shelter, a lack of signposting, even a lack of flat surfaces to walk on. Gemma's gym-toned body was in good condition, but the strength and dexterity required to traverse this landscape comfortably came from something else – long hours of experience and slow, painful acclimatisation. As things were, her feet were swollen, her ankles aching, the cold and damp leaching into the very marrow of her bones. And of course it would help if she had the first idea where she was and which direction she had to go in. In that regard she had no option but to rely on Hazel, an unlikely Calamity Jane by almost any standards, but someone who, if nothing else, had spent most of her life here.

'So how far do you estimate we have to go?' Gemma asked.

'It's probably another mile down to the Race Bridge,' Hazel said. 'After that, a mile to the Boat Club. Then another to the Keld.'

'What's the Race Bridge? Not another death-trap I hope?'

'No, it's just an arched stone bridge at the tarn's southern tip. Whenever we have heavy rain, the tarn overflows and it pours downhill in what we call the Cragwood Race. It's like a fast, steep river with lots of turns and rapids. The Boat Club use it for white-water rafting, kayaking, all that sort of stuff.'

'And where does that lead to? The Race, I mean.'

'Down into Great Langdale. At the bottom, it joins Langdale Beck.'

'How far down into Langdale from the Race Bridge?'

'Another couple of miles.'

'Another couple?'

'Maybe more.'

'Great,' Gemma said. But the path progressively steepened as they descended, and gravity began to assist. Gemma's ears popped as the pressure changed. It felt as if they were getting somewhere, at last.

Heck fell a distance he estimated as being close to a hundred feet.

As he plummeted through the fog, the quad-bike turning over and over alongside him, engine yowling, heat and fumes pouring off it, it fleetingly struck him that he wasn't absolutely sure of his location, or what he was descending towards. It could have been another shallow river full of rocks and cobble-stones, or even a dry valley bottom, or a moor, or mountainous heap of scree. But he had no time to ponder these dread possibilities before the vapour cleared beneath his feet and the flat, black surface of the tarn came racing up towards him.

Instinctively, with only a second to spare, Heck straightened his body as much as possible, ankles extended downward, arms raised on high, head turned, chin tucked behind the bulwark of his shoulder.

He struck clean, toes first, but the impact was phenomenal.

His body shuddered at the blow, the water all but dragging his clothes over his head as he crashed through a surface hard and yet brittle as glass, and plunged deep, deep into the icy, unlit depths below. He sank at least fifteen feet, maybe more, and the pressure change was shocking; his ear-drums felt as if they'd blow out, his teeth as if they'd explode. At first he was so dazed that all he could do was float in that turgid embrace, his clothes filling with water, ballooning around him, dragging him ever further down into brackish murk – but then it seeped past his lips, and forcefully revived him. Though even then, it took every inch of strength he had, and wild, explosive kicks to propel himself upward.

When Heck finally broke the surface, he vented his lungs in a single eruption of air, and greedily sucked fresh chestfuls as he wallowed amid seething, hissing bubbles. He was still groggy, with no clue which direction he was supposed to take to find the nearest shore, but then, just to his left, he caught a last glimpse of a fading luminous orb far beneath the tea-coloured surface, before it dwindled entirely from view. Witch Cradle Tarn was seven hundred feet deep, or so he'd been told. Whoever that handy ATV had belonged to, they weren't going to see it again.

At least it gave him a marker. The quad-bike had fallen to his left, which meant the cliff was behind him, so the other shore – the populated west shore – was directly in front, albeit a considerable distance away. At first, Heck was so bruised and tired that all he could do was wallow there, gasping, treading water, which now at last was settling, lapping rather than frothing.

He'd have liked to keep doing this, taking time to rest, but knew he couldn't risk it. The big problem now was the very low water temperature inducing hypothermia. He remembered hearing in a training session once that the projected survival time for a healthy adult in fifty degrees of water or less was a maximum of about two hours, but of course during that time the body would get weaker, the thinking process turn progressively more muddled. So he couldn't afford to mess around. It was tempting to head for the unpopulated east shore, as that was closest, but then he'd be exposed to the near-freezing night air in sodden clothes, miles from any kind of shelter. The only real option was to head for the more distant west shore. As such, he rolled over onto his back, and commenced a slow, heavy frog-kick, which propelled him steadily across the tarn. Within minutes his limbs were so leaden it was more like forging through treacle, but with gritted teeth he persisted. Maybe half an hour passed before he felt ribbons of weed billowing around his legs. By this time his scalp was numb. He placed an exploratory hand on it, and was shaken to feel a patina of wafer-thin ice on his hair. He quickly scrubbed it loose, then turned properly to look over his shoulder. The fog still obscured the shore, but not the entrance to the corridor that led through the rushes to the boatshed. It seemed he'd crossed the tarn diagonally rather than heading straight to the other side. A longer and more indirect route, but at least he could get help in the Ho. Bill Ramsdale had a landline.

Heck turned onto his front and breast-stroked his way along the corridor. The fog was still so thick that the shed only materialised when he was almost at the end of it, at which point he stopped in the water, bobbing there, regarding the open entrance in bewilderment. It was too dark to be absolutely sure, but it looked as if the police launch had been returned, and yet now was sitting extremely low in the water – so low, in fact, that it had to have sunk.

Heck poked his toe at the lake-bed, but it was out of reach. He covered the final twenty yards at a front-crawl, before seeking the floor again and this time finding it.

Chest-deep, he waded forward into the shed, edging his way around the launch's starboard gunwale. When he peeked over the top, the craft was indeed full of murky water. Various items – bits of wood and weed, but also materials from the first-aid kit – were floating in there.

The loss wasn't a complete disaster. The boat was old, and most of the time they barely had cause to use it. But more of a worry was how this had happened. It was possible Mary-Ellen had accidentally holed it earlier on, when she went back to mark out the crime scene, but if that was the case, how had she brought it back?

He reached up, fitting both palms on top of the starboard pier, and with a grunt, levered himself out of the water, swinging around and planting himself on his backside. He slouched there for almost a minute, regaining his breath, which came in ragged gasps – not that there was any time now for taking five.

Concern for his fellow officer was nagging at him badly.

By the looks of it, the boat had been taken possession of elsewhere – the far side of the tarn maybe. Whatever had happened, it must have been some time ago, because the killer had then gone straight up the Cradle Track in pursuit of Hazel. But what had he done with Mary-Ellen before then? Had the bastard simply stolen the boat while she was busy securing the crime scene, effectively marooning her over there? Or had he attacked her too? It seemed highly improbable the ruthless killer they were dealing with tonight would miss the opportunity to add to his tally. Heck felt queasy at the mere thought of Mary-Ellen – who, for all her confident athleticism, was still only a young lass – having to face this guy on her own.

With such fears in mind, it was probably not the ideal time for him to spot the writing on the far wall of the boat-house interior. This only happened slowly, as his eyes adjusted to the deep gloom, but once the piece of crude graffiti had swum properly into view, he jumped to his feet.

Now that he was fully out of the water, it was bitterly cold. Ice felt as if it was forming inside his clothes, but fleetingly Heck was too distracted to notice that. He limped around the interior to the far pier, so that he could examine it up close.

REMEMBER ME?

There was no question about who'd written it or what it meant. In the dimness he was colour-blind, so though he didn't immediately realise that the sentence had been inscribed in blood, the idea struck him hard when he dabbed at it with a fingertip, and it felt both slimy and congealed.

He backed away a couple of steps, heart thumping.

This didn't necessarily mean Mary-Ellen had been attacked. The blood might have come from one of the two hikers. Even from Annie Beckwith. Of course, standing here ruminating wasn't going to help. And nor was it going to warm him up. Heck's joints were now stiffening; the dampness in his hair turning again to flaky ice. Realising he was in dire need of dry clothing and a hot drink, he plodded quickly out of the boatshed and across the sloping lawn to the rear of Bessie Longhorn's house. He banged on the rear door for several minutes. But there was no response. It was pitch-dark inside.

Frustrated, but hoping Bessie had gone down to the Keld to seek the company of others, he circled the house, crossed the garden and climbed through the rockery and over the barbed wire fence onto Ramsdale's property. The lights in this building were still on, and when Heck made his way around its exterior, the front door stood wide open. He halted, uncertain, at any moment expecting the householder

272

to emerge. But as the seconds ticked by and no one emerged, new alarm bells began sounding. It was a foggy, frozen night at the start of the winter . . . and this guy was prepared to leave his front door wide open?

No chance. No chance at all.

Chapter 21

When Heck ventured inside Bill Ramsdale's cottage, the first thing he saw was the blood-caked figure seated upright in the office swivel chair. Unsurprisingly, it was dead, its throat hacked wide open. Equally unsurprisingly, its eyes had been stabbed to jellied ruin. Despite these ghastly mutilations, and the cataract of congealing gore that had resulted, Heck was still able to identify the scruffy jeans and t-shirt that Bill Ramsdale had been wearing the previous day.

But now his attention was drawn somewhere else – to a large item of furniture on the far side of the room, just to the left of the foot of the staircase. In any normal household it would be a dining table, though in this one it was cluttered with old papers, bits of food-crusted crockery, a few items of discarded stationery – and something else.

Heck advanced towards it, unsteadily.

He remembered the comments Hazel had made about the 'ungodly wailing' she'd heard coming down the length of the Cradle. And what was it he'd said in response? That it would have taken an 'astonishingly powerful' pair of lungs to project over such a distance.

Or maybe an astonishingly tortured pair.

It was highly unlikely that sound had issued from Bill Ramsdale – the initial assault to his throat would have been swift and purposeful: to silence him as much as kill him. As always with the Stranger's male victims, Ramsdale had been despatched quickly and without fuss. But Bessie Longhorn . . . well, that was a different story.

The girl was now splayed out naked on the table like a frog in a Biology class. Except that no laboratory incisions had ever been as cruel or as jagged, or had criss-crossed each other as repeatedly and crazily as these did. Heck was reminded of the crime scene glossies in the Devon and Cornwall MIR, and how it looked as if the maniac was progressively working himself to such a state with his female victims that he was finally committing acts of human evisceration.

It was anyone's guess how long this ordeal had lasted. But Bessie – a younger woman, of course, and more the Stranger's type than Annie Beckwith – had been bound securely in place, her own bootlaces fastening her left and right wrists to the table legs at the head of the table, while a belt, possibly Ramsdale's, and her own worn-out brassiere, accounted for her feet at the other end – so the perpetrator had been able to drag it out at his leisure. Heck could only hope that the usual gouging of the eyes, done with such viciousness here that the bones of the sockets had been exposed, had occurred well after death.

Heck couldn't remember the last occasion he'd shed a tear for a murder victim. Neither could he remember the last time he'd used a tea towel, or any piece of material for that matter, to cover a victim's terribly contorted face. But today they'd reached a point where all the rules of common decency, common sense, and even normal existence no longer applied.

His own phone, of course, had been dunked in the lake and was no longer functioning, so he trekked back across the cottage to the landline, barely concerned that in leaving his own footprints on the carpet of blood, he was again compromising the crime scene. But Heck had just enough mental wherewithal left to dig through the cutlery-crammed drawers in the kitchenette, and find himself an oven glove with which to put the telephone receiver to his ear – only to hear nothing on the other end.

This was more or less what he'd expected.

To say they were isolated here would actually be a euphemism. They were marooned, trapped, cut off from the rest of civilisation, and the maniac in their midst clearly intended to take advantage of every second this afforded him.

Heck slumped onto the only stool at the breakfast bar that wasn't draped with old clothes or further bits of half-finished manuscripts. His vision was no longer blurred by tears, but he struggled for a further minute to get his thoughts together.

One major problem was that he was receiving mixed messages.

Taken alongside the writing out in the boathouse, there was no question what the atrocity on the dining table signified: the Stranger was back. And yet, other things still didn't add up. After a disorderly start, the original Stranger crimes in the West Country had fallen into a pattern of Ripper-like sex murders, each individual offence clearly recognisable as such. And yet now, despite the near-evisceration of Bessie Longhorn, the bulk of the offences here seemed to lack any such rhyme or reason. The maniac was showing great industry, but without an obvious remit, eliminating those who were a threat to him, like the police, by shooting, and butchering those whose vulnerability allowed him some leeway to enjoy himself. But it wasn't like he was on a traditional series, with cooling-off periods in between each attack. It was more like he was on a rampage, and that had definitely *not* been the original Stranger's style.

Heck glanced at the front door, which, still standing ajar, was a slice of silent blackness. The only movement beyond it were twists of eddying mist. He blundered over there, slammed the door closed and threw its bolts. Then he headed upstairs, where he intended to shower and get changed. It seemed a tad indelicate. It also seemed rash. Again, Heck was thinking of the crime scene. He was always thinking crime scene – preservation was the vital role of any first responder – but on this occasion he was thinking pneumonia as well. And he knew which had the greater priority overall.

Heck stood under a hot spray for five minutes, then towelled down and entered Ramsdale's sordid bedroom, where, after rummaging through several disordered wardrobes, he pulled out some clean underwear, a fresh pair of jeans, an old moth-eaten jumper and a camouflaged flak-jacket of the sort worn by hunters. They weren't a perfect fit; Ramsdale had been a physically larger specimen than Heck, but they would do for the time being. He also found a pair of worn-out training shoes. These did fit, which was a relief.

He retrieved his essentials from his own sodden clothes – wallet, warrant card, keys and such, and went back downstairs. It occurred to him that Ramsdale might have some kind of weapon, but he didn't want to disrupt the crime scene anymore by turning the house upside down in what could be a futile and time-consuming search. He tried the landline one more time, but it was still dead. Heck glanced again at the householder's corpse still propped in the swivel chair, and then across the room at the dismembered husk of the odd young woman who'd thought he'd never noticed her blushing bright red whenever he favoured her with a smile.

When he left the cottage, he was newly enveloped in cloying vapour. Heck locked the house first – he could take that preservative measure at least – and walked up the garden path. At the top, he turned right across open, frost-speckled turf, and followed the short-cut path to the car park. When he got there, as he'd hoped, both his Citroën and the police Land Rover, plus Hazel's Laguna, were still parked. The only problem was that all three of their bonnets had been forced open, by the looks of it with a crowbar, and their engines mangled. He gazed into the disordered guts of his Citroën. Sliced pipes and shredded cables lay in a spaghetti-like tangle. It was the same with the Laguna and the Land Rover.

The latter implied even more that Mary-Ellen hadn't come back across the tarn in the boat. It seemed ever more likely that she had been bushwhacked on the far shore. Even if she was uninjured over there, she was currently out of reach. While Heck himself, incommunicado, had to tramp his way back to Cragwood Keld, all three miles of it, along a narrow, fog-shrouded road, lined down both sides with impenetrable trees and brush.

Talk about ambush alley.

Chapter 22

It wasn't too long, maybe another half-hour or so, before Gemma and Hazel were back on level ground, surrounded by hints of trees and leafless shrubs, all redolent with that loamy autumnal scent: fungus and decay, dankness in every shivering bough. Somewhere to the right, they could hear the faint lapping of water, indicating they were back alongside the tarn.

This gave them new heart, Hazel hurrying ahead, albeit with an awkward, limping gait.

'It's only a few hundred yards to the bridge from here,' she said.

'No problem.' But Gemma then glanced over her shoulder, wondering if she'd just heard a crackle of foliage. She flicked her torch on.

'Something wrong?' Hazel asked.

Gemma didn't immediately reply. The pall of rapidly dimming light – her torch's battery was finally failing – speared into the gloom, but revealed nothing. 'Let's keep moving, eh?'

They walked on, Gemma glancing over her shoulder several times more. The lapping of wavelets soon gave way to an ongoing rumble of rushing water.

'Hear that?' Hazel said. 'That's the Race. There's actually a barred gate they lower from the bridge to stop people going over the top of it by accident. They only raise it for competitions.'

'Okay . . .' Despite her better judgement, Gemma allowed Hazel's increasingly upbeat mood to affect her. As the torch now emitted little more than a weak, yellow glow, she switched it off and shoved it into her pocket. 'I don't suppose anyone lives near the bridge? There are no houses or anything?'

'No. As I say, even from here it's still a couple of miles to the Keld.'

The rushing of water was now thunderous, as if it was pouring in a waterfall. The direction from which it emanated appeared to have changed; it no longer came from their right, but from somewhere to their left, just ahead.

Then Gemma heard something else. And this time there was no error.

It was another crackle of twigs, from close behind.

She spun around, by instinct going for her torch and thumbing its button, but the bulb failed; the battery had finally died. She kept hold of it nevertheless, clamping it in her left fist. It wasn't especially heavy, but anything would do that felt like a weapon.

Hazel hobbled up beside her.

They were silent for several seconds, their breaths pluming in milky clouds.

'Do deer ever come down to the water's edge to drink?' Gemma asked quietly.

'I suppose . . . I've known sheep do it too.'

What Gemma would have given at that moment for a loud and reassuring *baaa*! But the lakeside woods remained silent.

'Keep walking,' Gemma murmured, turning and steering Hazel along the path. 'And don't look back.'

'What do you mean?'

'Go over the bridge if you want to. Act like there's nothing unusual.'

'You sound like *you* won't be with me.'

'Like I say, don't look back.' Gemma edged towards the left side of the path. 'If you hear anything bad, start running.'

'You can't hide!' Hazel hissed. 'Mark said this guy might have some kind of heat-vision device.'

'We don't know anything about him. We don't even know if this is him. If it was, I'm sure he'd be whistling his happy tune . . .'

'So why are you . . .?'

'Don't argue, Hazel, okay!'

They strode on, Gemma still veering casually left and then, without warning, darting away into the fog-shrouded undergrowth. Hazel almost whimpered aloud, but managed to suppress it, and strolled on alone as calmly as she was able.

In the brush, Gemma dropped to a crouch, and waited. Pine needles and cones were scattered around her feet, but no heavy stone lay close to hand, no broken branch she could wield as a club. She hefted the torch again, this time in both hands, and strained her ears as Hazel's stumbling footfalls receded.

Seconds passed as she tried to subdue her breathing, which wasn't easy – her throat was sore and her lungs ached from the frigid air and constant exertion. She knew she wasn't particularly well concealed. Only a few clumps of naked foliage separated her from the path. But hopefully she was close enough to hear the footsteps she now confidently expected to come crunching along it. Until it occurred to her that what she'd heard had been the crackling of *twigs*. Which did not signify someone proceeding along a path – but through undergrowth.

She spun around. The figure standing directly behind her was a black outline in the gloom. Before she could move or even shout, a torch flicked on and searing light glared over her. If Gemma hadn't just walked so far and over such rough ground, she might have been able to respond more effectively. As it was, her legs were cramped and cold, so she wasn't able to leap to her feet and go into her unarmed combat routine. The blinding light rendered her opponent all but invisible anyway, so, though she flung the torch, it flew wide, the figure easily able to step aside.

'Whoah!' came a sharp voice, with a distinct Irish twang. 'Do that again, miss, and I'll break your fucking arms!'

'PC . . . PC O'Rourke?' Gemma said warily.

There was a brief, surprised silence. 'Who are you? Hey . . . keep your hands where I can see them!'

'I'm a police officer too . . . from Scotland Yard.'

The figure behind the torch regarded her with prolonged suspicion.

'If you'll let me,' Gemma said, lowering her right arm again. The wallet containing her warrant card was inside her jacket.

'I said don't fucking move!'

The tone was attack-dog aggressive. If this was the famously tough and resourceful Mary-Ellen O'Rourke, she sounded highly on edge. But then, even the most affable officers were likely to be out of sorts tonight. Gemma's eyes had now adjusted to the bright light. She detected a sturdy stature, black clothing and a luminous slicker of some sort. A pale face hovered just above the torch. By the looks of it, the officer had drawn her extending baton, and held it at her right shoulder, ready to strike.

'You say you're Scotland Yard . . .?'

'Yes.' Gemma kept her arms outstretched. 'And I'm guessing

you're PC Mary-Ellen O'Rourke, from Cragwood Keld police office. If it helps, my name's Detective Superintendent Gemma Piper . . . from the Serial Crimes Unit. I came here at the request of DS Heckenburg.'

There was another long, near-eerie silence from the figure behind the torch. Then the light was inclined downward, so it no longer shone into Gemma's face. The newcomer emerged fully into view. It was indeed a policewoman.

'I'm sorry, ma'am.' She offered a hand to assist.

Gemma waved this away and rose stiffly to her feet. She reached under her coat and produced her ID. Mary-Ellen only gave it a cursory examination.

'Heck mentioned your name, but . . .'

With wild shrieks, a third figure lurched from their left, carrying an enormous knotted tree limb, which it swung like a baseball bat. Gemma fell backward and rolled. Mary-Ellen dodged nimbly aside, the limb whistling harmlessly past the pair of them. Their female assailant staggered, and almost fell herself. Mary-Ellen jumped forward before she could strike again.

'Easy, Hazel! It's me! Mary-Ellen!'

'Oh my God!' Hazel stammered, half-collapsing. She sank to her knees. 'I'm sorry . . . I, I didn't realise . . .'

'So one of you is lying in wait for me,' Mary-Ellen said. 'The other comes at me with a shillelagh. Who needs enemies with friends like you lot?'

Gemma got slowly to her feet. 'You can't totally blame us, PC O'Rourke.'

'What you doing this end of the tarn?' Mary-Ellen asked.

'What are *you* doing here?' Gemma retorted. 'Aren't you supposed to be on the east shore, marking out a crime scene?'

'I was there a few hours ago. But I kept hearing noises. Like there was someone circling around. Eventually I went and looked. I couldn't find anything. I was about a hundred yards away when I heard the bloody boat start up. I ran back there, but by then the sodding thing had gone. So I've had to walk it back. It's taken me ages just making it this far. The east shore's pretty difficult to negotiate.' Mary-Ellen displayed torn gloves and skinned fingertips. 'Had to climb more than a couple of rock-faces. Soon as I got to this end, I heard voices. Didn't have a clue who it might be, so I hid and followed you. The rest you know.'

'Well . . . you won't believe what's happened to us,' Hazel said.

Wearily, in faltering, disjointed fashion, she related their own experiences. Mary-Ellen listened, initially incredulous, her face visibly lengthening, her green eyes losing their lustre when she heard about PC Heggarty's death.

'Dan Heggarty?' she said slowly.

'I'm afraid so,' Gemma replied.

'Oh, Christ . . .' Briefly, the Irish lass sounded too upset to speak. 'I mean, he wasn't a bad bloke, Dan Heggarty. Shit . . . who am I kidding? He was a total prick. But shot, you say? Through the head?'

'Point-blank range,' Hazel confirmed. 'Or so Mark said. He saw it, we didn't.'

'And then the bastard chased you two all over the fells? How far?'

'At least to the other side of the Via Ferrata.'

Mary-Ellen looked astounded. 'You climbed over that ancient thing? It's a bloody disaster waiting to happen!'

'Tell us about it.'

'So . . . where's Heck now? Do you think he's in trouble?'

'We're all in trouble, PC O'Rourke.' Gemma had started walking. The others followed. 'And so are the people in Cragwood Keld. The best thing we can do is get back there now.'

'So do we actually know what's going on here?' Mary-Ellen asked.

'The only thing we can be certain of,' Gemma said over her shoulder, 'is there's an extremely dangerous person loose, who's decided to subject your local community to a vicious and prolonged attack.'

'But why would anyone do that?'

'They don't all need a reason, PC O'Rourke. Just an opportunity.'

A minute later, they approached the bridge. It was a flat-topped, slate-built structure, covered at its lower levels with moss and pondweed, but the tarn was higher than normal, so at present only a couple of feet of the arch underneath it was visible. A rusty iron grille, operated by a chain and pulley system, had been lowered down over this, and the water – brackish-green in the gloom – was pouring noisily through it. As they trooped over the top of the bridge, Gemma glanced left, catching her first glimpse of the Cragwood Race. It was a foaming torrent, plunging steeply down a narrow gully formed between jutting roots and heaped, slimy boulders.

'People take their chances down there?' she said.

'It's not as bad as it looks,' Mary-Ellen answered. 'The channel widens out further down. In the right boat you'll go all the way to the bottom, though Switchback Canyon, which is about halfway down, is a bit of a challenge. I won't pretend it isn't a pretty rough ride overall.'

They walked on in desultory silence, the echoing roar of the Race falling away behind, until the only sound was the clumping of their boot-soles on the grit. Eventually, the trees thinned out as the path angled left. Gemma felt as if they were headed away from the tarn. But then, abruptly, it bent right again, keeping them roughly parallel to what she assumed must be the west shore. Without warning, they came to a T-junction, their route bisected by a smooth tarmac surface running south to north.

'Cragwood Road,' Mary-Ellen said. 'It's another couple of miles from here back to the nick, but at least it's all flat. Anyone need a rest first?'

'We've rested enough,' Gemma said, striding on.

There were a few more nervous moments as they passed between thick belts of trees, where the fog seemed to linger at its absolute deepest. Mary-Ellen shot her light several times into the roiling depths. The faintest noise set them on edge, whether it was the patter of an autumn leaf belatedly falling or the whisper of frosty sedge as a fox needled its way through. At one point, a lesser road, made from compacted dirt, branched away on the right, vanishing not just into the fog but down a tunnel formed beneath tangled skeletal branches.

'That leads to the Boat Club,' Mary-Ellen said, anticipating Gemma's question.

'Don't suppose there's anyone down there?' Gemma asked.

'Not between October and March.'

'There's a spare set of keys to it behind the bar at The Witch's Kettle,' Hazel added. 'But that's only in case of emergency. It's closed for the off-season.'

They clumped on. Soon the trees and undergrowth were pushed back from the road by dry-stone walling, grassy verges replacing them. When they reached another turn, a single road-sign pointed right.

Cragwood Keld

They'd just started down Truscott Drive when they were hailed by a voice.

Shocked, they spun around. An indistinct male figure had

turned into the road from the opposite direction. By his slouched posture, he too was exhausted. But instantly Hazel recognised Heck. Tearfully, she dashed the forty yards towards him, and threw herself into his arms with such force that he almost toppled.

'Hey . . . hey,' he said, hugging her. He saw Gemma and Mary-Ellen approaching. 'What a bloody night this has been. At least you're all okay.' He focused on Mary-Ellen. 'I'm particularly glad to see *you*.'

'And me *you*,' she replied, looking startled by his appearance. 'At what point of the evening did you get the chance to change clothes?'

'I ended up in the tarn again,' he said. 'Don't ask how.'

'Did you find the launch?'

'Yeah. It's back at the Ho. But it's been sunk.'

'Fuck,' she said.

'That's not the only thing. Your Land Rover, M-E, your Laguna, Hazel, and my Citroën have all gone to that great scrap dealer's in the sky. Same with Bill Ramsdale's Honda Civic. But listen, there's worse. Let's get back to the nick. I'll tell you on the way.'

They walked down the road as he described the abattoir at Ramsdale's house. With Hazel present, a civilian, he tried to omit some detail – but not much, as Gemma had witnessed the Stranger's original crime scenes for herself and was their resident expert. She listened in grim silence. Even Mary-Ellen looked shaken by what Heck told them, especially when he mentioned the fate of Bessie Longhorn, while Hazel clapped a hand to her mouth and wept softly.

'There's a message too,' Heck said, before elaborating on the graffiti in the boatshed.

Gemma nodded and contemplated this. Ahead of them now, the first houses of the village arose through the mist.

'"Remember me?"' Heck reiterated. 'I know we can't necessarily read too much into that, ma'am,' Heck added. 'But whoever this guy is, it's pretty obvious that he's playing for keeps.'

Gemma nodded again. 'From this point on, DS Heckenburg, so are we.'

Chapter 23

PC Mick McGurk was sitting in the main office at Cragwood Keld nick as if it was any ordinary night shift. In fact he was dozing, slumped in the chair alongside the radio, his brawny arms folded. But he jumped to his feet when two people entered noisily through the personnel door. It was Heck and Gemma, Mary-Ellen having accompanied Hazel back to The Witch's Kettle.

'Nothing tae report,' he said with a shrug. Any normal copper would have had the good grace to look sheepish, but PC McGurk didn't seem to do emotions.

He listened in stoic, stony silence as Heck explained what had happened on the fell. Even the news about PC Heggarty made little immediate impact on McGurk, as he hadn't known the guy that well. However, his expression sagged when he learned about Bessie Longhorn.

'That wee daftie who used to come down to Bowness to see her ma?'

'It wasn't an easy death for her,' Heck said, able to give a fuller description of the crime scene now that Hazel was no longer with them.

'Christ preserve us,' McGurk said slowly.

'Christ preserve us indeed.' Gemma banged the telephone receiver back on its cradle. 'This landline's dead.'

Heck glanced at McGurk, who suddenly seemed to remember something. 'Internet went down some time back. I presumed it was the network. Was gonna give it half an hour . . .'

'And then you fell asleep,' Heck interrupted.

'Hey, sarge,' McGurk replied in a flat tone. 'I've been on all day and it's now after three in the morning, okay? And you lot were gone God knows how long. I had nae idea there was any kind of emergency. I didna know the phone was dead because I had nae call to use it.'

They tried to reboot the internet but got no change from it, which was no surprise if the phone line was at fault.

Mary-Ellen now entered the nick. 'All the villagers are still down at the pub,' she said. 'Most of them are asleep, or dozing . . .' Her words tailed off as she saw their faces. 'What's the matter?'

'He's been here,' Heck said. 'First he did the phone lines in the Ho. Now he's done them in the Keld.'

'What . . . all of them?'

'It would make sense. The easiest way would be that telephone mast at the top of the green, wouldn't it?'

'That'd be the only way,' Mary-Ellen said.

'You've got a couple of messages left from earlier,' Gemma said, having checked the station answering-machine.

In fact there was only one they hadn't already listened to. It was an update from DI Mabelthorpe, pointing out that the firearms team were only making slow progress from Penrith. It wasn't just the fog apparently; it was constant hold-ups on the motorway due to a lengthy procession of accidents. At one point they'd veered off and tried to progress via the back-lanes, but that had been even worse. It didn't require a crashed HGV to block a narrow mountain road – a three-wheeled milk float would do it – and in those isolated spots there'd likely be no response from the rescue services all night. So now they were back on the motorway, sitting again in grid-locked traffic.

'*They're on their way, Heck, but there's nothing moving at present,*' Mabelthorpe concluded. '*Could be another two . . . maybe* three *hours. Sorry about that.*'

That message had been left on the answering-machine at quarter-past midnight.

Heck turned to McGurk. 'Why didn't you take this call?'

'I've nae just been sitting in here,' McGurk explained. 'You asked me to check around the village and the pub.'

'Yeah, suppose I did . . . okay.'

'The main thing is they're en route,' Mary-Ellen said brightly. 'Even if it's taken them three hours, they should be here anytime now.'

'Well that's the first good news we've heard all night,' Heck said. 'At least then we'll have an armed response available right on the spot should the bastard decide to show his face. In the meantime, I want to find out what's happened to the phone.'

Mary-Ellen had been in the process of opening her anorak, but now she zipped it back up. 'I'll come with you.'

She and Heck exited the station, crossed Hetherby Close and rounded the corner to the edge of the village green. The mast in question was located at its northwest tip. Telephone wires spanned out from it in every direction, servicing all the houses and businesses in the village – or at least, ordinarily they did. Though it was a tall mast, Mary-Ellen only needed to shine her torch up there to expose a distinct absence of cabling. Nearby, an extendable aluminium ladder lay in the leaf-littered grass.

'The bastard just climbed up there and chopped them

down?' she said, amazed. 'Tell me it's not that easy to take an entire community off the grid.'

'It looks like it was that easy tonight,' Heck said, feeling visible again despite the fog. 'Back to the nick, quickly.'

'Shouldn't we tape off the ladder . . .?'

'If it was going anywhere, it would have gone. Which means it'll probably be no use to us. Come on, quickly.'

Before re-entering the station, they quickly checked the Astra brought up by Heggarty and McGurk. It was the only police vehicle they now had at their disposal, but it was big and spacious, and, if necessary, would serve the purpose of transporting at least four of their charges back to safety. But the Astra was beyond use; the glistening pool of brake fluid underneath its belly was proof of that.

'No mangling of the engine in this case, like we saw up at the Ho,' Heck observed. 'No banging, no hammering . . . too noisy with McGurk just inside the nick. So our boy did a bit of quiet surgery underneath instead – sliced the brake cables. What are the odds he's done the same to every other vehicle in the village?'

'He can't have,' Mary-Ellen said. 'Can he?'

'There's only a handful, and all the owners are cooped up in the pub.'

'Bloody glad those firearms lads are coming. At least all we have to do now is wait.'

'Let's get inside,' Heck replied. 'We can count our chickens when we're behind locked doors.'

They hastened up the station path, and entered again through the personnel door. Heck explained what they'd found.

'So wha' is this, a siege?' McGurk wondered, blank-faced.

None of them bothered to reply. They hadn't thought

292

about it in those terms, but now that McGurk mentioned it, a siege seemed to be exactly the predicament they faced.

'We need to get over to the pub,' Gemma decided. 'We're still police officers, even if we are deaf, dumb and blind. Protecting those civilians should be our priority.'

'Plus it'll be more easily defensible,' Heck said. 'It's the sturdiest building in the village. It's got smaller windows than the nick as well.' He indicated the glass door opening into the police office porch and the front desk, and the large plate-glass window alongside it. 'We can close the blinds, but let's not pretend this guy isn't armed. From what I saw, he had a Colt Python. That's a .357 Magnum revolver, which explains why it sounds like a cannon. Dirty Harry eat your heart out, and all that. The main thing is he can easily shoot his way into here.'

'Hang on,' Mary-Ellen said. 'If we all go down to the pub, the firearms team won't know where we are.'

Heck gave this some thought. 'Suppose we could leave a note . . .'

'And have the killer remove it as soon as our backs are turned?'

Heck glanced at Gemma.

'She's right,' Gemma said. 'Someone should stay behind. This is a police station, after all. We shouldn't just abandon it. Whoever it is, we can lock them in . . . they'll be reasonably safe in the short time between now and the shots arriving.'

'I'll stay,' McGurk offered. They all looked at him. He returned their gazes indifferently. 'Sitting around in foxholes all night, waiting tae get sniped – won't exactly be a new experience for me. Plus I've got body-armour on. You lot havena. Don't worry, I'll lie low with the lights out. He won't see me.'

'You'll be on your own,' Heck advised him. 'Out of contact.'

McGurk shrugged; that blank, stony-faced visage of the war veteran again. 'Wha's a few minutes between friends?'

'Okay,' Heck said, 'but just remember . . . this guy's got a gun and he's not afraid to use it. If he tries to come in through the front door, you go out the back. No heroics.'

McGurk gave a toothy half-smile; the first they'd seen from him, and a rather odd-looking thing it was. 'Don't worry, sarge . . . I'll leave those tae you.'

Heck, Gemma and Mary-Ellen circled around from Hetherby Close to the top of the green, and there halted.

The grassy surface glistened with frost as it stretched away into dimness. At this deepest part of the night, there was no sound. The houses along either side were dark, vaguely definable shells, more like mausoleums than habitations. It was astounding how completely the grey shroud of fog had changed the look and feel of the place – it now stood silent and sepulchral, like some forgotten rural necropolis. And yet even by the standards of ever-scenic Lakeland, the Keld normally held 'chocolate box' appeal. Its permanent residents might number only a handful, but they were mostly retired, so they looked after it religiously. Its lawns were always mown, its verges trimmed, its fruit trees pruned. In summer, the cottage gardens were a riot of rainbow flowers.

It was all still here, of course. It was only a matter of months until spring. But just surviving the next half-hour or so, while they waited for the firearms team to arrive, felt like a task in itself. They started forward, stepping softly as they progressed down Truscott Drive.

'Why is this always the worst time?' Mary-Ellen wondered quietly. 'When it's only a few minutes 'til the cavalry shows up?'

'Human nature,' Heck replied. 'If you always expect the worst, it prevents you ever being disappointed.'

'I'll be honest, I've no clue what I'm going to put in my report,' Gemma said. 'If this *is* the Stranger, I've no idea what script he's working to.'

'It's a very different process from last time,' Heck agreed.

'Do you see *any* process here?'

'These are opportunist killings. But there's an element of organised planning too. This guy couldn't control the actions of the people living in Cragwood Vale; he couldn't pre-empt what they were going to do next. But he's obviously been watching them and taking notes. He's hung very close indeed, so he can make counter-moves at the drop of a hat. He's hellishly organised, and he's working to *some* kind of a plan.'

'Still doesn't sound like the Stranger to me.'

'Not as you knew him in 2004 . . . but a lot may have changed since then.'

'What's his end-game, though?' Mary-Ellen asked.

'Isn't that obvious?' Heck replied 'To kill us all?'

Ahead of them, The Witch's Kettle materialised through the vapour.

'In which case, is it really a good idea we all pile into the pub at the same time?' Gemma said.

Heck considered this. 'You mean is he waiting 'til he's got us all in one place?'

'Isn't that what he did up at Annie Beckwith's farm, hole us all up in one building, then herd us into a single room, before pouncing? It would make life easier for him when he's got multiple targets.'

295

Heck mulled that over. Such a thought was unnerving, primarily because it made good sense. But ultimately, the potential disadvantages of using the pub as a base of ops had to be weighed against its very real advantages. They kept on walking. Warm firelight now glimmered from the pub's curtained windows. 'The way I see it, we've no choice,' he said. 'I mean, we surely can't send everyone back to their individual houses. He could pop them all just as easily that way. Probably even more easily. There's still got to be safety in numbers.'

'Agreed,' Gemma replied. 'But we've got to turn this place into a fortress.'

Lucy answered the pub door when they knocked. She looked pale and sallow-faced. Inside, the fire had burned low, casting a dull reddish light which nevertheless filled the taproom and bar. The rest of the villagers, many of whom looked stiff and dazed as if they'd just been woken, were sitting where Heck had left them. One or two muttered together, but immediately on seeing the cops, sat up, alert again, watching and listening intently.

Hazel appeared behind the bar from the kitchen. She'd changed into a grey, slim-fit tracksuit and wore a cardigan over the top. She'd also brushed her straggly hair back and tied it into a pony tail. She didn't exactly look fresher – faint hints of mascara still marked her cheeks – but she seemed calmer to be back on home turf.

'All windows and doors secured?' Heck asked her. 'Back door, back gate?'

She nodded.

'How many rooms upstairs?' Gemma asked.

'Eight in total,' Hazel said.

Gemma gave that some thought. 'The probability is we're going to be okay. But we don't want any last-minute disasters. So I suggest we lock all the rooms that have locks on them, and keep checking on the others for as long as we need to. This place is sturdy, but it isn't invulnerable. Nowhere is.'

'I can start that now,' Lucy said, glancing uneasily at the darkened stairway. 'Haven't been up there for half an hour at least, so it's about due.'

'I'll come with you,' Mary-Ellen said, drawing her baton.

Lucy looked relieved and they went up the stairs together.

'Hazel, we need to damp that fire down,' Heck said. 'I know the room's nice and warm, but if this guy's outside and he sees our shadows moving past the windows, he could easily take a pot-shot at one of us.'

Hazel nodded and went to deal with it.

'The rest of you!' Heck said, turning to the taproom. The villagers listened attentively. 'The best thing you can do is stay exactly where you are. We're much safer in here together. And it's probably not going to be for much longer. We've got armed reinforcements on the way, and they'll be here anytime now.'

'Have you been up to the Ho?' Sally O'Grady asked in a querulous tone. Clearly no one had broken the bad news about the recent murders yet.

'Yes, I have.'

'And did you speak to them? Did you tell them they should come down here?'

'Listen . . .' Heck hesitated, but these people weren't dumb; he knew they'd be able to read his body language and conclude something was wrong. Besides, hiding unpleasant truths didn't always help if you wanted to gain compliance. 'I'm sorry, but we've had one or two casualties tonight.' They regarded him, glassy eyed. 'I wouldn't be doing you any favours if I lied to you about this. I'm very sad to tell you that Bessie Longhorn and Bill Ramsdale aren't with us anymore.'

There were muffled whimpers in response.

'And neither is Annie Beckwith.'

Ted Haveloc swore under his breath.

'Is anyone keeping firearms in the village?' Heck asked. 'Forget whether they're legally or illegally held. We're not looking to prosecute good citizens for minor breaches of the law. If you've got a gun and you've got ammunition, please tell us now. So we can go and get it.'

There was a painfully long silence.

'Sergeant Heckenburg, we're none of us farmers here, or gamekeepers,' Bella McCarthy said, which particularly disappointed Heck, as she and her husband, with their apparent remit to fill their early retirement with every kind of activity on the country sports calendar, might have been most likely to assist in this matter.

'We hate guns,' Burt Fillingham added, as usual taking it upon himself to make a moral point on behalf of everyone else. 'We live in the mountains for our health.'

Heck glanced at Haveloc. 'Ted, you're a native Cumbrian and a lifelong outdoorsman. You don't do a bit of poaching on the side?'

Haveloc stiffened. 'Never have, Mr Heckenburg, never will.'

'I assure you, no one will get in trouble.'

'I should think we won't!' Burt Fillingham blurted. 'Aren't *we* the targets here? And why do *you* need guns if there are armed officers about to arrive?'

Heck wasn't quite sure how to respond to that. The firearms team was a bit overdue by now. It was past three hours since Mabelthorpe had left his message – not long past, but past. It was still the case they could arrive at any moment. But there was something else. Maybe it was that old nagging instinct thing, but Heck increasingly felt there was something about this killer they hadn't yet accounted for, some factor currently concealed from them. After everything that had already happened, and the energy they'd expended just managing to keep a few of their number alive, it didn't compute that it could suddenly be so easy to save everyone else.

Mary-Ellen now reappeared at the foot of the stairs with Lucy, and made a beeline for the hatch in the bar-top, passing through it and indicating to Heck and Gemma they should accompany her into the kitchen. They did so, with Hazel also in attendance.

'Listen,' Mary-Ellen said in a low voice, 'I don't think this pub is quite as secure as we'd like to think. None of the rooms upstairs can be locked from the outside, so it's not like we can create containment areas if the bastard manages to get in.'

'At least tell us the windows can be locked?' Heck said.

'Well yeah, most of them.'

'*Most* of them?'

'There's a broken catch on one of the guest bedroom windows.'

'That's no problem,' Gemma said. 'We can nail that one shut.'

Hazel nodded, implying they had her full permission.

'Yeah, but look,' Mary-Ellen said. 'Outside this building there are sheds, outhouses, lower sections of roof. Easy access to the top floor. If miladdo really wants to get in, he's in. And then what happens . . . panic down here, everyone running around in a tizzy. Meanwhile, he comes downstairs and picks us all off with his Magnum.'

'Maybe we should use one of the other houses?' Hazel suggested.

'No house is safe from a determined burglar,' Mary-Ellen replied. 'And the closer we get to morning, the more determined he's gonna be. Either that or he's gonna leg it. Problem is, we don't know which.' She paused. 'Seriously guys, the sooner those shots get here the better.'

There was no immediate response. Heck in particular

found it difficult to conceal his growing sense of concern. Gemma was the first to notice this.

'What's the matter?' she asked.

'I don't know.' Heck chewed his lip. 'I don't like being passive. Just sitting waiting for help that may never arrive . . .'

Mary-Ellen frowned. 'But Mabelthorpe said . . .'

'Mabelthorpe isn't up on the motorway, where it's Carma-bloody-geddon,' Heck retorted. 'Mabelthorpe was trying to be helpful, but he doesn't have the first clue what's going on with the firearms team. And if by some miracle he's found out a bit more since the phone lines were cut, there's been no way for him to tell us. The shots may still turn up. They're . . .' He glanced at his watch, 'they're only forty minutes late. But then again, they may be sitting in a traffic jam 'til dawn. Twenty miles away, thirty, tops. But it might as well be thirty thousand.'

'So what do you propose?' Gemma asked quietly.

'That we get these civvies out of here ourselves. I mean right out of the Cradle and down to civilisation.'

'Mark, how can you do that?' Hazel asked.

'We're only working on the *assumption* the other cars in the village have been sabotaged,' he said. 'I mean it's a reasonable assumption – but we should at least check. I know it means someone has to go back out there, but I don't see any other way.'

'Well . . . I'll be honest, I don't like sitting around doing nothing either,' Gemma said, which rather surprised Heck, because he tended to be the risk-taker, while she usually counselled caution. 'Especially as we can't secure this place,' she added. 'Until the firearms lads get here, and Heck's right – we don't know they're coming until they actually arrive – we're still vulnerable.'

'But we've only got one dodgy window,' Hazel argued. 'Surely, together, we can defend that?'

'No, on reflection I think Heck's right too,' Mary-Ellen said. 'This guy's got a .357 Magnum. He can shoot out every window in the pub if he wants, and the lock off every door.'

'But the firearms officers are on their way,' Hazel protested.

'And the killer's already here,' Heck said.

'You don't know that . . . I mean, just because he cut the phone lines . . . You're going to go outside and risk your lives again for that?'

'Hazel . . . he's already murdered five people that we know about,' Mary-Ellen said. 'He's obviously on a bender. Let's be realistic, the only way he's not going to extend it to Cragwood Keld is if he decides he's had enough. And what are the chances of that, eh? Until support arrives we're easy meat for him . . . easy meat.'

Heck didn't comment on that, because it was a discomfortingly accurate assessment of their situation. Whether or not their opponent had started his criminal career as a serial sex-slayer, he'd now morphed into that most dangerous and unpredictable of felons – a spree killer. Throughout the modern history of the world, odd, disaffected men had simply gone crazy, grabbed guns and other weapons, and started cutting people down for no easily identifiable reason. In most cases, it went on and on until it ended with the perpetrator's own death, either self-inflicted or at the hands of law officers. The problem was, in this fog, with whatever advantage it was he'd given himself, even the arrival of a firearms unit would be no guarantee of safety. Suppose they drew up in front of the pub, and jumped out in the usual swaggering SWAT-team fashion – only for him to emerge from the mist behind them, Magnum blazing? It would be over in seconds.

There was one other certainty too: the more they dithered here, the more the threat would grow.

'I agree it's a risk,' Heck said, glancing through the kitchen door at the subdued crowd seated around the dull embers in the pub fireplace, and then out through a narrow gap afforded by a slightly displaced curtain. It only hinted at the blank miasma shrouding the village. 'But I'm sorry, it's a risk we're going to have to take.'

Chapter 24

There were dumbfounded expressions when Heck asked which of the villagers had their car keys with them. Faces previously haggard from lack of sleep jerked into full wakefulness.

'Sorry guys, but this is important,' Heck said.

Still there was no instant response. Expressions were now worried as well as mystified.

'Let me explain,' he said. 'PC O'Rourke and I are going to sneak around the village, checking on your vehicles. If possible, we're going to bring a couple back here and drive you all out of the Cradle. We've decided not to wait.'

'So does this mean the invisible men of your firearms department are going to remain that way?' Bella McCarthy asked. 'Invisible?'

'No,' Heck said. 'They're on their way, and they're doing their damnedest to get here. But *we* can be a bit more proactive as well.'

'Do you think that's actually necessary?' Burt Fillingham asked. 'Or will it just make you feel better about yourselves? Bear in mind it's *our* motor vehicles you'll be smashing up.'

'I'll be honest with you,' Heck replied. 'I've reason to believe your cars may all have been disabled already. Perhaps extensively. But we won't know unless we go and look.'

'Is this for real?' Bella McCarthy wondered. 'A few minutes ago you told us we'd soon be safe. That reinforcements were coming. Even if they aren't, it's only just over four hours to sunrise. Can't we just sit it out here?'

No obvious reply suggested itself to Heck. It was that tightrope again, where you don't want to fall on the side where everyone panics and gets hysterical, but likewise don't want to fall on the other side, where everyone is too complacent because they think there is no danger. Gemma solved the problem for him.

'The weather forecast has changed,' she lied. 'The fog is going to linger all day tomorrow and maybe tomorrow night as well. That means whatever problem may be hampering the specialist firearms unit may persist. As we said before, we've no reason to believe anyone who stays in this pub is in imminent danger. But as police officers, we can't just sit around indefinitely.'

'The best thing we can do is see if we can find our own way out of the Cradle, guys,' Mary-Ellen added. Our shooters will likely still turn up, but we don't want to take any chances. All we need is access to a few cars so we can make a decision.'

There was another silence as the villagers took this in. As usual, the chirpy Irish lass who they dealt with on a more regular basis than their local detective, appeared to have a reassuring effect. One by one, five sets of car keys clattered onto the table.

'Thanks.' Heck circled around and scooped them up. 'Don't worry, Mr Fillingham. We won't smash anyone's vehicle. They're no use to us if they're not roadworthy.'

The three cops moved back into the kitchen, where Hazel,

with an astonishing degree of domestic thoughtfulness, had now made a pile of cheese sandwiches for them. She shrugged, almost embarrassed. 'You guys can't run on air all night.'

Gemma, who would be the least useful out there as she didn't know the layout of the village, was staying behind in the pub. So she stepped aside while Heck and Mary-Ellen, who hadn't eaten since the morning before, wolfed the snack down. Mary-Ellen then accompanied Hazel out into the rear yard to see if they could improvise any tools into weapons. Heck polished off the last sandwich, and then turned to face Gemma, who regarded him with a vaguely troubled expression.

'Everything okay?' he asked. 'I mean apart from the obvious . . . that I'm about to do something massively against my better judgement.'

'Look . . . Mark, if you've genuinely been looking for some kind of leadership from me in this, I'm sorry I've not delivered.'

'I'm sorry I asked you up here in the first place.' Heck mopped his lips with a napkin. 'And I mean that in a nice way.'

'You think it would have been kinder *not* to tell me you thought the Stranger was in town?'

'You'd have found out in due course through the normal channels. But . . . oh shit, I might as well admit it.' He blushed. 'I suppose I saw an opportunity to create a kneejerk response . . . to pull you out of your comfort zone.'

Rather to his surprise, Gemma smiled. 'You mean like, where I'd be at your mercy?'

'Sort of.' He shrugged. 'I didn't do it deliberately, you understand. It was all in the back of my mind. I must have liked the idea of watching you try to take charge of a situation where you didn't know the lie of the land, didn't know the people . . . all set in the worst weather, in the wildest place imaginable. I thought even Gemma Piper, Scotland

Yard's Little Miss Perfect, will screw that up.' Heck paused for thought. 'I ought to have known you'd have the sense to take a back seat and let someone who supposedly knows what he's doing take all the difficult decisions, only chipping in now and then with useful stuff – like that fib about the weather forecast.'

'I hope that doesn't backfire on us.'

'Well, the alternative is telling the villagers there's a maniac out there who's gutting people alive and cutting the eyes out of their heads.'

'I know, I know . . . the thing is, you and Mary-Ellen going out there again isn't just against *your* better judgement, it's against mine as well. But I've never known anything like this. We really are between the devil and the deep blue sea. I think there's at least as much chance he'll attack the pub while you're out as there is that he'll attack you two.'

'Maybe just one of us should go and check the cars . . .?'

'Oh, do me a favour. One of us, two of us, three, four . . . the fact is, he's armed and we're not. Just go and find some wheels, and get back here pronto, alright?'

Mary-Ellen and Hazel reappeared in the doorway.

'Nothing more than a few spades and rakes,' the former said, having found nothing out in the yard they could use in self-defence. 'Not even a decent pick-axe.' She patted the baton and CS canister on her utility belt. 'I think I prefer my traditional appointments.'

Heck nodded. 'Good call.'

'Still no sign of the firearms team?' she asked.

'No, still no sign. In which case . . . you ready?'

Very solemnly, Mary-Ellen saluted.

'Don't mess around out there,' Hazel said brusquely.

'Not likely,' Heck replied, as they coated up, pulled their gloves on and stepped out into the yard. The other two women followed.

'Hazel's right,' Gemma said quietly. 'Be careful. Don't even think about splitting up. Not for any reason.'

Hazel's message was to embrace Heck and kiss him on the lips, even forcing her tongue between his teeth. Aware of Gemma watching, he gently resisted that. There was reproach in Hazel's eyes as he pulled away.

'Gotta go,' he said.

She gave a short, terse nod.

He and Mary-Ellen slipped out through the back gate, which was closed behind them. A second later, they heard the pub's back door slamming as well, and a double-thunk as its bolt was thrown and the barrel-lock turned. They moved one behind the other to the edge of the building, peering over the white picket fence and across the pub beer garden and the leaf-cluttered emptiness of its car park. On all sides, banks of curdled mist corralled their vision. The next nearest building from here was a vaguely visible slate structure housing the pumping equipment that processed water from the tarn.

They crouched to deliberate.

'The way I see it, we make a circuit of the village anti-clockwise,' Heck whispered. 'Start in this northeast corner and work our way around.'

Mary-Ellen nodded.

They clambered over the fence, crossed the pub garden and car park, and circled around the back of the pump-house, following an east–west path which eventually brought them to the low wall at the rear of Dulcie and Sally O'Grady's property. Here, they paused again – but heard nothing. The fog lay in a deep, motionless gloom. They jumped over the wall, and crept through Dulcie's frost-hardened flower beds. Beyond that, around the right side of the house, was a car-port wherein sat Sally's Volkswagen Polo.

All four of its tyres had been sliced to the core.

'Shit,' Mary-Ellen said. She hunkered down, fingering the brutal gashes. Before commenting further, she glanced sharply into the murk at the end of the drive.

'Something wrong?' Heck asked.

She rose to her feet. 'Thought I heard something . . .'

'What?'

'Nothing.'

'No, what did you . . .?'

'Seriously, Heck. Nothing. Just getting a bit jumpy.'

He understood that, but couldn't help wondering if she'd heard another of those faint whispers or nasty little snickers.

Be under no illusion . . . there are some very weird offenders.

They circled around to the front of the house, and crossed a paved area covered with potted plants, doing their level best not to kick any over, before taking a side entry hemmed on the left by spruce firs. This brought them to Dulcie O'Grady's Mini One, which was parked on Lakeside Row, a gravelled cul-de-sac at the other side of the property. This car too was sitting on its trims, each tyre hacked clean through.

'Bastard's been thorough,' Heck muttered.

Giving up on the O'Grady house, they nipped along a ginnel back to Truscott Drive, emerging at the village green's northwest corner.

'Where to next?' he wondered.

'Why not try the Fillinghams?' Mary-Ellen suggested. 'They've got a big Rover. If that's running, we could probably get everyone out of here in one go.'

This made sense. They headed west up Truscott Drive, bypassing the entrance on their left to Hetherby Close – no lights from the police office were visible, as McGurk had agreed – and moved to the next road on their left, Highview. All the way, the thick vapour retreated ahead of them but filled in the emptiness behind. It was impossible to shake off the sensation they were being watched, but both were experienced enough to know this was common in situations when danger was known to be close by.

The Rover was parked in a narrow entryway at the back of the small terraced cottage/corner shop where the Fillinghams lived. It sat there, lopsided, its tyres again sliced and its bonnet forced open, the engine inside trashed. The Rover belonged to Burt. His wife, Mandy, had a Renault Clio, which was parked at the other end of the alley. But this too was out of service, all four tyres punctured – they saw that before they even reached it.

And they saw something else, too. Or rather, Mary-Ellen did.

Without warning, she grabbed Heck's shoulder, dragging him down behind a low back wall. They crouched there face to face, barely breathing.

'Okay, what is it?' he asked quietly.

She struggled to contain her excitement. 'There's someone in Ted's cottage.'

'You sure?'

'I just . . . I just glanced right. Totally by accident. And his downstairs curtain was twitching. Heck, Ted's down at the pub. There shouldn't be anyone in there. It's *got* to be him. It's *got* to—'

'Wait a minute.' He clamped a hand on her shoulder. 'Remember, if it is him, he's armed.'

'Okay . . . alright.'

Very warily, Heck peeked up and over the wall. Mary-Ellen did the same, removing her hat in the process. Before them stood the rear of a row of three small, detached cottages. Two of these, those at either end, were holiday lets and currently empty. But the one in the middle belonged to Ted Haveloc, who, as Mary-Ellen had said, was currently

309

ensconced in The Witch's Kettle. His downstairs curtain now hung very still – almost too still, if such a thing was possible.

'The main question is, did he spot us?' Heck whispered.

'I dunno . . . I just glimpsed a fraction of movement. What do you think?' Mary-Ellen asked him.

Heck held his crouch as he pondered. The house was ten yards away from them. If someone had been looking out, surely all he'd see was a darkened, foggy alley. But there was no way to be sure.

'Was he even looking?' Mary-Ellen wondered. 'Or just drawing the curtain? Could be he's taking five in there. It's been a long night for everyone.'

Heck chewed his lip.

'You're the one giving the orders,' she reminded him. 'How do you want to play it?'

Ultimately, it wasn't a difficult decision. For the first time that night, they felt empowered; they finally knew where their opponent was. Not only that, he was indoors while they were out; now *he* was the one who'd been cornered.

They were going to have to go in there, but still they waited.

'You don't suppose . . .?' Mary-Ellen began. 'Nah . . .'

'Go on.'

'You don't suppose he'd go to all this trouble . . . I mean, having us running around like blue-arsed flies, thinking the most heinous killer in Britain is here, and all the while it's just a fucking burglary? It's a ploy to strip the houses while we're hiding in the pub?'

Heck didn't take this idea completely seriously, but he gave it some thought, again wondering what the real motive behind this crime-wave might be. It was so out of the blue – and yet so unremittingly brutal. Was it really possible some schizoid had been wandering the Lake District fells and had

310

happened across this little settlement, which he'd immediately fixed on and had devised a strategy to depopulate, for no real reason? And that wasn't even considering the possibility it was the Stranger.

'None of this makes sense,' he said to himself.

'I know,' Mary-Ellen agreed. 'If he's got it in for us, why is he sitting in some cottage, letting the minutes tick by?'

'I don't mean that. I mean . . . never mind. Look, I'll do the back, you do the front.'

'What, just knock on the door?'

'Well . . . maybe check the property out first. He's obviously found a way in, so there must be a loose window or something. But come and find me before you go in the same way.'

She nodded and scuttled off. Heck waited until she'd vanished from sight, and then waited another couple of minutes just for good measure, before heaving himself up and over the wall, dropping down the other side into another semi-frozen flower bed. From here, he crawled alligator-style across the lawn. It was a slow, cautious process, and all the way his eyes were fixed on the curtained window. When he was halfway across, the hanging material twitched slightly. Not dramatically, but he saw a ripple pass through it. Heck froze on the grass – slow seconds dragged past before he glimpsed movement again, but this time it was to the left, in the corner of his vision.

Mary-Ellen had appeared in the side passage. She signalled to him.

When he reached her, she grabbed his combat jacket, hauling him into the passage. Halfway along it, the rear entrance to the house stood open by a couple of inches, blackness skulking on the other side.

'Like this when you found it?' Heck whispered.

She shook her head. 'Closed, but not locked.'

311

He slid his gloved fingers around the edge of the door, pushing it slowly open, dreading that it should suddenly creak. Fortunately the hinges proved to be well-oiled, and they slipped inside. They found themselves in a short, slant-roofed corridor under the main stair. There was an immediate scent of must and human sweat; vaguely rancid – outdoorsman Ted wasn't the cleanest chap in Cragwood Keld.

The gap at the end of the corridor opened into the hall. A pair of work-pants hung on the radiator opposite, while a donkey jacket was draped over the newel post at the foot of the stairway. Beyond that, mist swirled behind the frosted glass panel on the front door. To their right, at the other end of the hall, stood the entrance to the kitchen – and something else. A dim form, which at first looked like a motionless figure, though they soon recognised it as the shadow of a coat stand. Also on the right, on the far side of the passage, was another open door, which they expected would lead into the lounge, where the curtain had twitched.

Mary-Ellen drew her baton. Instead of snapping it out, she eased it open with her fingertips. She nudged Heck, handed him her CS canister, and they padded down the hall together, stopping one to either side of the lounge doorway.

There was a faint noise in there – like a soft, slow breathing.

Heck glanced at Mary-Ellen, bemused.

She mouthed exactly what he was thinking: 'Asleep?'

Heck was hardly able to believe it. But it sounded as if they were listening to someone snoring. He sucked in a deep breath and held it, then turned his body, stepping through into the room beyond. Mary-Ellen went with him, lithe and stealthy.

The room was so dark with the curtain drawn that it was initially difficult to see anything. They'd still expected to distinguish a humanoid form slumped in the low-slung armchair, or lying on the settee to their right.

But nobody was there.

Bewildered, Heck glanced left. Towards the front of the house, the lounge was being used as a dining room. There was a table there and some chairs, but also a few boxes, overflowing with discarded clothing. He squatted to check if someone was under the table, but spied only a forest of table and chair legs.

They could still hear it – the snoring, or breathing. Whatever it was.

Heck turned a full circle, and saw Mary-Ellen heading for the rear curtain. Immediately, it struck him that whoever was here, he'd stepped around that curtain the moment he'd heard them enter the house, and was now lying in wait.

Heck darted after her, but before he could stop her, she'd reached the material and dragged it back. With an ear-piercing squawk, Buster, Ted Haveloc's scruffy old ginger tom, flew off the cushion positioned for him under the window radiator, and streaked past them into the hall.

Their own shouts still echoed through the house as, with a resounding crash, the cat exited by the rear door. They stared dumbly at each other, before Mary-Ellen collapsed in fits of guttural giggles. Despite everything, Heck laughed too. Briefly, all concerns about stealth absented themselves.

'What a pair of pillocks,' he said, slumping onto the settee.

'Oh fuck!' she cackled. 'Your face. I'm surprised you didn't mace the poor little sod.'

'You can talk, I saw your staff go up . . . I thought you were going to brain him.'

'Some chance. Fastest cat in the Cradle, that Buster . . . shit, I should have remembered. He always sleeps under that radiator.'

'Yeah . . . well, let's not forget what we're here for,' Heck said, pulling himself back together.

Mary-Ellen made an effort too. 'Ted's Volvo's round the front. It's kaput.'

Heck nodded, having expected nothing less. 'Which just leaves Bella's BMW X5. What's the chance our resident maniac so admires expensive motors that he's left that one intact?'

'At a guess, not much?'

Heck sighed. 'We've still got to check.'

Chapter 25

The clock behind the bar in The Witch's Kettle said it was eighteen minutes past four. Only three and a half hours before daylight, but maybe several more after that before the fog cleared.

Gemma pivoted on her stool. A couple of feet away, behind the bar, Lucy was slumped forward asleep, head resting on her folded arms. Across the taproom, only lit now by the faint green glow of the low-key emergency lighting, Dulcie and Sally O'Grady were asleep on the settle, huddled against each other. Ted Haveloc sat across from them in an armchair. His back was turned, but by his slouched posture, he too was sleeping. It was the same with Burt and Mandy Fillingham and Bella and James McCarthy, both duos reclining at opposite ends of the lengthy leather sofa near the door to the vault.

Gemma yawned and stretched, and wondered how long it was since any of these couples had actually slept in each other's arms. They'd probably be surprised to find they were doing it now, but in her experience unspoken human instinct was an overriding factor in times of fear and stress, and thank God for that.

She dabbled her fingers in the glass of tap-water Lucy had served her earlier, and sprinkled it on her face. She'd been on the go now for over twenty hours, which included the torturous four and a half she'd spent on the fell. Almost certainly the arduous exercise involved up there explained the ache in her thighs, calves and back. Meanwhile, torpor was creeping up again. She was supposed to be on guard duty here. It was essential she stay awake in order to protect these people, but second by second her wakefulness was slipping away.

Gemma stood up, shook herself and rubbed more water on her face.

No one else stirred, which was probably a good thing. As their vigil had worn on, some truly ridiculous suggestions had been made; Mandy Fillingham wondering if they all ought to sit on the roof – even if the killer broke in, he would never know where they were. Gemma had replied that, in the unexpected event the killer did not possess thermal imaging and was not able to pick them off the roof with embarrassing ease, hypothermia would have less of a problem. Burt Fillingham had agreed with Gemma that his wife was talking 'ludicrous crap', though Gemma hadn't actually used that term, and suggested they go on the offensive instead: smash up the furniture, arm themselves with clubs and charge from house to house, banging on doors, shouting, trying to smoke the guy out. It hadn't taken Gemma to remind him the average bullet would be more than a match for a broken chair leg; Ted Haveloc had made that contribution, pretty scathingly.

At this point Gemma had intervened, advising them to keep the noise down and stay focused on the real problem, which was the dangerous individual outside. Twenty minutes had passed since then, and everyone now was snoozing – aside from Gemma.

She patrolled the downstairs, visiting each and every room, including both sets of toilets, checking every window, occasionally stealing a peek from behind the closed drapes, seeing only the monotone blankness of the fog.

At length, she ventured upstairs, the creak of each tread amplified in the deep quiet. At the top, a single passage ran the full length of the building, various rooms leading off it, all standing open and in darkness. She proceeded slowly, poking her head into each one separately, but always waiting for her eyes to attune before entering to check the window. In most cases, with the exception of Hazel's flat, they contained nothing more than a sideboard, an armchair and a bed, so it wasn't like there were many hiding places. Even so, it was a far from agreeable experience, evoking memories of her days as a young constable in Limehouse, where she'd spent many a night shift property-checking at the backs of shopping precincts, along rows of garages or underground lock-ups, or among the sheds on desolate urban allotments. This had been as much to fill the long, lonely hours as anything else, though occasionally she'd discovered a break-in or the odd tramp or junkie dossing where he shouldn't. Of course, it had never entered her head that she might be about to encounter a deranged killer.

Even now, such thoughts only occurred to Gemma as she approached the bedroom at the far end of the passage, the one with the broken window-catch. Partly this was because it struck her that, in all the fuss, they'd forgotten to nail that offending window shut – but primarily it was because for some reason the door to that bedroom was now closed.

She halted in front of it, wondering if it had been closed the last time they'd looked, which had been at least an hour ago. Her memory was too fogged by fatigue to recall accurately. But it didn't make sense that this door had been left closed while all the others were open.

She glanced behind her. The corridor dwindled through darkness to the top of the stairs, where only a very faint ambient light filtered up from below. The complete silence down there suggested no one was going to come to her aid quickly if she called out. She turned back to the closed door, remembering the door in Fellstead Grange, how it had virtually been blasted from its hinges. When she'd told Heck earlier there was at least the same chance the perpetrator would attack the pub as there was he'd attack them, she'd meant it truthfully, but perhaps deep down she hadn't held it as a real and conscious fear. But now . . .?

'Oh sod it!' Gemma blurted, reaching out a weary hand, depressing the handle and pushing the door open, exposing the pitch-darkness beyond.

She wondered what she would do if the window was wide open, but it wasn't – and neither was there anybody in there, at least nobody she could see.

She circled around the neatly made bed, dropped to her knees to glance underneath it – even though she was barely able to see anything down there – and even checked in the wardrobe, which was the same, though at least she was able to grope around inside, hands bashing the empty coat-hangers. Feeling ridiculous, and relieved she hadn't called one of the civvies to assist, she closed the room up again, this time making a mental note that she *had* shut the door, and sloped back along the landing and down the stairs.

Everyone was still asleep, so she lifted the hatch and passed through the bar, intending to get herself another glass of water.

It was in the kitchen where she had her next fright. She was at the sink, filling a glass, when she sensed someone behind her. She spun wildly around – to find Hazel sitting bleary eyed on the floor against the units at the other side of the room, knees drawn up under her chin.

'You gave me a turn,' Gemma said.

'No sign of Heck or M-E?'

'I wouldn't expect them for some time yet.'

'If ever.'

Gemma sipped water. 'I understand your concern, Hazel, but pit some demented gunman with loads of ammunition and the biggest grudge going – against Heck, with no gun, no wheels, no idea who he's up against . . . I still make it even money. And that's not taking into account Mary-Ellen, who's just about the most efficient and energetic uniform I've come across in quite some time.'

'Nice speech. I appreciate the attempt to reassure me.'

'Well that's partly what I'm doing, but there's no reason to despair. They're both good at their jobs, and however late they are, we've still got a firearms unit en route.'

Hazel nodded tiredly, as if that was of no consequence at all. 'Everything alright upstairs?'

'Won't deny that I freaked myself out a little bit . . . but basically, yeah. How come you've not got your head down?'

'Don't know how anyone can sleep, to be honest. Mind you, they didn't see what we saw up at Fellstead Grange, did they?' Hazel struggled to suppress a shudder. 'I know I look like shit, Gemma, but there's no way my eyelids are closing tonight.'

'Laudable ambition.' Gemma placed her glass of water on the unit, and then slid down until she too was seated on the floor. She yawned. 'You have my full permission to extend it to me if you catch me nodding off – give me a good hard dig in the ribs.'

Chapter 26

'Bit more excitement than we've been used to, eh?' Mary-Ellen whispered.

'Yep,' Heck said, equally quietly, ensuring he was flat against the wall behind him. 'I'd almost forgotten how much fun all this stuff was.'

They were waiting just around the corner from Truscott Drive. Only a few dozen yards north of their position, on the opposite side, was the turn into Baytree Court. This was the small cul-de-sac that constituted the village's most westerly residential road. There were three holiday cottages along there, but dominating the turning circle at its end was a large detached house belonging to the McCarthys.

Heck wasn't sure why, but the sense of impending threat he'd felt before they'd entered Ted Haveloc's place seemed to have dissipated, though that wasn't necessarily a good thing. The incident with the cat had certainly lightened the mood, but it might also have created a false sense of security. If anything, the squawking beast could have alerted the madman to their presence on the village streets – if he wasn't already aware of that. They thus held their position a little longer, waiting and watching.

'Any ideas yet?' she wondered.

'Lots,' he said. 'None that make sense.'

'Changed your mind about the Stranger?'

'My mind's never actually been made up on that. I think the Stranger's the key to all this. But whether the Stranger is the perp is another matter.'

'Don't get you?' Mary-Ellen replied.

Heck pondered again. 'First, I thought it was a hell of a coincidence, me being up here and the Stranger turning up as well. I mean, I wasn't involved in the original investigation. But it was a near-certainty I'd recognise the whistling . . .'

'Admittedly, that would be a *real* coincidence. And a lucky break for us.'

'Unless it's been contrived,' Heck said. 'Unless I was *supposed* to recognise it and conclude we were dealing with the Stranger. Because if I did, what was the next thing I was going to do?'

'Call for supervision and support, I suppose.'

'Of course, but this very convenient fog has prevented any of that arriving.'

'Heck, whoever this guy is, he can't control the weather . . .'

'No, but he can control his own timetable . . . like watch the weather forecasts and wait for some really bad stuff to come along before he kicks everything off.'

She mused on that.

'So what would I do next?' Heck said.

'Well . . . call DSU Piper.'

'That's right. Gemma was a key investigator on the original case. She even fired the fatal shot . . . assuming it *was* fatal. You don't get much more involved than that.'

He set off walking, heading diagonally across the road towards Baytree Court.

Mary-Ellen scurried to catch up. 'You think this whole thing's been what, a ruse . . . to bring Gemma up here where he can attack her? Does that fit the Stranger's profile? Would he still be looking for revenge ten years later?'

Heck shrugged. 'We don't have any kind of profile for him. Except that we had him down as a local man who worked outdoors. And we know for sure that at least one of those assumptions was wrong . . . he turned out to be a Scot. From his build, his voice, his manner, Gemma reckoned he was a husky bloke . . . but she also reckoned he wasn't a young man. Now okay, I don't know how accurate that assessment could be . . . he was in heavy clothing and it was dark, but sometimes it's the way people breathe, the way they position their body.'

'Well if it's true he wasn't young, say he was middle-aged, and this was ten years ago, how could he be running all over the fells like a March hare now?'

'Exactly my point.'

'Plus he might have suffered severe damage from the gunshot.'

'That too.'

'But Heck, if it isn't the Stranger . . .?'

'Shit!' he hissed.

They were only halfway along the short cul-de-sac that was Baytree Court, but already that was close enough to see that Bella McCarthy's BMW X5, which was parked outside the front of her house, had also been disabled. Only tatters remained of its tyres, and its bonnet had been jacked open.

'That's that,' Heck said irritably.

'I suppose we should have expected it.'

'Yeah . . . let's get back.'

They returned to Truscott Drive, walking quickly.

'Heck, if it isn't the Stranger,' Mary-Ellen said again, 'who the bloody hell . . .?'

Ptchuuung!

The shot was fired from somewhere to their left.

322

The first they heard of it was the ricochet from the road surface, because even though the gun was fired from close range, it had been silenced. Instinctively, Heck ducked towards the nearest line of brush, which lay on the right. He crashed through it and threw himself onto his face, and only then noticed that Mary-Ellen hadn't followed.

He glanced over his shoulder.

She was still in the middle of the road, crouched but apparently frozen rigid.

'M-E, get over here!' he hissed.

This jerked her into action, panic driving her onward up the road rather than across it towards him. A second later, the fog had enveloped her, but he heard her feet hammering away into the distance.

'M-E!' he hissed again, pointlessly, as she was almost certainly out of earshot.

Somebody else wasn't.

There was a second *pop*, and a slug tore through the leafage just above his head. A third followed, smashing a branch about three inches from his right ear.

Heck scrambled further from the road, unavoidably threshing twigs and mulch, but remained on his belly, propelling himself with his elbows and his knees. Several yards later, he halted, holding his breath, fresh sweat streaming from his brow.

Now there was silence.

Several seconds passed before he rolled onto his back, knelt up and coiled his legs beneath him so that he could spring to his feet. But instead, he waited again. He was deep amid the foggy trees, but though he'd gone to ground left of the blacktop, he'd now been turned around a couple of times so he didn't know which direction was which, only that he was somewhere in the extensive triangle of woodland between Truscott Drive and Cragwood Road.

Still, there was no sound. But it was impossible not to imagine the killer wasn't somewhere very close. Perhaps inevitably, Heck's ears began to play tricks. Was that the faint shuffle of someone moving slowly through the vegetation about twenty yards to his left? Was that almost imperceptible *click* over on his right the cracking of a twig, or the cocking of a firearm?

Heck hunkered down as low as possible, eyes scanning the unfathomable vapour, reminding himself that even if he *did* hear something, he was deep in the heart of nature. Just because there was a madman on the loose, that didn't mean animals wouldn't forage, birds wouldn't flutter.

More sweat dripped from his forehead as he held his ground.

The seconds became minutes, which in their turn became tens of minutes. But Heck remained alert, twirling at the slightest hint he might not be alone. In normal circumstances, he'd gradually get used to the dark, his natural night-vision soon penetrating the deepest corners of the woodland, but the fog refused to surrender its secrets. He wondered where Mary-Ellen was and if she might have been been hit. The guy hadn't followed her – at least not initially, as he'd hung around to peg another two off at Heck. Of course, if he was now using a silencer, Heck wouldn't know whether or not he'd gone after her later, firing off more rounds.

That in itself was confusing. Why had the son of a bitch started using a silencer? He hadn't been concerned to conceal his gunfire when he was up on the fells. Unless that was all part of his game?

There was a rustle of undergrowth somewhere to Heck's rear.

He manoeuvred himself around again, muscles tensioned like coiled springs. Something was definitely happening just beyond the scope of his vision. The killer was prowling, searching out his victims. It *had* to be him. It could *not* be anything else. For which reason, Heck determined to stay where he was. If the maniac *was* in his vicinity, as soon as he broke cover a thermal imager would locate and target him easily and cleanly. Several times again, he fancied he heard motion, and yet when he glanced at his watch he saw that forty minutes had now elapsed since he'd gone to ground. Surely, if the killer knew where he was, there'd be no reason to let him sit here?

Slowly, quietly as he could, Heck started forward, still moving at a crouch, leaves and twigs barely rustling as he slid past them – only to realise, some twenty-five yards later, that he wasn't headed back for the road.

He halted again, trying to think.

And a black-gloved hand clapped his shoulder.

Inadvertently, Heck gave a hoarse yelp. He twisted around, but another hand clapped across his mouth and forced him backward to the dirt, a strong body pressing on top of him.

'Shhhhhh!' Mary-Ellen hissed into his ear.

'What the hell?' he spluttered. 'Jesus, you almost gave me a coronary!'

'Heck, this guy's a fucking lunatic!'

'No shit, Sherlock . . .'

'No, listen!' Her bright green eyes bugged almost unnaturally. Her face had turned waxy-pale. 'There's a marked police car about seventy yards from here, just off Cragwood Road. Half-hidden in the undergrowth.'

'A marked car . . . anyone inside it?'

She nodded dumbly. 'I think it's the firearms team.'

By her tone alone, he knew this wasn't going to be good.

Chapter 27

'You must see this kind of thing all the time?' Hazel asked.

They were seated opposite each other at the kitchen table, stirring mugs of tea. Gemma watched quietly as Hazel rubbed at her brow. Now the pub landlady had had some time to reflect on the events of earlier, she almost looked dazed. For a second or two, fresh tears had trickled from her eyes.

'I suppose the answer you want, Hazel, is "yeah, sure . . . but we always get the right result in the end".' Gemma shrugged. 'Thankfully, this kind of extremely violent psychopath is a rarity. Most of the criminals we encounter are desperate nobodies who've just lost their way in life.'

Hazel arched a scornful eyebrow. 'So they murder people as a solution?'

'The majority don't murder anyone. Even hardened career criminals basically want an easy time. They're a bunch of pathetic losers who haven't got the personal integrity to do any work. They prefer to acquire stuff they want by taking it from others, be it money, property, sexual gratification, personal dignity. But ultimately, they all pay for it. They do long stretches inside, they get criminal records that'll hang around their necks for the rest of their lives, preventing them ever getting a proper job, a bank loan, or ever being able to live anywhere again without the police knocking on their door each time there's an incident. I mean, they come out of jail acting the big "I am", but the reality is they've been shagged in the showers, got a habit they won't shake off easily, and the only people who still know them are the last guys on Earth you'd ever want to be your mates.'

'But we're not talking about those people, are we?' Hazel said. 'Not up here. Not tonight. We're talking about that other small per cent: the weirdos, the aberrations.'

'We don't know *what* we're dealing with here, Hazel. Truth is, we never really knew what we were dealing with during the Stranger enquiry. Our psychological profile was way off . . .'

'You think it could be the same person? Seriously? After all this time?'

Hazel wasn't sure what response she hoped to get. Whoever it was out there, they were doing horrible things, but the thought it might be some kind of monster from the distant past was somehow even more disturbing, perhaps because it hinted at an unnatural longevity.

Gemma shrugged again, affecting an air of nonchalance – the public always felt safer if their police officers were calm and analytical.

'It could be the same person. The evidence suggests it is. But common sense says something else. The real issues at present are not who he is, but *what* he is . . . why is he doing this? How much is he actually capable of? Will he decide enough's enough, or just carry on? I'm sorry . . . for all my experience, I just don't know.'

Hazel nodded and sniffled. Gemma noted that her earlier tears had been short-lived. She'd endured a terrible experience this night, the sort few civilians could emerge from unscathed, but thus far at least she was on top of it.

'I never thought this kind of thing would ever come up here,' Hazel said. 'I mean don't get me wrong, the Lake District isn't Fairy Land . . . we have problems up here, of course we do. But people murdered in their homes, a madman roaming the fog!'

'Like you called it before, it's an aberration. It probably won't happen again in your lifetime.'

'But it shows how fragile the world is, doesn't it? Every morning, I get up and go outside. I see the tarn lying flat as a millpond, reflecting the sky and the clouds. I see our beautiful mountains. The stillness, the serenity. It feels so good to be alive. But is all that a façade? Is it just a pretty smokescreen?'

Gemma leaned forward. 'Hazel, I've dealt with hundreds of murders, rapes, woundings . . . and I've met thousands of victims. I'll say to you what I always say to them: it happened, it's real, we can't pretend otherwise, but don't be frightened to enjoy life just because of this. The moment you do that, these petty, inadequate bastards have won.'

'I won't be frightened,' Hazel said, perhaps not looking totally convinced. 'When it's over, I mean. At least, I don't think I will. I'm not a coward, Gemma.'

'Never said you were.'

'I'm not easily scared . . .'

'You proved that when you went up to the farm.'

'I don't know . . . maybe. I'm a fighter by origin. My dad, Will, was a farm-hand who worked every hour God sent, labouring in all kinds of weather. His older brother was Jim Barrett. Played loose forward for Workington Town . . . they used to call him "the Mangler". Once smashed the Australian Rugby League captain's jaw in an absolute bloodbath of a Test match in Sydney. That's my line of descent, Gemma. But, hell . . .' Hazel paused long and hard. 'After tonight I'll feel a little bit safer if Mark's here too.'

'Heck is a handy guy to have around,' Gemma admitted. 'But he's no white knight. You need to know that.'

'I do know it.'

'He's always got his own agenda – though some would call it an "obsession" – and it rarely involves anyone else.'

'I also know he's going to leave at some point. Or he's contemplating leaving . . .?'

Gemma shrugged as if she couldn't help with this.

'I heard everything you said about him earlier,' Hazel said. 'Marooning himself up here to punish you, cutting off his nose to spite his face and all that. And I've no reason to disbelieve any of it. But at some point soon he's going to make a decision. The thing is . . .' her tone became earnest, 'now that *you're* here, Gemma, there's no conceivable way you won't be part of it.'

'That's not why I'm . . .'

'*Why* you're here is irrelevant. When a guy talks about a previous girl in his life as much as Mark does about you, that's not because you were just friends. He's a warrior, and I can see you are as well. And that's got to be an enormous attraction to him . . . even if he won't admit it to himself. So he's going to make his decision, and you'll be part of it.'

'Okay.' Gemma sat back tiredly, sensing the ball was still in her court. 'What do you want me to do?'

'If you want to offer him his old job back because you value his work, you want a good man on your team . . . that's okay. I can't quibble with that. But please guarantee me one thing. That you're not going to offer him something you can't or, after what you were saying up on the fell, *won't* deliver. Please give me that guarantee, Gemma. Because it'd hardly be fair on Mark, would it?'

Gemma eyed her with fascination. 'Heck doesn't bloody deserve you, Hazel.'

Before Hazel could respond, there was a thunderous

knocking on the pub's front door. They stared at each other blankly, then struggled to their feet. By the time they'd entered the taproom, all the others had woken. Burt Fillingham and Ted Haveloc were already at the door.

'Who is it?' the postmaster asked through the wood.

'McGurk,' came a muffled voice. 'PC McGurk . . . I need either PC O'Rourke or DS Heckenburg.'

'Why?' Fillingham asked.

'Just open the sodding door, alright!'

'It's okay, thank you, Mr Fillingham,' Gemma said, sliding past and turning the lock, but ensuring to keep the door on its chain, only releasing this when she saw McGurk outside. He was bug-eyed and rubbing tiredly at the back of his neck.

'What's the problem?' she asked.

'I'll tell you wha' the problem is, ma'am . . . the power's out up at the nick.'

'What . . . a full blackout?'

'Yeah, the whole thing's gone. I'm not so bothered about the lights, because I'm not using them anyway. But the electric heaters are on the same circuits, so it's like a deep freeze inside there, and it's getting worse . . .'

'Mark's said that's happened before,' Hazel said, appearing at Gemma's shoulder. 'It was designed to be a house not a police station, so the circuits get overloaded.'

'Whatever, it's pitch-dark and I can't find the breakers,' McGurk replied.

'The breakers will be in the cellar,' Burt Fillingham said, standing close by. 'It's the same all over the village. There's a cellar underneath, and all the circuits and meters and such are down there. But if it's anything like our house, you can't get into it through the actual building. There'll be a doorway around the back.'

'Same at my place,' Ted Haveloc agreed. 'But it won't be easy to find in the dark.'

'I'll find it,' McGurk said. 'Cheers . . .'

He backed away, but Gemma followed him out, pulling on her coat. 'I'll come with you.'

'It's okay, ma'am . . .'

'No, two pairs of eyes are better than one.' She glanced at the half-open pub door, and then specifically at Hazel, who seemed the most likely to assume an effective leadership role in her absence. 'You guys going to be alright for a couple of minutes?'

Hazel simply nodded.

The door banged closed, and Gemma and McGurk set off up Truscott Drive.

'No disrespect, ma'am, but I don't need babysitting,' he muttered.

'We've already lost one officer tonight. What kind of guv'nor would I be if I sent another one into a dangerous situation alone?'

'I'm looking for a switch so I can turn the power on. Hardly gonna be dangerous.'

'That depends on how the power was turned off, doesn't it? How long before you realised, anyway? You look frozen.'

'I don't know. But I'm alright.'

She believed that, even though he *did* look frozen. McGurk might be a taciturn individual, but there was something vaguely elemental about him. He had granite features, a burly, apelike stance. As he walked now, he'd hunched forward, hands thrust into his pockets as if this whole late-night business at Cragwood Keld was more a personal inconvenience than a ferocious crime-spree that had claimed five lives. Presumably this owed to his past as a Royal Marine and combat veteran. In some ways it was reassuring he could be so fearless, but though he'd actually said very little since she'd first met him – that exchange at the pub door had been the first proper conversation they'd had – Gemma couldn't help thinking there were deep, dark currents inside McGurk.

'I'm guessing you've seen a bit of action?' she said.

He shrugged. 'Some.'

'Comrades getting slotted left, right and centre?'

'Some.'

It was difficult, if not impossible, to read anything into such determinedly monosyllabic responses.

'Well I don't need to remind you of all people about procedure when an offender's carrying firearms,' she said. 'But let's remember . . . Heggarty got shot through the head from point-blank range. This suspect is for real.'

'We'll see how real he is, ma'am, when I get my hands on him.' That was the closest thing to an emotional statement she'd heard from McGurk all night, though again it was delivered in a flat monotone that was vaguely unnerving.

She remembered the unconfirmed story that McGurk had been demoted from the rank of detective sergeant for ill-treating prisoners. She thought about those numerous members of the military who'd also been disciplined for this kind of offence, and she wondered if McGurk had only been continuing a habit he'd picked up in the theatre of war. She also wondered what this kind of thing revealed about a man's character. Did he not handle tough experiences well, or was it more a case that life in the security services gave him opportunities he wouldn't otherwise have to do exactly what lurked in his nature?

You could never tell at first glance, especially with a laconic figure like Mick McGurk.

Chapter 28

Heck and Mary-Ellen moved through the wood for about seventy yards, though it might have been further. Mary-Ellen admitted that she'd only guessed the actual distance. The first they saw of the wrecked police car were rotating spears of misted blue light flickering through the undergrowth.

They slowed down as they approached.

The vehicle, which was about three yards off the blacktop on this side of Cragwood Road, thinly concealed by leafy branches, was exactly as Mary-Ellen had described: a Ford Focus bearing Cumbria Constabulary markings, with extra roof details to indicate it was an armed response car. It was now sitting on four flat tyres.

Almost immediately an answer to one of Heck's earlier questions struck him. Why had the killer not used a silencer before? Maybe because he hadn't been able to – until a police firearms unit had provided him with all the additional kit he needed.

As with most of the other vehicles, the car's tyres looked as if they'd been repeatedly sliced, reducing them to ribbons, negating any possibility it could be driven anywhere else.

Up close, Heck noticed the front passenger window had been powered down. Someone had probably appeared on the verge, waving to the vehicle as it had cruised through the fog. It had braked alongside them. Down went the panel as the firearms lads sought an explanation. *Bang bang bang* went the assassin's gun.

Heck stuck his head inside.

It was another abattoir, blood and brain spatter streaking the dashboard, the upholstery, the insides of all the windows, even the ceiling. The officer in the passenger seat, a youngish, stocky guy with a shaven head, had taken one in the left temple and one in the throat. The officer behind the wheel looked about the same age, but was slimmer; his face was unrecognisable because most of it had been blown away. There was one other officer in the back, an older man with a mop of iron-grey hair. He'd taken one in the forehead and one through the cheek.

Head-shots in all cases, Heck noted. So the killer had expected an armed response, and had acted accordingly, even allowing for the body-armour they'd be wearing. He leaned further in, resisting the temptation to open the door and interfere with yet another crime scene. Despite the half-dark, he could see empty pistol holsters. He glanced towards the boot, realising it had been jacked open. No doubt the strongbox in there, used to transport additional arms and ammunition, would also have been pillaged.

'Funny thing,' Mary-Ellen said, sounding subdued. 'Me, Gemma and Hazel walked down this road only two and a half hours ago . . . and, well, we didn't notice this.'

'Would you have noticed in the dark and the fog?' Heck wondered. 'With the blue light switched off?'

'Probably not if the beacon was off, no.'

'That'll explain it. If this ambush had happened since you came past, we'd have heard the shots.'

Unless of course, the gunman had had access to a silencer *before* he'd launched this ambush. Heck no longer knew what to think on that score. He leaned further in and assessed several of the blood dribbles down the inside of the windshield. They'd congealed to the point where they were cracking and flaking.

'No,' he said slowly. 'This incident happened quite a bit earlier. These lads got bushwhacked a good while ago. The car was then pushed into the bushes so they were out the way in time for you lot to walk innocently past. The beacon's only been switched on in the last hour or so.'

'Why?'

'Presumably to ensure that this time we found it.'

'Found it?' Mary-Ellen sounded incredulous. 'Again . . . why?'

Heck shook his head. 'To let us know what our fate is going to be. And that now no one is coming to prevent it.'

Only the darkened outline of the police station was visible as McGurk and Gemma stumped towards it. They switched their torches on as they strode up the path, but with no power now to utilise, the key-pad was no longer functioning on the personnel door at the side.

'Great, now we're locked out of our own nick,' Gemma said quietly.

If McGurk felt any responsibility for this, he didn't show it. 'They said we could get into the cellar from the outside, didn't they?'

They followed the drive to the back of the building, the area that had once been a garden but was now an impromptu storage space for boxes, tyres and traffic cones. They searched the immediate area, but saw no entrance that might lead

335

down to a cellar. McGurk shone his torch through an open door into the rear of the garage, which stood to the right. More bits and pieces met their gaze: a couple of rusty bicycles, and some ropes and harnesses that might be used in mountaineering, various spare parts for cars, plus several rolls of fibreglass lagging.

'What's all this for?' Gemma toed the nearest roll. 'Attic need insulating, or something?'

'That'll be for winter,' McGurk replied. 'It's bad enough now, but get into December, January and February, ma'am, and it doesn't get much over zero at this height. They get feet of snow as well . . . any time up to April.'

A row of Calor Gas bottles stood against the far wall. They were made from moulded steel and beige in colour. The stencilled lettering on each one read:

3.9 kg Propane

'Propane?' she said.

'Empty, most probably.' McGurk pushed one of the canisters over. It rolled across the garage with a series of hollow clanks. 'Yeah. Again, they're for winter. Pipes freeze up here, power lines come down. You can end up with no heating, so a lot of the villagers in these isolated communities keep propane cylinders for gas appliances. There'll be more of these in the cellar. Full ones.'

'Interesting . . . if we could find it.' They wandered again into the main storage area, spearing their lights back and forth. This time, Gemma's beam alighted on a heap of bulging bin-liners at the southwest corner of the building. They wandered over there, threw some bags aside and exposed a small, letterbox-type window at ground level, its frosted glass thick with grime. 'At least we know there *is* a cellar,' Gemma said. 'Won't be easy wriggling in though . . .'

'Door's here, ma'am.'

McGurk had worked his way past the bin-bags to find a partially concealed recess just around the corner. The cellar door was set inside that. When McGurk tested it, it wasn't locked. Beyond it, a flight of concrete steps dropped into darkness. He shone his torch down, illuminating another single door at the bottom. This one resembled a fire door; it was made from heavy oak with rubber seals around its trims.

'Bingo,' Gemma said – and then she glanced once over her shoulder. It had suddenly occurred to her that, during the course of their search, they'd neglected to keep a look-out for company. But the storage yard lay as dingy and motionless as they'd found it. There was still no sound in the foggy night.

'You don't feel a bit exposed out here?' Mary-Ellen wondered.

Heck was busy circling the firearms car, shooting as much footage with Mary-Ellen's mobile phone as he could, both inside and out, and at the same time relaying his on-the-spot observations. He glanced around at Mary-Ellen. She was standing rigidly a couple of feet away, breathing painfully, almost wheezing – clearly it wasn't just the revolving blue light that left her a little off-colour. Only now did it strike him that the young policewoman hadn't attended any other of the murder scenes in the Cradle thus far. In fact, she was only twenty-three and had done about four years in the job, so she couldn't have attended too many murder scenes during her service. Almost certainly none involving the mass slaughter of fellow officers.

Mary-Ellen prided herself on being an energetic and resourceful cop, mentally strong and physically tough. But clearly and very abruptly, she'd discovered the limit of that toughness. And she wasn't wrong about their vulnerable position either. Standing out here in this misty woodland, bathed in bright light, talking aloud – it struck Heck that he might have got too absorbed in preserving the crime scene.

'You're right,' he said, handing her the phone. 'Time to get back, perhaps. Our pal's a bloody lunatic, but he's also clever. The only way out of the Cradle before daylight now is to walk, and we're hardly likely to try that after seeing this.'

'So not only is no help coming,' she said, 'we're not getting out of here under our own steam either.'

'No.' He pushed on through the undergrowth, heading back the way they'd come. 'Best go and break the bad news.'

They descended the cellar steps with McGurk at the front and Gemma following close behind. She'd entered numerous dark, dank buildings in this way, but it never ceased to amaze her how such a confined space could swallow up so much light. Both their torch-beams had retracted into brilliant dots on the closed door below them.

And yet, she didn't think this was the reason why she suddenly felt uncomfortable. It puzzled her. If anything, she should feel good. All they had to do now was push the breakers back into line, and the job was a good 'un. Heck would be back soon, maybe the firearms team as well. Then the odds would be back in their favour.

But wasn't all this a little too easy?

Where was the killer while these measures were being taken?

She only voiced this fear when a sudden, sour odour pricked her nostrils.

'McGurk!'

McGurk's nose also wrinkled – as he pushed the door at the bottom open.

'*No!*' Gemma shouted.

In the flashing torchlight, she caught a fleeting glimpse of the five or six matchboxes that had been taped together along the door-jamb. She didn't see the two dozen matches taped to the door itself, only heard them striking as they swept over the boxes' coarse outer surfaces.

Heck and Gemma had progressed forty yards back through the woods when they heard a dull but resounding *CRUMP* from the direction of Cragwood Keld.

They stopped short, glancing around at each other.

Heck was long enough served to know exactly what he'd just heard, while Mary-Ellen, though a junior officer compared to Heck, had seen plenty of war movies. They could both of them identify the distant tone of a powerful explosion.

Chapter 29

Heck and Mary-Ellen threw caution to the wind as they sprinted back through the foggy woods towards Cragwood Keld. Long before they got there, even deep amid branches so tangled they managed to lose sight of each other, they could see the wavering glow of a huge fire some distance ahead.

When Heck finally staggered, panting, into Hetherby Close, he found that Hazel and the rest of the villagers had also discarded concern for their personal safety and were milling all over the pile of burning rubble where the police station had once stood.

He advanced into the chaos, goggle-eyed.

Up close, the debris mainly consisted of shattered timbers and scorched bricks, and had heaped itself around a central crater – what had once been the cellar – from out of which cloying black smoke was pouring.

'What happened?' Heck shouted, wafting his way back and forth. He snatched at someone. But it was dizzy old Sally O'Grady, who could only respond by shaking her head and fixing him with a fishlike stare, her cheeks blackened with soot.

'What happened?' he said, blundering over the hot wreckage to the next figure. This was Hazel. She too was in a state of stupefaction. He grabbed her by the wrists. 'Hazel, what happened?'

'I . . . I don't know.' She shook her head. 'We just heard it . . . and now the whole building's gone.'

'I can bloody see that!'

'Mark . . . Gemma was in there.'

'*What?*'

Hazel's red-rimmed eyes filled with tears. 'And PC McGurk.'

'*Gemma . . .?*'

'There was a power cut at the station, and they came up here to try and fix it.'

At first Heck played it cool, determined to show no obvious distress. And that wasn't difficult because Gemma wouldn't have been in there, she couldn't have been. There was no way Gemma would have been . . . in *there*.

'*Mark!*' Hazel shrieked as he tore himself away.

He flung himself up and over the nearest embankment. His throat was too raw from the smoke for him to scream Gemma's name as he staggered down into the pit at the heart of the conflagration. More rubble lay scattered, though very little was identifiable. A few warped fragments of blistered metal were all that remained of the propane tanks, but there were puddles of fire between them, which Heck knew defied the laws of nature – unless they were eating up the remnants of spilled petrol.

The propane canisters *and* petrol.

Someone had done a number on them this time, alright.

'Gemma!' he cried, meandering through the flames, the intense heat drying the sweat on his face, searing his skin, the smoke filling his lungs, causing him to retch. 'Gemma! Christ almighty, don't you dare do a runner on me . . .'

341

A muffled moan sounded in response.

He spun around. 'Gemma . . .?'

'Heck,' a voice croaked. It was breathless, pained beyond belief.

He spun again, and fleetingly, through billows of smoke, spied two pillars of blackened concrete in the far southwest corner; all that was left of the cellar's reinforced door-frame.

Heck scooted over there, kicking flaming planks aside.

Beyond the gateposts, a concrete stair led upward. There was no roof above it anymore, no walls to either side; most of the stair itself was buried in bricks and masonry. But right at the foot of it lay the smouldering hulk of a heavy oaken door. More to the point, it was shifting slightly, as if something was pinned underneath.

Heck took hold of the wood. Its edges were ragged, glowing embers, and his fingers were scalded even through his gloves, but the strength of desperation was a potent force. Shoulders straining, he heaved the door up and tossed it behind him. But his gut lurched when he saw what lay underneath it: a hideous mess of broken limbs and charred flesh.

A choked whimper escaped from him. But his eyes were attuning fast to the dense smoke and crimson firelight, and as he blinked away tears, what at first had looked like a single person reduced to a mangled, faceless horror, slowly resolved itself into two people, both thick with dust and debris; one lying over the top of the other, back turned upward – which explained the lack of face. The POLICE insignia stencilled into the partially melted hi-viz slicker revealed that this was McGurk.

If the burly Scot had been wearing his hat at the time, he no longer was now – his bull-neck and the back of his head were not just singed black, they were thickly bloodied. Presumably they'd taken the brunt of the impact as the door flew from its hinges. Heck hunkered down and felt at the side of the PC's neck. There was a pulse, but the injured cop was lifeless, a deadweight. It didn't stop Heck hauling him off to get to the person underneath. This one was equally coated in dust and dirt, but more animated, coughing and writhing as she struggled to breathe.

'Thank God,' he said, slumping down onto his knees. 'Oh, thank God . . .'

'Oh hell, Heck . . .' Gemma coughed again, hawking out wads of gritty saliva. Her face too was a mask of dirt and blood, but her focused gaze indicated full consciousness.

'Don't try to move,' he advised.

'I'm . . . I'm alright.' She tried to get up.

'Yeah, but just be careful . . .'

'Ow, shit . . . *I'm not alright!*' She stiffened in agony. 'My back . . .'

'Is it bad?'

'Just a bang, I think.' She wriggled where she lay, grimacing again, and then eased herself up into an awkward sitting posture. 'Hell of a bang . . .'

'This whole thing went with a hell of a bang. Must have slammed you back onto those concrete steps like a bundle of laundry.'

'McGurk?' Gemma asked.

Heck turned to the dusty figure lying motionless alongside them. 'He's alive. And it's a bloody miracle. Good job this was a heavy door.'

Gemma mopped a sleeve of grimy sweat from her brow. 'Propane, yeah?'

'Yeah. Some maniac must have opened the valves on all the cylinders.' Heck glanced around. Treacly-black smoke still snaked from several pools of liquid fire, wreathing into the mist topside to create a hellish, stinking smog. 'Looks like he doused the floor with petrol as well. Turned the whole nick into a time-bomb.'

There was a clatter of bricks as Hazel scrambled down the side of the crater. The other villagers were now gathered along the top. Heck's gaze roved across them. Despite everything, it was important to remember the civvies they were trying to protect here. Thankfully, it looked as if all were present and correct.

McGurk now stirred, giving a dull groan.

'Mary-Ellen!' Heck called. 'I need you.' There was no response. He glanced up, expecting to see her hastening down the brick slope towards him. But nobody moved among the spectators along the rim. *'M-E!'*

'I didn't see her with you,' Hazel stammered. 'You arrived here on your own.'

'She was right behind me when we were back in the trees.'

'I didn't see her.'

Heck was about to let forth on the subject of people doing disappearing acts just as you needed them most, when he was distracted by a louder groan from McGurk, who now tried to turn over.

'Lie still,' Gemma instructed, leaning across the injured cop and prodding at the side of his neck, as if to assure herself that Heck's diagnosis hadn't been wrong.

McGurk lay still again, breathing slowly but heavily.

'Nightmare scenario, this,' Gemma said. 'He could have a dozen broken bones that need immobilising . . . but we can't leave him here.'

'Agreed,' Heck replied. 'We need to get him back to the pub. If we do more damage to him en route, we apologise afterwards.'

Even so, they checked McGurk over quickly before moving him. The workable first-aid knowledge all police officers were

344

required to possess didn't come close to matching that of qualified medical personnel, but it was frequently the only thing available in situations like this. Aside from a deep, nasty gash zigzagging across the back of McGurk's head, which was responsible for most of the blood and for his groggy state, he wasn't manifesting any other obvious injuries.

'Good enough to go, I reckon,' Heck said.

Gemma winced as they tried to lift the guy upright.

'Here,' Hazel said, stepping in. 'Let me.'

The casualty groaned all the more. His face was unrecognisable it was so black, but mainly this was soot adhering to congealed blood.

'How the devil could this bastard benefit from blowing up the police station?' Gemma wondered, as Heck lifted the casualty's left arm over Hazel's shoulders, and then manoeuvred the right one over his own.

'Hard to say, but he probably set it up earlier . . . a lot earlier,' Heck said. 'Might have thought we'd pack all the villagers in there for safekeeping. Alternatively, he might just have wanted to wipe the cops out . . .'

'I thought he liked to get hands-on,' she said, limping after them as they sidled clumsily up the steps, McGurk's booted feet dragging.

'Seems to be a jack of all trades,' Heck grunted. 'Where the hell is Mary-Ellen?'

'I told you, I haven't seen her,' Hazel said. She too was smoky-faced, tears smudged down her cheeks.

'Wha' . . . the fuck happened?' McGurk mumbled. He was slowly becoming coherent, but his head drooped onto his chest as though his own bodyweight was pulling him down. The ex-Marine might be in his forties now, but he was still a solid hunk of bone and muscle.

'You got front-row tickets to the Stranger's barbecue,'

Heck told him. 'Think you can walk? You weigh a sodding ton.'

'I'm blo— bloody sorry . . .' McGurk stuttered.

It was several minutes after they'd got up onto the flat before the casualty was able to find his feet properly. Even then, his knees buckled as they tried to skirt the exterior of the rubble.

'Don't . . . don't think I'm gonna make it,' McGurk said.

'Yes you are,' Heck replied.

'Totally . . . messed up . . .'

'Look on the bright side. You'll get six months' sick leave for this. Full pay.'

The rest of the villagers had now convened on Hetherby Close, their faces stark and pop-eyed in the firelight, stained with smoke.

'Okay, that's all of us,' Heck said. 'Back to the pub, everyone. Come on, another two hours and a bit, and it's daylight.'

They shuffled along Hetherby Close in a disorderly group, heading for the junction with Truscott Drive. It was far from easy. McGurk still hung semi-lifeless from Heck and Hazel's shoulders, and none of the other villagers were prepared to walk ahead, instead clustering around the cops for safety but at the same time impeding progress.

The smoking ruins of the police station and the surrounding buildings fell slowly behind and vanished in the mist, but that was no comfort.

'Come on, people,' Gemma urged them. 'Make way, eh . . . we've got to get this injured man to shelter.' But she too looked strained; her voice was weak with pain.

'Where the bloody hell is M-E?' Heck said for the umpteenth time. 'We couldn't half bloody use her now!'

'You sure she wasn't injured too?' Gemma said. 'She couldn't be buried under wreckage?'

'We were nowhere near the blast when it went off. We ran back towards the village together, but got separated in the woods . . .'

Almost on cue, a shrill voice sounded from their left. 'Heck . . . Heck!'

They glanced around as Mary-Ellen emerged from between the houses north of Truscott Drive.

'Where the hell have you been?' he demanded.

Mary-Ellen was as sooty, dusty and bug-eyed as the rest of them, her spiky black hair gleaming with sweat. 'I think . . . think I almost caught him . . .'

'What . . . where?'

'Baytree Court.'

'Yeah . . . well, "almost" doesn't help us. Come on everyone, stop standing around. Back to the pub!'

'Heck, he was right *there* . . . I almost nabbed him.'

'Tell me on the way. McGurk's hurt and we've got to get these people under cover.' Heck glanced at Hazel as they stumbled on. 'Please don't tell me you've got propane cylinders in *your* cellar too.'

She shook her head. 'Ours are in the shed out back. There's only beer in the cellar.'

'Thank God for beer.'

'I'm not kidding, Heck,' Mary-Ellen said excitedly. 'After we got split up in the woods, I came out on Truscott Drive a bit further up from you . . . just across from Baytree Court. And I thought I heard something down the far end . . . like breaking tiles . . . like stuff was falling off Bella's roof. It made me think there might be someone up there, you know . . . next to the tower.'

'That was more important than finding out what had happened at the nick?' Heck said.

'Think about it,' she said. 'If you wanted to survey this

347

whole village with thermal imaging, where would be the best place?'

Heck couldn't deny the logic of this. The McCarthys' house didn't just boast a higher, steeper roof than most of the properties surrounding it – its features also included a mock-Victorian bell-tower. In addition, it sat on raised ground. Anyone perched on top of there with heat-detecting vision would have a grandstand view of the neighbourhood and the chaos slowly engulfing it.

'And did you see anything?' he asked.

'I couldn't *see* anything, could I? But I heard him, I'm sure. It was like a cracking, breaking sound. When I ran over to the McCarthy house, bits of slate and other shit were falling off the roof.'

'And that's the bloody extent of it?' he snorted. 'You know explosions create shockwaves that cause structural damage?'

'What . . . you think I should have ignored it?'

'No . . . no, course not.' Heck was now acutely aware of the other villagers clustered around them, listening, and therefore not looking to their own safety. 'Look, we've got to get these people under cover. Give us a hand here, M-E!'

Mary-Ellen hastened to assist with McGurk, replacing Hazel, who now looked exhausted. 'There was no sign of the bastard anyway,' Mary-Ellen said. 'Then I heard you screaming for Gemma . . . so I didn't hang around.'

'Come on everyone, move it!' Heck shouted, McGurk still a sagging weight on his shoulder. They recommenced shuffling down the hill in a disorderly gang. 'Christ's sake, PC McGurk,' Heck complained. 'Can't you put one foot in front of the other?'

Before McGurk could mumble a foul-mouthed reply, a familiar refrain, rendered harmonious by the most tuneful whistling they'd ever heard, came drifting downhill towards them. They stopped and glanced back at the station, which was blanked out by smog, though flickers of orange firelight were visible. Whoever was whistling *Strangers in the Night* to them, he was standing right there, right in the midst of the obscured ruin. But of course, just because they couldn't see him, didn't mean he couldn't see them.

Chapter 30

'Into the pub, all of you,' Heck said, expecting a fusillade of shots to roar out of the fog. 'Right now!'

The villagers jerked to life again, dashing down Truscott Drive to The Witch's Kettle. Lucy unlocked the door, and, despite Gemma's advice that everyone take it easy and try to stay calm, the rest of them piled through in a frightened mob. Burdened with McGurk, Heck and Mary-Ellen brought up the rear. It took no more than forty seconds to get down the road and scramble inside, but Heck's heart was jackhammering for those last few yards. Gunfire from behind felt imminent, and it was only when he heard the pub door slam closed and the bolt ram home that he allowed himself to breathe.

'Everyone down . . . sit down or lie down!' Gemma shouted to be heard over the gabbling voices. 'Away from the windows!'

The villagers complied, while Hazel and Lucy shoved stools and tables away, so Heck and Mary-Ellen could lay McGurk on a leather-topped couch. He'd recovered sufficiently now to start pushing off hands. 'I'm alright . . . you can stop fussing.'

'Pity you didn't decide that at the top of Truscott Drive,' Heck said, rubbing his shoulder.

Hazel glared at him. 'For God's sake!'

'Wha' happened?' McGurk tried to touch his brow, but the mere act of lifting his arm brought a grimace to his battered face. 'IED?'

'Something like that,' Heck said.

Gemma approached, pale-cheeked herself. 'You don't remember the cellar, PC McGurk . . . under the police office?'

McGurk looked vague. 'I don't . . . I'm nae sure.'

She reminded him of the events leading up to the explosion; how he'd been looking to fix the power, how he'd said he hadn't needed her help, but how they'd gone up there together anyway. 'Then, at the last second you seemed to realise something was wrong. You slammed the door again, before we took the full blast in our faces.'

McGurk shook his head, bewildered – which made him wince all the more.

'Can I get you a drink, PC McGurk?' Hazel asked.

'Just water for the moment, please . . .'

Heck tapped Gemma's shoulder. 'I need a word.'

Leaving Mary-Ellen to apply what first aid she could in the dark, Gemma followed Heck across the pub to a distant corner. As they huddled together, he quickly and quietly relayed the info about the SFO vehicle, the trio of corpses inside, and the missing cache of police firearms. Under normal circumstances, even Gemma Piper, DSU at Serial Crimes, might have reeled with shock at hearing this, but tonight it seemed to be par for the course. Instead, she slumped onto a bench, cringing with pain. 'This is getting ridiculous,' she said. 'I mean, Cragwood Vale is hardly small. How's this guy getting here, there and everywhere?'

'I think I can help with that, ma'am,' Mary-Ellen said,

joining them and sitting down. 'That quad-bike you mentioned, Heck? The one he chased you on? I think it's parked in the back garden of Bella McCarthy's house.'

'You saw it?' he asked.

'Yeah. When I went over there, investigating that noise on the roof, I nipped around the back, just to see if someone was climbing down the other side. The quad was there . . . parked on the lawn.'

'And was it drivable?' The import of this was quickly dawning on Heck.

'Can't say for sure. There were no punctured tyres, I can certify that. But it could explain how he's been getting around so fast, don't you think?'

'Except that we'd have heard its engine,' Gemma replied.

Mary-Ellen shook her head. 'Not necessarily, ma'am. This fog, it eats everything . . . sound as well as vision.'

'She could be right,' Heck said. 'Get out there in the middle of it and it's like cotton wool's stuffed in your ears.'

'Look . . . why don't I just go back and check it out properly?' Mary-Ellen said. 'Maybe bring it back here. I'm not frightened. And I know exactly where it is.'

Heck and Gemma glanced at each other. The implication of this was obvious: if they managed to obtain the quad-bike, one of them could easily get out of the Cradle and ride for help. But how had this opportunity suddenly arisen?

'Sounds fishy,' Gemma said. 'He goes to all this trouble, and then leaves us a way out?'

'It doesn't seem like our lad, I agree,' Heck said. 'I mean, this guy's organised to the nth degree.'

'But if he doesn't know we know it's there . . .' Mary-Ellen argued.

'He might have drawn our attention to it deliberately,' Heck interrupted. 'Look, whoever he is, he's been planning this whole thing for a while. He's taken every eventuality into consideration. I mean, how much homework did he do to find out we had propane bottles in the police station cellar? This isn't some everyday nutter getting his rocks off, I can tell you that.'

'We should at least check it,' Mary-Ellen persisted. 'I can be there and back in no time.'

'I don't like the idea of anyone going out there now,' Heck said. 'Not when we know he's right here on the plot, whistling his little heart out.'

'Heck . . .'

'No, M-E! Let's have a breather and take stock of where we are . . .'

'Which is fucked, if we don't do something!' Mary-Ellen retorted. 'Heck, he's just blown the fucking police station sky high, not to mention wiped out the firearms team . . .'

'Keep your voice down!' he admonished her with a hiss.

She clamped her mouth shut, but her eyes shone with defiance, her face gleaming with sweat. She looked even more wired than usual, though this was hardly a surprise.

'Whatever we do, we don't go at this thing like a bull at a gate,' Heck said more quietly. 'Let's try and keep a level head for a second or two, because this guy's not just outgunning us, he's outthinking us as well.' He paused before turning to Gemma. 'I'll be honest, ma'am, I've been trying to work out his motivations . . . and needless to say it's a dog's breakfast. We can only guess at it. But regardless of whether or not this guy is the actual Stranger, I reckon *you're* his primary target.'

She eyed him curiously. 'This another flight of your imagination, Heck?'

'Imagination is all we've got at present. But here it is, for what it's worth. Suppose this guy's been following recent events, I mean in relation to your and my careers. Suppose he saw where I got transferred to after the Nice Guys business, looked the place over and decided it was ideal for his purpose, especially with winter coming. We were bound to get bad weather at some point, whether it be fog, heavy snow, anything that would make it difficult to get reinforcements up here. And after that, well . . . what was more likely to draw *you* to this place than a suspicion the Stranger had showed up?'

Gemma mulled this over. 'On that basis, if this *isn't* the Stranger, say, it's another major player who wants to get even – and I've upset plenty of them in the past – he could have an entire hit-team with him.'

'Christ,' Mary-Ellen breathed. 'That'd be all we need.'

'For which reason I doubt that's the case,' Heck said. 'Look . . . a team of killers would have slaughtered us out on the road just now. Either that or they'd move on the pub. No one's coming to help us. There's still two hours of darkness and fog, and if they weren't armed to the teeth before, they are now. There'd be nothing we could do to resist them. I still think we're only dealing with a small number of adversaries, two at the most. Though to be honest . . .' He recollected the grisly murder scene at Bill Ramsdale's cottage. 'It's pretty difficult to envisage even two men coming together who'd willingly participate in a death as sadistic as Bessie Longhorn's. I think we're only facing one person here, an extreme type of psychopath – rare, even in the criminal fraternity. But that still gives us a bit of an advantage, because contrary to appearances, he *cannot* be in half a dozen places at once. So let's assess what we *do* know. First of all, he's fit and energetic. He's also a local guy – if he wasn't born and raised here, he's made it his business to get to know the place. He knows which houses are occupied, he knows where the local cars are kept, he knew where the police motor launch was housed. Trouble is . . .' Heck drummed his fingertips on the table. 'There's one thing that doesn't even fit into this picture.'

'Go on?' Mary-Ellen said.

'This has been bugging me for the last hour or so, but I've not really had time to sit down and give it any thought . . .'

'*Go on!*' Gemma said impatiently.

'How did he know that when we were up at Fellstead Grange we only had two shotgun cartridges?'

Gemma frowned. 'Are we sure he knew that?'

'Absolutely. Hazel fired one shot through the door, and he still didn't launch a frontal assault. That only happened after he used that mannequin to fox you into loosing off the second and final round.'

Mary-Ellen, who hadn't been present during the fight at Fellstead Grange, listened to this in bafflement. 'So what exactly are we looking at here?'

Heck sat back. 'The only person I can think who could conceivably have known about that is Hazel's ex-husband.'

'Who no longer lives anywhere near here,' Gemma said.

'So? Does that mean he doesn't harbour grudges?'

'From what Hazel's told me, he's a long way from being athletic enough to get up into the fells,' Mary-Ellen said. 'What about someone else she might have told? Some punter maybe?'

Gemma shook her head. 'She'd have to be a real flake to trust that info to blokes she doesn't know, and a flake is one thing Hazel isn't.'

'Someone Lucy might have told? An old boyfriend? A college pal?'

Heck mused. 'If it does turn out to be someone from round here, that kicks my theory into touch about Gemma being the target.'

'We're all basically targets,' Gemma said. 'Whoever he's really got it in for, the rest of us are going to cop it as collaterals if we don't do something. So perhaps we should save the theorising for later, and concentrate now on saving the lives of everyone here.' There was a brief silence, which she finally broke herself. 'I hate saying this, but I think M-E's right. It's going to *have* to be that quad-bike.'

Heck didn't immediately reply.

'I don't like it either,' Gemma added, 'but the way things are looking, that's our only option. We've got to try and get the word out that we need help right now, not in two or three hours.'

'I agree,' Mary-Ellen said firmly.

Reluctantly Heck nodded. 'Okay, okay . . . if we don't have any other choice.'

'How far is Bella McCarthy's house from here?' Gemma asked.

'On a good day, if you weren't worried about getting shot, you could make it in under a minute,' Mary-Ellen said.

They pondered this glumly. In their collective mind's eye, the idyllic Lakeland village had transformed into a dystopian landscape, its blanket of fog tainted by brackish, semi-toxic smoke, a yawning, burning wound at its heart, the fallout from which had rained across the surrounding properties, smashing windows and roofs, strewing the paths and gardens with unsightly debris. And if that wasn't enough, they now knew for a fact the unseen menace that was lurking there. The question was, where exactly? Around a corner, behind a dry-stone wall, in some darkened niche, or leeward of some rickety old outbuilding? In any of those cases, they wouldn't see him until he'd lined them neatly in his sights.

'This time I'll go,' Gemma said. 'You guys have taken your share of risks.'

She stood up, only for her face to etch with agony. She promptly sat again.

'The only place you're going is X-ray,' Heck said. 'Soon as we get you out of here. Looks to me like you might have fractured a vertebra.'

'I've got full movement,' she said. 'It can't be that serious.'

'You're still staying put.' He turned to Mary-Ellen. 'It's me and thee again.'

'Hurray.'

'Hey, we can't always choose the tasks fate sets before us.'

'Very Tolkienesque.'

'I like Tolkien.'

'So do I,' she said. 'See . . . you've inspired me again.'

He smiled tiredly.

Outside, the fog waited.

They went out the same way as before, through the back. It was now quarter past six in the morning, and the temperature was still hovering just above freezing. The cobblestones at the rear of The Witch's Kettle glistened with frost. Heck and Mary-Ellen's breath hung in dense, white clouds. It might have been Heck's imagination, or the result of sheer exhaustion – he'd been on duty now for more hours than he could count – but ·despite the all-pervading dark, the fog itself seemed to be paler.

This time they followed a different route through Cragwood Keld, intending to come around on the McCarthy house by circling the village clockwise. Without speaking, they darted along the access lane between the pub and the shingle beach, where the humped forms of boats and kayaks lay. The village jetty jutted away into dimness, the dark waters of the tarn lapping sluggishly around its pilings. Past the jetty, they diverted southwest across the green, the grass of which was sparkling with frost. Beyond the green, they skirted the Section House, scaled its rear fence and approached what remained of the police station from the south end of Hetherby Close. All the way, they saw extensive rubble and damage: the holiday lets had been bombarded; the road surface itself was gashed and broken.

Even when they stood alongside the black, smoking hole where the nick had formerly been, the last of the petrol fires having burned themselves out, Heck found it difficult to comprehend that the office where he'd been posted since he'd transferred up here no longer existed. Fortunately, there hadn't been much inside it of value. His laptop, he supposed, but he could always get another of those; all its files were backed up. His scrapbook of faces would be harder to replace; not that its absence would matter very much if none of them made it out of here.

The icy mist oozed around them as they struck a diagonal path across the top of Truscott Drive. The whistling had fallen silent, at least for the time being, but that in itself was no solace. For one thing, it meant they didn't know where the madman was. Okay, they couldn't pinpoint him exactly even when he was whistling, but when he wasn't he could be following three yards behind and they wouldn't know about it.

More fog eddied past them as they entered Baytree Court. Rather than walking along the centre of the small cul-de-sac, they nipped up a drive and proceeded via the empty holiday homes' front gardens. These too were strewn with bricks and bits of blackened timber. At the end of the Court, they accessed the McCarthy property by slithering through an evergreen hedge.

Here, at the front of the palatial residence, they paused, bodies damp with sweat.

'If we can get it started, just get your foot down and go,' Heck said quietly.

Mary-Ellen nodded.

They'd agreed that she would make the journey, while he remained behind. It would be no soft option for her. Miles through the fog on a quad-bike was a big ask, and there'd be no guarantee the killer wouldn't launch himself at her before she'd left the vicinity.

'Don't worry about trying to reach Windermere,' Heck reminded her. 'Just get yourself down to Chapel Stile and start knocking on doors.'

'No problem.'

'Okay. You ready?'

Mary-Ellen nodded again, tense. It seemed pretty transparent that if the killer knew they'd spotted the quad-bike, he could easily be using it as bait with which to lure them, but as so often on this night of nights it was a case of needs must.

'Same as last time?' she whispered. 'Me around the left, you around the right?'

Heck nodded. 'No heroics. You see or hear anyone, you holler, okay?'

She winked and moved away through the mist, heading to the entry-passage that led to the rear of the premises on its far side. Heck took the right-hand passage, conscious of his feet echoing and so attempting to tread stealthily, constantly glancing overhead. Mary-Ellen had mentioned earlier that she'd thought she'd heard movement on the roof, but there were plenty of broken slates and bits of guttering strewn underfoot.

Then his progress was halted.

He was almost at the rear of the house when the passage was suddenly blocked by a tall gate made from oak planks. He pressed against it, but it was solid and wouldn't budge.

'Fuck,' he said under his breath, backing away, only to hear a clanking of metalwork on the other side. Involuntarily, he backed away further. He glanced behind him. The far end of the entry was filled with fog, but there was nowhere to actually take cover. With a *clunk*, a bolt was disengaged. Heck continued to back away as the gate swung inward.

And Mary-Ellen stood there.

'You okay?' she said.

'Yeah,' he replied, relieved, walking forward.

'Sorry . . . forgot about this gate.'

'It's okay. All clear?'

'Seems to be.'

Despite the gloom, they were confronted by the broad expanse of the rear lawn, the mud-caked shape of the quad-bike sitting in the middle section of it, which now was churned to slurry where the vehicle had spun to a halt. They scanned all surrounding parapets before striding out towards it. The quad wasn't leaning or slumped over, and at first glance looked to be in working order – until a scent of petrol assailed them. Before they'd reached it, Heck spotted what looked like the handle of a screwdriver jutting from the fuel tank located beneath its handlebars.

'Crap!' He dropped to a crouch. The soil and grass underneath the machine was slick, glimmering with greasy liquid. What remained of the tank's contents was still stringing out, albeit slowly.

'Bastard beat us to it, eh?' Mary-Ellen said.

'Yeah. Left us a present though.' Using only his gloved left thumb and index finger, Heck waggled the screwdriver loose. When he held it aloft, its tip had been machine-honed to a pencil-like point. 'Don't suppose you've got an evidence bag?'

'Think that could be one of the murder weapons?'

'It's exactly the kind of weapon the Stranger was believed to have used – not just to stab his victims, but to gouge their eyes.'

'Well, as it happens, I do have evidence bags.' She unzipped a pocket on her tunic's upper sleeve and whipped out a roll of clear sterile sacks. 'Take your pick.'

He peeled one loose, and slipped the screwdriver inside, before sealing it and shoving it into one of his own pockets.

'Okay . . .' Mary-Ellen stood up. 'If there's no way out of

here, we should get back to the pub, shouldn't we, and dig in? I'm sure we can make it through 'til dawn . . .'

'Hang on . . . whoa.' Heck reached down into the tangle of wires and circuitry their opponent had left behind after jacking the machine to life. 'Looks like he may have left us more than one present.'

Very carefully, he extricated a long, pale, rubbery object, which at first resembled a deceased earthworm. Mary-Ellen leaned down, none the wiser.

'I don't . . . I don't bloody believe this,' Heck muttered, as he rose to his feet. 'I know we said no torches, but give us some light, eh?'

She switched her torch on – and there was no mistaking what he'd found. It was a rubber wristband, beige in colour, torn at one end. A *Help For Heroes* logo was imprinted on it. They turned to face each other, their expressions mirroring disbelief.

'Please tell me Mick McGurk was still wearing his wristband when we carried him back to the pub,' Heck said.

Mary-Ellen looked agog with shock, but shook her head. 'He wasn't. I noticed it was missing when we laid him on that couch. I just assumed he'd lost it in the explosion. But, hang on, Heck . . . this maniac can't be Mick McGurk! Can he?'

Heck didn't want to believe it either, but wanting to and being forced to were nearly always different things. He dangled the band gingerly, as if it was something vile. 'He must have lost this when he was hotwiring the quad-bike on Fiend's Fell. That's the only explanation.'

'And he's a Scot too, isn't he?' she said. 'Good Christ . . .'

'Not only that,' Heck added. 'He's had the time. I mean, most of tonight he's been on his own. He was supposedly manning the nick, but there was no one there to check. He could have got up to all sorts . . . he's had hours and hours.'

'No, no . . .' Mary-Ellen shook her head. 'Mick McGurk's

a copper. A bona fide copper. He's been in Cumbria Constabulary for years.'

'Which means he knows the lie of the land.' Heck's mouth dried as the hideous idea grew on him. 'He could have scoped out Cragwood Vale a dozen times. He might even have known about Hazel's ammo . . .'

'Yeah, but wait a mo . . . why would he do all this? Why would Mick McGurk have it in for DSU Piper?'

Heck didn't reply. Initially he couldn't.

With indecent speed, his certainty of a half-second ago was replaced by the inevitable flood of doubt. On the face of it, it was surely preposterous to think Mick McGurk could be the guy. For all these possibilities and odd coincidences, what Mary-Ellen said was true: he *was* a bona fide copper; before that he'd had a career in the military, and it must have been hassle-free, else he wouldn't have been accepted into the police. What would he have to gain by all this?

But then, what would anyone have to gain by this?

That thorny question remained unanswered. And then there was the evidence – the wristband. In any normal circumstances, that clue alone would be sufficient for Heck to make an arrest. Which, if he was honest, was what they were going to have to do now. Or something along those lines. Perhaps they shouldn't be too hasty – because if McGurk was the guy, injured or not, he could easily be packing concealed firearms.

'We're going to have to play this carefully, M-E,' Heck said. 'Very, very carefully.'

They bagged the wristband and set off back to the pub, circling the house and darting through Bella McCarthy's front garden and along Baytree Court.

'The more I think about this, the more I think it's him,' Mary-Ellen said.

Heck was still trying to weigh everything up.

'Mind you,' she added, 'he was inside the nick when it exploded. Shouldn't that rule him out?'

'Not necessarily. From what Gemma said, McGurk led the way down there, he opened the door that lit the fuse . . . and then at the very last second he closed it again, providing himself with a shield.'

'It could still have killed him, Heck.'

'A risk he was prepared to take to put himself in the clear? And look how it all actually happened. Like you say, McGurk's been part of Cumbria Police for years, and yet he needed an officer on a daytrip from London to show him where the cellar was? He must've visited a hundred mountain villages like this one.'

'Yeah, but he said he didn't want Gemma to go with him. He even got vexed.'

'There are subtle forms of coercion, M-E. McGurk's out there in the cold, shivering, while Gemma's in a nice warm pub. I know Gemma. It wouldn't have taken much more to prick her conscience, to make her go and offer help.'

'So you think it's McGurk . . . for sure?'

'We have to suspect it's him. We can't just assume . . .' Abruptly, Heck stopped talking; halted in his tracks. They were now on a level with the turn into Hetherby Close. Heck peered past it, towards the blast site.

'What?' Mary-Ellen asked.

'What about the whistling we heard after the explosion? We were carrying McGurk down the road to the pub at the time.'

'Shit . . . we did, you're right!'

Heck headed urgently over there. Mary-Ellen followed. The heaped rubble was still smouldering as they sidled around it, picking through the gutted shell that once had been the station garage; most of its corrugated roof had caved in, owing to the weight of debris on top.

'What exactly are we looking for?' she asked.

'That whistling sounded as if it was coming from around here,' Heck said.

'Yeah . . . so?'

'So . . . maybe McGurk *is* our boy, but maybe he's got an accomplice, someone who whistled at us out of the smog to try and cover for his mate.'

'You said earlier you didn't think it could be a hit-team . . .'

'And I stand by that,' Heck replied. 'A team of professional assassins would have done for us all by now. But if you recall, I didn't discount the possibility of a *couple* of guys, non-pros maybe.'

Though they kicked their way around what had once been the storage yard, it was little more now than a heap of burnt, twisted junk.

'We'll be lucky to find evidence anyone was hanging around here,' Mary-Ellen said. 'Who could the other fella be, anyway? Who'd join a serving copper on a mindless murder spree?'

Heck shook his head as he scanned the wreckage. 'It's only a theory. But an awful lot went on last night that needs explaining. Was Mick McGurk even up here in the Cradle when Bill Ramsdale and Bessie Longhorn got murdered? The first time I saw him yesterday was down at Westmorland General Hospital just before five p.m.'

'Yeah, but we haven't got times of death for Ramsdale and Longhorn yet.'

'True, but if he only got up here for around seven, and then went on to pinch your boat, attack us up at Fellstead Grange and kill the occupants of the Ho as well . . . that's an awful lot to cram into one evening.'

'Suppose so. But I never thought there might be two of them.'

364

'And then again . . . maybe there isn't.'

Detecting a change of tone, Mary-Ellen glanced up, to find Heck pointing across the rear of the yard at the slatted wooden fence, which had now been flattened by shrapnel – except for a single concrete post. On top of that sat a small rectangular device about the size of a mobile phone, with a pad of key-controls at the front. Heck took it down and examined it.

'What the hell . . .?' Mary-Ellen said.

'It's a Dictaphone.'

'A Dictaphone . . .?'

Heck thumbed at a plastic, funnel-like appendage in its top left corner. 'A Dictaphone with a loudspeaker.' He fiddled with the keys. There was a whirring sound as the tape inside rewound itself. Mary-Ellen switched her torch on again so he could access the keypad properly. He hit the 'stop' button, and then 'play'.

The volume of the music surprised both of them, though the tune didn't.

It was *Strangers in the Night*, melodiously whistled.

Heck ran his thumb down the side, found the volume control and decreased it. He looked at Mary-Ellen.

'So it could just be McGurk after all?' she said.

'That possibility has never gone away. One thing's for sure, whoever it is . . . he's never actually been whistling to us. He's been playing a tape.'

'And McGurk set that up on the fence . . . when? Just before he and Gemma went down into the cellar?'

'Why not?' Heck said. 'They were poking around here, looking for a door. She wouldn't have been watching him all the time. I'll need another evidence bag . . .' Mary-Ellen handed one over. He slipped the device inside, sealed it, and zipped it away into another inside pocket. 'With luck, this'll be the one that'll either clear PC Michael McGurk's name, or send him to prison for the rest of his life.'

'What do you mean?'

'Well, he's a copper, isn't he? So he knows the ropes.' They set off walking again, Heck leading the way. 'He'll almost certainly have worn gloves when he was handling the murder weapons. But the chances are damn good his dabs will be on this Dictaphone, and that's all we're going to need.'

'In that case, why would he have left it out here, where any Tom, Dick or Harry could find it?'

Heck shrugged. 'Perhaps he intended to reclaim it afterwards, but wasn't able to. That would put McGurk even more firmly into the frame.' They were now back on Truscott Drive, heading down towards the pub.

'If it is McGurk, do you think he was the original Stranger?' Mary-Ellen wondered.

'If it is him, we'd have to consider that. How well do you know him?'

'Not very. He's been a bobby eight or nine years. Tarnished his record up in Carlisle, but not sufficiently to get himself sacked.'

'I wonder if there was a window of opportunity between him leaving the military and joining the job.'

'You mean to go and kill people on Dartmoor?'

'Maybe in other places too. Depends where he was posted.'

'Well, you said something about him perhaps committing murders before he even came to the West Country.'

'That was never official, it was my own hypothesis.'

'Heck, are we really about to arrest a serial killer?' Mary-Ellen looked stunned by the prospect.

'I don't know. But let's not get too excited, eh?'

'If nothing else, it should be easy,' she said. 'I mean, at present he's just lying there, too knackered and injured to move. All we've got to do is slip the cuffs on him.'

However, when they were readmitted to The Witch's Kettle, Mick McGurk, all rough, rugged fourteen and a half stones of him, was sitting upright at the bar, a little pale in the cheek, but wide awake; in fact sipping a whisky and warm water. He nodded at them when they entered, and raised the glass high; as if toasting his own remarkably improved health.

Chapter 31

'I'm alright,' McGurk said. He'd smeared the sooty grime away from his eyes, but still looked like a man who'd been steeped in oil. 'Head's banging a bit.'

He probed at the back of his skull, where a jagged laceration, perhaps nine inches long, meandered across his scalp, bright crimson amid his sweat-damp bristles. It would almost certainly require stitching, though for the moment it had been cleaned and smeared with Germolene, presumably by Hazel.

McGurk remained hunched on his bar stool. He was still clad in armour and bulky waterproofs. There was plenty space there for concealed weapons.

'I take it you weren't able to retrieve any of our vehicles?' Burt Fillingham called from his chair. He'd adopted a weary, peevish look. His voice was strained by irritation.

'All the vehicles in the village have been sabotaged, I'm afraid,' Heck admitted. 'And in the light of that, there's a bit of a problem.'

Once again, pale-smudge faces were fixed on him from different corners of the darkened interior. Only in the toilet corridor, where Mary-Ellen was quietly conferring with Gemma, were other matters under discussion.

'Without vehicles, there are no means to evacuate any of us from Cragwood Keld at the present time,' Heck said. 'Or even send anyone for help.'

'We're trapped here, then?' Ted Haveloc said.

'That's about the strength of it.'

'Oh my God!' Sally O'Grady whimpered.

'None of that,' Dulcie chided her.

'But isn't help already on its way?' Hazel asked quietly. 'What about the police firearms team? Why have you suddenly stopped talking about *them*, Mark?'

'Yeah?' Mick McGurk also looked interested in hearing an answer to this. If he was responsible for massacring the firearms unit and his curiosity was just an act, it was convincing.

'Well, Sergeant Heckenburg?' Burt Fillingham asked. 'What about it?'

'Sorry . . . what about what?'

'About the fact this madman's trapped us here, about the fact he obviously wants to murder us all.'

'That's an assumption, not a fact.'

'Have you found any evidence to indicate he doesn't?'

'There's no evidence of anything, Mr Fillingham. But I understand why you're all frightened. I'm going to have a chat with my colleagues, and we'll make a decision about what to do next.'

'Let's hope it's a more effective decision than the various others you've reached so far tonight,' Fillingham said.

Heck ignored that and walked into the corridor by the toilets. Gemma and Mary-Ellen glanced around as he approached. Behind him, civilian voices rose as they began to dispute with each other. He heard McGurk making some comment about people needing to keep it together. Hazel joined in, saying the last thing they wanted was to fall out among themselves.

'M-E put you in the picture about McGurk?' Heck asked Gemma quietly.

Gemma nodded but didn't look totally convinced. 'This wristband may not be his.'

'If it's not him, the forensics will clear him.'

'Heck, you theorised this perpetrator is here to get me. If so, how does that tie in with McGurk saving my life over at the police station? Saving it at considerable risk to his own. Once those matches struck, he did everything he could to get that cellar door closed. And even then he shielded me with his own body.'

'You sure?' Heck asked. 'Or was it more the case he couldn't help but shield you in that tiny corridor?'

'Can he be in two places at once?' Gemma asked. 'While he was supposedly shooting at you two on that road near the firearms truck, he was also down here at the pub telling me we'd had a power cut.'

'There's a time discrepancy there,' Heck said. 'Only three shots were fired at us on that road, and we laid low for . . . I don't know, forty minutes, maybe more. Easily long enough for him to get back to the village and tell you the lights had gone out.'

'Ma'am,' Mary Ellen said, 'there were prolonged periods when Mick was in sole charge of the nick. That would have given him ample opportunity not just to pinch my boat and chase you guys up the fells, but to cause damage to phone lines, vehicles . . . not to mention murder potential witnesses.'

'How did he get over to the far shore to pinch your boat, Mary-Ellen?' Gemma wondered. 'Did he *walk* around? It would have taken him hours.'

Mary-Ellen shook her head. 'Two minutes from here, down at the village jetty, there are kayaks, canoes . . . and he's an ex-Royal Marine. It wouldn't have taken him very long to paddle over to the east shore.'

Gemma gazed at Heck searchingly. 'Are you *really* sold on this?'

He shrugged, sighed. 'Truth is I don't know. I really don't. There are lots of questions to answer . . . would McGurk have had time to kill all these people? Possibly not. Heggarty was with him at least part of that time. Was he even up here when the first of yesterday's murders were committed? I don't know that either, not yet. I considered earlier that he might have had an accomplice . . . I mean that would explain a lot, but even then it wouldn't totally add up. There are all sorts of contradictory messages here. But the point is, ma'am, we can't pretend we didn't find that wristband on the quad-bike. In evidential terms, that's pretty overwhelming. Mick McGurk has *got* to be involved in this somehow.'

Gemma still seemed undecided. 'Look . . . think about *this*. We put McGurk under arrest now – on suspicion only – and if it's not him, it reduces our fighting potential by a quarter. And what if the real bad boy then shows up?'

'I'd much rather the real bad boy was still out there,' Heck said. 'Because if it *is* McGurk, he's right where he wants to be – in our midst. And he's done that pretty damn cleverly, making everyone think he's just another victim.'

'Ma'am,' Mary-Ellen said, 'this Stranger guy – the original one down in the West Country. You heard him speak, didn't you?'

'It was ten years ago, remember.'

'Yeah, but I'm sure that voice must be printed on your memory.'

'If you're going to ask does the voice sound similar to Mick McGurk's, the answer is no. Not in any obvious way.'

'Didn't you say something about the Stranger not speaking with a full Scottish accent?'

'That's true . . .'

'Well, McGurk's from the Borders. He hasn't got a full Scottish accent either.'

Gemma pondered that. Behind them, the argument in the pub had risen, Fillingham exchanging words with Dulcie O'Grady and Ted Haveloc, neither of whom were prepared to fall in line with his criticism of the police, who, in Dulcie's opinion, were 'trying to cope with a horrible and unprecedented problem', while Burt's 'scathing tone was neither helpful nor appropriate'.

Mary-Ellen leaned even closer. 'Look . . . there's three of us. He's a tough nut for sure, but like I say, he's out on his feet. Why don't we rush him?'

'Only two problems with that,' Heck said. 'Firstly, unless he coughs, we're not going to know for sure we've got the right guy. So we'll then have a prisoner to watch as well as all these innocent bystanders, and we'll still have to keep an eye open for a dangerous presence outside. Secondly, if it *is* him, he could easily be packing a pistol right now . . . maybe more than one.'

Mary-Ellen looked sceptical. 'So, he's going to pull a brace of pistols and gun us all down if we jump him from behind? He won't even see us coming.'

'He doesn't need to gun us *all* down,' Gemma said. 'He gets any shots off in here at all, it's a potential nightmare.'

'We've got to get the civvies out first,' Heck said.

'I love the way you think you know better than the coppers!' Ted Haveloc hooted from the taproom. 'You're only a bloody postman.'

'I'm a postmaster, actually,' Fillingham retorted. 'There's a big difference.'

'Oh, excuse me, your worship . . .'

Rotten with fear and fatigue, the rest of the pub were still arguing. It sounded as if Hazel was trying to offer reason, though McGurk, aside from voicing his disapproval a couple of times, hadn't contributed much.

'If we're not going to jump him, what's to stop him pulling his guns anyway and taking everyone out?' Mary-Ellen wondered. 'He's ideally placed to do it.'

'We certainly need to act quickly,' Heck agreed. 'If it is McGurk, I don't know why he's delaying. It looks like he's waiting for something, and having closed down all our avenues of escape, he wants us to wait with him . . . and that can't be for anything good.'

'You got something in mind?' Gemma asked.

'It's another long shot,' Heck said. 'But if it comes together, it may get all the civvies safely away from here and at the same time, put McGurk right in our hands.'

His new idea had first germinated once they'd realised the quad-bike was out of commission, and had been evolving ever since. It was hardly a risk-free strategy, but it had become increasingly clear to Heck that they had to do something. Gemma and Mary-Ellen listened attentively while Heck outlined it to them. When he'd finished, they regarded him with blank expressions.

'I told you it would be a long shot,' he said.

'There are an awful lot of variables there,' Gemma said. 'A lot of stuff we'll have no control over.'

Even Mary-Ellen looked uncertain. 'It's very dangerous, Heck.'

'More dangerous than hanging around here for another few hours?'

'It's almost seven,' Gemma reminded him. 'The sun rises just after eight.'

'Yeah, but realistically, ma'am, how manymore hours after that before DI Mabelthorpe and his various search teams start arriving? The fog isn't due to shift until midday at the earliest. And all that time we've got a well-tooled, highly motivated sociopath right in our lap?'

Behind them, the villagers were still at each other's throats. Mandy Fillingham was in the midst of a bitter exchange with Dulcie O'Grady.

'You can damn well talk,' she said. 'You think you're some lady of the manor! Lady bloody Muck, more like . . .'

'This lot aren't going to hold it together much longer anyway,' Heck murmured.

'Wait 'til you put this bloody plan to them,' Mary-Ellen replied.

'You resentful little cow!' Dulcie O'Grady snapped. Abruptly, Gemma strode out into the pub. 'Alright everybody, *put a sock in it!*'

Surprised at her strident tone, the villagers fell quiet.

'Keep a close eye on McGurk,' Heck said to Mary-Ellen from the side of his mouth. 'At all times from this moment on.'

'DS Heckenburg has come up with an idea which is hellishly dangerous,' Gemma said, addressing everyone in the pub. 'Though I think it's just about workable, given that we've no real alternative.'

She stepped aside, and Heck came forward.

'Let's face it, folks,' he said. 'Whoever this guy is, and for whatever reason he's doing what he's doing, he's obviously not going to stop now. I'm afraid you were right earlier, Mr Fillingham. He's trapped us in this valley because he intends to liquidate us.'

This time there was no response, not even a whimper.

'It may feel as if we're reasonably secure here,' Heck added. 'But I'd have thought we'd be secure in the police station. The fact is, our opponent has planned all this in advance and is highly proficient, technically as well as everything else.

He was able to create a highly destructive bomb out of little more than household appliances. The same plan won't work here, because there are no explosive materials stored in the pub cellar. But we've made the decision that we can't just sit around and give him time to hatch another scheme. Are we at least agreed on that?'

'What do you want us to do, sergeant?' Dulcie O'Grady asked.

Heck glanced at McGurk, who was watching and listening with interest. His eyes caught a hint of radiance from the murky light outside, glinting like chips of steel.

'We can't drive out of the Cradle,' Heck said. 'And we certainly can't walk out of it. So we're going to sail out.'

The silence that greeted this was the silence of bewilderment.

'Let me explain,' he said. 'In a couple of minutes, if we're all in agreement, we're going to walk out of this pub's back door and go down to the jetty, where, as you know, there are several kayaks available.'

'My God, you're not talking about the Cragwood Race?' Dulcie interrupted.

It was a new experience for any of them to hear the elder of the O'Grady sisters sound shaken, and it kick-started an immediate clamour from the rest.

'Bloody madness!' Burt Fillingham intoned, amid the tumult of disbelief. 'We don't have helmets, we don't have life-jackets . . .'

'I can't swim,' Sally O'Grady wailed.

'There are some life-jackets down at the jetty,' Heck replied.

'We'll be safer hanging on here, surely?' Mandy Fillingham cried. 'Those armed officers might still show up!'

'Hear me out, please!' Heck raised his arms. 'Everyone . . . *shut up!*'

The room fell silent again.

'Now listen . . . I didn't want to mention this, but seeing as you've forced my hand; the reason we have to leave the Keld ASAP is because when we went looking for some vehicles earlier, we found the dead bodies of the police firearms team.'

Brief, stunned whispers filled the pub.

'Listen to me, people. Seriously . . . these are the highest stakes any of you has ever played for. Daylight is only one hour away, but our opponent cannot afford to let us reach it. We have got to get out of here *now*, and the Cragwood Race is the only way as far as I can see.'

'Why not go up the Track?' Mandy Fillingham said. 'Try and lose him on the tops.'

'We've already tried that,' Heck replied. 'Whoever he is, he's proved himself a vastly better fell-walker than we are. Look, I admit it won't be easy . . . but if we pull this off, we can be back in civilisation within the next hour.'

'Or in Davey Jones's locker,' Burt Fillingham grunted.

'Perhaps you'd better tell us wha' you've got in mind,' McGurk said quietly.

As usual, the injured PC's face was graven in stone. It was anyone's guess what was going on inside his head. If he was the killer, he'd displayed great improvisational skills during the course of this night. So was he already plotting another change of direction? Heck edged towards him, just in case that change involved pulling a gun and shooting.

'If memory serves, there are several kayaks down there,' Heck said.

'There are two three-man craft, two two-man craft and a single,' Bella McCarthy replied, and she would know, as she owned most of them. As big noises at the Boat Club, she and her husband had navigated the Race many times.

'We're going to take these craft, and paddle along the tarn until we reach the Race,' Heck said, 'which is flowing freely thanks to the October rain.'

'That's putting it mildly,' Burt Fillingham muttered.

'I'm under no illusions,' Heck added. 'This will be a dangerous journey. But the speed of our descent will help us, and the fog will cloak us. After that, once you get down to Langdale Beck, it's easy. The Beck's a gentle river you can paddle along all the way to Chapel Stile . . .'

'I'm sorry, sergeant,' Dulcie O'Grady said firmly. 'Sally and I can't possibly go down the Cragwood Race. We are far too old and set in our ways to be indulging in extreme sports.'

'I assure you, Miss O'Grady, today this is no sport . . .'

'We don't know the first thing about white-water rafting . . .'

'I've taken that into consideration.' Heck turned to the McCarthys. 'Bella . . . you and James are both dab hands at this, yeah?'

'That's correct.'

'Perhaps you can take Sally and Dulcie in one of the three-man kayaks. James, you could take Burt and Mandy?'

Bella didn't look hugely comfortable with the idea, but she nodded. 'I've taken passengers before. Not usually in darkness, but as you say, what alternative is there?'

She nudged her husband, who nodded in compliance.

Heck turned to Lucy. 'Lucy, you're an outdoors type. You ever done this?'

'Once,' she replied. 'When I first moved here. Bit dicey. Had to be brave.'

'You're going to have to be brave again. I want you to take your aunt.'

Lucy chewed on her bottom lip, but nodded. Hazel looked less than impressed, but made no objection, especially when Heck threw a covert wink in her direction.

'The current will carry us most of the way,' Bella McCarthy said to the two couples charged to herself and her husband.

'If you capsize, it's easy to right yourself again – it's called the Eskimo roll. But James and I can do that for you. All you do as passengers in that event is tuck yourself forward against the deck, and don't panic.'

'There we go,' Heck said. 'We don't panic. Gemma, you're in the single.' She nodded. He turned to Ted Haveloc. 'Ted, you're with Mary-Ellen in the two-manner.'

'Always fancied having a go at the Race, I suppose,' Haveloc replied dourly.

'Well that takes care of the kayaks,' McGurk said. 'But wha' about me and you?'

'We get the short straw, I'm afraid,' Heck replied. 'We're in the canoe.'

As well as the kayaks down at the village jetty, there was also a wood and canvas canoe that was just large enough to accommodate two travellers.

'We're going down Cragwood Race on a fucking canoe?' McGurk asked. He almost sounded amused.

'We can go down on our arses, if you want. But that'd be a tad more painful.'

'Slalom and wildwater canoeing are popular sports,' Bella McCarthy said. 'The Race is no stranger to canoes. In fact . . .'

'I know that,' McGurk interrupted. 'I've done it before. In the Marines. Not for a few years, though.'

'You can show me what to do.' Heck turned to face the others. 'So . . . are we all in agreement about this?'

There was hardly a belly-roar of enthusiasm. In fact, there was scarcely a sound. The array of canary-pale faces regarded him unblinkingly.

'I can't force this course of action on you, folks, but I strongly recommend it.'

Slowly, they began talking among themselves. Heck glanced around. Hazel was at the end of the bar, standing close to Mary-Ellen. He sidled over towards them.

'Do you want to tell me what the real plan is?' Hazel asked quietly.

He put a finger to his lips. 'All you need know is that it's going to be a doddle.'

She gave him a flat stare. 'That's got to be a joke.'

'Trust me. Oh, by the way . . .' He lowered his voice to a whisper. 'I need the keys to the Boat Club. Don't make it obvious.'

Puzzled, she slid them across the bar. He quickly stowed them in his pocket.

'There's something else, Hazel.' He leaned even closer to her. 'If, for any reason, this thing goes pear-shaped, and neither me, Gemma nor Mary-Ellen make it . . .'

'Mark, for heaven's sake!'

'No . . . listen, this is important! If none of us makes it out of here, Hazel, but the rest of you guys do . . . you watch Mick McGurk, okay?'

Her mouth dropped open.

'I can't tell you any more,' he added, 'but I can't stress it enough. Watch him.'

'Don't just watch him, Hazel,' Mary-Ellen said. 'Don't take your eye off him for a second.'

Hazel glanced wordlessly from one to the other, and then looked at McGurk's broad, hunched back.

'But that's only in the event we don't make it,' Heck said, sensing a lull in the general conversation. 'Which isn't going to happen.' He moved back into the centre of the room. 'Are we all decided then?'

'Should we not go home first and pick up some warmer clothing?' Sally O'Grady wondered tremulously. 'Maybe some waterproofs, some stout boots?'

'Sorry, Sally. There's no time for that now. Look, I appreciate this is a big decision, but we need to make it quickly. Anyone *not* prepared to take this chance? Because if there is, you'll be left behind here, most likely on your own, and then there'll be no way at all we can protect you.'

There was no response.

'I need to know, guys . . . is everyone okay with this?'

'We don't consider we have much option, sergeant,' Bella McCarthy replied. 'Given what you've told us.'

'Okay,' Heck said. 'Let's do it.'

Chapter 32

There was, of course, a significant part of the plan Heck hadn't revealed to his general audience. In fact, only Gemma and Mary-Ellen were in league with him on this.

To begin with, it was never the intention that any of the villagers would face the reality of the Cragwood Race. The mere proposal of this had been part of a deception by which to separate them from Mick McGurk, and it would be Mary-Ellen's job to bring this about. She and Ted Haveloc were to paddle ahead of the others, reaching the south end of Witch Cradle Tarn first, whereupon she would beach her kayak, climb out and mount the Race Bridge. Owing to the fog, none of the others would notice she had done this until they'd also arrived, at which point, with the gate still closed, she would direct them ashore. Hopefully this would be the full extent of the villagers' involvement, because from here Mary-Ellen would lead them into the trees, where they were to hide and await developments. Even if McGurk wasn't the killer, or wasn't the sole killer, this could only help; it would put significant distance between the civvies and the last place there'd been an actual attack. If a maniac was still out there, it would take him a long time to track them around the tarn, and it was now very close to dawn.

Meanwhile, Gemma, having been allocated a single-man kayak, would also have paddled ahead of the rest, and again making use of the fog as a smokescreen, would divert back across the tarn to its west shore, where, if she followed the shoreline closely, she would find Cragwood Boat Club. She would enter this by use of the club keys, which Heck had now covertly passed to her, and the alarm code, which was printed on a plastic tag attached to the key-ring. One inside, she was to infiltrate the Club Secretary's office, where she would acquire a starter pistol. It had only occurred to Heck after he'd realised they couldn't apprehend McGurk in the pub that the closest thing to a firearm they could find around here would be one of those noisy cap-guns used for sports galas. Okay, it wouldn't even be close to the real thing; a starter pistol couldn't hurt a flea, but in the dark and the mist their target hopefully wouldn't realise what it was. While Gemma was thus engaged, Heck, who'd have brought up the rear in the canoe with McGurk, would also steer towards the Boat Club, in the process of which he'd find a reason to go ashore, where Gemma would be waiting to bushwhack them, now armed. In the worst-case scenario and they ended up scrapping with McGurk, and he started shooting, at least the civvies would be out of the way. Mary-Ellen, meanwhile, in the event she heard repeated gunfire, was under orders to resume the evacuation and lead everyone down the Race – but only in that extreme case.

They moved into the pub's rear yard in a group, where there were several moments of disorganisation. For one thing, McGurk was none too steady on his feet, and Mary-Ellen had to assist him, wrapping both arms around him to keep him upright. Heck didn't know whether to be reassured by this or find it suspicious. Thus far the killer had used plenty of distraction tactics; it wouldn't be beyond him now to lure his foes into a false sense of security.

'Okay everyone, please!' Heck raised his voice, but only sufficiently for them all to hear. Again, the small crowd fell silent. 'Listen, folks . . . we can't afford this kind of kerfuffle when we get to the beach. This guy may be watching us from close range, or he may not. He may not be watching at all. But if he hears a commotion, he'll twig what's happening . . . and I very much doubt he'll be pleased.' He paused to let that sink in. 'Okay, now we all know what we have to do, so let's do it.'

Hazel unlocked the back gate, and they went out in twos, heading quickly and quietly along the lane towards the beach and jetty. Heck hadn't wanted them moving in a bunch for fear that one shot alone could damage maybe three or four of them, but likewise he didn't want individual duos slipping out of sight of each other, so the operation was enacted quickly. Gemma went first, setting the pace despite her throbbing spine and ungainly limp.

'You sure you can manage this?' he'd asked her quietly.

She'd nodded. 'Gonna have to.'

'If you're not up to it . . .'

'What? If I'm not up to it, what? We going to put the whole thing on hold until I feel better? Get real, Heck . . . I'll manage because I have to. Isn't that your motto?'

Heck, by necessity, was waiting until the end. The last two to go before him were Hazel and Lucy. Hazel glanced back at him once before stepping through the gate.

'No unnecessary risks,' she said.

'I'll be too busy taking the necessary ones.' He winked again, but she didn't smile. Then she was gone.

This left Heck alone with McGurk. He couldn't help wondering if this would be the moment for the madman to pull his guns. But the burly PC was otherwise occupied; he

383

still seemed dizzy, and Heck had to brace him as they prepared to set out.

'I'm okay,' McGurk mumbled as Heck took his arm. 'Wee bit groggy.'

The half-crazy notion flickered through Heck's mind that this was an opportunity to take him, just seize the advantage and clothesline the bastard. But that would be a risky deviation from the plan, with Heck's two main allies out of reach. Instead, he helped McGurk out through the gate, their combined breath wreathing around them.

The cobbled road was still covered with frost, and smooth and slippery as ice. Under Heck's stern instructions, the rest of them were keeping their wits about them and stepping warily. By comparison, McGurk was rickety.

'Listen,' he said, halting at the pub's southeast corner. His face was drenched with sweat. 'No' sure I'm up tae this . . . perhaps leave me here, eh?'

Was *this* the moment? Did the bastard see some advantage in being left behind? On the face of it, it didn't make sense, but then neither did the fact the killer wasn't killing. Had he stashed his weapons somewhere else maybe? Did he need to go and get them? Or was he on the verge of doing a runner? Did he suspect he'd been found out?

'Your call, Mick,' he said. 'But what else are you going to do?'

'Dunno.' McGurk chuckled without humour. 'Brain must've come loose . . .'

'I don't think it'd be a smart idea to stay behind.'

'Nah . . . me neither.' McGurk started forward unsteadily. 'I've missed a few butchers' bills in the past. Don't want tae be put on this one when the opposition's nothing more than some dickhead too scared tae show his face.'

'Just lean on me, you'll be alright,' Heck said.

384

'Bit fucking politer than you were earlier,' McGurk observed in a tone that was almost suspicious. 'Wha's changed?'

'Nothing. Just occurred to me you've taken more than your fair share of bumps for queen and country.'

'No more than you. And not just tonight.'

'Know my career, do you?'

'I read the bulletins.'

'Yeah?'

'Yeah. Nothing else to do when you're off-duty.'

'Well . . . I get you there.'

It was thirty yards from the pub to the beach, though there wasn't much beach visible given the high level of the tarn. When they arrived there, Heck was relieved to see Gemma already on the water, paddling inexpertly but with speed into the mist. The others had life-jacketed up and were climbing into their respective craft. It helped that Bella McCarthy was supervising, issuing curt but precise instructions, showing them how to fix their rubber skirts and wield their paddles to best effect.

The canoe that Heck and McGurk were to use was standing upright against the fence at the top of the pebbled slope. As they moved towards it, McGurk again stumbled. Heck grabbed him, an unconsciously caring gesture he realised, considering McGurk was the prime suspect.

'You okay?' he asked.

'Maybe . . . let's just do it!'

The guy was certainly dazed, the gash across the back of his head seeping a glutinous red stain. All of which should make this task easier. Unless it was another elaborate ruse. Hooking an arm around McGurk's body to stabilise him, and wondering what he'd do if his hand encountered something pistol-shaped under the waterproof packaging, Heck assisted him to one of the posts at the end of the jetty, and stood him against it while he dragged the canoe down to the water's edge. The rest of them were all now afloat and heading away from shore. Sally O'Grady audibly whimpered as they set off, hands clasped over her eyes, Bella McCarthy paddling at her rear. The two-man kayak, the one containing Mary-Ellen and Ted Haveloc, pivoted around some ten yards out, Mary-Ellen having pulled a handbrake-turn with her paddle. She stared at Heck silently. From this distance, he couldn't see her expression, much less read it. But it would almost certainly imply something along the lines of: 'Take it easy, pal. See you soon.'

Heck turned back towards McGurk, who'd lurched forward, unaided, and now pushed Heck away when he offered an arm. The PC's rugged features were written with pain, but maybe something else too – anger, frustration. He managed to climb into the canoe, squatting down near the back of it.

'You'll need to move up front,' Heck said.

McGurk didn't look around, but stiffened. 'You sure that's necessary?'

He's not happy about that, Heck thought. *He wants to sit behind me.*

'If you're dizzy, you can't paddle and expect to keep a straight course,' Heck explained. 'I'll paddle . . . and if I'm paddling on my own I have to go at the back.'

A second of disgruntled silence followed, and then McGurk shuffled himself forward until he was seated near the front. The black water was freezing as Heck waded out, pushing the canoe in front of him. When he jumped aboard, he landed on his knees – so heavily that the craft almost flipped over.

'Fuck!' McGurk hissed, grabbing the gunwales, his voice echoing across the empty tarn; already, there was no one else in sight.

Heck settled on his haunches and began to paddle, alternate strokes on either side, pushing them away from shore and into the vapour. It was much colder out on the tarn surface, as well as more otherworldly, the only sound the gentle rippling of the water, the mist swirling around them in shape-shifting phantoms. This time, though, he kept close to the west bank as they proceeded south. McGurk seemed to notice this.

'You're no' going tae run us aground, I hope.'

'Relax,' Heck said. 'We need to know where we're going, and that shoreline's the only marker.'

'Yeah, but if he's following us on foot, he can take pot-shots at us.'

Heck considered that, thinking it odd the actual culprit would make such a comment. It was an undeniable fact, of course, but the reason he was sticking close to shore was non-negotiable. He didn't want to miss the Boat Club jetty, which ought to be coming up on their right in only a few minutes' time.

He steered them a little further out, but only by a matter of yards. The fog-shrouded treeline on the shore remained visible.

'This'll do nae fucking good,' McGurk complained.

Heck didn't reply, his eyes straining through the shifting gloom – until he saw what he was looking for. The trees suddenly petered out on the rocky promontory at the end of Hermit's Bay, the small inlet in which the Boat Club was ensconced. If memory served, the end of the club's jetty was about thirty yards past that, and about twenty yards back towards shore. Surreptitiously, he dipped his left hand into his combat jacket, feeling for the screwdriver he'd retrieved from the quad-bike. It was still sealed into its evidence bag. Though it wasn't easy one-handed and wearing a glove, he managed to twitch the bag open and slowly worked the tool out.

'You stopped paddling, or wha'?' McGurk said, half glancing around.

Heck froze. 'Gimme a second . . . okay?'

McGurk looked front again.

Heck slid the screwdriver loose. As improvised weapons went, it was well-balanced. It wouldn't be difficult to lean forward and drive it between McGurk's shoulder blades, penetrating his cardiovascular system, killing him instantly. If only it wasn't for that one possibility McGurk *wasn't* the killer. Heck also had to wonder if recent cases hadn't brutalised him more than was good for him. Because even if the guy *was* the killer, bringing him to book by driving a blade through his spine was hardly likely to endear him to the judicial system. Instead, he lowered the screwdriver, and probed the bottom of the boat with its tip, before shifting his hand up its hilt, flattening his palm across its pommel – and leaning on it.

There was no splintering crunch, just a dull thud as the blade passed through. He wrenched it loose, before driving it down quietly, through the bottom of the boat, twice more.

'Wha' was that?' McGurk said. 'Like a vibration in the . . .'

'Shit,' Heck replied. 'Must've hit something.'

'Oh fuck, I told you we were too close . . . shit, look at this fucking mess!'

Ice-cold water was already sloshing around their legs.

'Something's pierced the hull,' Heck said, rather unnecessarily.

'I wonder what! Jesus, it's rising like the clappers . . .'

'Hang on,' Heck shouted, paddling them sharp-right. 'The Boat Club jetty's there.'

A flat-topped structure loomed through the mist. It was only ten yards away, but the canoe was submerging so fast, the water gurgling up past their thighs, that Heck wasn't sure they'd even make it that far. As it rose to the gunwales, the two men lurched over the side, McGurk striking madly for the wrought-iron ladder at the end of the jetty, now only three or four yards away. It seemed an unnecessarily panic-stricken measure, Heck thought, treading water. As the boat vanished underneath in a frenzy of brackish bubbles, McGurk ascended the ladder with hard, clattering impacts – his dazed state apparently a thing of the past.

'It'll be okay!' Heck shouted up as he breast-stroked in pursuit. 'There are other boats here.'

McGurk didn't reply, and in fact ducked out of sight.

Heck now swung himself up the ladder urgently, and clambered onto the top of the jetty – to find the guy standing about five yards along it, facing him warily. He'd pulled the canvas off a steel rack alongside him, revealing additional paddles and oars. Despite all his suspicions, it still jolted Heck to see that McGurk had already acquired one of these and was hefting it like a club.

'Just fucking stop pretending,' the PC said. 'I know your fucking game.'

Now would be the ideal moment for Gemma to come strolling down the jetty from the clubhouse, a vague boxy shape visible in the vapour some thirty yards behind them, produce her starter pistol and, as planned, tell the bastard to stick 'em up.

But that didn't happen.

Without warning, McGurk swung the oar at Heck's head.

Heck ducked and barrelled forward, slamming the top of his skull into McGurk's midriff and wrapping his arms around his thick torso. With shouts and struggles, the two of them plunged off the jetty and back into the tarn. At this point it was turning shallow, probably no more than five feet deep, and the violent wrestling match under its surface churned up a black tumult from the bottom. Blinded and gagging, smothered in weed and filth, they tore loose from each other and broke the surface together, staggering shoreward. McGurk seemed keener to make land than Heck did, so Heck jumped onto his back before he got there. They plunged under the surface again, but McGurk was a steely customer. He slammed a vicious elbow into the left of Heck's ribs, and then again into the side of his head. Heck was thrown off, and for a second was on his back underwater. If McGurk had grabbed the advantage then and jumped down on top of him knees-first, it would all have been over. But McGurk still sought the land.

He stumbled away, allowing Heck to scramble to his feet and reel after him. The shoreline was now visible. Kayaks, canoes and other boats were drawn up there, so it was impossible for Heck to tell whether or not the craft Gemma had taken was among them. But mainly he was focused on McGurk, who was knee-deep when he turned around again, this time having scooped up a leafy piece of driftwood, which he swung down like a poleaxe. Heck threw himself to one side, and it crashed through the water, shattering on the pebbles underneath.

Heck circled around him, fists clenched, boxer-style.

'Think you can fucking take me?' McGurk scoffed, backing away. 'If my skull hadn't already been cracked open, I'd beat you into the ground like a tent-peg.'

'You're going to have to,' Heck said, lurching onto dry land.

McGurk copied the manoeuvre.

'Give it up, pal,' Heck advised him. 'You've had it.'

'You fucking reckon?' McGurk's eyes gleamed. With his hulking shape and brutish face slathered in lake-mud, fleetingly he was a genuine monster. He took a threatening step forward. Heck held his ground, only realising at the last second that his opponent was still wielding the driftwood, and that the leafy end of it had broken off, leaving a thick, nobbled club some three feet in length. Raising it in both hands, McGurk aimed it down at Heck's cranium.

'Drop it!' came a harsh shout.

Both went rigid, then risked glancing right towards the clubhouse. Though a dim form in the mist, Gemma was limping across its side-garden, weaving between folded tables and chairs. She climbed stiffly over its low perimeter fence, clearly in pain, but never once lowering the pistol she was training squarely at McGurk's head.

'Ma'am,' McGurk said. 'Thank Christ!'

'I said, drop the club.'

'You don't understand . . .'

'Drop it!'

'Why don't *you* drop it, ma'am?' came a different voice. This time they glanced left.

Heck's mouth sagged open as Mary-Ellen emerged from the vapour coiling beneath the trees. She too was wielding a firearm, but this one didn't look like a starter pistol.

'No' before time,' McGurk said, relieved. He threw away his hunk of wood. 'You'd better enlighten the superintendent.'

'I will,' Mary-Ellen said.

Then she shot him.

Chapter 33

The first bullet hit McGurk in the throat, kicking out a divot of flesh and muscle. The second ripped through his forehead, bursting from the back of his skull in a deluge of blood and brains. It wasn't quite a double-tap, but it did the job.

He hit the ground like a sack of bones, like a puppet with its strings cut.

Silence followed. A fine crimson mist hung where he'd stood.

Heck staggered slowly forward. 'M-E . . . what . . . what the Goddamn hell! We didn't have any damn proof . . .'

'Uh-uh, Heck.'

Heck was so infuriated that he didn't initially notice the gun had been turned in his direction. Or that it was a very familiar make and model; a Colt Python .357. 'What's the matter with you? Don't you realise what you've just fucking done?'

'Stay where you are!' Mary-Ellen advised him.

He stumbled to a halt, baffled.

'And don't even think about raising that gun again, ma'am!' Mary-Ellen swung her weapon onto Gemma. 'I know it's only a toy, but well . . . I'd feel better if it was on the ground.'

Gemma had lowered her pistol in disbelief. Almost instinctively, she now made a half-effort to raise it.

'Uh-uh!' Mary-Ellen cocked her Colt.

Helpless, with no alternative, Gemma tossed the starter pistol down onto the shingle.

As she did, Heck's hand stole into his jacket pocket, but Mary-Ellen spotted this too, and levelled the weapon back on him. 'Don't be an arsehole, Heck! I mean what have you got in there, anyway? You gonna chuck a chisel at me, a screwdriver? Even if you've got one, I wouldn't take the chance . . .'

Heck's face lengthened as he raised his empty hands. 'You, you *can't* be . . .'

'Okay, the pair of you . . .' Mary-Ellen waggled the gun to indicate they should stand together. Reluctantly, they sidled towards each other. 'Excellent. Now . . . kneel down. So I can see you better.'

They complied, stiffly, like automatons, but Heck was still shaking his head. 'M-E, don't . . . don't tell me *you're* involved in this.'

'Of course I'm not,' she replied in a vaguely contemptuous tone. 'You know me, don't you, Heck?'

He glanced at McGurk's crumpled body. 'I thought I did.'

She surveyed him, her gaze oddly flat. Her lips puckered into a lifeless half-smile. 'You really couldn't see past Mick McGurk once he was in the frame, could you? Did you really think he'd set that police station to blow and then just walk into it . . . purely to give himself an alibi? You think even some hard-ass ex-squaddie would take a chance like that? Mind you, McGurk got it even more wrong. He thought *you* were the killer, and with no evidence at all. Purely because someone whispered it into his ear about an hour ago. And as for you guys thinking he might have an accomplice out there, because all this was, like, too good for one man. Well . . . I guess the real perp would be very flattered to hear that . . .'

'What have you done with the villagers?' Heck interrupted. 'You know, the ones you were supposed to be looking after down at the far end of the tarn.'

'Be fair, Heck. I wasn't supposed to look after them, I was supposed to send them down the Race. Isn't that right?' She feigned concern. 'That's what the villagers thought. That's what you told them. It'll be a wild ride for sure, but some of them might make it. In fact, I'm counting on that . . .'

'Irish,' Gemma said suddenly.

'What's that, ma'am?' Mary-Ellen wondered.

'All along I said the Stranger spoke with an off-kilter accent,' Gemma explained. 'Not quite Scottish.'

'And definitely not Border Scots, eh?' Mary-Ellen's mouth twisted into a full grin, but her eyes remained glassy, almost dead. 'They always used to say the Munster Irish dialect had some similarities with Scots Gaelic. But I suppose it would take a proper Sassenach to confuse the two. On which subject, I'm surprised at *you*, Heck! Throwing your lot in with Miss Piggy here, just because she's a handsome bit of tail. Didn't she piss on *your* life as well?'

'Munster,' Gemma said slowly and disappointedly, as if she couldn't believe she'd missed such an obvious clue. 'So who was he, the Stranger . . . your father?'

Mary-Ellen's grin faded. Her mouth trembled as she screwed it shut.

'Your father?' Heck posed it as a question because he still couldn't quite accept what he was hearing. 'Your father was . . . was the Stranger?'

'That . . . is a damn . . . fucking lie.' Mary-Ellen bared her teeth. 'My father . . . my fucking father was the kindest, sweetest man in the world. My mother died giving birth to me, so I grew up with one parent . . . but he was the best you could hope for. The gentlest, the most caring, the most loving . . .'

'And a vicious sexual sadist,' Gemma said.

Mary-Ellen swung the pistol around, finger tightening on the trigger. 'Say that one more time, you bitch, and I'll take those baby blues out while you're still fucking alive! It isn't bad enough you shot him dead, now you think you can denigrate his name!'

'So it *was* your father,' Heck said, breathing slow and steady, trying to stay calm and at the same time to draw her attention back to him.

It worked; Mary-Ellen switched again, but slowly. 'I'm sure even *you* would like to think that, Heck. A nice easy answer. A nice *acceptable* answer. Now we know who the Stranger was . . . that thieving Gypsy bastard who nobody liked. That fucking Irish tinker who even got kicked out by his own people . . .'

'They had their suspicions too, did they?' Gemma said.

'Don't make this worse for yourself, Piper. All my Dada's life he got picked on, blamed for stuff he didn't do, and for why . . . because he was foreign, because he didn't have any kind of education! And now you think you're going to pin a series of sex murders on him? When it's plain as mustard the real killer is still here, doing the same thing all over again . . .'

'Why don't you tell us what really happened then?' Heck said.

'What does it matter to *you*?' Mary-Ellen wondered.

His thoughts raced as he tried to play for time. 'Hey, if there was a miscarriage of justice, if Gemma shot the wrong person, it's important we know about it.'

'It won't make any difference if *you* know about it, Heck! You won't be walking away from here!'

'I'm sure if it didn't matter to you that we know the truth, you'd already be pumping that trigger, M-E.'

'You think I'm not going to, is that it?'

'Hardly. The evidence you're ready and willing is all around us.'

'Evidence . . . that's a great word.' Mary-Ellen turned back to Gemma with reptile speed. 'There was never any evidence against my father, was there, Miss Piper? But you put lead in him all the same. You found a scapegoat, someone no one would care about . . .'

'You said your own people kicked your father out,' Heck said. 'If you and he were part of a travelling community, something must've gone badly wrong. Those guys are pretty tight.'

Mary-Ellen's eyes brimmed with tears, yet her features remained rock solid. When she licked saliva from her lips, it was with tiny, darting strokes of her tongue. These were minor details of course, yet the physical transformation alone was quite fantastic. The affable, energetic young policewoman of earlier had completely gone, replaced by something . . . well, by just that, *something*.

'I was a child at the time,' she said uncertainly, as though she possibly shouldn't be breaking these confidences. 'I don't know the reason they sent him away. I don't even know where we were . . . somewhere in Europe maybe. But I didn't care. It suited me. Just me and him together in our battered old car, in our little caravan. That was the way I liked it. When we came back to Britain, I liked it even better. Felt like I was home. Not that you native Brits ever had much time for us. Even down in the West Country, where our kind were common, Dada couldn't get work anywhere. When he did, he soon got sacked. The usual thing . . . accusations of theft, accusations of drunkenness. Always unproved.'

'Never your dad's fault, eh?' Gemma said.

'You bitch, Piper! What would you know of life on the road? No one wanting you around, people disliking you on principle. Dada couldn't even go for a drink at night without men picking fights with him. The number of times he came home late, and I saw him washing blood from his clothes . . .'

'Never occurred to you where that blood really came from?' Gemma asked.

Unexpectedly, Mary-Ellen smiled at this. But it was almost a deranged smile, the corners of her mouth hooking upward, globs of saliva oozing out.

'It never entered your head he might be the Stranger?' Heck asked. 'You must have known those murders were going on?'

'Oh, I was very aware of the murders, Heck. I was thirteen in 2003, I was no child. Dada would even talk to me about it, warn me about the sin of going off with lads I didn't know . . .'

'Who was he?' Heck asked. 'What was your father's name?'

'Nice try. But you didn't get it at the time, and you aren't getting it now.'

'You understand the circumstances in which he was shot?' Gemma said.

'Oh, I've immersed myself in the case since then, Miss Piper. Buried myself in it. And your account of that night's events would be very impressive . . . if you hadn't completely fabricated it.'

'M-E,' Heck said. 'You don't know anyone fabricated anything . . .'

'*I know enough!*' she hissed. 'Namely that late one night, when he'd been out for ages, Dada almost crashed his car as he pulled onto the derelict lot where we were camped. I managed to get him out, only to find him filthy with mud and blood, and suffering the most terrible gunshot wound . . . and then, without saying anything, not even a simple "goodbye", proceeding to die in my young arms.'

She paused, breathing harshly, as though it required a momentous effort.

Neither captive said a word. Neither dared.

'Can you imagine what it was like, Miss Piper . . . to experience that at such a tender age? Can you imagine the depth of shock and despair? Crying 'til there was no fluid left in my body . . . for the loss of the man who'd done everything for me since I was a little girl, my guardian, my best pal, the bloke who'd nurtured me, who'd looked after me so lovingly despite the world putting constant obstacles in his path.'

Heck listened in fascination as Mary-Ellen slipped briefly into a kind of recitation mode. It was almost lyrical, the way she recounted these events – as though she'd revisited them over and over in her head, and had religiously rehearsed the speech by which she'd put them right. Only now did it truly strike him how absorbed by this terrible experience she'd been, how it had come to dominate her life – and worse.

'Trust me, guys, the word "bereft" doesn't quite cover it,' Mary-Ellen added. 'And then, less than two hours later, while I'm still sitting there, rigid with shock, Dada lying in my lap, I hear on the radio that a young policewoman is believed to have lured the Stranger into a trap, and shot him!'

'M-E, you must've known what all this meant,' Heck said. 'Even in that wretched state, you must've known . . .'

'I knew the Stranger was still alive!' she replied tautly. 'I also knew you fuckers were not going to pin his series of murders on my dead father. No, sir.'

She relapsed into silence. More harsh breathing followed. Her eyes streamed copious tears.

'So let me guess,' Heck said, '. . . you buried him?'

'Bang on, Heck. I buried him. Somewhere no one would ever find him. Along with his name, just to make sure *you* couldn't besmirch it further, Miss Piper.'

'You knew the truth,' Gemma said coolly. 'You were just deluding yourself . . . by the looks of it to a point where you went stark staring mad!'

'There are lots of reasons why people go mad, Miss Piper. I'm sure you know plenty of them. But not me. No, I made an effort to keep it together. Even during the months after, when I was living rough on the streets of Plymouth. Even when I got arrested as a teenage vagrant. Just in case you're wondering, Heck, I gave them a very convincing sob-story. About parental abuse in the itinerant community, about how I'd run away from home because anything was better than that. I even gave myself a new surname – O'Rourke – just to make sure they wouldn't get any joy when they checked it all out. Not that they tried very hard, I'm certain.'

'Mary-Ellen,' he said. 'None of this . . .'

'I also kept it together in the British care system!' she snapped. 'Can you fucking believe that, Heck? Five years in those fucking pits of Hell. Something else I owed to my Dada, because one thing he *did* teach me was how to look after myself. Oh, I put the word out at an early stage, you can bet . . . "Anyone fucks with me and it's your fucking life!" They believed me.'

'I'm sure,' Heck replied.

'It helped me at school too. Particularly on the sports field . . .'

'I suppose you had to divert all that pent-up hatred somewhere . . .'

'Oh no, Heck.' Despite her tears, she grinned again. Broadly. Showing rows of pearly teeth. 'No . . . I had to reserve *that*. Can you guess who for, Miss Piper?'

'Never in a month of Sundays,' Gemma said.

'You see, by then I'd read all about you in the papers. What a hero you were. How you lay in wait for the Stranger, how you put yourself in the most terrible danger, and how you shot him in self-defence. After that, I followed your career with fascination. All your promotions, all your big arrests. Apparently you inspired a lot of young girls to join the police service. Well . . . you certainly inspired me. I joined the Met in 2010, but then they stuck me in Richmond, which put me a bit out of the way. I could have sought a transfer to one of the inner-city boroughs . . . to get closer to you, ma'am. But, I wouldn't really have got close, would I? You, cosseted in that ivory tower they call Scotland Yard, me working the streets . . . no more important than the shit on your shoes, if we'd ever by any chance attended the same crime scene. So I stayed at Richmond, planning it out. I knew something would show up, some opportunity. And eventually, lo and behold, Heck came along – on his usual tide of destruction.' Mary-Ellen's grin spread even more as she focused back on him. 'I heard all about you refusing your commendation for the Nice Guys business, Heck. About you transferring out of NCG. And when I saw where you'd finished up . . . well, how could I resist sharing a piece of that cake?'

'So you really did transfer up here because you were following me?' he said.

'Put my papers in straight away. It was still risky. I requested Central Lakes, and ended up in Ulverston, but it wasn't difficult to push for the Langdales. No one else wanted it . . .' She gave a burst of guttural, raucous laughter. 'Come on, Heck, you never thought all this was coincidence, did you?'

'I knew it couldn't be that.'

'Timing was always going to be crucial,' she added. 'But it started well. Me and you both arrived in the early autumn, set up the new office. As the year waned, I knew the weather would deteriorate. I was waiting for the first snow, just like you suspected back in the pub. But then, when a severe fog blotted out the district, I saw an early chance. And when I spotted that email about the two missing hikers in the Pikes, well . . . it was a sure sign the time had come.'

'You went all the way up onto Fiend's Fell to attack two lost girls?' he said.

'No . . . no, don't get it fucking wrong, Heck, when you were doing so well. I went up there to observe.'

'To observe? Observe who?'

'Who do you think, knobhead? . . . The fucking Stranger!'

'The Stranger . . .?'

'He was the one did those two hikers. Just like he did those hikers back near Glastonbury all those years ago . . .'

'M-E, think what you're saying . . .'

'I know perfectly well what I'm saying.' Her grin never faltered, as though it was fixed in wax. 'You see I'm very familiar with the Stranger. I've made it my business to get to know him. He's the other end of you, Heck. Determined. Dangerously obsessive. There's nothing he won't do, no distance he won't cross, no amount of time he won't wait.'

'And no limit to the softness of the targets he'll tackle, eh?' Heck said, increasingly torn between the urge to sympathise with the abused child and either humour or hate the soulless maniac she'd grown up into.

'Heck . . . he's a serial killer. What do you expect?'

'Did he kill Jane Dawson?' Gemma asked. 'She was the one we couldn't account for.'

Mary-Ellen gave this apparent serious thought. 'My understanding, ma'am, is . . . yes. I believe her body's lying in a rocky cleft up on Fiend's Fell somewhere.'

'And how did the Stranger find her and Tara Cook in the first place?' Gemma wondered. 'In all that fog?'

'I suspect he had one of these.' Mary-Ellen produced her mobile phone, at the same time snapping a small plastic fitting to the back of it. 'Familiar with this, Heck? You ought to be. You've mentioned it often enough.'

'Thermal imaging?'

'Bang on again. For two hundred quid you can buy this specially adapted iPhone case with a thermal camera on the back. In the worst fog you can imagine, this'll do the business for you. Mind you, it isn't perfect. I mean, you ever tried walking around looking through a phone? You think that's bad, you want to try hitting targets while you're staring through one. But if nothing else, this kind of gimmick clearly helped the Stranger keep tabs on the rest of us while we were all blundering around like kids in blindfolds, eh?'

'He didn't keep tabs on Tara Cook?' Gemma said.

'Seriously, DSU Piper?' This time Mary-Ellen roared. '*Seriously?* I thought you were the ace homicide detective, not a fucking Barbie doll. And you can't even second-guess a guy you once hunted for months across the moors of the West Country?'

'He foxed me the first time. Is it a surprise he did it again?'

'Oh, spare me your fucking excuses, Barbie. Surely you understand how important it was that at least one of those girls survived? Someone had to set the ball rolling, spread the word about *Strangers in the Night*. Mind you, that tape-recording and the heat camera are the only bits of tech he needed. Good old Heck did the rest. Reported straight to you . . . made such a song and dance about the Stranger that you couldn't resist rushing up here and seeing for yourself, could you? It couldn't have gone better.'

'He certainly did his homework on us,' Heck said.

'And how!' Mary-Ellen chuckled. 'But don't beat yourselves up too much. You kept him well busy . . . when he wasn't sinking the police launch, he was otherwise engaged around Cragwood Ho. Had quite a bit of work to do there.'

'Yeah, really came into his element at the Ho,' Heck commented.

'That was quite a challenge, I'd imagine,' Mary-Ellen agreed. 'Of course, it was made a tad easier for him by a certain local policewoman pretending she'd made telephone calls warning the Ho's occupants about the killer on the loose, and actually having done no such thing.'

Heck nodded sagely. 'Like minds, our killer and this local policewoman.'

'Not that a message wasn't left in due course.'

'Yeah, we got that,' Heck said. 'Bessie Longhorn's blood, was it?'

'More likely Bill Ramsdale's.'

'I see . . . well at least that's one way Bessie wasn't violated. Because let me tell you, Mary-Ellen, only a complete fucking lunatic could've been responsible for what happened to that poor kid.'

Mary-Ellen's smile tightened. 'I guess he felt the notice on the boatshed wall just wasn't enough . . . that it was *vital* you knew who you were dealing with. Much, much more important than the lives of a few Lake District bumpkins.'

'And just out of interest, M-E, how did you divest yourself of the rest of these bumpkins' blood? It must have been all over you.'

'Not me, Heck . . . I wasn't there. But I'd imagine the Stranger washed off in the tarn. It's so conveniently close. Plus, if he was mainly wearing waterproofs . . .'

'Like you are, you mean?'

'Whatever, it worked . . . more or less.'

'"More or less" seems to be the way this whole thing has gone,' Gemma said. 'It's almost morning, most of the villagers have escaped . . . and we're still alive.'

Mary-Ellen shrugged. 'My reading is that it's never been as simple as killing everyone, Miss Piper. Sure, bit-players like Dan Heggarty could croak it, but I doubt the Stranger wanted *you* dead. Not initially. Look at the moment when

403

you and I first ran into each other at the south end of the tarn. He was so very close to us then. That was probably the first time he'd seen you in the flesh since you last met on Dartmoor. For a few seconds he must have been *sooo* tempted . . . but at the end of the day, the plan was that you'd be the only one he *didn't* kill. Don't you see it? Famous Scotland Yard detective, now famous for all the wrong reasons . . . especially after that Nice Guys debacle. I mean, okay you got the Nice Guys, but the broadsheets didn't think much of you and your team, did they? All those dead people on Holy Island . . . and then imagine, a load more dead people over here in the Lakes. On *your* watch again, with you on site in fact . . . and you the only survivor.' Mary-Ellen's smile took on a ghoulish intensity. 'I think "national humiliation" and "career suicide" are the phrases you're looking for.

'But of course, all this could only happen after he'd run you around a bit . . . like the set of blue-arsed flies you surely are. Keeping you on the move, never letting you rest. Just like my father couldn't rest that last night of his life on Dartmoor, staggering soaking wet for miles through the dark and the cold before he finally made it to his car, suffering, slowly bleeding out, no one to turn to . . .'

'Who are you trying to kid, M-E?' Heck scoffed. 'Keeping us on the run? Only killing selectively? The Stranger's a total fuck-up. He's been firing shots at us all night, trying to kill us at every turn. What about that incident on the Via Ferrata?'

'That's easily explained,' she said. 'I guess neither you nor Hazel were quite as important as Gemma. He must have seen you crossing the bridge, Gemma at the front, and thought chopping it down would nicely take care of the two at the back – plus it might look like an accident, which could be an advantage when all this was over. As it happened, the bridge was probably sturdier than he expected. And of course everything they say about you is true, Heck . . . you don't kill easily.'

'Sorry about that . . .'

'Don't be. It's made things more interesting. You see, after that, the Stranger was really up against it. First he had to get back to the Ho, disable the cars – pain in the arse doing the police Land Rover, I'd imagine, but he had to start thinking about putting himself in the clear. Not to mention me. I mean, what did I have to do with all this? The main thing is, he had the quad-bike by then, which helped him skedaddle down to the Keld to do the vehicles and phones there, then dash off to the south end of the tarn on foot, to try and intercept us ladies on our way back. Tough shit for the firearms team he met en route. They'd arrived from Penrith at just the wrong moment. Mind you, getting rid of *that* evidence wasn't quite as tough – all he had to do was drive the car into the undergrowth.'

'If it was all going so well, why blow up the police station?' Heck asked.

Again, Mary-Ellen paused. 'I'd imagine he'd prepped that explosive the moment he learned about the two hikers on the fells.'

'He just walked into a police station cellar and turned it into a giant bomb?'

'Why not? It was unlocked. We were all of us tucked up in bed. A bit lax of me, I'll admit. May get a ticking off for that.'

'And *why* would he turn it into a bomb?' Gemma wondered.

'A kind of insurance policy. If things weren't going totally his way, he'd probably think it couldn't hurt to keep closing down your resources. Claim a few more lives in the process, remove another safe haven for you and the villagers – which is basically what happened.'

'That must've been the trickiest part of the operation, M-E,' Heck said. 'You must have had to get your timings smack-on.'

'Not me, Heck.'

'It was also damn clever of you to support me when I suggested we shouldn't wait for the firearms lads but should go out and get a couple of cars. That would *prove* you were one of the good guys, wouldn't it?'

'I *was* one of the good guys,' she said. 'You should actually thank me. I drew the bastard's fire at the top of Truscott Drive. I kept you alive.'

'Well, it certainly wouldn't have suited you if I'd died at that stage,' Heck replied. 'I know you wanted me dead earlier, but not then. I mean, if I'd died then I couldn't have gone back to the pub and told everyone how brave you'd been. You looked equally brave when we got distracted by Ted's curtain twitching. Whether you actually saw that curtain twitch or not, you knew Buster would be in there, so you'd have an excuse when we finally forced entry and only found the cat. The main thing was it gave you a few minutes away from me. Just enough time to nip across the road to the police station, climb through the cellar window, hit the breakers, open the propane tanks, and then climb out again. Done and dusted inside what . . . three, four minutes? Course, the real stroke of genius came a few minutes after that, when you shot the road surface alongside us.'

'Now you're just being silly,' she said, but her fixed grin had hardened into a kind of sneer.

'The gun was up your sleeve, I suspect,' Heck said. 'And that's why you used a silencer. I'm guessing that, earlier on, the sound of roaring gunfire suited your plan. Had to keep us running scared, like you said. But I'd never have fallen for an unmuffled gunshot when the weapon was in your hand and you were right next to me. Of course, while we were both supposedly lying low in the trees, all you had to do to draw our attention to the ambushed firearms car was nip up there and switch its beacon on. A tight schedule, I agree, and it's kept you on your toes, M-E, but ultimately all very manageable.'

'You're so wrong,' she said. 'It was the Stranger. It's been the Stranger from the beginning.'

'You think saying that over and over will make it true?' he asked her.

'Ultimately, Heck . . . it won't matter what you believe.'

'Or what *you* believe, M-E. Because they'll still go over this place with a fine-tooth comb, and at some point they'll uncover the truth.'

'Which is that all the evidence implicated Mick McGurk, isn't it?'

'Neatly planted evidence, I'll give you that. I guess you snaffled the wristband while you were applying first aid to McGurk back in the pub. It's also telling that only *after that* did you mention the quad-bike to us. You were certainly thinking on your feet, love. Which led neatly to the next stage of the operation . . . you sending me around the side of the McCarthy house where you knew there was a closed gate. That would give you just enough time to plant the wristband on the quad-bike, wouldn't it?'

'Aren't you forgetting I was with you and all the other villagers when the Stranger whistled to us from the fog, Heck?'

'That Dictaphone was neatly planted too,' Heck said. 'Except I wasn't meant to find that, was I?'

Mary-Ellen gave a low whistle. 'You see, Miss Piper. Heck's luck strikes again. You really were a fool to let him leave SCU.'

'Winners make their own luck,' Gemma replied. 'For Heck's luck, check no further than his habit of chasing a lead to its very end, of doing the job more thoroughly than anyone else. And that's what's undone you, isn't it, Mary-Ellen? The discovery of the Dictaphone meant you had to complete your mission at any cost.'

'Yeah,' Heck said. 'After that, you couldn't just cut your losses and run. You couldn't simply lead the villagers down the Race and then bask in the safety of their innumerable testimonies that you'd been such a friend. Maybe letting so many of them go wasn't your plan in the beginning, but I bet you had half an eye on it as a contingency when you saw time was running out. I mean, enough damage had been done to this place to register it as a disaster on the seismic scale, and the senior officers on site would get dragged over the coals for it. It wouldn't be perfect, but it would keep *your* ass out of a sling. And you could go after your real foes again at a later date. But no . . . once we had possession of the Dictaphone, which was covered in *your* prints and DNA, all that went by the wayside. You *had* to come back here and finish us.'

Mary-Ellen shrugged innocently. 'My decision to come back here was entirely the right one, DS Heckenburg, for all sorts of reasons . . . even though it won't have a happy outcome. Thanks to you confiding in Hazel about Mick McGurk, no one will ever now query my own witness state-ment, which will be that I got worried about you guys and came back with Ted Haveloc to the Boat Club – only to discover that McGurk had already killed you two, and that in the ensuing fight he killed Haveloc as well . . . before I managed to get his gun and use it on him.'

Heck shook his head. 'So you've killed Ted Haveloc too?'

'*No Heck, you killed him!*' Mary-Ellen barked, froth spurting from her lips. 'By fucking things up for everyone. By allocating Ted to *my* kayak. I told you, you fuck, by this time I was happy to send the rest of that rabble down the

Race. Ted could have gone too, but by sticking him with me you signed his death warrant. What choice did I have . . .'

'By sticking him with *you* we signed his death warrant?' Heck said, wonderingly. '*You* had no choice?'

Briefly, her mouth slammed shut, her jaw trembling violently. A fresh tear snaked a zigzag course down her left cheek.

'Careful, M-E,' he said. 'You're moving off script.'

'The Stranger killed Ted Haveloc,' she said tightly. 'Everyone will see that. And I've had enough of this bullshit!' She focused on Gemma again, raising the gun until it was level with her face. 'The Stranger's plan was to break you, DSU Piper, to ruin you professionally . . . but I'm sure he'll be equally happy to see you dead . . .'

'Course he will!' Heck butted in. 'He's the lowest of the low, a sadistic pipsqueak!'

'Shut up, Heck,' she shouted. 'You're next, but how you get it is my choice.'

'*You* know what a scrote he was better than anyone, don't you, M-E!'

Fleetingly, Mary-Ellen was distracted between the two of them; more tears poured profusely; tears of rage, regret, angst . . . who knew?

'All those lonely years in that dirty, decrepit caravan,' Heck said. 'Just him and his perverted fantasies. And you of course. The little girl with the perfect dad.'

'*I said, shut the fuck up!*'

'Except no one could ever have been that perfect, Mary-Ellen. Especially not someone with a track record for sexual violence. Like I say . . . *you* know that better than anyone!'

Her eyes flared like pits of burning oil as she swung the Python around, at which point Gemma snatched her own firearm from the shingle and levelled it with both hands. 'Drop that weapon, PC O'Rourke! Right now!'

Heck had been counting on this. Only a few seconds earlier, he'd glanced again at Gemma's gun, and had suddenly thought its chunky black outline and big cylindrical barrel all wrong for a harmless starter pistol.

Mary-Ellen smirked at Gemma with disbelief. 'You on crack, ma'am? Thinking you can take me down with that silly toy?'

Gemma locked gazes with her. 'Don't make me do it, Mary-Ellen.'

And only now did Mary-Ellen seem to recognise that something might be wrong. That somehow or other she might not be fully in control of this situation.

'You sneaky bitch!' She swung the Colt Python back around.

But Gemma fired first.

The 'starter pistol', which was actually a single-shot flare gun, bucked in her hand, a ball of blistering light flashing the twenty yards between them, hitting the policewoman clean on her left side and engulfing her in flame; igniting her like a Roman Candle. With flames roaring up her legs and the whole left side of her body, Mary-Ellen ran headlong into the tarn, uttering muffled, incoherent shrieks, but still managing to get three thunderous shots off before the waters enveloped her in clouds of steam. Thanks to her frantic, stumbling flight, and the massive recoil of the Python, all three slugs went wide, though the two cops still threw themselves to the ground.

As the tarn roiled and hissed, Heck snatched Gemma's hood and yanked her to her feet. 'This way,' he said, hauling her along the shingle towards the clubhouse.

'Tell me you got all that?' Gemma shouted.

Heck stuck his hand into the same pocket as before, where the Dictaphone was still running on 'Record'. He hit the 'Off' switch through the sealed evidence bag.

'Just hope it picked up something,' he said. 'It's a souped-up model, so it ought to have. Good job these bags are airtight too. Otherwise, this thing would have died when the canoe went down . . .'

They scrambled over the Boat Club fence, but there now came a squawk of outrage behind them. Whatever the fire had done to Mary-Ellen, they couldn't tell – despite glancing back, in the murk and the smoke and the steam they had no detail. But she hadn't relinquished her Python and now appeared to be kneeling upright in the water, levelling the weapon with both hands. Two more deafening shots followed, an entire plate-glass window on this side of the clubhouse disintegrating.

Heck and Gemma ducked sideways, struggling and tripping between tables and chairs. The next thing they were on slick timber decking. Ahead of them, the Boat Club jetty tapered off into the fog.

'You bitch!' Mary-Ellen screeched behind them. 'He'll do you for this!'

At that shrill pitch, her voice barely sounded human; it was frothy and distorted. It was easy to picture the effects of the flames on her face and mouth. Not that she'd lost any of her demented rage. She was armed with a revolver, which only contained six shots. She'd now fired five. But if she was concerned about using her last, it didn't show. The Python roared again, and the wooden handrail alongside them exploded.

'You fucking bitch, Piper!' Again, it was a barely human sound, as if her mouth was stuffed with sand.

It was a near-certainty that having raided the strong-box in the firearms car, she'd have another weapon to hand, and indeed, as Heck and Gemma started along the jetty at a faltering, hobbling gait – not only was Gemma injured, but neither of them really knew where they were going – she opened fire again, and instead of the deafening *bang* of the Magnum, this time they heard the duller, flatter *blam* of a police-issue Glock nine millimetre. The shot whistled past, with inches to spare.

'Heck, where the hell are we going?' Gemma stammered. 'I can't even stand up, never mind swim . . .'

'There are other boats along here.'

'Another bloody boat!'

'You got a better idea?'

The only boat they found was about two-thirds of the way along the jetty, on its starboard side. It was a canoe, smaller than the previous one but with two paddles inside it. Quickly, Heck untied its line, and lowered Gemma down the ladder. Behind him, heavy feet were advancing along the jetty, along with a hoarse, raw breathing.

He'd expected Mary-Ellen to open fire again by now, but they had a good fifty yards on her, and presumably, her thermal-imaging device had died either in the fire or the tarn.

'You sodding bastards,' she blathered. 'He'll scalp you for this . . . he'll scalp you and he'll fucking skin you . . .'

Heck contemplated lying flat on the top of the jetty, hoping she'd have come alongside him before she realised he was there. He felt he could take her. Even with Mary-Ellen hurt, it would be a hell of a fight, but he'd have the element of surprise. However, when she started shooting again, blindly and indiscriminately, he changed his mind. With boards erupting and splintering around him, he rolled over the edge and swung himself down the ladder like an ape.

'Nice touch with the flare gun,' he said, as he paddled them away. Gemma was attempting to help, but was in so much pain that her efforts were sluggish and uncoordinated. 'Just get comfortable,' he said. 'I've got this.'

The Glock detonated thirty yards behind, and a slug slapped into the water a few feet to their left.

'Are you kidding!' Gemma said through gritted teeth. She struck hard with her paddle. 'It's two of us or none at all.'

Heck didn't argue. He was already breathing hard, feeling the strain in his chest and shoulders, though the canoe was moving swiftly and smoothly, cutting cleanly out into the south-central waters of the tarn. He still didn't know where they were going, the fog slithering on all sides, masking everything. 'Anyway, like I say, nice touch with the flare . . .'

'Yeah, I heard you the first time.'

'Better than a starter pistol.'

'I couldn't find the sodding starter pistol! But the flare gun was in an emergency kit in the club's first-aid locker. I trashed the Club Secretary's office in the process!'

'That'll be the least of his problems when the new season starts.'

There was another bark of gunfire. A bullet whizzed closely past.

'I don't believe it,' Heck said, glancing over his shoulder.

Another boat was already on the water behind them. Barely visible, but gaining.

'Don't tell me,' Gemma said. 'She's back in her kayak.'

'Looks like she's in yours, the single-hander. Doesn't give up easily, does she?'

'How can she afford to?'

'I've met some headcases in my time . . .'

'It's about survival now, Heck.'

'Call it what you want, she's mad as a hatter!'

They'd now managed to find a mutual rhythm, though Gemma winced with the pain and effort. Ahead of them, the fog seemed to be shifting. Heck had the feeling they were approaching a landmass of some sort; the southeast shore maybe.

'Just think about it,' he panted. 'All this time, she's been waiting her chance. I mean, it might never have come. But

413

she was patient, infinitely patient, just biding her time . . .
month after month, year after year.'

'Yeah, yeah . . . just keep that tape recording safe . . .'

'It may be classified as unreliable evidence, don't you
think?'

'Improperly obtained,' she replied, 'but real enough. I think
they'll admit it . . .'

The Glock barked again. But they barely heard. A rising
rumble from somewhere ahead now drew all their attention.
The fog broke apart like dim, dusty curtains, to reveal rising
slopes clad with trees, and yet directly in front, a cleft in
this hillside, and across that at ground level, a stone footbridge. The steel grating of the gate was raised, a cloud of
spume hanging over it.

Gemma grabbed the gunwales as she felt the current take
them. 'You think we can handle the Race?'

'If the others made it, why can't we?'

'We don't know whether they made it or not.'

'We will in a few minutes . . .'

They ducked down as they were sucked under the bridge.
The white-water boomed in their ears. And then they were
dropping, nose-diving downward into a chaos of noise and
spray and rolling, tumbling waves.

Chapter 34

At first glance, Cragwood Race was like something manmade, the river roaring steeply downhill between high earthen banks and heaped, slab-like rocks, but with no central obstructions, nothing to impede the velocity of the water.

The initial experience was of a frantic downhill chase through roaring foam. Little or no paddling was needed. In fact, the best thing was to keep one's arms firmly to one's body as the boat swerved around bends, constantly sideswiping the moss-clad embankments. Oftentimes Heck and Gemma hit rocks, only the thick layer of vegetation covering these hard surfaces preventing serious damage to the canoe, but the sheer force and noise of these collisions made them realise why modern day wildwater enthusiasts wore crash helmets. It was certainly impossible to steer. Wind hit their faces as well as spray, forcefully and constantly. Heck was already wet through, but now Gemma was drenched too, from head to foot.

The foggy darkness persisted even down this hectic channel, which made all attempts to gauge the speed they were moving at pointless, though it was clear they'd quickly travelled several hundred yards downhill, merely having allowed the torrent to take them. The trouble was that they were now hitting a series of natural platforms, the river boiling monstrously over every level stretch before dropping sharply downward again. On each of these occasions, there was a tremendous backward surge which required strenuous paddling to get through and which always saw them deluged from behind, gallons of frothing, icy water pouring over them in sledgehammer cataracts. No sooner were they free of this than the canoe was driven forward furiously, rising, falling and rocking, bumping and scraping its way across submerged stones. For several seconds on the third platform, they were travelling sideways, like an airbed on an ocean wave. They shrieked in unison as they began to tilt, hurling their bodies the other way to right themselves, and paddling frantically for fear the boat would turn around and take them down the rest of the Race backward, or even worse, upside down. They pulled it around just in time as the gradient re-steepened, water like frothing milk exploding past and over the top of them, and shot down the next stretch like a cork from a bottle, battering the rocks along its sides, bodies jerking left to right, necks whiplashing.

But it was only when they entered a deep canyon between pitted granite walls, with a tangle of roots, mosses and hanging grasses interlaced overhead, that they understood the true meaning of peril. Initially it was so dark in here that it was virtually a tunnel, but then a fiery flash seared the dripping walls, and though the roar of the torrent was amplified a hundred times, they still heard the dull *blam*.

A slug whipped past Heck's shoulder, ricocheted from the gully wall about twenty yards ahead, and with a flash of sparks, caromed from the opposite wall before vanishing into the maelstrom.

'Jesus!' Gemma shouted.

'Guess again!' Heck craned his neck to look behind.

A dim form was descending the foam-filled channel at their rear. There was another flash-bang, and the slope dipped just in time as the round zipped past overhead. In front, the canyon turned sharply. This was the Switchback, Heck realised, the one Mary-Ellen had mentioned – supposedly the only really dangerous section. For several seconds, the rolling waterway turned glass-smooth, the current moving so fast it was broken by little more than ripples. But as they approached the turn, the river level rose rapidly and they were jolted upward and to the left, clinging for dear life as the Race banked around the tight corner. Briefly, they were horizontal, as if they were riding the Wall of Death in some crazy amusement park. But then they were dropping again, descending a muddy, root-filled throat, bouncing over another series of steps, the canoe elevating into mid-air with each one, then crash-landing again, the echoing impacts deadening their ears, the river raining over them from behind, rollback buffeting them from every side.

If that wasn't enough, as soon as Mary-Ellen rounded the Switchback, she opened fire again, twice. Both projectiles struck blistering sparks along the underside of a leaning, egg-shaped boulder even as Heck and Gemma were bowing their heads to pass beneath it.

'You're right!' Gemma cried. 'She's out of her bloody mind!'

The river now veered to the left, but beyond this, the descent flattened out, and the route unexpectedly broadened. They decelerated as the canyon walls fell away, and found themselves in open space. They were back on a level stretch, and this time it persisted, though they were still moving fast. They got to it with their paddles, doing the best they could to create another effective rhythm. The problem was they were novices at this, while Mary-Ellen had done it several times before. Heck glanced back again, though now saw only white-water and fog. Had she come unstuck?

The answer came quickly, with another dim gun-flash, and the whining impact of lead striking a boulder, this one tooth-like and jutting up just ahead of them. In anticipation of rapids, the water began to boil. They swerved around the obstruction, but could see more outcrops beyond it.

'Shit!' Heck shouted. If Switchback Canyon was the only dangerous part, he didn't know what this was supposed to be.

They attempted to steer with their paddles, but crashed and bounced around one boulder after another. If they got through this, he reckoned, it would mainly be due to the force of the flow, which rose and fell and swelled and burst over them in storms of spray. And yet shortly, when they *had* passed it, the downhill race recommenced, shunting them over another series of stair-like platforms, the heavy edges of rock hammering the underside of the canoe with such nauseating force that it left them groggy. When a brackish wave swamped them from the left, all but capsizing them, it did less to revive them and more to half-drown them. They now drooped limply in their seats, lifeless and exhausted like broken dolls, when the course of the river changed dramatically, surging around a few more S-bends but now at a gentler, almost meandering rate.

Heck mopped water from his face, but had to blink to make sure he wasn't seeing things. The fog had lessened. It was still a notable presence, but not as all-enveloping as it had been. It helped that they were suddenly on very level ground, but he realised he could see tens of yards beyond the banks of the river, into sparse woodland, skeletal under-brush and the pillars of ivy-clad tree-trunks stretching away in all directions.

There was another hairy moment when the boat grated

over hidden surfaces, lurching side to side – it seemed they were among rapids again – but these were actually a minor issue: a few scattered cobblestones cluttering the decelerating flow.

'I think . . . I think we've made it,' Heck risked saying. 'Look, there!' Some thirty yards ahead, a stone-built structure arched over the channel. 'That bridge carries the B5343. The other side of that and we're into Langdale Beck.'

'You sure?' Gemma gasped. Again, she was rigid with pain, her torso angled left.

'It must be . . . there's no other road along here.' His jubilant tone faltered. 'Trouble is . . .' He glanced back. Despite the receding fog, there was no sign of Mary-Ellen, but how far behind could she be? 'Now we've *really* got to work.'

They paddled strenuously again, passing under the B5343. It was tempting to try and run the vessel aground, get out and climb up to the road. But the embankment looked steep and in any case, even if they made it, they'd still be in the middle of nowhere, with miles to go before the next habitation.

Perhaps forty yards past the bridge, now amid open, flattish farmland, increasingly more of which was visible thanks to the dwindling fog, they joined Langdale Beck, a broad, slow-moving stream. Even in the dimness, it was so shallow – no more than two or three feet – and so clean and clear they could see the layers of pebbles at the bottom. However, its eastward current was laboriously slow, so they had to paddle even harder – until Gemma stopped abruptly, the paddle slipping from her shuddering grasp, dropping into the water. 'Shit, Heck . . . I've really hurt my back . . .'

'I know,' he said. 'Don't worry. We're almost there. We'll get you to hospital ASAP.'

But neither of them believed that.

'You know . . . she's gonna catch us if we stay on this river,' Gemma gasped.

'I'm open to suggestions.'

'How far . . .' She'd hunched sideways against the port gunwale, both hands clawed into fists. 'How far to the next village?'

'That would be Chapel Stile. A few miles. But it's only a church and a handful of cottages.'

'You think the others will have got there?'

'Bella McCarthy will most likely have headed there.' Heck was guessing, but it seemed reasonable. They hadn't seen any trace of the others yet; no wreckage or bodies, which had to be a good sign, but no beached craft either, which meant they were all still on the water. 'She knows the owner of the Wainwrights' Inn, which is a popular pub around here. She might be there already. Trouble is, Chapel Stile's not necessarily any refuge. We could call for help from there, but Mary-Ellen will have killed everyone by the time it arrives.'

'You really think she'd go that far?'

'Count on it. Like you said, it's all or nothing for her now. She's not gonna start this whole thing again somewhere else at some later date.'

'If Bella and the others have made it to Chapel Stile, they might've called for help already. M-E's going to get caught . . . she must know that.'

'I doubt she cares about herself anymore,' Heck said. 'She's been planning all this time to punish you, Gemma – if not ridicule you in the eyes of the nation, to kill you. Brutally, slowly. And now look . . . you've got most of the villagers away, plus you've survived. Not only will you be a hero, you'll be a *live* hero.'

He glanced behind – just in time to see the distant blip of Mary-Ellen's vessel come veering around the bend into the beck, its passenger working furiously with her two-bladed paddle. Again, even though there was maybe eighty yards between them, he could see that she was gaining ground. In normal circumstances, two to one, they ought to be outpacing her with ease, but Gemma was too stiff with pain to help in any way. On top of that, Mary-Ellen was the ace athlete and an experienced kayaker.

Heck looked around frantically. They were currently passing leafless trees on the north bank and quiet waterside meadows on the south, but some thirty yards back from the river on this latter side, vaguely misted by vapour but still identifiable, stood a row of four hollow, half-built structures. Holiday maisonettes almost certainly, being adapted from more ancient farm buildings. The area around them was cluttered with prefab cabins, cement mixers, piles of building materials, hand-tools and the like, the ground muddy and slashed by caterpillar tracks.

Without conferring on the matter, Heck turned the blade of his paddle, bringing them towards the south bank, the canoe grounding itself on sand and shingle.

'What're we doing?' Gemma asked.

'Sorry, but you're right.' He took her by the elbow and helped her out. 'Once she gets close, we'll be sitting ducks on this river . . .'

'Is there somewhere here we can hide?' Gemma asked, as he hustled her forward.

'We'll see . . .'

The maisonettes swam fully into view, their river-facing side covered with scaffolding and hanging plastic.

'Hell, Heck . . . what is this, a bloody building site?'

'It'll do!'

'Just so you . . .' Gemma's bottom lip was bloodied, she'd bitten it so hard. Though he dragged her forward mercilessly, she could barely even hobble. 'Just so you know . . . I can't go much further . . .'

'With luck, you won't need to.' He forced her under the site's single boundary rope.

'Maybe . . . maybe there's a security guard who can make a call,' she stuttered.

'Nope. They tend not to need security up here.'

The gaunt shadow of the maisonettes fell over them.

'Course not,' she replied. 'Not a bad 'un for miles, eh?'

Chapter 35

The Stranger's scorched uniform clung to her in tatters, adhering to the blistered, purulent flesh underneath. She couldn't imagine what she looked like, but for the moment that mattered no more than the pain itself: it was something she could deal with later. If there was going to be a later. Not that she cared one way or the other, so long as she finished the task she'd set herself.

Pointed statements had been made about her earlier on: that she was scum, a sadistic pipsqueak.

Well, she couldn't deny it. What she was and what she did revolted her. This very night alone she'd several times puked as her innate self-loathing had threatened to overwhelm her. But they were far past the stage of backing out now. The task was everything – to show the world she was here, she was back, that she'd never gone away, that they couldn't attribute her work to anyone else, no matter how hard they tried, no matter how blind they were to the innocence of those they despised, especially that one whose life they'd so callously taken. The one known only as 'Dada', with all the wonderful things that had entailed: the affection, the care, the shield against a hostile world, the endless, unconditional love. So what if he'd had demons inside him that he'd needed to extinguish? All men did.

The Stranger herself did.

And she was about to extinguish them right now.

She stooped under the rope and limped into the building site. She'd only caught a fleeting glimpse of them before they'd dodged out of sight. But they couldn't have gone far. She might be hurt, but she had the edge on them in everything: fitness, aggression, guile. She'd toyed with Heck, the strongest among them, all night, running rings around him in the fog, chasing him along the Cradle, knocking off his friends and helpers one by one, even blowing up his police station. Oh, *that* had been a hoot.

But this was no time for dwelling on past victories.

The Stranger stood and listened, but heard only her own breathing as it rasped between her teeth. The echoing structures of the half-built maisonettes with their vast exoskeleton of scaffolding, were the obvious place to start. They might contain a hundred niches where two injured, weary creatures could hide. But before she could commence searching, she heard something: a low mumbling.

She flattened herself against a stack of polythene-covered house-bricks to listen.

There was no question: it was voices. A man and a woman conversing quietly.

At least, they thought it was quietly. Their heads were probably still ringing after their violent trip down the Race. In addition, they'd have no clue how much an animal of the night the Stranger was – how superior she was in the dark, how sharp her senses, how acute her hearing. How this was *her* hunting ground, *her* natural home.

She slid to the first corner of the bricks and glanced up. The voices emanated from one of the higher floors of the maisonettes, the first or second storey. The Stranger had no idea whether there'd be stairs inside the big, half-built structures. But a stair would be a risk anyway; using the most obvious route up would make her an easier target than she cared for. Of course, there was another way to approach.

She nipped across the open ground at the foot of the scaffolding, and stepped underneath it to avoid being seen from overhead. The maisonettes were open at the front, so from here she could see right through to the back of them. They were indeed empty shells, nothing but bare, grey concrete inside their outer carapace of Lakeland slate, their floors and walls blank except for the odd builder's chalk-mark, their only contents a few heaps of cement sacks in the far corner of the ground floor beyond the brand-new fireplace. She glanced upward again. Nothing was clearly visible: too many cross-beams, wood and metal interspersed, too much polythene sheeting. But she could still hear that subdued conversation, so clearly she could even distinguish the man and the woman's individual voices.

The Stranger checked the Glock she'd used on the way down the Race; its magazine carried seventeen shots, and she'd fired at least twelve. The five remaining might not be enough to ensure she'd take Heck down, so she ejected the clip, slammed another into place and tucked the Glock into her belt. Reaching back under her burned jacket, she drew out a second Glock, another gift from the armed police car. This one was already fully loaded. She'd reserve that one for Piper, she thought, tucking it into her belt alongside the first, and beginning to climb, ascending slowly and painfully through the framework, the bars and pins creaking, juddering, but all the way hearing that unbroken conversation overhead.

It sounded as if Piper was in pain. The Stranger smiled; the bitch didn't know the meaning of real agony yet. Seventeen rounds from a Glock would change all that, starting from the legs up.

425

She reached the first timber catwalk, which lay roughly parallel with the first floor of the maisonettes, and paused to listen. Still they were muttering together. She glanced around. About ten yards behind, a ladder slanted up to the next catwalk, vanishing through a hatch. She hobbled down to it, halting at the bottom, listening. Their tones were fraught. Drawing the first Glock, she clamped it between her teeth. It hurt appallingly – just opening her blistered mouth was torture, but anything was endurable at this stage. She started up slowly, watching the hatch overhead like a hawk, but from the ongoing murmur she was confident they hadn't yet realised she was here.

The Stranger emerged through the hatch, unscathed. They were very close – she could now hear them clearly.

'Try and relax,' Heck said. 'It may be you've just slipped a disc . . .'

'Are you a doctor?' Gemma replied sharply. 'How can you damn well tell?'

At the extreme end of the catwalk hung a sheet of opaque polythene. The voices were on the other side. A pistol in either hand, the Stranger zeroed in.

'Why have a go at me?' Heck protested. 'I've kept you alive this long, haven't I?'

'*You've* kept me alive? That's a good one!'

'Hey, it's time you were told what's what . . .'

The Stranger grinned again. The timber walk seemed loose beneath her feet. In fact the entire scaffold wobbled, but that didn't matter.

Nothing mattered now.

She yanked the polythene curtain back.

And found herself confronting not Heck and Gemma, but a builder's sawhorse, and standing on top of it, a Dictaphone.

'You're such a smartarse,' Gemma's voice intoned.

'You think you're someone special,' Heck's voice added,

426

'but in fact you're a demented little nobody who's totally lost the plot . . .'

Taking his cue from Mary-Ellen's screeches of birdlike outrage, Heck stepped out from the ground-floor room, shook off a layer of cement dust from the bags he and Gemma had been hidden under, and swung with a sledgehammer at the nearest scaffolding support, the one whose nuts and bolts he'd already carefully loosened.

Three heavy blows were all it took, and the support fell away.

Heck leapt backward into the interior of the building, as the entire scaffolding structure began to collapse in on itself. It seemed to happen in slow motion, and yet resulted in a monumental deluge of smashing wood and twisting, screaming steel.

Mary-Ellen didn't fall straight away. The catwalk beneath her collapsed immediately, but she snatched at a parallel bar and hung there, some thirty feet up. However, her gloves had no real grip, plus more and more pieces of metalwork plummeted past from above, several clouting her en route, so at last she dropped with them, vanishing without a sound into the dust-enshrouded mass of clattering poles and booming, shattering timber. Even then it didn't end; section after section crashing down, each landing on top of the one before with shuddering force, sparks flying, fountains of mud and dirt exploding as the earth was brutally gouged.

When Heck and Gemma finally emerged from their shelter several minutes later, wafting at dust, it was only when they were sure the avalanche of steel was over. They beheld a building site flattened beneath mounds of contorted wreckage, which seemed to stretch as far in every direction as the diminishing fog would allow. It took several more minutes for Heck to locate Mary-Ellen, and pick his way through to her.

427

She wasn't so much submerged beneath the heavy, broken materials, as mangled by them; beaten, torn, hammered into the churned, bloody ground. The mere glimpses of her body permitted by the tangled metal told him all he needed to know.

Ironically, the only part of her untouched by falling steel was the only part properly exposed, which was her face, and yet the earlier fire had already scoured this clean. All her female features had gone. A sexless, skinless visage stared unblinkingly up at Heck as he sat alongside her. Initially there wasn't a lot he could say. But then he spotted something lying nearby. He rooted through the debris and produced the Dictaphone, which he was pleased to dust off and find was still in working order.

'Lucky . . .' Her voice was a hoarse croak; the mere act of trying to speak inducing a choked cough; thick, purplish syrup oozed from her gash of a mouth. 'Lucky again, uh . . . Heck . . .?'

'Winners make their own luck, M-E, haven't you heard? But let's not waste anymore time when there are so many people in need of assistance this morning.' He hit the 'Record' switch and held it down to her. 'Do you want to make a dying declaration?'

'Just this . . . he's still out there . . .' More bloody ichor dribbled down her blistered jaw. 'He'll always . . . always be out there . . .' She gave a throaty gurgle, which Heck didn't at first identify as a chuckle.

'Okay, I hear that,' he said. 'How about your father then? Anything you can tell me about him. His name, where you buried him . . .?'

'That . . . won't do you any good.'

Gemma now appeared, looking weak and pale, leaning on a broken scaffolding pole. 'It's the best chance you've got to put things right, M-E.'

'And you . . . you needn't look so happy, Miss Piper . . .'

'Nothing I see here is making me happy,' Gemma said.

'Saint Barbie, eh?' Mary-Ellen treated them to a ghastly jack-o-lantern smile. 'The . . . gun-toting Barbie doll whore. This isn't over . . .' Her lidless eyes rolled in agony. 'Not . . . for *you* . . .' More brackish red gunk welled from Mary-Ellen's mouth as her breathing faltered. Her voice had fallen to a hoarse, barely audible whisper. Heck almost had to touch his device to her mouth. 'The Stranger . . . is still . . . out there . . . in the dark. That's . . . where he lives. You'll try to avoid it, Gemma . . . I know. But sometime . . . in the future, you too will be out there . . . on your own. And then . . . then you'll learn.' She looked away, but her crooked smile remained unnaturally fixed, as if the dying nerve-ends had locked it in place.

Gemma shook her head. 'You silly, vindictive child.'

'No wisecracks, sarge . . .?'

Heck sighed. 'If you've genuinely nothing to offer this world but hatred, M-E, you're probably better off out of it.'

'Doesn't look like . . . like . . . got much choice . . .'

At which point Mary-Ellen's fire-damaged eyes glazed over, her grinning mouth froze, and the last breath exhaled slowly and foully from her dismembered body.

Chapter 36

The fog had cleared by two o'clock.

Not a wisp of it remained, not even on the highest peaks. Once it had gone, the eerie, almost mystical atmosphere went with it, leaving behind another drab November day, cold and damp, autumnal-brown hillsides lowering under a slate-grey sky. Yet this was still the busiest afternoon in Cragwood Keld's history, at least as far as Hazel could remember.

Helicopters lofted by overhead, while search teams – police, military and civilian – were trawling the surrounding fells. Rescue and emergency vehicles of every description were parked in numerous parts of the village, though mostly in those areas that hadn't been taped off by groups of men and women in forensics garb. The air crackled with radio static and echoed to the yipping of police dogs. Hazel didn't think she'd ever seen as many officers, either uniformed or in plainclothes, at one time. It all seemed terribly chaotic, though she supposed there must be some level of organisation.

It still seemed incredible to her that all this appalling mayhem – life-changing events in so many ways, afflicting so many people – could have taken place in just twenty-four hours. At roughly this same time yesterday morning she'd arisen as usual, yawning, stretching, expecting another easy, uneventful day in the Lake District off-season. If it wasn't for the grim detritus littered on all sides of her, it was possible she could still be persuaded that it had been an unreal dream.

That was evidence perhaps that she was still in shock, although she'd been looked over by a senior paramedic first thing that morning. She'd assured him she didn't need it, and that she didn't feel too bad – in fact that she didn't feel anything at all. His response had been that this was abnormal and that in due course she'd realise this and would take the pills he recommended.

Maybe. For the moment though, she continued to wander what remained of the village, finally finding Heck at the bottom of the crater where Cragwood Keld police office had once stood. Both the Bomb Squad and the Fire Brigade had now cleared it for inspection, and apparently Heck had been one of the first ones down there. That had been half an hour ago, and he was still burrowing through the rubble.

The scraping of bricks as she descended alerted him to her presence. He turned, brushing his grubby hands on his sweatshirt, and half-smiled when he saw the big ginger tom-cat in her arms.

'Gemma's in hospital, I hear,' Hazel said.

'Damaged disc. No surgery required. Just rest. She'll be fine.'

'And how are you?'

'The usual . . . bit frazzled round the edges, but I think I'll be okay. How's Buster?' he asked, indicating the cat. With Ted Haveloc gone, it would now be minus one very caring owner.

'Lost . . . a bit sad.' In truth, the cat didn't look either of those things, snuggling against her bosom as she squeezed him. 'Not to worry, we'll house him at the pub from now on.'

Heck smiled, and went back to his rooting and digging. She saw that he'd already retrieved one item; what looked like an old scrapbook. Its cover was badly charred, but the edges of the pages inside looked to be intact. She'd never seen his photo-record of all those murder victims he'd gained results for, and she'd never wanted to – but it seemed a reasonable guess that this was it.

'How did you find the Race?' she asked.

'Wet.'

'Me too. So did everyone else. Burt Fillingham had a heart attack going through Switchback Canyon.'

Heck glanced up. 'I heard that. How is he?'

'He'll recover. Something to tell his grandkids . . . a red badge of courage from the battle of Cragwood Vale.'

Heck brushed his hands again, surveying the scorched rubble. 'Sure looks like a battlefield.'

'And yet you're still here, Mark . . . right in the middle of it.'

'Just salvaging what I can.'

She nodded at his scrapbook. 'Looks like the important thing survived.'

He picked it up, flicked its pages. Many had browned in the heat and smoke, but the images they contained were just about identifiable. 'None of these poor people survived the attacks that really mattered, I'm afraid.'

'You know, Mark . . . you have to draw a line somewhere. You can't live this job like you seem to.'

'That's been said,' he agreed.

'It's going to send you to an early grave.'

'That's been said too.'

'By Gemma, no doubt. But if you won't listen to it from her, what're the chances you'll listen to it from me?'

He didn't reply, just regarded her guiltily.

'You know I can't go with you, don't you?' she said.

432

'And that means . . .?'

'When you return to the world.'

'I'm not returning to . . .'

'Don't lie to me, please. We've been through an awful lot together this last day and night. I'm just about still on my feet. But I don't think I could take it if you started lying to me.'

'Okay . . . I won't.'

'That world you yearn to be part of is not mine, I'm afraid. And don't tell me you *need* to be part of it, because that isn't true. If you need anything, Mark Heckenburg, it's a clip around the ear from time to time, from a woman who loves you. But you're a grown-up. You have to make this decision for yourself.'

'You know, Hazel . . .' Heck kicked the last few bricks he'd been searching back into place. 'You've been the only nice thing that's happened to me in an awfully long time.'

'But not nice enough, is that it?'

'In some ways you've been too nice. I'd say you're too good for me, but that would be a cliché. What I actually mean is . . . you'd make it very difficult for me to do the job the way I do it.'

'You mean you wouldn't be able to risk your life every day?'

'I don't risk my . . . well, not *every* day.'

'Just now and then?'

'Yeah, now and then.' He shrugged. 'Most of the time I'm buried in routine stuff. Hours and hours of it.'

'You're telling me you'd never come home?'

'I would come home because I'd *have* to, but that'd be the problem . . . it would reduce my effectiveness as an operator.'

She shook her head. 'So not only are you not prepared to stay here, in this place, you're not prepared to be with me? Not in the long term anyway.'

433

'Look, I've always known I have this problem with commitment . . .'

She pointed at his scrapbook. 'But you're committed to *those* people, who are actually dead. They can't be hurt anymore than they already are, can they?'

'Hazel, come on . . .'

'But maybe that's what you like about them.'

'That's a low blow.'

'Sometimes low blows are deserved. And required.' She turned and headed back up the slope. 'I'm reopening the pub in half an hour, if you fancy a drink. A few of your colleagues have been commenting about what thirsty work all this is.'

'Hazel . . . for what it's worth, I'm really sorry.'

She glanced down from the top. 'You'll get over it, I'm sure. Life goes on, the future beckons and all that. Who knows what it holds, Mark. For either of us.'

Are you #HOOKEDONHECK? Tell us all about it @CrimeFix and @paulfinchauthor.

And if you can't wait for your next Heck fix, read on for a sneak peek of Paul's next book, *Hunted*, which hits the shelves in May 2015.

Chapter 1

Dazzer and Deggsy didn't give a shit about anyone. At least, that was the sort of thing they said if they were bragging to mates in the pub, or if the coppers caught them and tried to lay a guilt-trip on them.

'We do what we do, innit? We don't go out looking to hurt people, but if they get in the way, tough fucking shit. We pinch motors and have a laugh in 'em. And we're gonna keep doing it, because it's the best laugh ever. No one's gonna stop us, and if they get, like, really pissed off because we've just wrecked their pride and joy, so what. We don't give a shit.'

Tonight was a particularly good night for it.

Alright, it wasn't perishing cold, which was a shame. Incredible though it seemed to Dazzer and Deggsy, some numbskulls actually came outside, saw a bit of ice and snow and left their motors running for five minutes with the key in the ignition, while they went back indoors for a cuppa; all you had to do was jump in the saddle and ride away, whooping. But if nothing else, it was dank and misty, and with it being the tail-end of January, it got dark early – so there weren't too many people around to interfere.

437

Not that folk tended to interfere with Dazzer and Deggsy.

The former was tall for his age; just under six feet, with a broad build and a neatly layered patch of straw-blonde hair in the middle of his scalp, the rest of which was shaved to the bristles. If it hadn't been for the acne covering his brutish features, you'd have thought him eighteen, nineteen, maybe twenty – instead of sixteen, which was his true age, though of course even a sixteen-year-old might clobber you these days if you had the nerve to give some indication that his behaviour affronted you. As was often the way with juvenile duos, the second member of the tag-team, Deggsy, though he wasn't by any means the lesser in terms of villainy, looked more his age. He was shorter and thinner, weasel-faced and the proud owner of an unimpressively wispy moustache. His oily black thatch was usually covered by a grimy old baseball cap, the frontal logo of which had long been erased by time and had been replaced with letters written in dayglo orange highlighter, which read: *Fuck off*.

There wasn't thirty years of experience between them, yet they both affected the arrogant swagger and truculent sneer of guys who believed they knew what was what, and were absolutely confident they did what they did because the world had been a bastard with them and fully deserved whatever they gave it back.

It was just around nine o'clock that night when they spied their first and most obvious target: a Volkswagen estate hatchback. A-reg and in poor shape generally: grubby, rusted around the arches, occasional dents in the bodywork; but it ticked all the boxes.

Posh motors were almost impossible to steal these days. All that top-of-the-range stuff was the sole province of professionals who would make a fortune from ringing it and selling it on. No, if you were simply looking for a fun time, you had to settle for this lower quality merchandise – but that could also be an advantage, because you went and smacked a bit of rubbish around on the streets, the coppers would tow it away afterwards but would rarely investigate; so, if they didn't catch you in the act, you were home free. In addition, this one's location was good. Leatherhead boasted several sprawling industrial estates with lots of service and retail parking, not to mention numerous supermarkets, pubs, clubs and restaurants in the town centre, which also had 'own risk' parking lots attached. Most of these were covered by cameras, which made the punters feel it was relatively safe to leave their motors overnight, and in many cases that was true – it was certainly safer in Leatherhead than it had been in the pre-CCTV era – but there were black spots as well, all of which Dazzer and Deggsy were intimately informed about, and the old Volkswagen estate was sitting right in the middle of one.

They watched it from a corner, eyes peeled for any sign of movement, but the dim sodium glow of the sparsely located streetlamps illuminated only a rolling beer can and a few scraps of wastepaper flapping in the halfhearted breeze.

Still, they waited. They'd been successful several times on this patch – it was a one-lane access way running between the back doors of a row of old shops and a high brick wall, and ending at three concrete bollards. No one was ever around here at night; there were no tenants in the flats above the shops, and even without the January miasma this was a dark, dingy place – but all such apparent ease of opportunity did was make Dazzer and Deggsy more suspicious than usual. The very fact that motors had been lifted from around here before made the presence of this one seem curious. Did people never learn? Maybe they didn't. Though maybe there were other factors as well. The row of shops was a bit of an eyesore. Only one or two were occupied during the day, most of the others 'to let', a couple even boarded up as if they'd just been abandoned. God bless the Recession. When folk were at their wits' end, they stopped caring – and that was always the best time to hit them.

The lads ventured forth, walking boldly but stealthily, alert to the slightest unnatural sound – but no one called out, no one stepped from a darkened doorway.

The Volkswagen was locked of course, but Deggsy had his screwdriver with him, and in less than five seconds they'd forced the driver's door open. No alarm sounded, which was just what they'd expected given the ramshackle state of the thing; another advantage of pillaging the less well-off. With rasping titters, they jumped inside, to find that the steering column had been attacked in the past – it was held together by wads of silvery duct-tape. A few slashes of Dazzer's Stanley knife and they were through it. Even in the pitch darkness, their gloved but nimble fingers found the necessary wiring, and the contact was made.

The car rumbled to life. Laughing loudly, they hit the gas.

It was Dazzer's turn to drive today, and Deggsy's to ride, though it didn't make much difference – they were both as crazy as each other when they got behind the wheel. They blistered recklessly along, swerving around bends with tyres screeching, racing through red lights and stop signs. There was no initial response from the other road-using public. Opposing traffic was scant – another good thing about January; most folk, having spent up over Christmas, would prefer to slump in front of the telly rather than go out on the town. They pulled a handbrake turn, pivoting sideways through what would ordinarily be a busy junction, a stink of burnt rubber engulfing them, hitting the gas again as they tore out of town along the A246. They had over half a tank of petrol and a very straight road in front of them. Maybe they'd make it all the way to Guildford, where they could pinch another motor to come home in. For the moment, though, it was fun fun fun. They'd probably veer off en route, and cause chaos on a few housing estates they knew, flaying the paint from any expensive jobs that unwise owners had left in plain view.

Some roadworks surged into sight just ahead. Dazzer howled as he gunned the Volkswagen through them, cones catapulting every which way – one struck the bay window of a roadside house, and demolished it. They mowed down a 'keep left' sign, and took out a set of temporary lights, which hit the deck with a detonation of sparks.

The blacktop continued to roll out ahead; they were doing eighty, ninety, almost a hundred, and briefly were mesmerised by their own fearlessness, their attention completely focused down the borehole of their headlights. When you were in that frame of mind – and Dazzer and Deggsy nearly always were, it was part of their legend – there were almost no limits. It would have taken something quite startling to distract them from their death-defying reverie – and that came approximately seven minutes into this, their last ever journey in a stolen vehicle.

They clipped a kerbstone at eighty-five. That in itself wasn't a problem, but Deggsy, who'd just filched his mobile from his jacket pocket to film this latest escapade, was jolted so hard that he dropped it into the foot-well.

'Fuck!' he squawked, scrabbling around for it. At first he couldn't seem to locate it; there was quite a bit of junk down there – so he ripped his glove off with his teeth and went groping bare-handed. This time he found the mobile, but when he pulled his hand back he saw that he'd found something else as well.

It was clamped to his exposed wrist. Initially he thought he must have brushed his arm against an old pair of boots, which had smeared him with oil or paint. But no, now he could feel the weight of it and the multiple pinprick sensation where it had apparently gripped him. He still didn't realise what the thing actually was, not even when he held it close to his face – but then Deggsy had only ever seen scorpions on the telly, so perhaps this was unsurprising. Mind you, even on the telly he'd never seen a scorpion with as pale and shiny a carapace as this one had – it glinted like polished leather in the flickering streetlights; or as big – it was at least eight inches from nose to tail, that tail now curled to strike; or with as menacing a pair of pincers – they were the size of crab claws, and extended upward in the classic defensive pattern.

It couldn't be real, he told himself distantly.

Was it a toy? It had to be a toy.

It stung him.

At first it shocked rather than hurt; as though a red hot drawing pin had been driven full length into his flesh, and into the bone underneath. But that minor pain quickly expanded, filling his suddenly frozen arm with a white fire, which in itself intensified – until Deggsy was screaming hysterically. By the time he'd knocked the eight-legged horror back into the foot-well, he was writhing and thrashing in his seat, frothing at the mouth as he struggled to release his suddenly restrictive belt. At first, Dazzer thought his mate was play-acting, though he shouted warnings when Deggsy's convulsions threatened to interfere with his driving.

And then something alighted on Dazzer's shoulder.

Despite the wild swerving of the car, it had descended slowly, patiently – on a single silken thread, and when he turned his head to look at it, it tensed, clamping him like a hand. In the flickering hallucinogenic light, he caught brief glimpses of vivid, tiger-stripe colours and clustered demonic eyes peering at him from point-blank range.

The bite it planted on his neck was like a punch from a fist.

Dazzer's foot jammed the accelerator to the floor as his entire body went into spasms. The actual wound quickly turned numb, but searing pain shot through the rest of his body in repeated lightning strokes.

Neither lad noticed as the car mounted an embankment, engine yowling, smoke and tattered grass pouring from its tyres. It smashed through the wooden palings at the top, and then crashed downward through shrubs and undergrowth, turning over and over in the process, and landing upside down in a deep-cut country lane.

For quite a few seconds there was almost no sound: the odd groan of twisted metal, steam hissing in spirals from numerous rents in mangled bodywork.

The two concussed shapes inside, while still breathing, were barely alive in any conventional sense: torn, bloodied and battered, locked in contorted paralysis. They were still aware of their surroundings, but unable to resist as various miniature forms, having ridden out the collision in niches and crevices, now re-emerged to scurry over their warm, tortured flesh. Deggsy's jaw was fixed rigid; he could voice no complaint – neither as a mumble nor a scream – when the pale-shelled scorpion re-acquainted itself with him, creeping slowly up his body on its jointed stick-legs and finally settling on his face, where, with great deliberation it seemed, it snared his nose and his left ear in its pincers, then arched its tail again – and embedded its stinger deep into his goggling eyeball.

Chapter 2

Heck raced out of the kebab shop with a half-eaten Doner in one hand and a carton of Coke in the other. There was a blaring of horns as Dave Strickland swung his distinctive maroon Astra out of the far carriageway, pulled a U-turn right through the middle of the bustling evening traffic, and ground to a halt at the kerb. Heck crammed another handful of lamb and bread into his mouth, took a last slurp of Coke and tossed his rubbish into a nearby bin, before leaping into the Astra's front passenger seat.

'Grinton putting an arrest-team together?' he asked.

'As we speak,' Strickland said, shoving a load of documentation into Heck's grasp, and hitting the gas. More horns tooted despite the spinning blue beacon on the Astra's roof. 'We're hooking up with them at St Ann's Central.'

Heck nodded, leafing through the official Nottinghamshire Police paperwork. The text he'd just received from Strickland had consisted of thirteen words, but they'd been the most important thirteen words anyone had communicated to him in several months:

Hucknall murder a fit for Lady Killer
Chief suspect – Jimmy Hood
Whereabouts KNOWN

Heck, or Detective Sergeant Mark Heckenburg, as was his official title at Scotland Yard, felt a tremor of excitement as he flipped the light on and perused the documents. Even now, after seventeen years of investigations, during so many of which shocking twists and turns had been commonplace, it seemed incredible that a case that had defied all analysis, dragging on doggedly through eight months of mind-numbing frustration, could suddenly have blown itself wide open.

'Who's Jimmy Hood?' he asked.

'A nightmare on two legs,' Strickland replied.

Heck had only known Strickland for the duration of this enquiry, but they'd made a good connection on first meeting and had maintained it ever since. A local lad by birth, Dave Strickland was a slick, clean-cut, improbably handsome black guy; at thirty, a tad young for DI, but what he may have lacked in experience he more than made up for with his quick wits and sharp eye. After the stress of the last few months, even Strickland had started to fray around the edges; 'frazzled' would have been one way to describe him, but tonight he was back on form, collar unbuttoned and tie loose, but careering through the chaotic traffic with skill and speed.

'He lived in Hucknall when he was a kid,' Strickland added. 'But he spent a lot of his time back then locked up.'

'Not just then either,' Heck said. 'According to this, he's only been out of Roundhall for the last six months.'

'Yeah, and what does that tell us?'

Heck didn't need to reply. Roundhall was a low security prison in the West Midlands. According to these antecedents,

Jimmy Hood, now aged in his early thirties, had served a year and a half there before being released on licence. However, he'd originally been held at Durham after drawing fourteen years for burglary and rape. As if the details of his original crimes weren't enough of a match for the case they were currently working, his time back in the community put him neatly in the frame for the activities of the so-called 'Lady Killer'.

'He's a bruiser now and he was a bruiser then,' Strickland said. 'Six-foot-three by the time he was seventeen, and burly with it. Scared the crap out of everyone who knew him. Got arrested once for chucking a kitten into a cement mixer. Him and his mates did time for bricking a couple of builders who'd given them grief for pinching tools. Both workmen were knocked cold; one needed his face reconstructing.'

Heck noted from the paperwork that Hood, the mug-shot of whom portrayed shaggy black hair fringing a broad, bearded face with a badly broken nose – a disturbingly similar visage to the e-fit they'd released a few days ago – had led a juvenile street-gang that had involved itself in serious crime in Hucknall, from the age of twelve. However, he'd only commenced sexually offending, usually during the course of burglary, when he was in his late teens.

'So he comes out of jail and immediately picks up where he left off?' Heck said.

'Except that this time he murders them,' Strickland replied.

Heck didn't find that much of a leap. Certain types of violent offender had no intention of rehabilitating. They were so set on their life's work that they regarded prison time – even prolonged prison time – as a hazard of their chosen vocation. He'd known plenty who'd gone away for a lengthy stretch, and had used it to get fit, mug up on all the latest criminal techniques, and gradually accumulate a head of steam that would erupt with devastating force once they were released, and he could easily imagine this scenario applying to Jimmy Hood. What was more, the evidence seemed to indicate it. All four of the recent murder victims had been elderly women living alone. Most of Hood's victims when he was a teenager had been elderly women. The cause of death in all the recent cases had been physical battery with a blunt instrument, after rape. As a youth, Hood had bludgeoned his victims after indecently assaulting them.

'Funny his name wasn't flagged up when he first ditched his probation officer,' Heck said.

Strickland shrugged as he drove. 'Easy to be wise after the event, pal.'

'Suppose so.' On reflection, Heck recalled numerous occasions in his career when it would have paid to have a crystal ball.

On this occasion, they'd caught their break courtesy of a sharp-eyed civvie.

The four home-invasion murders they were officially investigating were congregated in the St Ann's district, east of Nottingham city centre, and an impoverished, densely populated area, which already suffered more than its fair share of crime. The only description they'd had was that of a hulking, bearded man wearing a duffle-coat over shabby sports gear, and 'smelling bad', which suggested that he wasn't able to bathe or change his clothes very often and so, maybe, was sleeping rough. (Heck had since lost count of the number of raids they'd made on homeless shelters, subways and cardboard cities, rounding up everyone with a beard – which was usually most males there, only to discover that none of them owned either a shell-suit or a duffle-coat.) However, only yesterday there had been a fifth murder in Hucknall, just north of the city, the details of which closely matched those in St Ann's. There'd been no description of the perpetrator on this occasion, though earlier today a long-term

Hucknall resident – who remembered Jimmy Hood well, along with his crimes – reported seeing him eating chips near the bus station there, not long after the event. He'd been wearing a duffle-coat over an old tracksuit, and though he didn't have a beard, fresh razor cuts suggested that he had recently shaved one off.

'And he's been lying low at this Alan Devlin's pad?' Heck asked.

'Part of the time maybe,' Strickland said. 'What do you think?'

'Well . . . I wouldn't have called it "whereabouts known". But it's a bloody good start.'

Alan Devlin, who had a long record of criminal activity as a juvenile, when he'd been part of Hood's gang, now lived in a council flat in St Ann's. These days he was Hood's only known associate in central Nottingham, and the proximity of his home address to the recent murders was too big a coincidence to ignore.

'What do we know about Devlin?' Heck said. 'I mean above and beyond what the paperwork says.'

'Not a player anymore, apparently. His son Wayne's a bit dodgy.'

'Dodgy how?'

'General purpose lowlife. Fighting at football matches, D and D, robbery.'

'Robbery?'

'Took some other kid's bike off him after giving him a kicking. That was a few years ago.'

'Sounds like the apple didn't fall far from the tree.'

As part of the National Crime Group, specifically the Serial Crimes Unit, Mark Heckenburg had a remit to work on murder cases across all the police areas of England and Wales. He and the other detectives in SCU (as it was abbreviated) tended to have a consultative investigating role with regard to the pursuit of repeat violent offenders, and would bring specialist knowledge and training to regional forces grappling with large or complex cases. They were usually allocated to said forces in groups of four or five, sometimes more. On this occasion, as the Nottinghamshire Police already had access to experienced personnel from the East Midlands Special Operations Unit, Heck had been assigned here on his own.

SCU's presence wasn't always welcomed by the regional forces they were assisting, some viewing the attachment of outsiders as a slight on their own abilities – though in certain cases, such as this one, SCU's advice had been actively sought. At the outset, Heck had been personally contacted by Strickland on the orders of Taskforce SIO Detective Chief Superintendent Max Grinton, who had solved many crimes off his own bat, but was a keen student of those state-of-the-art investigations carried out by other bodies, SCU figuring highly on his approved list.

Grinton was a big man with silver hair, a distinguished young/old face and a penchant for sharp-cut suits, though his most distinctive feature was the patch he wore over his left eye-socket, having lost the eye to flying glass during a drive-by shooting fifteen years earlier. He was now holding court under the hard halogen glow of the car park lights at the rear of St Ann's Central. Uniforms clad in full anti-riot gear, and detectives with stab vests under their jackets and coats, stood around him in attentive groups.

'So that's the state of play,' Grinton said. 'We're moving on this quickly rather than waiting 'til the crack of dawn tomorrow, firstly because the obbo at Devlin's address tells us he's currently home, secondly because if Jimmy Hood is our man there's been a shorter cooling-off period between each attack, which means in plain English that he's going crazier by the minute. For all we know, he could have done two or three more by tomorrow morning. We've got to catch him tonight, and Alan Devlin is the best lead we've had thus far. Just remember . . . for all that he's a scrote from way back, Devlin is a witness, not a suspect. We're more likely to get his help if we go in as friends.'

There were nods of understanding. Mouths were set firm as it dawned on the Taskforce members just how high the stakes now were. Every man and woman present knew their job, but it was vital that no one made an error.

'One thing, sir, if you don't mind,' Heck spoke up. 'I strongly recommend that we take anything Alan Devlin tells us with a pinch of salt.'

'Any particular reason?' Grinton asked.

Heck waved Devlin's sheet. 'He hasn't been convicted of any crime since he was a juvenile, but he wasn't shy about getting his hands dirty back in the day – he was Jimmy Hood's right-hand man when they were terrorising housing estates around Hucknall. His son Wayne is half way to repeating that pattern here in St Ann's. Try as I may, I can't view Alan Devlin as an upstanding citizen.'

'You think he'd cover for a killer?' Strickland said doubtfully.

Heck shrugged. 'I don't know, sir. Assuming Hood is the killer – and from what we know, I think he probably is – I find it odd that Devlin, who knows him better than anyone, hasn't already come to the same conclusion and got in touch with us voluntarily.'

'Maybe he's scared?' someone suggested.

Heck tried not to look as sceptical about that as he felt. 'Hood's a thug, but he's in breach of licence conditions that strictly prohibit him from returning to Nottingham. That means he's keeping his head down and moving from place to place. He's only got one change of clothes, he's on his own, he's cold, damp and dining on scraps in bus stations. Does he really pose much of a threat to a bloke like Devlin, who's got form for violence himself, has a grown-up hooligan for a son and is well ensconced on his own patch?'

The team pondered, taking this on board.

'We'll see what happens,' Grinton said, zipping his anorak. 'If Devlin plays it dumb, we'll let him know that Hood's mug-shot is appearing on the ten o'clock news tonight, and all it's going to take is a couple of Devlin's neighbours to recognise him as someone they've seen hanging around. The Lady Killer is going down for the rest of this century, ladies and gents. Devlin may be the hardest bastard in Nottingham, but he won't want a piece of that action.'

They drove to the address in question in a bunch of unmarked vehicles; five cars, one of them Heck's metallic-blue Peugeot 306, and one plain-clothes APC. They did it discreetly and without fanfare. St Ann's wasn't an out-of-control neighbourhood, but it wasn't the sort of place where excessive police activity would go unnoticed, and mobs could form quickly if word got out that 'one of the boys' was in trouble. In physical terms, it was a rabbit warren of crumbling council blocks, networked with dingy footways, which, at night, were a mugger's paradise. To heighten its atmosphere of menace, a winter gloom had descended, filling the narrow passages with cloying vapour.

The address was 41, Lakeside View (there might have been a lake sometime in the geological past, perhaps with a stunning view across it, but no one who lived here now remembered that). It was a boxy, redbrick structure, accessible by a short cement ramp with a rusty wrought iron railing, and then a single corridor running through from one side to the other, to which various apartment doors – 41a, 41b, 41c and 41d – connected.

Heck, Grinton and Strickland regarded it from a short distance away. Only the arched entry was visible in the evening murk, illuminated at its apex by a single dull lamp; the rest of the building was a gaunt outline. A clutch of detectives and armour-clad uniforms were waiting a few yards behind them, while the troop-carrier with its complement of PSU reinforcements was about fifty yards further back, parked in the nearest cul-de-sac. Everyone observed a strict silence.

Grinton finally turned around, keeping his voice low. 'Okay . . . listen up. Roberts, Atherton . . . you're staying with us. The rest of you . . . round the other side. Any ground floor windows, any fire-doors, block 'em off. Grab anyone who tries to come out.'

There were nods of understanding as the group, minus two uniforms, shuffled away into the mist. Grinton checked his watch to give them five minutes to get in place, then glanced at Heck and Strickland and nodded. They detached themselves from the alley mouth, ascended the ramp and entered the brick passage, which was poorly lit by two faltering bulbs and defaced end to end with obscene, spray-painted slogans, which also covered three of its four doors. The only one that hadn't been vandalised in this fashion was 41c – the home of Alan Devlin.

There was no bell, so Grinton rapped on the door with his fist. Several seconds passed, before there was a fumbling on the other side. The door opened as far as its short safety chain would allow. The face beyond was aged in its mid-thirties, but pudgy and pock-marked, one eyebrow bisected by an old scar. Whoever the guy was, and he looked like Devlin – though the last police photographs taken of him were a decade and a half out of date – he was squat and pot-bellied, with a shaved head. He'd answered the door in a grubby t-shirt and purple Y-fronts, but even through the narrow gap they spotted neck-chains and cheap, tacky rings on nicotine-yellow fingers. He didn't look hostile as much as puzzled, probably because the first thing he saw was Grinton's eye-patch. He put on a pair of thick-lensed, steel-rimmed glasses, so that he could scrutinise it less myopically.

'Alan Devlin?' the chief superintendent asked.

'Who the fuck are you?'

Grinton introduced himself, displaying his warrant card. 'This is Detective Inspector Strickland and this is Detective Sergeant Heckenburg.'

'Suppose I'm honoured,' Devlin grunted, looking anything but.

'Can we come in?' Grinton said.

'What's it about?'

'You don't know?' Strickland asked him.

Devlin threw him an ironic glance. 'Yeah . . . I just wondered if *you* did.'

Heck observed the householder with interest. Though clearly irritated that his evening had been disturbed, his relaxed body language suggested that he wasn't overly concerned. Either Devlin had nothing to hide or he was a competent performer. The latter was easily possible, as he'd had plenty of opportunity to hone such a talent while still a youth.

'Jimmy Hood,' Grinton explained. 'That name ring a bell?'

Devlin continued to regard them indifferently, but for several seconds longer than was perhaps normal. Then he removed the safety chain and opened the door.

Heck glanced at the two uniforms. 'Wait out here, eh? No sense crowding him in his own pad.' They nodded and remained in the outer passage, while the three detectives entered a dimly-lit hall strewn with crumbs and cluttered with piles of musty, unwashed clothes. An internal door stood open on a lamp-lit room from which the sound of a

453

television emanated. There was a strong, noxious odour of chips and ketchup.

Devlin faced them square-on, adjusting his bottle-lens specs. 'Suppose you want to know where he is?'

'Not only that,' Grinton said, 'we want to know where he's been.'

There was a sudden thunder of feet from overhead – the sound of someone running. Heck tensed by instinct. He spun to face the foot of a dark stairwell – just as a figure exploded down it. But it wasn't the brutish giant, Jimmy Hood; it was a kid – seventeen at the most with a mop of mouse brown hair and a thin moustache. He was only clad in shorts, which revealed a lean, muscular torso sporting several lurid tattoos – and was carrying a baseball bat.

'What the fucking hell?' He advanced fiercely, closing down the officers' space.

'Easy, lad,' Devlin said, smiling. 'Just a few questions, then they'll be gone.'

'What fucking questions?'

Strickland pointed a finger. 'Put the bat down, sonny.'

'You gonna make me?' The youth's expression was taut, his gaze intense.

'You want to make this worse for your old fella than it already is?' Grinton asked calmly.

There was a short, breathless silence. The youth glanced from one to the other, determinedly unimpressed by the phalanx of officialdom, though clearly unused to folk not running when he came at them tooled up. 'There's more of these twats outside, Dad. Sneaking around, thinking no one can see 'em.'

His father snorted. 'All this coz Jimbo breached his parole?'

'It's a bit more serious than that, Mr Devlin,' Strickland said. 'So serious that I really don't think you want to be obstructing us like this.'

'I'm not obstructing you . . . I've just invited you in.'

Which was quite a smart move, Heck realised.

'We'll see.' Grinton walked towards the living room. 'Let's talk.'

Devlin gave a sneering grin and followed. Strickland went too. Heck turned to Wayne Devlin. 'Your dad wants to make it look like he's cooperating, son. Wafting that offensive weapon around isn't going to help him.'

Scowling, though now looking a little helpless – as if having other men in here chucking their weight about was such a challenge to his masculinity that he knew no adequate way to respond – the lad finally slung the baseball bat against the stair-post, which it struck with a deafening *thwack!*, before shouldering past Heck into the living room. When Heck got in there, it was no less a bombsite than the hall: magazines were scattered – one lay open on a gynaecological centre-spread; empty beer cans and dirty crockery cluttered the table tops; overflowing ashtrays teetered on the mantel. The stench of ketchup was enriched by the lingering aroma of stale cigarettes.

'Let's cut to the chase,' Grinton said. 'Is Hood staying here now?'

'No,' Devlin replied, still cool.

Too cool, Heck thought. *Way too cool.*

'So if I come back here with a search-warrant, and go through this place with a fine-tooth comb, Mr Devlin, I definitely won't find him?'

Devlin shrugged. 'If you thought you had grounds you'd already have a warrant. But it doesn't matter. You've got my permission to search anyway.'

'In which case I'm guessing there's no need, but we might as well look.' Grinton nodded to Heck, who went back outside and brought the two uniforms in. Their heavy boots thudded on the stair treads as they lumbered to the upper floor.

'How often has Jimmy Hood stayed here?' Strickland asked. 'I mean recently?'

Devlin shrugged. 'On and off. Crashed on the couch.'

'And you didn't report it?'

'He's an old mate trying to get back on his feet. I'm not dobbing him in for that.'

'When did he last stay?' Heck asked.

'Few days ago.'

'What was he wearing?'

'What he always wears . . . trackie bottoms, sweat-top, duffle-coat. Poor bastard's living out of a placky bag.'

The detectives avoided exchanging glances. They'd agreed beforehand that there'd be no disclosure of their real purpose here until Grinton deemed it necessary; if Devlin had known what was happening and had still harboured his old pal, that made him an accessory to these murders – and it would help them build a case against him if he revealed knowledge without being prompted.

'When do you expect him back?' Heck asked.

Devlin looked amused by the inanity of such a question (*again false*, Heck sensed). 'How do I know? I'm not his fucking keeper. He knows he can come here anytime, but he never wants to outstay his welcome.'

'Has he got a phone, so you can contact him?' Strickland wondered.

'He hasn't got anything.'

'Does he ever come here late at night?' Grinton said. 'As in . . . unusually late.'

'What sort of bullshit questions are these?' Wayne Devlin demanded, increasingly agitated by the sounds of violent activity upstairs.

Grinton eyed him. 'The sort that need straight answers, son . . . else you and your dad are going to find yourselves deeper in it than whale shit.' He glanced back at Devlin. 'So . . . any late-night calls?'

'Sometimes,' Devlin admitted.

'When?'

'I don't keep a fucking diary.'

'Did he ever look flustered?' Strickland asked.

'When didn't he? He's on the lam.'

'How about bloodstained?' Grinton said.

At first Devlin seemed puzzled, but now, slowly – very slowly – his face lengthened. 'You're not . . . you're not talking about this Lady Killer business?'

'You've got to be fucking kidding!' Wayne Devlin blurted, looking stunned.

'Interesting thought, Wayne?' Heck said to him. 'Is that *your* bat out there . . . or Jimmy Hood's?'

The lad's mouth dropped open. Suddenly he was less the teen tough-guy and more an alarmed kid. 'It's . . . it's mine, but that doesn't mean . . .'

'So if we confiscate it for forensic examination and find blood, it's *you* we need to come for, not Jimmy?'

'That won't work, copper,' the older Devlin said, though for the first time there was colour in his cheek – it perhaps hadn't occurred to him that his son might end up carrying the can for something. 'You're not scaring us.'

Despite that, the younger Devlin *did* look scared. 'You won't find any blood on it,' he stammered. 'It's been under my bed for months. Jimbo never touched it. Dad, tell 'em what they want to fucking know.'

'Like I said, Jimbo's only been here a couple of times,' Devlin drawled. (*Still playing it calm*, Heck thought.) 'Never settles down for long.'

'And it didn't enter your head that he might be involved in these murders?' Grinton said.

'Or are you just in denial?' Strickland asked.

'He was a good mate . . .'

'So you *are* in denial? Can't see the judge being impressed by that.'

'It may have occurred to me once or twice,' Devlin retorted. 'But you don't want to believe it of a mate . . .'

'Even though he's done it before?' Grinton said.

'Nothing this bad.'

'Bad enough . . .'

'You should get over to his auntie's!' Wayne Devlin interjected.

That comment stopped them dead. They gazed at him curiously; he gazed back, flat-eyed, cheeks flaming.

'What are you talking about?' Heck asked.

'He was always ranting about his Auntie Mavis . . .'

'*Wayne!*' the older Devlin snapped.

'If Jimbo's up to something dodgy, Dad, we don't want any part in it . . .'

These two are good, Heck thought. *These two are really good.*

'Something you want to tell us, Mr Devlin?' Grinton asked.

Devlin averted his eyes to the floor, teeth bared. He yanked his glasses off and rubbed them vigorously on his grubby vest – as though torn with indecision, as though angry at having been put in this position, but not necessarily angry at the police.

'Wayne may be right,' he finally said. 'Perhaps you should get over there. Her name's Mavis Cutler. Before you ask, I don't know much else. She's not his real auntie. Some old bitch who fostered Jimbo when he was a kid. Seventy-odd now, at least. I don't know what went on – he never said, but I think she gave him a dog's life.'

So Hood was attacking his wicked auntie every time

he attacked one of these other women, Heck reasoned, remembering his basic forensic psychology. *It's a plausible explanation. A tad too plausible, of course.*

'And why do we need to get over there quick?' Strickland wondered.

Devlin hung his head properly, his shoulders sagging as if he was suddenly glad to get a weight off them. 'When . . . when Jimbo first showed up a few months ago, he said he was back in Nottingham to see her. And when he said "see her", I didn't get the feeling it was for a family reunion if you know what I mean.'

'So why's it taken him this long?' Strickland asked.

'He couldn't find her at first. I think he may have gone up to Hucknall yesterday, looking. That's where they lived when he was a kid.'

Cleverer and cleverer, Heck thought. *Devlin's using real events to make it believable.*

'Someone up there probably told him,' Devlin added.

'Told him what?'

'That she lives in Matlock now. I don't know where exactly.'

Matlock in Derbyshire. Twenty-five miles away. Quite a diversion.

'How do you know all this?' Grinton sounded suspicious.

Devlin shrugged. 'He rang me today . . . from a payphone. Said he was leaving town tonight, and that I probably wouldn't be seeing him again.'

'And you still didn't inform us?' Strickland's voice was thick with disgust.

'I'm informing you now, aren't I?'

'It might be too late, you stupid moron!' Strickland dashed out into the hall, calling the two uniforms from upstairs.

459

'Look, he never specifically said he was going to do that old bird,' Devlin protested to Grinton. 'He might not even be going to Matlock. He might be fleeing the fucking country for all I know! This is just guesswork!'

And you can't be prosecuted for guessing, Heck thought. *You're a cute one.*

'Don't do anything stupid, Mr Devlin,' Grinton said, indicating to Heck that it was time to leave. 'Like warning Jimmy we're coming. Any phone we find on Hood with calls traceable back to you are all we'll need to nick you as an accomplice.'

Out in the entry passage, Strickland was already bawling into his radio. 'I don't care how indisposed they are . . . get them to check the voters' rolls and phone directories. Find every woman in Matlock called Mavis bloody Cutler . . . over and out!' He turned to Grinton and Heck. 'We should lock that bastard Devlin up . . .'

Grinton shook his head, ignoring the door to 41c as it slammed closed behind them. 'He might end up witnessing for us. Let's not chuck away what little leverage we've currently got.'

'What if he absconds?'

'We'll sit someone on him.'

'Excuse me, sir,' Heck said. 'But I won't be coming over to Matlock with you.'

'Okay . . . something on your mind?'

'Yeah. Alan Devlin. Good show he put on in there, but I don't think Hood has any intention of going to Derbyshire. I reckon we're being sent on a wild goose chase.'

Strickland looked puzzled. 'Why would Devlin do that?'

'It's a hunch, sir, but it's got legs. Despite the serious crimes Jimmy Hood was last convicted for, Alan Devlin let him sleep on his couch. Not once, but several times. This guy is not too picky to associate with sex offenders.'

'Come on, Heck,' Strickland said. 'Devlin's in enough hot

water as it is . . . he's not going to aid and abet a multiple killer as well.'

'He's in lukewarm water, sir. Apart from assisting an offender, what else has he admitted to? Even if it turns out he's sending us the wrong way, he's covered. It's all "I'm not sure about this, I'm only guessing that" . . . there aren't even grounds to charge him with obstructing an enquiry.'

'We can't *not* act on what he's told us,' Grinton said.

'I agree, sir. But while you're off to Matlock, I'm going to chase a few leads of my own. If that's okay?'

'No problem . . . just make sure you log them all.'

While Grinton arranged for a couple of his plain-clothes officers to maintain covert obs on Lakeside View, the rest of them returned to their vehicles and mounted up for a rapid ride over to the next county. Strickland was back on the blower again, putting Derbyshire Comms in the picture as he jumped into his car. Heck remained on the pavement while he too made a quick call – in his case it was to the DIU at St Ann's Central. As intelligence offices went, this one was pretty efficient. It was regularly utilised by the East Midlands Special Operations Unit, so its functionaries tended to know what they were doing.

'Heck?' came the hearty voice of PC Marge Propper, a chunky uniformed lass, whose fast, accurate research capabilities had already proved invaluable to the Lady Killer Taskforce.

'Marge . . . am I right in thinking that, apart from Alan Devlin, Jimmy Hood has no other known associates in the inner Nottingham area?'

'Correct.'

'Okay . . . I want to try something different. Can you contact Roundhall Prison in Coventry? Find out who's been visiting Hood this last year and a half. Any regular names that haven't already cropped up in this enquiry, I'd like to know about them.'

'Wilco, Heck . . . might take a few minutes to get a response at this hour.'

'No worries. Call me back when you can.'

He paused before climbing into his Peugeot. The other mobile units had driven away, leaving a dull, dead silence in their wake. The surrounding buildings were little more than blurred, angular outlines, broken by the odd faint square of window-light, most of which leached into the gloom without making any impression. The passage leading towards Lakeside View was a black rectangle, which bade no one re-enter it.

Heck climbed into his car and switched the engine on.

It was impossible to say whether or not they were on the right track, but it *felt* right. He still didn't trust Alan Devlin, but the guy's partial admissions had revealed that Jimmy Hood had been in this district as well as Hucknall – which put Hood close to all the identified murder scenes and in roughly the right time-frame. Of course, with the knowledge of hindsight, it was all so predictable and sordid. As Heck drove out of the cul-de-sac, it struck him that this decayed environment, with its broken glass and graffiti-covered maze of soulless brick alleys, seemed painfully familiar. So many of his cases had brought him to blighted places like this.

His phone rang and he slammed it to his ear. 'Talk to me.'

'We could have something here, Heck,' Marge Propper said. 'In his last three years at Roundhall, Jimmy Hood was visited nine times by a certain Sian Collier.'

'That name doesn't ring a bell.'

'No . . . she hasn't been on our radar up to now, though she's got minor form for possession and shoplifting. She's white, thirty-two years old and a local by birth. Her last conviction was over five years ago, so she may have cleaned up her act.'

'Apart from the bit where she gets mixed up with sex killers?'

462

'Yeah . . .'

Heck fiddled with his sat-nav. 'Where does she live?'

'Mountjoy Height, number eighteen . . . that's in Bulwell.'

'I know it.'

'Heck . . . if you're going over there, you might want to speak to Division first. It's a lively place.'

'Thanks for the warning, Marge. But I'm only spying out the land. Anyway, I've got my radio.'

The murkiness of the winter night was now to aid Heck – mainly because it meant the roads were empty of traffic, but also because, once he arrived in Bulwell, he was able to cruise its foggy, rundown streets without attracting attention.

When he finally located Mountjoy Height, it was a row of pebble-dashed two-storey maisonettes on raised ground overlooking yet another labyrinthine housing estate. First, he made a drive-by at the front, seeing patches of muddy grass serving as communal front gardens, with wheelie-bins dotted across them and litter strewn haphazardly. There were only a couple of other vehicles present, but lights were on in most of the maisonette windows. After that, he explored at the rear, working his way down into a lower, winding alley, which ran past several garages. Some of these stood open, some closed. The garage to number eighteen didn't have a door attached, but was of particular interest because a large, good-looking motorcycle was parked inside it.

Heck glided to a halt and turned his engine off.

He climbed out, listening carefully; somewhere close by voices bickered. They were muffled and indistinct, but it sounded like a couple of adults; he wasn't initially sure where it was coming from – possibly number eighteen itself, which towered behind the garage in the gloom and was accessible by a narrow flight of steps running upward.

He assessed the motorbike through the entrance, and

despite the darkness was able to identify it as a new model Suzuki GSX, an expensive make for this neck of the woods.

'DS Heckenburg to Charlie Six,' he said into his radio. 'PNC check, please?'

'*DS Heckenburg?*' came the crackly response.

'Anything on a black Suzuki GSX motorcycle, index Juliet-Zulu-seven-three-Bravo-Foxtrot-Alpha, over?'

'*Stand by.*'

Heck moved to the side of the garage and glanced up the steps. The monolithic structure overhead was wreathed in vapour, but lights still burned inside it, and the argument raged on; in fact it sounded as if it had intensified. Glass shattered, which wasn't necessarily a bad thing – it might grant him the right to force entry.

'*DS Heckenburg from PNC?*'

'Go ahead.'

'*Black Suzuki GSX motorcycle, index Juliet-Zulu-seven-three-Bravo-Foxtrot-Alpha, reported stolen from Hucknall late last night, over.*'

'Received, thanks for that. What were the circumstances of the theft, over?'

'*Fairly serious, sarge. It's being treated as robbery. A motorcycle courier got a bottle broken over his head outside a fish and chip shop, and then had his helmet stolen as well as his ride. He's currently in IC. No description of the offender as yet.*'

Heck pondered. This sounded more like Jimmy Hood by the minute. On the basis that he was now looking to make an arrest for a serious offence, Heck had the power to enter the garage – which he duly did, finding masses of junk littered in its oily shadows: boxes crammed with bric-a-brac; broken, dirty household appliances; even a pile of chains, several of which were wrapped around an upright steel girder supporting the garage roof.

'DS Heckenburg . . . *are you saying you've found this vehicle, over?*'

'That's affirmative,' Heck replied, pulling his gloves on as he mooched around. 'In an open garage at the rear of eighteen, Mountjoy Height, Bulwell. The suspect, who I believe to be inside the address, is Jimmy Hood. White male, early thirties, six foot three inches and built like a brick shithouse. Hood, who has form for extreme violence, is also a suspect in the Lady Killer murders. So I need back-up ASAP. Silent approach, over.'

'*Received sarge . . . support units en route. ETA five.*'

Heck shoved his radio back into his jacket and worked his way through the garage to a rear door, which swung open at his touch. He followed a paved side-path along the base of a steep, muddy slope, eventually joining with the flight of steps leading up to the maisonette. When he ascended, he did so warily. Realistically, all he needed to do now was wait until the cavalry arrived – but then something else happened.

And it was a game-changer.

The shouting and screaming indoors had risen towards a crescendo. Household items exploded as they were flung around. This was just about tolerable, given that it probably wasn't an uncommon occurrence in this neighbourhood. Heck reasoned that he could still wait it out – until he got close to the rear of the building, and heard a baby crying.

Not just crying.

Howling.

Hysterical with pain or fear.

'DS Heckenburg to Charlie Six, urgent message!' He dashed up the remaining steps, and took an entry around to the front of the maisonette. 'Please expedite that support . . . I can hear violence inside the property and a child in distress, over!'

He halted under the stoop. Light shafted through the frosted panel in the front door, yet little was visible on the other side – except for brief flurries of indistinct movement. Angry shouts still echoed from within.

Heck zipped his jacket and knocked loudly. 'Police officer! Can you open up please?'

There was instantaneous silence – apart from the baby, whose sobbing had diminished to a low and feeble keening.

Heck knocked again. 'This is the police . . . I need you to open up!' He glimpsed further hurried motion behind the distorted glass.

When he next struck the door, he led with his shoulder.

It required three heavy buffets to crash the woodwork inward, splinters flying, bolts and hinges catapulting loose. As the door fell in front of him, Heck saw a narrow, wreckage-strewn corridor leading into a small kitchen, where a tall male in a duffle-coat was in the process of exiting the property via a back door. Heck charged down the corridor. As he did, a woman emerged from a side-room, bruised and tear-stained, hair disorderly, mascara streaking her cheeks. She wore a ragged orange dressing-gown and clutched a baby to her breast, its face a livid, blotchy red.

'What do you want?' she screeched, blocking Heck's passage. 'You can't barge in here!'

Heck stepped around her. 'Out the way please, miss!'

'But he's not done nothing!' She grabbed Heck's collar, her sharp fingernails raking the skin on his neck. *'Can't you bastards stop harassing him!'*

Heck had to pull hard to extricate himself. 'Hasn't he just beaten you up?'

'That's coz I didn't want him to leave . . .'

'He's a bloody nutter, love!'

'It's nothing . . . I don't mind it.'

'Others do!' Heck yanked himself free – to renewed wailing

from the woman and child – and continued into the kitchen and then out through the back door, emerging onto a toy-strewn patio just as a burly outline loped down the steps towards the garage. The guy had something in his hand, which Heck at first took for a bag; then he realised that it was a motorbike helmet. 'Jimmy Hood!' he shouted, scrambling down. 'Police officer . . . stay where you are!'

Hood's response was to leap the remaining three or four steps, pulling the helmet on and battering his way through the garage's rear door. Heck jumped as well, sliding and tumbling on the earthen slope, but reaching the doorway only seconds behind his quarry. He shouldered it open, to find Hood seated on the Suzuki, kicking it to life. Its glaring headlight sprang across the alley. The roars of its engine filled the gutted structure.

'Don't be a bloody fool!' Heck cried.

Hood glanced around – just long enough to flip Heck the finger. And then hit the gas, the Suzuki bucking forward, almost pulling a wheelie it accelerated with such speed.

But the fugitive only made it ten yards, at which point, with a terrific *BANG!*, the bike's rear wheel was jerked backwards beneath him. He somersaulted over the handlebars, slamming upside down against another garage door, before flopping onto the cobblestones, where he lay twisted and groaning. The bike came to rest a few yards away, chugging loudly, smoke pouring from its shattered exhaust.

'Bit remiss of you, Jimmy,' Heck said, emerging into the alley, toeing at the length of chain still pulled taut between the buckled rear wheel and the upright girder inside. 'Not checking that something hadn't got mysteriously wrapped around your rear axle.'

Flickering blue lights now appeared as local patrol cars turned into view at either end of the alley, slowly wending their way forward. Hood managed to roll over onto his back, but could do nothing except lie there, glaring with glassy, soulless eyes through the aperture where his visor had been smashed away.

Heck dug handcuffs from his back pocket and suspended them in full view. 'Either way, pal, you don't have to say anything. But it may harm your defence . . .'

Want more? Read the rest of
Hunted
when it hits the shelves in May 2015.

'All he had to do was name the woman he wanted. It was that easy. They would do all the hard work.'

Dark, terrifying and unforgettable. *Stalkers* will keep fans of Stuart MacBride and James Oswald looking over their shoulder.

A vicious serial killer is holding
the country to ransom, publicly – and
gruesomely – murdering his victims.

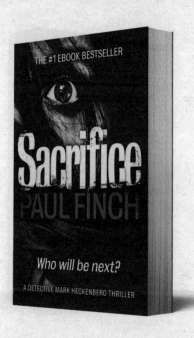

A heart-stopping and unforgettable
thriller that you won't be able to put
down, from bestseller Paul Finch.

DS Mark 'Heck' Heckenburg is used to bloodbaths. But nothing can prepare him for this.

Brace yourself as you turn the pages of a living nightmare.

Welcome to The Killing Club.